Wrong

"A unique plot, crisp dialogue and well written characters make this a standout read."

—Cayacosta72—Book Reviews

"In her gripping debut novel, *Wrong Place, Wrong Time*, Tilia Jacobs explores, with wisdom and grace, the complex ethical and religious questions surrounding a brutal kidnapping and its aftermath. This absorbing, masterfully structured suspense is infused with delightfully wicked humor and shimmers with vivid descriptions, sharp dialogue, and fascinating, multi-dimensional characters. With *Wrong Place, Wrong Time*, Ms. Jacobs made me laugh, made me cry, and, while drawing me into a complex web of human frailty, desperation, resilience and ultimately survival, both inspired me and urged me to think."

—Terri Giuliano Long,
author of *In Leah's Wake* and *Nowhere To Run*

"Heroine Tsara Abrams is edgy swagger with an overlay of happily ever after thrown in—think Angelina Jolie and Naomi Watts morphed together. Add a smidgen of Katniss Everdeen thrown in for that fun, action/adventure read we all crave, and you've got this great debut novel. Pick it up NOW."

—Mary Kennedy Eastham,
author of *Squinting Over Water* and *The Shadow of a Dog I Can't Forget*

"This is a book that manages to include fast-paced, adrenaline-pumping action, thoughtful ponderings about morality, and a witty sense of humor all in one novel, an impressive feat.... The author's wry humor pervades the novel, adding substantially to its entertainment value.... This is a book that can be dramatically suspenseful, heartrendingly emotional, and laugh-out-loud funny all at once. It's well worth a read. "

—IndieReader.com

"Part action and adventure drama and part psychological thriller, *Wrong Place, Wrong Time* keeps you turning pages. The complex characters are woven into a many-layered conflict with as many turns as the mountain roads on which they travel. This is a must read book."

—Allyson Walker,
co-author of *The Pen is Mightier than the Broom*

"Witty and engrossing, *Wrong Place, Wrong Time* is a genuine page-turner."

—Joanna Catherine Scott,
Judge, Soul-Making Keats Literary Competition

"With sharp, clear prose and a refreshing lack of sentimentality, Jacobs tells her tale with compassion, humor, compelling characterization, and intense drama. Eschewing literary pyrotechnics, Jacobs delivers a taut, suspenseful thriller, layered with detail and rich in theme. *Wrong Place, Wrong Time* is full of surprises and twists, yet always puts the human drama front and center. In Tsara Adelman, Jacobs has created an unforgettable heroine for our time. During her harrowing ordeal, Tsara is forced to dig deep within herself to survive, and emerges both stronger and wiser—but with strength and wisdom that are hard-earned, and leave emotional scars. In the end, *Wrong Place, Wrong Time* turns out to be more than a ripping yarn—although it is that, indisputably—but also a thoughtful, profound mediation on the eternal themes of vengeance, honor, and, above all, redemption."

—Peter Ullian,
critically acclaimed, award-winning author of
Flight of the Lawnchair Man, Black Fire White Fire, and *Eliot Ness in Cleveland*

"A page-turner for brainiacs!"

—Lisa Moricoli-Latham,
TV sitcom writer

"*Wrong Place, Wrong Time* is a genre-shifting story. On one hand, it is a classic tale of suspense: a beautiful woman is kidnapped and taken on a frightening trek through the mountains of New Hampshire. On the other hand, her kidnapper is not a brute, and as the reader becomes more aware of and sympathetic to his story, the novel takes on the uncomfortable nuances of a romance. In the end, this is an exploration of forgiveness, beautifully crafted through dialogue and built on the perennial themes of love and loyalty."

—Sarah Jordan, Ph.D., Professor of Language and Literacy

Wrong Place, Wrong Time

Tilia Klebenov Jacobs

LINDEN TREE PRESS
—— For Those Who Love to Read ——

LINDEN TREE PRESS
For Those Who Love to Read

First published 2013 in the United States of America by Linden Tree Press

ISBN-13: 978-0-9898601-1-6 (Linden Tree Press)

To Doug and Nate and Elwyn
All my love,
for ever and always.

A woman of valor, who can find? Her worth is greater than rubies.
—Proverbs 31:10

Wrong Place, Wrong Time

She almost hadn't gone that weekend.

The invitation had come as a complete surprise, a heavy, cream-colored envelope looking much too classy to be rubbing shoulders with the bills and Netflix movies that crowded the mailbox. Tsara opened it outside, leaning against the mailbox. When she shook it gently upside down, a rectangle of thick paper slid out with cloud-colored tissue protecting it on either side. The cursive letters were raised, and the ink was a cross between gold and platinum that caught the light and wore it like jewelry.

Mr. and Mrs. Castle Thornlocke
Request the Pleasure of Your Company
At a Fundraiser for the Red Dress Brigade
The First Friday in October
Chateau Thornlocke, Libertyville, NH

Below that were the time and date. A second piece of paper in the envelope had directions as well as a slightly different address for anyone using a GPS. It noted that the fête was black tie, and ladies were encouraged to wear red. On the invitation itself in a familiar, slanting hand was written, "Tsara, I do hope you can come. It has been far too long, and I am trying to atone. Much love, Uncle Cass."

Like she even needed the signature. An invitation like that could only have come from Cass.

— ❋ —

"You should totally go," said David. He was sitting at the dining room table paying bills on his laptop.

"Why?"

"Because my *God*, if this invitation is anything to go by, this party is going to be epic."

"Of course it'll be epic. It'll be a Castle Thornlocke extravaganza."

"No, I mean really epic," said David. The history teacher in him took over and he set down the invitation. "I mean, this will put the funeral of Patroclus to *shame*."

"David."

"Poets will write about it. It'll become part of the fabric of the culture."

"David."

"Peasants will chant about it around their fires at night."

"*David.*"

"Unless, of course, you have some reason for not wanting to go," he said, showing how sensitive he could be.

"Gee. What could that possibly be?"

David looked at her, thinking how green his wife's eyes were. And how sad they got when the subject of her uncle came up.

"The half-life of a grudge?" he suggested, but his voice was softer.

"I would have called it the statute of limitations on avuncular bullshit. But I won't fight you for it."

David closed his computer. "You always say he was nice to you and Court."

"He was. Always. And our mom."

He picked up the invitation again. "Dang. This thing is actually engraved." He flipped it over and showed her the dents on the back where the plate had punched the letters in.

She was unmoved. "Sweetie, the whole event's going to be engraved."

He put it down again. "So why don't you want to go?"

Tsara looked through the dining room windows. The roses were soft poofs of pink and red, their scent drifting through the window with the velvet hum of sun-sated bumblebees. Past the lawn and behind the fence was a stand of maple trees, the beginning of the town's forest. They were dark green, but by the first weekend in October they and every tree in Libertyville would be shouting with color. "Don't know if I do or not."

He waited.

"Did I ever tell you about the surprise party he threw my mom for her fortieth birthday?" she said.

"Yes."

"There was an improv group," she said dreamily, "and a strolling magician. She loved it." She frowned. "Were there fireworks? I think there were fireworks. Unless that was some other time."

"So you want to go?"

"And I do have that dress."

"So you want to go?"

"The cool red one."

"Very cool."

"On the other hand." She looked back at him.

David said nothing. But he thought, *That was so long ago.*

"And the kids."

David nodded sagely. "The kids."

"Long drive," she said.

"Strange grownups in a strange house," he said. "Weird food. The carrots might be touching the peas."

"God, yes. They might." She sighed. "Ah, screw it. I'll just RSVP no." She squeezed the ends of the envelope so it gapped open, and pulled out a small card with a matching, stamped envelope.

"Before you do that." David spoke in a tone that had made generations of high school students snap to attention. "Seriously, just ask yourself if you'd like to go. Because if you do, we can make it happen."

"But—"

"Look. Do you want to go to this engraved event?"

Tsara sighed. "Well … it would be *fun*. And Court says Cass has mellowed a bit. I think Alicia has been good for him. And I've never met my cousins. But still …."

"Is Court going?"

"I don't know."

"Find out," he said.

"What if I'm being disloyal to my dad?"

"Your dad's been gone a long time, honey," he said gently.

"Cass said my dad—"

"I know." He waited until Tsara's shoulders dropped. "How long are you going to cling to that?"

"You don't know what it's like."

David tapped the invitation. "Looks to me like he's trying to say he's sorry."

Tsara stared far away, her fingers drumming. There were Cheerios on the tablecloth. She'd have to sweep those up. Or just change the tablecloth.

David watched her, thinking, *Oh, honey. Just go. Have fun. Take a few days off from diapers and laundry.*

"Call the rabbi," he suggested. "See what she says."

"Nah. Adara comes from one of those *functional* families." She rolled her eyes.

"Want to know what I would do?" he said.

"Enlighten me."

"Call Court and see if he's going. If he says yes, ask him why. And then I would take a long look at that red dress. And then I would go."

Tsara considered this. "What about Josh and Abbie?"

"If Court is going, you can go with him and I'll stay here with the kids," said David. "You have a great time with your family and test the waters. If it looks like something Josh and Abbie would enjoy next time, then there will be a next time. If not, you haven't just subjected them to a boatload of ick."

"You don't want to go?" said Tsara. The red dress faded a couple of shades in her mind.

David hesitated. "It sounds crowded." The apology was in his tone. "I think you'd have more fun by yourself."

He was probably right, thought Tsara. Though practically perfect in every other way, her guy was a bit of a clamshell at large gatherings. She pulled her cell phone out of her pocket.

"Calling Court?" David opened his laptop again.

"Calling Court."

Her brother was indeed going to Castle's fundraising bash. "Oh, hell yeah. It's going to be amazing, it's for a great cause, and plus, look, I hate to say it, but Dad's dead."

"True," said Tsara. "I like to think that shit between him and Cass died when he did."

"Why don't you come, sis?" he urged. "Cass is Cass and he's always going to be, but Alicia's nice and the kids are fun. And look, he's at least trying to reach out."

"And I have this amazing dress," she said. "It's floor-length and red, with—"

"Yeah, yeah, whatever. I'm wearing a tux. It's black with a bow tie. Look, are you coming or not?"

"I guess I am," she said brightly. "Wow. This will be fun."

— ❊ —

The first Friday of October was perfect for driving. The sky was azure, wisped with occasional brushes of clouds, and the trees were rocket bursts of fall color. As Tsara drove north, the soft rise and fall of the land gave way to hills that roiled before her in a succession of orange and blue and a transparent grey that was hard to tell from the clouds. Presently they heaved themselves into mountains with rocky shoulders, shaggy at the bases with their scruff of bright trees. Ski slopes waiting for snow draped the hillsides like emerald ribbons.

At a late lunch in Tilton, she checked her phone. There was a message from Adara.

"Hey, there. Sorry I missed your call. Really quickly, the term you're looking for is *shalom bayit*, and it means 'peace of the house.' It's a general principle that encourages people to be flexible and patient with family members so the home is a calm, safe, nurturing place. Sometimes it's better to be kind than right. And in answer to your second question, reaching out to an estranged member of the family absolutely counts. So

5

you go, woman! Jewish values in action. Have a great time and tell me all about it when you get home."

Tsara put the phone away and finished her lunch, pleased that she was now the official embodiment of Jewish values.

A couple of hours later she drove through Trapper's Notch, a giant V where the mountains cascaded to the highway in a silent thunder of granite. Beyond the Notch the Silver Mountains began. She was officially in North Country.

As if to mark the passage, a truck passed her pulling a flatbed trailer carrying a female moose. She almost covered the floor. Her glassy eyes stared vacantly ahead and her hooves danced along the edge with the movement of the road. As it went by Tsara could see the gash on the animal's belly where the guts had been removed.

The sun was getting lower in the sky, and it flashed in her eyes through the trees on her left. Tsara pulled the shade over to one side, which didn't help much, and put on her sunglasses. The road and mountains lay ahead.

"You have arrived at your destination," intoned the GPS. "Guidance is now finished."

Tsara turned the steering wheel to the right and drove slowly onto the driveway. Trees formed a leaf-thick arch over the iron gates, their branches glowing in the fading memory of daylight. Gravel pinged the undercarriage of the minivan. Almost immediately the driveway broadened into a semicircle edged with cars that had done their best to park parallel to a curve. It framed the big house with Cartesian elegance. Tsara pulled in behind a wine-dark Mercedes sedan, and cut her engine.

She smiled. The trees that edged the courtyard were tall and broad. They must have been planted when the house was new. Tonight they were dressed for a party. Their lower boughs hung with Japanese paper lanterns glowing white, rose, and dusky yellow. The luminous globes drifted at their moorings with the heat of their invisible candles. The movement set the nearest and slenderest branches in motion, but the trunks and broader limbs were still. They were stately yet welcoming, like grand arboreal butlers pleased at her arrival.

It wasn't dark yet, not quite, but lights were on in and around the house. A street lamp above the minivan bathed it in a warm cone of light. Through Tsara's windshield the chateau's white walls gleamed, lit by soft floodlights hidden in the hedges and flowerbeds encircling the building. Brightness poured from the ground-floor windows, many of which looked big enough to drive through. Half a dozen men in tuxedoes walked past inside, carrying black cases shaped like trumpets and cellos. A woman led them, smiling as she talked backwards over her shoulder.

Tsara's uncle hadn't skimped. Then again, he never did.

Tsara glanced in the rear-view mirror. She could see the gates at the end of the driveway where she had turned off the state road, here called Libertyville Lane. Outside, tarmac. Within … this.

She stepped out of the car as the elegant double doors of the chateau flew open. Three figures hurried toward her, surrounded by an undulation of dogs barking joyfully. The lead figure gave shout.

"Tsara!" Castle was a bulldog of a man with a powerful chest and strong limbs. His hair was thin, Tsara noted with surprise, and greying. She remembered it as an abundant sweep of chestnut combed back from his forehead. But his blue eyes were clear and his square face strong. One might easily mistake him for an athlete in his sixties, not a man within striking distance of eighty.

Cass used a cane, ebony topped with a silver wolf's head; but it was mainly for show. He dropped it to the ground to give her a bear hug. "Goodness gracious me, just *look* at you." He held her at arm's length before crushing her again. The dogs, who had sorted themselves into a German shepherd and two huskies, ran around them grinning, their tongues curling in their mouths. "You look splendid. *Exactly* like your mother. Hans, can you believe this is the same teenager we used to see every summer? Tsara, you remember Hans, don't you?"

Tsara pushed away from the embrace and scooped up Cass's cane, handing it to him as she planted a kiss on his cheek. "Mwah!" She turned to the other man, feeling a smile lift her cheeks. "Of course. Hello, Mr. Freihoffer. Nice to see you again."

"Hans, please." The elderly gentleman shook Tsara's hand, grasping it with both of his. They felt like warm parchment paper wrapped around chicken bones. "I think at this point we can call each ozer by our first names, yes?" Hans was Austrian, and despite a flawless command of English he spoke with a slight accent others considered charming and he found an annoying imperfection.

"Sure, Hans. It's nice to see you. Court!"

"Hey." Three years younger than his sister, Court was dark to Tsara's bright. His brown, wavy hair was cut short, and his eyes were hazel. Tsara's blonde head came only to his shoulder, and he bent to give her a quick half-hug with one arm.

"Don't get mushy on me," she teased.

Court grinned. "Okay."

"Ah, ze bond of siblings," said Hans. "Humbling, isn't it, Castle?"

"I see her all the *time*," protested Court. "Geeze."

"Sure you do, little bro."

"And it gives you the advantage over us, no question," said Cass. "When you two are done being thicker than water, why don't you come inside? Alicia and the children are very excited to meet you, Tsara. And thank you so much for the flowers you sent—they're in the front hall. Absolutely lovely."

"Oh, I'm glad they arrived," said Tsara. "Let me just get my stuff out of the back and I'll follow you in."

"Fine, fine," said Cass heartily. "I'll ring the porter for you. No, don't you dare." He cut off her protest. "None of my other guests has carried luggage, and it's not going to start with you." He turned, pulling a cell phone out of his pocket and hitting a single number as Tsara walked to the door of the van.

Court sidled up to her. "You sent flowers?"

"Yeah, so?"

Court rolled his eyes. "Way to make me look good, sis."

Tsara tried to hide her smile as she turned to open the side door of the minivan. She pulled her duffel close, brushing past the dress that hung from the dry-cleaning hook.

The dogs erupted into a rolling broadside of barks, dashing between Castle and the edge of the shadows. From around the corner of the house two forms appeared, a large man followed by a smaller one. The figure in front was shouting, walking sideways so he half-faced the man behind him. A baseball cap was jammed low on his forehead, shadowing his face. The second man was dark, and wore a blue uniform. Under his cap his hair was almost black. As he stepped into the light Tsara noticed that his nose was spectacularly broken—not recently but thoroughly, with lumps and flat spots in the most extraordinary places. His right hand was on his hip holster, as though he had just replaced the gun, and with his left arm he made a violent gesture. "Clear out!" he snapped.

"Oh, for God's sake," said Cass in disgust. "Sit!" The dogs' haunches smacked the gravel as one. The huskies' tongues lolled from their mouths and their eyes sparkled. Next to them the German shepherd was still, but his ears lay flat against his skull and a low mutter came from his closed mouth.

Cass strode over to the two men, cane in hand. In the still mountain air every syllable carried clearly. "What seems to be the problem *this* time, Arnold?"

"Sorry for the disturbance, Mr. Thornlocke," said the security guard grimly. His voice was nasal. "He was trying to break into your wine cellar."

"Oh, he was, was he?" Cass raised his voice so the group by the minivan couldn't help but hear. "I've about had it with you. If you're that interested in the contents of my wine cellar, you can pay for them the same as anyone else. Now get off my property, and stay off."

"Want me to book him for breaking and entering, Mr. Thornlocke?" asked the guard. Tsara thought he sounded hopeful.

Cass glanced at the cluster by Tsara's car. Shadows misted purple and black around the house. The street lamp cast Tsara in a pool of light, one hand on her duffel bag still in the minivan. Cass's eyes met hers and he smiled, a smile of many yesterdays. He turned back to the guard and spoke more quietly.

"No ... I don't want to spend the evening filling out paperwork." He raised his voice again, looking up at the intruder. "But as for you—don't ever set foot on my property again. Now get out!"

The big man looked down on Cass, saying nothing. At his sides his fists clenched and unclenched. Tsara caught her breath. She felt Court stiffen next to her. The security guard stepped forward, hand on his gun. The big man jammed his fists into the pockets of his jacket and walked onto the driveway, making his way to the iron gates at the edge of the property. His steps were hard. As he passed through the light, he turned toward Tsara. His face was twisted, the eyes snaps of cold light. Over her shoulder she heard Hans draw in his breath as the fellow passed, the gravel grating beneath his feet.

Hans laid a hand on her arm. "Never mind him," he said quietly. "Local troublemaker. Every community has a few, eh? Nothing to worry about."

But Tsara kept her eyes on the figure as he strode down the driveway, almost dissolving into the shadows under the sycamore trees. Just past the gates a small pickup truck rolled up with its lights off, and the man climbed in. As he opened the door, yellow light filled the cab and she caught a glimpse of the driver's wide eyes and dark, curly hair. The door banged shut as the truck drove away.

After the briefest of conferences with the security guard, Cass rejoined them, cane swinging jauntily from one hand. "Some unexpected excitement, eh? I'm so sorry you had to see that," he said to Tsara and Court. "No need for concern. I've doubled security, and I can't imagine we'll see him again."

"What was he—" began Tsara.

"Just one of the local dipsomaniacs," said Cass airily. "Harmless except when sober, so you have nothing to worry about. Come on into the house, do, and meet Alicia and the kids." A young man with broad shoulders came out of the house and stood at the edge of the group. Castle nodded to him. "This is Christopher—he'll take your bags. Court? Hans?"

Christopher lifted Tsara's duffel and gown from the car. Tsara clicked on her keychain and the minivan's door slid shut. She wondered if Castle would be insulted if she locked the car. Then she locked it anyway and turned to follow her bags into the house. The security guard walked past her, rubbing his bulbous nose.

Hans fell in place beside her and stopped, so she did too. "Tsara, I wanted to make a suggestion about your room."

"My room?"

"Yes, here for the weekend. About an hour ago I got a phone call from my wife. One of the kids is sick and they won't be able to make it."

"Oh, I'm sorry. Nothing serious, I hope?"

"No, not at all. Just the sort of thing that keeps a child clutching a toilet for a day or two. But the reason I bring zis up is that your uncle was kind enough to give my bride and me a suite on the first floor. Since she will not be joining us I thought perhaps you might like to have it? It's quite lovely, with a terrace and a private bathroom. I think you would be more comfortable there than anywhere else."

"Oh, you don't have to do that," Tsara protested. "I'm sure wherever Cass put me is fine."

"I am sure of that, too," laughed Hans. "Especially since Alicia was in charge of rooms. But I am just one old man, and I don't need such splendid accommodations. Please take the room. Really, I insist."

Tsara smiled. "Well, I guess if you insist I don't have much choice. Sure, I'll take it."

"Wonderful!" Hans was elated. "I should tell you that in anticipation of your acquiescence I took the liberty of moving a few things to the room. Just small things," he added as she opened her mouth to ask. "A couple of items your uncle thought you might enjoy."

"Well, now you have me curious," said Tsara. "Excuse me." And she hurried ahead to tell Cass of the change in plan, lest the porter take her bags to parts unknown.

Castle held the door open and the group stepped into the hallway, all lights and warmth and movement. By the time Court let the door shut behind him, Castle's wife Alicia was hugging Tsara as though they were twins separated at birth. The older woman laughed at her own exuberance and straightened up to brush her hair from her forehead.

"—to meet you after all this time—" said Tsara.

"—to meet you, finally—" said Alicia at almost the same moment. They both stopped, each waiting for the other to go on, then laughed when they realized they had reached mutual courtesy paralysis. The porter shifted his weight. Tsara smiled at him and disentangled herself from Alicia.

"I'll see you at dinner, Court," she called as she and Christopher walked down the hall. "Gotta check out my lovely accommodations."

The family was so thrilled to see her, she thought. Alicia was charming, tall with a stylish sweep of silver-grey hair and dark eyes. Her pleasure at meeting Tsara was clearly genuine, and it made her irresistible. And Hans—God, it had been ages.

— ※ —

The big man crouched at the base of a massive oak with shaggy bark. Bushes and coppice growth gave cover, and he had darkened his face with dirt to blend with the shadows. He breathed when the trees moved, and kept still in their stillness.

Arnold stumped past the shrubbery at the end of the driveway. He was talking into his cell phone and holding it low so the bright screen blinded him in the dusk.

Mike could have touched him.

13

He watched Arnold go past, then fixed his eyes on the brightly lit house and the rich people in its big, fancy windows.

Mike was going to make Castle Thornlocke and everyone around him very sorry they had ever crossed him.

"Here you go, ma'am." Christopher held open the door for her—a neat trick, considering how full his arms were—and Tsara walked into her room.

The heavy wood door opened soundlessly onto a polished granite floor scattered with embroidered rugs. One depicted a unicorn lying by a tree, chained to the trunk by a collar buckled around his neck. He looked rather morose. On another, medieval peasants stomped on grapes, their shins stained with juice, while behind them wenches poured wine from jugs.

The walls, too, were stone, rising to a cathedral ceiling far overhead; but track lighting made the chamber elegant instead of Gothic. Even so, Tsara had a sudden urge to brush her hair over the parapets so the local prince would have some way of meeting her for their rendezvous.

By one wall was a reading nook, complete with plump easy chair, ottoman, and standing lamp; a crimson throw hung over one arm. Next to the chair a small bookcase held hardcovers and paperbacks, artfully interspersed with vases, ivory elephants, and a single bookend in the shape of a cowboy on a bucking horse. Tsara mentally pulled the throw around her shoulders and planted herself in the chair with a chunky novel some winter night when snow flashed past the windows.

On the other side of the chair was a cheval glass with beveled edges. A king-sized canopy bed overloaded with pillows dominated the rest of the room; a twin bed would have been lost, like a dingy at sea. Behind the bed, French windows had been left open to reveal a flagstone terrace. Velvet drapes of pine green framed the doors, heavy enough so the breeze coming through did not stir them. Tsara felt stiffness from her long drive drift away. She hadn't known it was there until it left.

A door opposite the chair was slightly ajar. Through it Tsara could see a bathroom gleaming with white and blue tile.

"Where would you like your bags, ma'am?" Christopher still stood in the doorway.

"On the bureau, please." As he settled the bags she stepped out through the French windows.

The breeze came off the lake, which lapped at one side of the terrace. On the other side a set of stairs led down to the beach. Past the stairs to her right was the rest of the house, curving along the lakeshore and reflected in its waters. It was magnificent, a thing of turrets and windows and dark red tile roofs crowning white stucco walls. They gleamed, floodlit in the purple dusk. Just beyond the lights a collage of rocks tumbled to the water in shades of sand and grey, topped with Halloween-colored maples. The oaks were further in, then a thin band of birches. Above them would be pines, then scrub and bare rock as the mountains ascended to the sky.

An iron guardrail enclosed the lake side of the terrace, but on the shore side it was open. The kids would like jumping off that onto the sand, she thought wistfully. Maybe next time.

"Ma'am?" The porter spoke to her from the threshold. "I've put your things on the bureau."

"Thanks." She re-entered the room. "Sorry. I've never been here before, and it's pretty wow."

The porter smiled. He looked young, in his twenties maybe, and his nametag read *Christopher Sweet.* "Yes, ma'am, it is that. This has been a labor of love for Mr. Thornlocke over the past few years."

"I can see that." She hesitated. "Okay—I never know how to do this, so I'll just ask. Am I supposed to tip you?"

"Oh, no, ma'am. Mr. Thornlocke was very specific about that." He grinned. "Any tips and I'm out on my ear. But it's okay—he's making sure we're well compensated for the weekend."

"So you don't work here full-time?"

"No, ma'am, just occasional things. Mostly it's just the family here, and I guess they carry their own bags." He smiled again.

16

"Do you live in Libertyville?"

"Yes, ma'am. Most of the time I work at the lumber store."

"And did Mr. Thornlocke tell you to call all his guests sir and ma'am?"

"Yes, ma'am, he did," replied Christopher, his eyes twinkling. He gestured at various parts of the room. "You've already found the terrace, and over there is the bathroom. These switches here control the lights." He stepped over to the doorway and moved a small button up and down. The room blurred into darkness and back again. "They're all on dimmers. Oh, and one more thing." He walked over to a small table where a telephone sat. "You can dial direct for long-distance, but if you need the housekeeper just hit zero three times."

"Why would I need the housekeeper?"

"It's pretty far away from the rest of the house. I think Mr. Thornlocke had that feature put in just in case someone got sick in the middle of the night or something."

Tsara was impressed. "He really did think of everything, didn't he?"

"Yes, ma'am. Mrs. Thornlocke had a lot of input too, is my understanding. This place was just an abandoned wreck before they took it over. Now it's something the whole community can be proud of."

"So they didn't build it from scratch?"

"Oh, no, ma'am. This has been here since the 1890s. Built by a railroad millionaire before there was income tax. I don't think anyone has that kind of private wealth anymore, even around here." He grinned again. "It probably would have been cheaper to tear it down and start over, but I guess they just fell in love with the place."

"I can see why. It's gorgeous." Tsara had passed other imposing homes on the way in, but nothing as majestic as this.

"My dad says when he was a kid he and his buddies used to explore in here. Of course, like I said, it was a wreck then." He gestured toward the long wing of the house visible through the French windows. "Wait till you see the ballroom. I did some of the work on it. The detail is all walnut from an orchard that got flattened in a storm a few years ago. The owner was pretty happy to find a buyer for the lumber."

Tsara thought of the two men in the driveway. "Is Mr. Thornlocke—popular in town?"

"With all the jobs he's brought in? You bet." He lowered his voice. "You maybe don't know, but he and Mrs. Thornlocke do a lot for the town. They donated a computer room to the library—just gave it, 'cos there wasn't one before. My mom says that's the only reason I finished high school. She's probably right. 'Course, there's no pleasing some people."

"What do you mean?"

"Oh, you hear crazy rumors. Like, why is the family so wealthy? Sour grapes. Anything else I can help you with?"

Interesting, thought Tsara. "No thanks," she said. "I think I've got a handle on the place, and I should probably get unpacked and ready for dinner."

"Enjoy your evening, ma'am."

"I'm sure I will. Thanks."

He left, pulling the door closed behind him. Really, she thought, for such a massive structure it was astonishingly silent.

Tsara went to the bureau, homing in on the dress that lay draped across the bags. She straightened the clingy dry-cleaner bag and gently hung the gown in the closet. *Red*, she thought happily. Then she unzipped the duffel. Early fall in New England could mean anything, and she had packed for everything. She hoped. Sunscreen and deet went into the bureau, along with a swimsuit and a heavy sweatshirt. Slacks, jeans, shorts, T-shirts, two turtlenecks and long underwear followed. The windbreaker went into the closet, next to the gown. You never knew.

Finally she extracted her toiletries bag and went into the bathroom. White tile glittered under halogen lights. The door to the shower stall was clear, and the interior was a glass tile mosaic of a waterfall, sea-green and blue, crashing over granite boulders cemented into the wall. The showerhead was approximately the size of a manhole cover, and the stall was so wide she could stand in the middle and stretch out her arms without touching the sides. She sighed in deep satisfaction.

A sunken tub took up the far end of the room; she could see Jacuzzi jets on the sides. A bottle of green bubble bath stood on the side of the tub next to a bar of soap still in its paper wrapper.

"Oh, wow," she murmured. She hung up the bag and crossed over to the tub. Sitting down on the edge, Tsara unscrewed the bottle cap and sniffed deeply, feeling the shock of transport across decades. Pine and rosemary mingled with something floral, a little like jasmine. It smelled of summers at Cass's old house, of her mother bathing her when she was a little girl. Of being five years old and taken care of.

Cass remembered.

Wandering out again she noticed a small cardboard box on the end table next to the armchair. Two or three envelopes poked out of the top, along with several dog-eared postcards. Curious, she sat down in the chair and picked up the folded card next to the box. In Cass's familiar script she read, "I thought you might enjoy these. They were all I could find. Much love, CT."

Putting down the card she reached for the nearest envelope and pulled it out. With a jolt she recognized the bold loops of her mother's handwriting. It had been on every birthday card and shopping list and note by the phone till Tsara was seventeen years old.

The postmark was over four decades old.

"Oh," she breathed. All else forgotten, she removed the letter and unfolded it, feeling vaguely prurient. In her family, one did *not* read other people's mail. But this must be okay. Cass had left them for her. She could almost hear her mother's voice as she read.

> ... *Thanks so much for the little dress. Rina looks beyond adorable in it, and as soon as the photos are developed I plan to prove it to you—not that I suspect you of doubting such a thing.*

Tsara wondered how long she had been "Rina," since she had no memory of it. She went on to a second letter.

> ... *Court turns out to have been aptly named, you will be pleased to know. He is really the consummate gentleman, even if he is only ten months old. Now that we have both a Court and a Castle in the family, I wonder what the next one should be called. Turret, perhaps, or Portcullis.*

There hadn't been a next one, which based solely on this letter might be just as well. Not that Tsara's mom would really have named a kid Portcullis. Would she?

19

The first postcard was from Denmark and showed a fortress overlooking slate-colored water. "Spent the day at Elsinore. Much grey stone and quite drafty. No spectral visitations, drat the luck."

Tsara chuckled silently. She had been fourteen on that trip, which would make Court about eleven. Her mother had reread Hamlet on the flight to Copenhagen and talked it up to both her kids, with varying levels of success. She pointed out to Court, who was deeply into superheroes at the time, that the Prince of Denmark was much like Peter Parker: "They both worry about doing the right thing, to the extent that they often manage to do nothing at all." Court conceded the similarity, but Hamlet's lack of web shooters was a deal-breaker for him and he went back to his comic book. Tsara was fascinated with the fight at the end, and she and her mother spent much of the remainder of the flight reenacting the duel with the plastic swords from their drinks and crying out, "Have at you now!" and "A touch, a touch, I do confess't!" while Tsara's father hid behind his Wall Street Journal and tried to pretend he didn't know them. Eventually the stewardess came by and demanded an immediate cessation of hostilities. Apparently not all the passengers were bardophiles, and her mother's comparisons with Shakespeare in the Park fell on deaf ears.

No wonder Tsara had become an English teacher.

"To a large extent we write our own scripts," her mother used to say. It was her favorite life metaphor, though she also meant it literally. Misplaced apostrophes sent her into a tizzy, and she considered any confusion between its and it's a signifier of the apocalypse. "If you're writing your own script it might as well be punctuated correctly," she sniffed once when Tsara needled her about it.

She'd certainly authored her relationship with Castle. Brother and sister had been so different—Tsara's mom had had the heart of an Eagle Scout. No compromises, at least not that Tsara could recall. And yet she'd maintained a close and loving relationship with her rebellious younger brother. Tsara wondered how she'd pulled it off. She tapped the postcard against her fingernails, then put it away and pulled out another one, then a letter, reading happily.

As she replaced the last of the papers in the box Tsara checked her watch. Whoopsie—time to get into that after five outfit, that's what time it was. She stood up, pulling off her clothes and reaching for gown and hose and jewelry.

Quickly she stepped into the bathroom to put on makeup. Her mother's classy WASP ideal was to apply just enough to make it appear she was wearing no makeup whatsoever. Well, Tsara thought, she would cheerfully cross that line. Bring on the eyeliner! Bring on the smoky shadows on the lids, the excited flush for the cheeks! And finally, everyone's best friend, lipstick.

After the makeup was on she stepped closer to the mirror and thrust out her jaw, turning her head slowly to search for those damn whiskers that had started sprouting as soon as she hit forty. She scrutinized furiously, searching out their every hiding place. Because let's face it: nothing wrecks a lady's evening ensemble like a goatee.

But if there were any whiskers that night they were too cowardly to show themselves. Satisfied, she ran a quick brush through her shoulder-length blonde hair and went back into the bedroom to see if the mirror approved.

It did. Tsara stood before it, utterly pleased. All five feet, four inches of her was ready for the ball and then some. Her face was round, with a softer version of Cass's square jaw, and her skin was clear—though she had often bemoaned the fact that nowadays she could have both zits and wrinkles. Her eyes were large and green, set over a straight nose and full mouth. The makeup added shadows and drama exactly where she wanted them.

And the dress! It was flame-red with rhinestones on slender straps that left her shoulders bare. A cowl draped over the neckline, hiding the mammary devastation wrought by nursing two babies. Below that a bias-cut bodice skimmed her tight waist. Tsara turned slightly, extending one foot in its sparkling, gold-colored dance shoe. A high slit on one side emphasized her trim, athletic legs, gleaming in iridescent hose purchased for the occasion. Well, truthfully, it emphasized one leg, she thought; but people could probably make the leap and assume there was another one much like it on the other side.

She had modeled it for the family the night before. Before she got dressed she had taken out one of her favorite pictures of her parents and propped it up on her dresser. It showed her father in a tux and her mom in a luminous gown whose ruby folds brushed the floor. Christina Thornlocke Abrams had loved red dresses.

When Tsara came downstairs in all her festive splendor Abbie had laughed and held up Mrs. Pinkie for a better look. (Mrs. Pinkie, in the manner of battered rag dolls the world over, had refrained from comment.) Big brother Josh said solemnly, "Mommy. You look like a superhero."

David said nothing, but his eyes gleamed; and as she brushed past him on the way back upstairs he muttered, "Need any help with the zipper?"

Looking in the mirror now she thought wistfully that it was a shame David wasn't there to threaten to rip the gown off her. Even after a dozen years together he could be counted on for such things. It made for a good marriage.

She and David had met as graduate students. He had been earning his teaching certification; she had been refreshing hers with a few courses. They had bonded over a required class they both loathed. Much of the curriculum had to do with getting in touch with one's emotions, the better to feel students' pain. (An assumption of most ed courses was that students are in an unremitting state of anguish.) One class project required making a timeline of their own emotional lives. In crayon. Tsara was trying to take notes that day, but eventually grew weary of waiting for the professor to say anything worth writing down; and in utter despair scrawled in her notebook, "*I can't stand it! This isn't even piffle—it's piffle lite!*" Leaning over to retrieve a dropped pen, David chanced to see it. His efforts to turn a guffaw into a cough nearly cost him his sinuses. It was at that moment, he told her later, he resolved to "get that woman no matter what I do." So he approached her after class and, screwing his courage to the sticking place, used his best line on her.

"Want to study together for the midterm?"

Tsara, who had always had a weakness for sensitive men with deep brown eyes, readily agreed. After they both aced the midterm (the professor feared inducing mass suicides by awarding anything lower than an A), they celebrated with dinner and a movie. The next weekend it was a folk concert at a tiny club in a brick basement off Harvard Square. They started calling each other, first once a week, then twice. Soon it was weird if they weren't talking every day.

It took him three weeks to kiss her, and when he did, it was glorious—his lips sliding smoothly over hers, one hand behind her neck gently pulling her closer. They were in her car; because of foul weather she had offered to drive him to the subway, and rain rattled like falling coins six inches above their heads.

After that he upped the ante. Dinner and a movie gave way to evenings of theatre and swing dancing, a marvelous whirl of rhythm and movement, hands slapping together at the perfect moment to keep each other in the music.

Finally one night he drove her home after seeing *King John* at the Huntington Theatre. He insisted on stopping for dessert after the show, and they had gourmet hot chocolates at a patisserie in Boston. It was like drinking a truffle. They went to her apartment and kissed on the couch until she couldn't stand it any more.

When she woke up next to him in the morning, she looked over at the soft, dark hair tumbling over his forehead and decided to marry him. Any nice Jewish boy who could woo a lady with Shakespeare, chocolate, and really superlative sex was a nice Jewish boy worth keeping. Two years almost to the day after they first met, Tsarina Abrams and David Adelman stood together under the *chuppah* and were joined in matrimony.

Five years later Josh inserted himself into the mix. He came out goopy and screaming like a Ringwraith, but after the initial shock they loved him anyway. Two years after that Abbie followed far more demurely, arriving a month after Tsara's fortieth birthday; and they loved her too. Now Tsara and David had just celebrated their tenth anniversary. They had a five-year-old boy and a three-year-old girl plus a house in the suburbs surrounded by a white picket fence. "Livin' the cliché" was Court's assessment, and Tsara was happy to agree.

She checked the watch David had given her for their last anniversary. It was slender and elegant ("Like you," he had said), encircled by tiny sapphires meant to mirror the ones that surrounded the diamond of her engagement ring. On the mother-of-pearl face were twelve more sapphires in place of numbers. The hands were black and lacy, matching the velvet band that held it on her wrist. The clasp was encrusted with Swarovski crystals.

The sapphires said it was just shy of seven-thirty. Not a good time to call him, she decided. He might still be putting the kids to bed, and besides, she would be expected in the main wing for cocktails. So, taking a last look at the mirror to make sure the back of the dress looked as good as the front (it did), she left the room, closing the massive oaken door behind her.

Two seconds later she walked back in and strode to the terrace doors, pulling them shut and locking them before leaving again. Cass's security was all well and good, but she had a thing about sociopaths wandering the grounds when she was on the first floor.

"A few things came for you," said David.

"From who?" Tsara was careful not to move as she spoke. Still in high heels from the party, she had had to walk around the room several times to find cell phone reception. It turned out that a certain flagstone to the left of the French windows was the magic spot, as long as she didn't twitch. The mountains were lovely, but they were hell on bars.

"Mm. *People* magazine. They say this will be your last issue."

"No, it won't. I renewed online a few days ago."

"Good. They seemed kind of panicky about it."

"What else?"

"Hold on." She heard him shift the phone. "Flyer from the women's center for some workshops next month."

"What kind?"

"Two financials and a self-defense."

"I'll take a look when I get home. Anything more?"

"Adara called."

"I got her voice message."

"She said to ask you when's the next time you can get together with her and solve the world's problems."

"I'll call her when I get back."

"You can't call her now anyway. It's after sundown."

"It's also after eleven. I'll give her a buzz when I can look at the calendar."

"You could use the one in your phone."

"I just want to make sure I'm not double-booking when I make plans to fix the world."

"I told her you suck at that, by the way," he said.

"At what?"

"This whole fixing the world thing. You guys get together all the time, and the world's still pretty screwy."

"You used the word 'suck' with our rabbi?"

"I used the word 'suck' with your good friend Adara. And I calls 'em like I sees 'em."

"The best plans take a while to come to fruition."

"So how are you enjoying Luxuryville?" asked David.

"It's *awesome,*" she crowed. "I haven't been into the town yet, but the chateau is pretty freakin' amazing."

"So how was dinner?" he said. "And how's Court? And the rest of your family?"

"Court's fine. He said to say hi. I met Alicia before dinner, and sat next to one of the kids during. Assigned seating."

Alicia's hand had been evident throughout the party. Every table had been perfectly balanced, guests grouped by common interests and husbands and wives separated so that by the end of the evening there were no strangers in the vast throng of the ballroom. Alicia knew everyone's name, including people she had never met before, and remembered their families, their jobs, and their hobbies.

"Is he or she nice?"

"He. Zachary. Yeah, seemed nice enough—a lot younger than me. I think he's still in college. The kid's a budding sommelier. I got a very detailed lecture about the table wine, and he's planted a vineyard on the grounds. He's going to give me a tour tomorrow."

"Really? They want to be vintners?"

"It has to be more of a hobby than anything else. He says he hopes they'll have wineable grapes in the next few years."

"Was dinner good?"

"Oh, God, yes. We started with this amazing lobster bisque with sherry in little hollowed-out pumpkin shells. Cass said that was so you got your vegetables."

"Ooooh—lobster bisque," sang David. "I'm gonna tell the rabbi."

"Yes, I'm pretty sure that would give her the vapors."

"Tell me how things are working out with the evil uncle."

"Well." She hesitated. "He seems really happy to see me. I think it meant a lot to him that I came."

"How often does he see Court?"

"Not as much as you might think. Court deals mainly with Alicia, and a lot of that's work-related."

Court ran an import-export business in Baltimore. His company was web-based, and with the anonymity of the Internet he had completed several transactions with Alicia before realizing that she was his uncle's wife. Alicia was the sort of driven entrepreneur who kept her own name for work but was perfectly content to be Mrs. Castle Thornlocke on weekends. "And geeze, it's not like we grew up with her," Court pointed out peevishly when Tsara laughed at him about it.

True enough: Alicia was the second Mrs. T., Castle's first marriage having ended in divorce. For a time Tsara's uncle had exulted in a raucous second bachelorhood alongside his friend Hans, also newly single. Both had subsequently remarried brides much younger than themselves who were able, as Tsara said, to "put on heirs." In this respect Alicia came fully loaded: at the time of their courtship she was a wealthy young widow with two toddlers, Zachary and his brother Alexander, who went by Zander. She called them "the twins" because they were eleven months apart.

"Hey, you know what's cool?" said Tsara. "Cass is a TV star."

"Then how come I've never heard of him?"

"You have so too heard of him."

"Not from TV I haven't. What makes him a star?"

"He does spots on local access cable—"

"Oh. *That* kind of star."

"Hush up. Zaylie was telling me and Court all about it."

David sighed. "I suppose if I wait long enough you'll tell me who Zaylie is."

"Zaylie," said Tsara with infinite patience, "is Cass and Alicia's daughter. She sat with Court."

"Ah."

"She's fourteen."

"And I'm supposed to know this how?"

"Because I *told* you. Before I left."

"Probably," said David. "What does evil uncle do on TV?"

"Stuff about guns. It's a hunting show." Zaylie's enthusiastic reports made it clear that the TV spots had established her father as a local celebrity. Firearms were something of a passion for Castle, and he was replete with anecdotes historical and personal about every weapon presented to him on-air or off.

"Is Court behaving himself?"

"Not really," admitted Tsara. "He kept trying to get the orchestra to play songs from *The Sound of Music* so he could give Hans stomach pains."

David snorted. "I always liked your brother."

"Me, too." Tsara thought over the dinner. It had been nice, really nice. Just that one moment of awkwardness.

She had been seated at the head table with Court and the Thornlockes. The only non-family member there was Hans, and he and Cass had regaled the assembled company with tales of their salad days, when Cass had been stationed in Germany in the early fifties and Hans had been trying to recoup his family's considerable wartime losses. One story involved a sporty red convertible they had stolen and sold three times. Another detailed an extortion ring they had run among the locals. "We never really broke anyone's legs," Cass said cheerfully. "Never had to. Any time there was an accident, we just put out the word we were behind it. Soon we were getting all kinds of credit for things we'd never done, and the lucre rolled in like a mighty stream." And Hans laughed uproariously as the three Thornlocke children gazed admiringly at their outrageous, dashing father with his fantastic stories of days gone by.

Tsara put down her soupspoon and glanced at Court. He smiled politely at the Thornlockes, but when he looked at Tsara his eyes were dark.

After dinner Cass pinged his wine glass with a fork for silence. He stood up, hair perfectly combed, tuxedo so crisp it looked die-cut.

"I want to thank you all for coming," he boomed. "And I shan't keep you from your conversations or the dancing which is about to start. But I wanted to let you know that thanks to the generosity of the ladies and gentlemen here tonight, as of this evening the Red Dress Brigade has capped off its fundraising year by breaking the one million dollar mark—thank you—for its parent organization, the Christina Abrams Cancer Center." He paused. *"Now* you may applaud."

Scattered laughter submerged under applause that thundered like a mountain waterfall. Cass raised his hand and it stopped. "We're especially fortunate that Christina's two children, Court and Tsara, could be here with us tonight." He indicated them with his champagne flute, and Tsara hastily sat up straight. "I hope you will join us as we raise a glass to their mother and my sister, Christina Thornlocke Abrams. May the good she did in life live on in the center that bears her name, and in our hearts." He raised his glass, and the company followed.

Tsara's chest tightened. It always hurt to think of her mother, whose death had had nothing at all to do with cancer.

She lifted her glass and drank. Champagne tingled down her throat.

Her musings were cut short as waiters swooped in on the tables, whisking them away and sweeping up any crumbs that had dared to transgress upon the hardwood floor that gleamed like glass. The ice sculptures punctuating the room were quickly arranged along one wall with tea lights behind them so the blood-red berries and orange leaves inside them jumped with light and shadow. Each member of the family had commissioned a statue. Castle's was a bear, rampant; Alicia had chosen a replica of the chateau, with lights in the miniature ballroom. Zachary and Zander's was an amusement park, complete with Ferris wheel. Zaylie had gone with a galloping horse, its frozen mane lifted in a breeze only it could feel. "She wanted a unicorn with pink hooves and a sparkly tail," confided Zachary as they stood to let the waiters push their chairs against the wall. "But Dad put his foot down."

The orchestra leapt into "Sing, Sing, Sing," and overjoyed wives heaved their husbands onto the floor. After that came a Beyoncé medley, followed by several Lady Gaga songs and an Adele cool-down. This got the younger crowd moving, and soon the band was moving effortlessly between Big Band classics and a finely tooled Top Forty playlist.

The music was splendid, but by eleven o'clock Tsara was happy enough to beg off. She had danced with Court, Cass, Hans, and the older Thornlocke boy. Cass and Hans knew how to waltz, but Hans's knees were arthritic and he had trouble staying on beat. And Court and her cousin were energetic but clueless on the dance floor.

"It's been a long day," she told Hans as they completed their second dance. "I think I'll call it a night."

"Must you?"

"It was a long drive. I'm about ready for bed."

Hans presented her with his arm. She placed her hand on it and they walked off the floor. "Good night," she called to Cass, who was dancing with Alicia. "I'll see you tomorrow."

"Breakfast whenever you want," roared Cass. "Sleep as late as you like." He twirled Alicia and she laughed, cheeks flushed.

Tsara smiled and waved. As she turned to leave the ballroom, Hans stopped, his hand on her elbow. His face was suddenly serious, and for just a moment she could see he was eighty. *When did that happen?* she wondered. He hadn't been eighty when she was a kid.

"Tsara," he said, "I don't know if you realize how much your being here means to Castle. He has always told me how much he hoped for a reconciliation between the families."

"Ah." Tsara floundered for something to say. "Well—it was so kind of him to invite me. Maybe next time I can bring the kids."

"That would make him very happy."

"Well." She paused again, wishing Hans would quit poking the elephant in the living room. "It's been a lovely evening. I'm already looking forward to tomorrow."

"Good night, then."

"Good night."

And so she had retreated from the bright gowns and dark tuxedoes, letting the pulse of the music fade behind her as she made her way down the long hallway to her room. She waved at Court, who was sitting with Zaylie and tying her napkin into cloth origami. He glanced from her to Hans.

"Nobody here dances as well as you," she told David.

"Poor bastards."

"Yeah. I told them all that, too."

"You didn't!" he said, aghast.

"Maybe I did, maybe I didn't." She wondered if he could hear her grin. "Are the kids in bed?"

"Kids are in bed, and I am curled up in front of a warm TV."

"Whatcha watching?"

"*The Seven Samurai*. With commentary." His voice radiated vast contentment.

"Excellent. It sounds like we're both having perfect weekends. Hey, quick question."

"What?"

"Why is there a pair of toddler socks, a stuffed monkey, and a dog biscuit in my suitcase?"

"Abbie was concerned your feet might be cold," he replied gravely.

Tsara giggled. "And the monkey?"

"Josh was afraid you might be lonely since you wouldn't be sleeping with Daddy."

"And the Milkbone is in case I need a snack?"

"No, that's for Great-Uncle Castle's dogs."

"I see. And what did Falstaff think of all this?"

"As I understand it, the entire scheme was his idea." David's tone was distilled gravitas. Tsara called it his Former Attorney Voice. Falstaff was the family dog, a hundred pounds of husky-Newfoundland mix. The kids treated him as half teddy bear, half sofa, and half galumphing best friend. If the math didn't quite add up, that was okay; neither did Falstaff. Like an old Hollywood movie star, he filled every room he was in. Naturally they would defer to his judgment.

"Well." Tsara considered this. "You can tell Falstaff the dogs seem quite well-fed. Noisy, though. Actually, I can hear them now," she added as a burst of excited barking came across the lake.

"How many are there?"

"Three, but that's twenty-one in dog years."

"Good point."

"And you can tell Josh I'll sleep with the monkey. But I'm not really sure what I'll do with the socks."

"You'll think of something. "

"I expect so. Well, I'll let you go. I'm sure Kurosawa is luring you with his siren song."

"See you Sunday evening."

"Love you."

"Bye."

31

"B—oh, wait, there's one more thing," she said. "You still there? Okay. I just wanted to tell you there's hardly any cell reception here, so don't panic if you don't hear from me much."

"I promise."

Tsara hung up and plugged the iPhone into its charger, setting it down on the table next to the telephone and her watch. As she straightened the door opened slightly.

"Hey," said Court, poking his head in. "Can I come in?"

"Sure."

"I wasn't sure you'd heard me knock," he said, closing the door behind him. "The door's so thick."

"I didn't, actually. But I was on the phone."

"Saw you leave the dance early," he said. "So what did Helmut von Blitzkrieg want?"

"To give me his room," she said brightly. "Like it?"

"Hell, yeah," he said, gazing around. "You should see where they have me. I think it used to be peon's quarters. You need a GPS and a team of Sherpas to find it."

"I'm much cuter than you."

"That, and you're the prodigal niece." Court sat down in the armchair and sighed. "Some party."

"Castle's castle," said Tsara quietly. She sat down on the bed, taking the weight off her high-heeled feet. "It's everything he always wanted."

"I guess all the good banana republics were already taken," said Court. He was silent, then turned toward her, eyes anxious. "Do you think Mom would want us to be here?"

"Oh, geeze. I have no idea." She brightened. "But Dad would *totally* hate it."

"Very funny. No, I'm serious. I mean, would she say—"

"Mom knew who Castle was, and she still took us to visit him every summer," said Tsara.

"Do you think she knew about his little operations after the war?"

"Honestly, I don't know." It was hard to imagine their mother overlooking something like that. But it was also hard to imagine she hadn't known about it. Cass wasn't shy.

"Do you think you'll come again?"

"Do you think you will?"

"I think I'll keep doing business with Alicia."

"She seems really nice."

"Yeah, I can totally see why he married her," said Court. "But you gotta be suspicious of anyone who would marry *him.*"

Far away the orchestra pulsed in a velvet undertone. Tsara shook herself. "Court, I'm beat. I'm going to get changed and go to bed."

"Okay." Court's eyes drifted to the iPhone. "Mind if I play Angry Birds?"

"Help yourself." Tsara retired to the bathroom as Court unhooked the phone from the charger. When she came out fifteen minutes later he was losing to a horde of sniggering green CG pigs.

"It's easier on an iPad," he muttered.

"I didn't say anything. You done?" Tsara walked to the closet and lovingly hung up the dress before turning back to her brother.

"Apparently." He handed her the phone and got up. "I think brunch is on the main terrace tomorrow."

"Is everyone staying?"

"No, I think it's just us and Freihoffer."

"Okay. See you tomorrow, then."

"Night."

As he closed the door behind him she replaced the phone in its charger, thinking about the *People* magazine and the workshops at the women's center.

She turned toward the cheval glass and adjusted it with one hand. "Howdy, belle of the ball. "

It was a different look from earlier in the evening. Her slight build was accentuated by bed attire: pink, fleece-lined Crocs and baggy plaid pajama bottoms of vivid blue topped with an Ohio Wesleyan sweatshirt that was old enough to drink. With the makeup washed off and her long bangs touched with dampness from the sink, she looked almost like a teenager. Her hair framed her face in a sleek bob. It was a buttery blonde that she and her hairdresser agreed was the color God would have given her if he'd really been paying attention. She had visited the salon that morning before hitting the road. Her stylist had wrought his elfin magic so that now her hair swayed as a single, glossy curtain whenever she moved her head. She tried it now, swishing the mass from side to side and enjoying the effect.

So even though her back was to the door, she saw it swing open to admit two men.

"*Oh*," she gasped, and tilted the mirror toward the floor to make it clear that she had not just been engaging in a love fest with her own reflection. She stepped toward the pair, who were looking at her with ninety-proof bewilderment. Likely they'd knocked and she just hadn't heard it.

They weren't guests. They hadn't been at dinner and they certainly weren't dressed for it. Jeans and black tee shirts weren't the same thing as tux and black tie. Probably more temporary staff. Poor guys—who could blame them for getting lost? "Can I help you?"

Her first impression was that the smaller of the two men looked like Mighty Mouse. He couldn't have been more than an inch taller than she, but his shoulders were vast for so short a man; and even through his shirt she could see his chest was solid and muscular. A tidy beard lined his pointed jaw. His hair was curly and black, and his eyes were the color of wet coal. He glanced from her to his companion, one eyebrow raised.

The second man shifted his weight. "Is—we're looking for Hans Freihoffer. Is he here?"

If the first man reminded her of Mighty Mouse, this one made her think of David—not hers, but Michelangelo's. It was all there: the grace, the athletic bearing, even the surprisingly big hands. One was over his shoulder, holding not a sling for Goliath but a grey backpack. It only heightened the resemblance. A sheath hung from his belt, and he had a red bandana knotted at his neck. His hair was sandy. He looked permanently windblown.

His face was familiar, but Tsara had met dozens of new people that night, so she felt she could be forgiven for not being able to place a particular individual. Even one who looked like that. She took a quiet breath to remind herself she was a happily married woman.

"I'm awfully sorry," she said. "He and I switched rooms. I don't know where he is."

The taller man's fingers flicked near the sheath at his belt. His friend glanced down, as if nodding with his eyes.

"Well." Tsara cleared her throat. "Well."

The men didn't move. Tsara reached for the phone on the bedside table. "The housekeeper will know where he is. Let me just call her for you."

As she turned to pick up the phone, she caught a flash of movement out of the corner of her eye. The small man leaped behind her, whipping one arm around her and slamming his hand over her mouth.

"No!" she shouted through the hand. She stomped on his feet, and he jerked backwards, his arm slacking. She smashed her elbow into his ribs. He grunted, letting go.

Across the room the door shut.

She whirled around, close to her attacker. "No!" she yelled again, and shot her hand, palm first, into the middle of his face. Blood sprayed out in a fan. His head snapped back and she grabbed his shoulders, smashing her knee into his groin.

It felt squashy.

He doubled over. She grabbed his hair, bringing her knee up to his head as hard as she could.

Behind her a lock clicked.

The man fell to the floor, arms flopping like empty socks. She gawped at him, astonished, then turned to run.

She had waited too long.

A hard body slammed into her and she crumpled. Her left cheek cracked onto the stone floor. She cried out. Her arm flailed over her head. She tried to push herself up. A hand grabbed her arm and held it down. The big man was lying on her, his body covering hers.

"Quiet!" he snarled.

She drew a breath to shout. Something flashed before her. His free hand held a knife, and the blade was an inch from her face.

She stopped.

"See this?" His fist held the bone handle, and he moved it slightly for emphasis. The edge of the blade glittered. It looked as long as her forearm.

She jerked her head yes.

"Do what I say and I won't hurt you. Understand?"

She nodded again.

"Say it!" The blade jumped forward.

Hating herself, she ground out, "You won't hurt me if I do what you say."

"Good." He straightened to a sitting position, his thighs straddling her hips, and pulled her arm behind her back with frightening ease. "Now be quiet and hold still."

The knife vanished and she heard a soft click as he returned it to its sheath. His grip rigid on her arm, he leaned past her and jostled the foot of the smaller man, who lay unmoving next to her.

"Wake up," he said, low and urgent. "C'mon, buddy, get up."

The figure did not stir. The big man shifted again and touched the hand that lay open on the floor. "Jim. Wake up."

Still the little man was motionless.

"Jesus Christ," said the big man. "What did you do to him?"

"I hope I killed him," spat Tsara.

The man tightened his grip and jerked her arm toward her head. She grunted with pain. Her heel throbbed where she had stomped on the smaller man's feet, and her free hand was slick with blood.

Oh, God—what's this guy going to do to me if I've killed his friend?

Just then the little man shuddered. Tsara heard him take a breath. His legs slowly swiveled around as he sat up. He shook his head, and blood splattered on the tiles before her in an arc of bright dots.

"Get the bag," said the big man's voice.

Jim stood and walked past Tsara. She felt a vicious stab of pleasure when she saw he was limping. He came back and dropped the grey backpack behind her. She heard the zing of a zipper flying open.

"On my count," said the big man. His voice was tight. "One—two—three."

He yanked her arm back to the floor, and as easily as though she had been a doll they flipped her onto her back. Jim wrenched her arms above her head. The big man sat just below her pelvis, his thighs gripping hers so she couldn't kick. The knife was at her throat again, but she didn't care. She tried to jerk one hand free to strike him. Jim pulled them back effortlessly, and loops of rope bit into her wrists. She opened her mouth to scream, and the big man's hand grabbed her jaw, digging into the muscles and forcing it to open wider. He dropped the knife to the floor, and with his free hand grabbed something small and red. She had just time to realize it was Abbie's sock before his hand was deep in her mouth, shoving it past her teeth.

His fingers tasted like dirt.

She gagged and jerked her head to throw the sock out, but now the massive hand was under her jaw, jamming it up and closed. A tearing noise, and strips of duct tape slapped onto her mouth. Jim held her hands, now securely bound, on the floor over her head.

The big man raised himself slightly and his hands patted her torso, his thumbs grazing the edges of her breasts before moving down her legs. Satisfied, he nodded at his companion. Once again they rolled her over, face to the floor. She caught a glimpse of herself in the downward-tilted mirror by the bed. Her eyes were wide, frantic over the bands of grey tape; her hair flew wildly. Jim stood over her, a small dark object in one hand. He whipped it down at her head. She screamed through the gag and lurched to one side. The big man's hand grabbed the back of her sweatshirt, pinning her.

A second passed. Two. Cautiously, Tsara raised her head to see the mirror.

Jim was still in striking stance, his arm halfway to the back of Tsara's skull. Around his wrist was the massive hand of his companion, who was glaring into his eyes. The big man shook his head. Jim shrugged and withdrew his arm, slipping the dark object into his jeans pocket.

Tsara dropped her head to the floor, breaths shuddering. From this angle she could partially see the reflections of the two men. The bigger one still gripped her sweatshirt. She could feel his knuckles on her back. He twitched his head toward the door, then at the French windows. His companion walked to the door and out of Tsara's sight. A click. The

38

lights went off. She shifted, wanting to get up, but the hand pressed between her shoulder blades.

"Don't move."

Jim's feet limped past her and paused for half a second by her head. With a soft swish he hoisted the backpack onto his shoulders. His footfalls were silent on the granite floor, but seconds later she heard the French doors open. The breeze moved the hairs on top of her head.

Keeping his hand on her back, the big man reached for the knife on the floor, replacing it in its sheath. But when she moved, his hand grew heavy. "Don't make me hurt you."

She was still.

Her eyes were adjusting to the darkness, and she wondered if he knew she could see him in the mirror. She glanced at it again without moving her head.

He was turned toward the windows, his face in profile. His hair stood up in billows. As she continued to stare he slowly turned his head toward the mirror. His face flattened to shadow. He was looking at her.

Tsara dropped her eyes. She thought desperately. Was there something valuable in the room? Did they think she was someone else?

Faintly across the expanse of lake, the orchestra sounded. Someone laughed, the sound perfectly preserved in the distance. And then—a clopping noise, and a trill that wasn't quite a night bird.

"Come on." The man heaved her to her feet, pulling her upper arm and moving toward the terrace.

He's leaving, she thought crazily. *Good, good, he's leaving—*

But as they approached the open windows his grip grew tighter. She pulled back, twisting her arm. For half a second it worked and she slid out of his grasp. He grabbed both her arms and slammed her into the wall. Her head snapped back and air pounded out of her. She gave a muffled moan. Her feet barely touched the floor. His hands were tight on her arms. He pushed them back and the ropes ripped her skin. He leaned in close, and she could feel the puffs of his breath.

"You're coming with me the easy way—or the hard way."

Right, she thought grimly. *The hard way.* Furiously she kicked at his knees. He sidestepped, pulling her off-balance as he heaved her from the wall and toward the open windows. She kicked again and her leg caught the bedside table, knocking it over. The phone and iPhone slid to the floor, crashing into each other. Ignoring the noise, he dragged her. She was only half-standing, and her Crocs scrabbled on the smooth floor.

Something small and flat slid under her foot. The watch! She smashed her heel down on it, feeling it shatter.

They reached the windows and as he stepped through she lurched at the floor-length drapes with her bound hands, grabbing the fabric so that as he yanked her through the opening the drapes came too. With a series of pings they tore free of the curtain rod. He turned his head at the sound. "Let go," he snarled. He dug his fingers into her wrists and her fists opened against her will.

He hauled her toward the beach side of the terrace where Jim waited, holding the reins of two dark horses. The big man pulled her toward the larger one and grabbed her below the shoulders, lifting her.

Don't let him!

Tsara twisted around and aimed a blow at his ear, hard and desperate. He turned his head aside, and her wrists hit his temple. She felt his hair on the blades of her hands. He grunted and set her down on the terrace, still holding her arm. With his free hand he stabbed his fingers deep into her shoulder muscle.

Pain blasted through her.

It hurt too much to scream.

Her knees gave way and she stumbled.

The pain stopped and the big man lifted her onto the horse, forward in the saddle, before climbing on behind her. His thighs were around hers and he reached forward, shoving her bound wrists down. "Keep those hands on the pommel and don't move 'em."

Jim tossed him the reins; Tsara felt him catch them. Then his hands were at her head. "Hold still." A dark band pressed against her eyes, and she realized it was the bandana from his neck.

Did I kiss David goodbye?

"Go." Saddle leather creaked as Jim mounted his horse, then a wild splashing surrounded them as they cantered into the lake. Water spewed up to Tsara's shins as she gripped the pommel. Everything was moving. She lurched to the side, one leg too high, sliding off the saddle.

Did I tell the kids I love them?

The big man's arm went around her, righting her and pinning her to his body as they galloped into the dark nowhere of the night.

The horses were noisy. Their cantering threw water everywhere, and their breath came in a cannonade of whooshes and snorts. Why on earth would anyone use them for a getaway? Wouldn't someone notice all this commotion?

But even as they crashed through the lake shallows, even as the music briefly grew louder then faded again, no voice called out to them.

They're going to kill me.

My family will never find my body.

The horses surged forward. The cold cut through Tsara's thin clothing.

But. I'm not dead yet.

Tsara kept her hands on the pommel and the man's arm stayed around her waist, firm enough that she felt it when she inhaled. He was literally aware of every breath she took.

But he couldn't feel her head. At least not the front of it. Carefully, Tsara pulled her jaw open against the tape. Slowly the adhesive peeled away from her skin, and soon one corner of her mouth was open to the night air. As the horses finally turned and left the water, their hooves clanging on stone, she thrust the little red sock out of her mouth and let it fall to the ground.

Somebody will find that, she told herself. *Somebody will find it.*

The sounds changed. Cricketsong receded and wind hissed through trees. The horses had slowed to a walk, and their hooves crunched when they lit. It sounded like leaves, not needles, which meant they must be entering the old-growth forest that had never been logged.

How long had they been going? She wondered abruptly. Impossible to say. But now she started counting, trying for a number a second and curling up one finger every time she had a minute.

She had used up both hands three times when the horses stopped.

The man slid off the saddle behind her, and she yanked off the bandana. A whirl of stars and branches spun overhead as rough hands pulled her to the ground. One knee gave way and she stumbled.

"Easy." He pulled her toward a dark shape in the trees, and she had to half-trot to keep up.

She heard a squeak, and white spilled from an oblong opening in front of her. By the time she understood it was a doorway she was through it, breathing hard and blinking in the light.

They were in a small room with a wood floor and low ceiling. The walls were logs, and there were no windows. A cabin. The furnishings were sparse: a wood stove sat pulled out from the wall, enclosed in a metal fence as though for childproofing. Two beds stood by the walls. A small, round table and two chairs completed the room. On the table sat a Coleman lantern, the source of the light. Jim stood next to it, his face dark and flecked with blood. He looked up and his fingers flew rapidly, like birds in different flocks. The big man replied with his free hand, his own fingers moving with grace and precision.

They're talking to each other, thought Tsara. And she couldn't understand a word they said.

Jim moved past them, brushing against Tsara. She cringed. He did not respond but walked out the door, closing it behind him.

The big man lifted a brass door key from a nail by the door. He put it into the lock and turned it. Tsara heard the snik of the bolt sliding into place, and with a sick lurch of panic she realized she was alone with him.

He slid the key into his back pocket and paused, rubbing the temple where she had hit him. There was an abrasion there, and a little blood. She was glad.

He pulled the chairs away from the table and set them facing each other in the middle of the room, before the wood stove. "Sit."

Tsara stayed standing. He pulled her over to the chair and kicked the back of her knee so she half-fell to the seat. "Do what I say," he said coldly. "Remember?"

He sat in the other chair and reached for her face. "I'm gonna take this off. Don't scream." He yanked off the duct tape, all three strips at once. Tsara couldn't help it; she gave a little shriek.

He stared at her. "Where's the sock?"

"I swallowed it," she snapped.

He stood up fast; the chair fell behind him. *"Where is it?"*

Oh, God, he was big, she thought helplessly. She raised her bound hands, but he pushed them down to her lap, thrusting his face into hers. *"Answer me."*

"I spat it out when we left the lake," she almost screamed.

He dropped her hands and strode to the door, pulling the key out of his pocket and thrusting it into the lock with one smooth movement. The door opened and Jim appeared. Once again their fingers sang to each other. Jim looked at Tsara. For a split second he was expressionless. Then his dark eyes glittered and a small smile came to his lips. He jerked his chin *Yes*, and withdrew.

The door closed again, locked. Her captor righted his chair again before her. He sat down, leaning close. "Now," he said, "we're going to have a little talk."

"What do you want with me?" she cried.

"I'll tell you what I want," he said. "I want my son."

Thoughts collided in Tsara's head. *Oh, good, there's been some mistake. Oh, shit, this guy's completely crazy.*

"I—don't have your son."

"I know you don't. But you're going to help me get him." He leaned back, arms folded across his massive chest. "How do you know Castle Thornlocke?"

"Cass? "

Once again he leaned forward, anger in his eyes. "Yes, *Cass,*" he spat. "They rolled out the red carpet for you when you arrived, and you got the best room in the house. *How do you know him?*"

Tsara thought fast. Clearly, this was about her uncle somehow. And just as clearly, this man was no fan. She chose her words with care.

"I knew him when I was a kid," she said, "but before tonight I hadn't seen him in over twenty years."

"Knew him how?"

"Our families were close."

He grunted, still looking at her. His eyes were grey-green, the color of a winter ocean. "And then what?"

"People drift apart." She hoped he would buy it. Being too closely associated with Cass right now might be very bad for her health.

"If you *'drifted apart,'*" he said, emphasizing the words, "why was he so excited to see you tonight?"

"Because it was the first time in twenty years. More." Twenty-five?

He looked at her, unblinking. "Do you know when he moved to Libertyville?" he asked.

"I heard about it," she said vaguely. "Um ... five or six years ago?" Her voice rose in a question. She was trying hard to give the impression of someone who had heard the news in such a roundabout manner that she scarcely remembered it. In fact, she recalled it vividly. It was two days after her father died. Cass had had the grace to pen a condolence note, and the new address had caught her eye.

"He employs a lot of people around here. "

"Yes," said Tsara, thinking of the porter who had helped her with her bags. Where was this going?

"So you knew about that."

"I found out today."

"Did you also find out about the loans he makes?"

Tsara shook her head, baffled. "What—I don't know about any loans."

"Let's say you don't," he said grimly. "I'll explain. He lends money, lots of it, to people who can't get it anywhere else, and charges interest that would make a Rockefeller bleed." He leaned close now, too close. "Know what he does if they can't pay it back?"

"No," she whispered. Oh, God, it was hard not to flinch.

"Neither did I." He sat up straight and ran his hand through his rumpled hair. "This is my house. I live here with my son. When I go into town I take him with me. That's what we did this morning, set out like normal. Usually I leave him with his grandmother, but today he wanted to play with some other kids he knows, so I dropped him off with them while I went to stock up. Came back a couple of hours later and you know what I found?"

Tsara shook her head again. Her heart was speeding up. It almost hurt her chest with its sharp, fast beats.

"Mom in the kitchen, hysterical. Dad in the yard, yelling like a damn fool. And the kids—my son and his friends—they were gone."

"Gone?"

"To Thornlocke's. You see, what I didn't know was this family owed him a pile of money plus interest. And when they didn't pay it back fast enough, he took their kids. And mine." He paused to let this sink in. "The parents are crapping their pants. When I left they were

46

trying to raise the cash. They can do what they want—I don't care. I would have never left my boy with them if I'd known they owed that scumbag. But I'm getting my kid back."

Tsara sat quietly, stunned. Either the man was completely delusional or the story was true. And it was almost too crazy not to be real.

Let's face it, she told herself. *It does sound like something Cass might do.*

There had to be a way out of this.

"Look," she said, "if this is about money—"

"Hell, no." He stood up abruptly and paced the room, scarcely looking at her. "I went to him—Thornlocke—and told him he could have every penny I got. But it wasn't—he laughed at me. I said *I* wasn't the one who owed him, and he said that wasn't the point, that giving me my *own kid* would set a *poor precedent.* And finally I got down on my knees and I *begged* him." He stopped, running both his hands through his hair till they clenched to fists. "I never begged any man for anything," he said in an undertone so soft Tsara wasn't sure he meant her to hear it. He turned to face her again, businesslike. "So I decided to bust my son out. Him and the rest of the kids. My buddy knows the grounds pretty good, we've both done work there, and he figured there was only a few places they could be. We went to the wrong ones first. Finally we figured it had to be the wine cellar—it's away from the house. My buddy went to get the truck. And I got there, and I could *hear* them inside—" He stopped, and drew a ragged breath. "But the guard was waiting, must've figured we were coming, so—"

"Oh," said Tsara, and stopped.

"What?" His voice was sharp.

"That—was you, wasn't it?" she said. "In the driveway this evening. And J—" She coughed. "Your friend. With the truck."

"That was us. Getting thrown out at gunpoint." He sat down again, anger still clouding his face. "We tried everything. We finally decided if Castle Thornlocke took mine, we'd take one of his. And obviously it had to be Freihoffer, so—"

"Why?"

"Why what?"

"Why obviously Freihoffer?"

"Because he was in on it," said the big man, as though it scarcely needed to be explained. "He knows all about it. Was there when I talked to Thornlocke. He *laughed*." The grey-green eyes flashed like the edge of a knife.

"But—why not go to the police?"

He gave a bark of a laugh. "Libertyville police," he spat. "Yeah. Jordan and Arnold Stone. Who do you think *took* those kids? Who do you think grabbed them like—like *garbage* and threw them into that hole? And who was holding a pistol on me tonight?"

Tsara stared at him, horrorstruck. "I didn't know," she whispered.

He looked at her silently. Appraising.

"Well—how about the State Troopers or something?"

"They wouldn't listen to someone like me."

"Why not?"

"Quiet," he snapped. "Why were you in Freihoffer's room?"

"He found out his wife and kids weren't coming, so he offered me the room. He said I'd be more comfortable there." The big man stared at her with deep skepticism. "It's true!" she protested.

"Maybe it is," he said. "I just wonder if the little prick knew I was coming."

Tsara gasped. Hans, who had always been so kind to her ....

"Can't see how he would have known," the man went on, more to himself than to her. He rubbed his chin. "But still. Maybe he just thought it would be safer somewhere else." He looked at her again, and one side of his mouth tightened. "Hell of a shock. We thought you were going to be an eighty-year-old Austrian with a God complex."

Tsara said nothing. After a moment the man continued. "We couldn't search the place for him, and we couldn't let you call the housekeeper. And you'd already seen us. So it was you. Wrong place, wrong time." He sighed and stood up, looking down at her. "So that's the deal. You'll stay here tonight. In the morning we'll do a quiet little prisoner exchange, and tomorrow night you'll be sleeping in your own bed." He pulled his chair back to the table. "I'll get the stove going. It gets cold here at night." He grabbed a handful of kindling from a small box on the floor next to the stove and sat down at the table. The hunting knife came out and he sliced into the branches, making small scales that curled away from the main stem.

"Ah—" She cleared her throat. "Um, excuse me—uh—"

"Mike."

48

She looked at him in terror, and when she did not speak he glanced at her. "What?"

"You're going to kill me," she gasped.

He shook his head. "Nobody's going to hurt you."

"But you—" She stopped.

"Told you my name?" He shrugged and returned to his whittling. "They'll figure out who I am in about five seconds anyway. And you already know Jim's name. Even though you're pretending not to."

Shit. "Well," she said carefully, "okay. Mike, then. Can I ask you something?"

"Go ahead. "

"How ... old is your son?"

Mike appeared to be concentrating very hard on the small branch in his hand. "Six. "

"Six," repeated Tsara in horror.

He turned to her, his face tight. "Why do you care? "

She opened her mouth and closed it. "I just—when you said the two of you lived here, I figured he was older for some reason."

Mike shook his head. "Six. Birthday was last week."

Six, thought Tsara.

Six is kindergarten or first grade. Six is apple juice and pinesap hands and favorite cartoon characters.

Six was a year older than her son.

"I'm sorry," she said awkwardly.

Mike did not answer. He stared at the branch and knife in his hands, and in the silence Tsara could hear the blade biting into the wood. After a moment she went on, "Um ... one other thing?"

"What?" His tone said this was the last question.

"Would you untie my hands? Please." She tried to speak in a neutral voice.

"Depends," said Mike.

She waited for a moment and when he neither answered nor looked at her she clenched her teeth and decided to play along.

"On what?"

"Are you going to fight me?"

"No," she said in a small voice.

He looked at her over the knife. "Why not? You did pretty good last time."

Because it wouldn't work, asshole, she thought. *I lost, remember?* But as this was probably not the answer that would convince him she deserved to be untied, she kept her voice as even as she could. "Because you're bigger and stronger than I am, and you have a knife. The door's locked and the key's in your pocket. I don't know where we are except that it's deep in the woods. Plus it's the middle of the night. The horses are gone, and anyway I don't know how to ride. So—no."

He grunted. "Got it all figured out, don't you?"

She didn't answer. After a moment he gathered the carved sticks and pulled his chair once more before hers, turning it toward the wood stove. He opened its glass door—which did not creak, Tsara noted; he must take good care of it—and dumped the kindling in. The rest of the fire must already have been laid, because as soon as he lit the twigs a bright yellow light fluttered forth. He shut the door again and turned to face her.

"Let's see those hands."

Tsara held up her wrists awkwardly and he began to work at the knots. It took some doing; they were tight. While he pulled on them she examined him, memorizing. The waves of his hair were the color of damp sand. Strong jaw, she thought. Full lips. Nose was straight, with a flare in the nostrils that broadened it at the base. From the small lines around his eyes she put him in his mid-thirties. She was close enough to make out a band of deep blue encircling his green-grey irises. His cheeks were leathery, and she could see black specks of beard along the clean-shaven jaw.

The face was not cruel. But it was determined.

"There." Mike unwound the rope from her chafed wrists, holding them briefly with one hand. "You promised. No fighting."

"No fighting."

He took away his hand. She stretched her arms slowly out, and her rings sparkled in the light from the fire.

"You're married," he said.

There didn't seem much point denying it. "Yes," she said, hoping that was good.

"Kids?"

Again, her thoughts leaped wildly. Lie? Tell the truth?

Truth. Easier to remember. Besides, it might make him like her.

"Two," she said. "Boy and a girl."

He nodded. "You'll be seeing them soon."

It was as though he had hit her. Tsara gritted her teeth and looked down, staring at the raw skin on her wrists. *Damnitdamnitdamnit!* She would not cry in front of this man.

He leaned back again, surveying her. "Where did you learn to fight?"

"I don't know," she muttered, not looking up.

"Bullcrap." Oh, this was not going well. "No one fights that good by accident. You cold-cocked Jim in about five seconds. Those were *moves,* my friend, which means you know what you're doing. So I'm going to ask you again, and this time I want you to remember that when I ask you a question you answer it with no shit attached. *Where did you learn to fight?*"

"Okay—okay," she said. "I took some women's self-defense courses."

There was silence for a moment.

"Women's self-defense courses," he repeated drily.

She opened her hands and looked up at him. "Yeah. I swear, that's it."

He looked at her until she blinked. He gave a short grunt and stood up. "Take whichever bed you want," he said. "Jim and I will take turns on the watch, so don't scream or try anything funny unless you want one of us to come in here and you can spend the rest of the night tied to a chair with a knife at your throat." He spoke matter-of-factly, as though telling her extra towels were in the hall closet. She nodded, not trusting herself to speak.

He turned to go. "No, wait," she said. She looked desperately around the small, windowless room. "I need the—I mean, where's the—"

"It's under the bed," he said. Then he was gone, locking the door behind him.

... under the bed?

Tsara reached under the bed closer to her and groped till her fingers hit something smooth and cold. She pulled it out. It was a white

51

porcelain bucket about nine inches tall, topped with a rubber-rimmed seal that sat snugly within the opening. A wire handle with a worn wooden grip was attached to the bucket itself.

Tsara bit her lip, forcing back a hysterical shriek of laughter. She had isolated his socio-economic stratum.

He wasn't so poor he didn't have a pot to piss in.

A ray of grey light woke Tsara. She blinked, wondering where it came from. There were no windows in the cabin.

She sat up on the bed, trying to swallow. The air was parched, and her tongue felt like a dead mouse. Her shoulders were cramped, and her back ached. She stretched, exploring the pain and wondering if her back were bruised or scraped. Or both.

Among the eddies of discomfort was a twinge under her left shoulder blade. At least that was familiar: a souvenir from her second pregnancy. Anyway, none of it was going to kill her. *Advil and a hot bath,* she thought. *Maybe a beer.*

She blinked again, peering up at the source of illumination. The last log before the slope of the ceiling began was missing, admitting the watery light. No, it wasn't, she discovered as she stood on the bed for a closer look. It was suspended below its opening by leather straps. Above the gap were pegs. The log could be rolled up into the opening and kept in place as soon as the straps were secured. On warm days it could hang as it was, admitting air and some light.

Everything about the cabin was sparse and efficient. She had looked around the night before, Coleman lantern in hand. There were two doors, both solid wood and both locked: the one she had come through, and one that must lead to another room. That would explain why there were no other furnishings in this one. By opening the door between the two rooms Mike could have his pantry or larder or whatever two steps away, and do the cooking and eating in here. Or maybe the other room was the kitchen, and this one was just for sleeping. Maybe the other room had electricity. Maybe it had a phone. But the door was locked, so it didn't matter.

Next she turned her attention to the material between the logs. It wasn't plaster or some sort of batting, as she had hoped. No, it was plastic foam, squirted between the logs for the best insulation money could buy. And there was no way to hack through those stone-hard bumps and bubbles, at least not with her fingernails.

The floor was solid wood—she tapped it gently a few times, hoping whoever was on guard outside the door couldn't hear; and the chimney wasn't a chimney but a hole about four inches across where the stovepipe met the wall.

So that was that. Short of setting the place on fire and hoping they got her out before she died, she was trapped. She cursed in a whisper and ran her hand through her hair.

Putting the lantern back on the table, she considered whether or not to take Mike up on his offer to sleep. Closing her eyes seemed dangerous. On the other hand, staying awake all night didn't make much sense either. It must be well past midnight.

So sleep it was; which led to the problem of where. She didn't like the idea of getting into *his* bed, even by accident. But damnit, they were identical: single pillow, striped wool blankets, white sheets. Hospital corners. Nothing about either one said adult or child. So she went to the one further from the door and with several angry yanks pulled the sheets free. She hoped it wouldn't irritate him, but the idea of being immobilized, even by bedclothes, was insupportable at the moment. Besides, she would need to dry off first. Her pajama bottoms were splashed with lake water and still stuck to her shins, and damned if she was going to stand around naked from the waist down. She took off her pants and socks, wrapping the sheet around her middle before draping the damp garments over the rail that surrounded the wood stove. She opened the glass door for more heat. The pants began to steam, and the stink of horses rose from them in a cloud.

While the pants dried, Tsara took the wad of duct tape from the table and dabbed it against her cheeks and swollen lips, pulling off the adhesive that still clung to her skin. Without a mirror she couldn't be sure she had gotten it all, but by the time she was done she felt less sticky. She flipped the socks and pajama bottoms over, letting them dry.

Before putting them on again she glanced down at her inner thighs where two dark red spots had blossomed from gripping the saddle. Her butt hurt, too, and her spine.

She dragged the sheet back to the bed and draped it loosely over herself with the blanket. The bed was a mess, bottom sheet wrinkled and pillow askew. She propped herself up in the corner with the pillow, half-reclining, and slid into a grey and restless twilight, pocked by night whispers and creaks that made her jump in her sleep.

Now it was morning. Tsara stood on tiptoe, peering out of the gap. They seemed to be in a small clearing: there were trees aplenty, but they weren't smack up against the cabin. One large oak grew close by, its branches hanging low. A tire swing hung from one. Off to one side was a low box one plank high. Sandbox?

Tsara sighed and rubbed her lower lip with her thumbnail. Here again was the mystery. Either Mike was telling the truth or he wasn't; which meant either he actually had a young son whom her uncle had abducted—or he was completely cracked. If the latter, he could easily have built the tire swing and sandbox for his phantom child.

In a way it barely mattered. That was his reality, so she would play along.

Laughter sounded through the trees. Mike and Jim strode into view, the smaller of the two men barely grazing his companion's shoulder. Jim was toweling off his hair, which glittered with droplets of water and stuck to his forehead. The air was chilly and he wore a plaid shirt over a tee shirt. Both were tucked neatly into his jeans. Hiking boots kicked the orange and gold leaves in front of him.

At his side strode Mike, also in jeans and boots. He was shirtless, towel draped over one shoulder, massive chest almost gleaming in the pearly light. He gestured to Jim with one arm, and muscles rolled under his smooth skin, through shoulder and torso. Tsara caught her breath.

The sound was not loud, but they both looked around at her anyway. Jim's expression was guarded, but Mike grinned and waved. Tsara hastily withdrew from the window, stepping off the bed and down onto the floor. *Bastard!* she thought. She ran her shaking hands though her hair.

Well, shit, she thought, looking around her prison. Her jailer was apparently something of a neatnik, so she might as well make the bed. No point risking his wrath. And when he came in, she would be completely expressionless. If he wanted to see her cowering, he was going to be bitterly disappointed. She bent to the bedclothes, molding her face into an unreadable mask.

Mike tucked in his shirt and fished the key out of his pocket. He pushed the door open, and the small room filled with dull light. The woman was sitting on his freshly made bed, staring at him.

Mike's conscience hit him like a body blow. She looked terrible. The circles under her eyes were dark as thunderclouds, and her left cheek was splotched with bruises. But worst of all was her expression—mouth a straight line, eyes a little too wide, a crease between her brows. She looked scared shitless.

Mike had been in charge of prisoners before. That was nothing new. But they had all been angry and unrepentant. And male. But this—this was something different.

Forget it, he told himself. The whole thing would be over in a few hours, and she'd have a hell of a story to tell her girlfriends.

More abruptly than he had intended, he set a bottle of water on the table. She looked at it but made no move to pick it up.

"It's unopened," he said.

She got up and took the bottle, inspecting the seal. It was indeed unopened, and she quickly snapped back the top and took a long drink, the bubbles slapping in the bottle as she tipped it up.

Mike waited till she was done, then took two apples from a paper bag and held them out to her. They were large and green, cheeks barely touched with red, and both fit in one of his hands.

"Choose one," he said. "I'll eat the other."

She pointed to the larger of the two. He set it down on the table and bit into the other one. The woman picked up hers and ate it, pausing frequently for more water. She finished the bottle and the apple at about the same time, and wiped her mouth on the cuff of her sleeve.

A shadow fell across the table. Jim was in the doorway, holding a pad of paper and a ballpoint pen. He handed them to Mike, who sat down and began to write, speaking out loud as he did so.

"Thornlocke," he said slowly, pen skating across the paper, "I have your—" he looked up at the woman.

"Guest," she said, too quickly.

He shook his head. "Girl," he said, writing it. "Release ... the kids ... and give ... Aiden Westbrook ... to the ... bearer ... of this note ... and I will ... return ... her ... to you." He shoved the paper and pen toward her. "Sit. Write what I tell you."

Dutifully, Tsara drew up the chair and sat down, pen in hand. She blinked, thinking longingly of her reading glasses, and took his dictation in slightly blurry letters.

"'Cass.'" ("That's what you call him, right?" "Yes.") "'I am okay but do what they say.' Now sign it. And no secret messages or other shit."

She signed. He took the paper and read it.

"Tara?" he said, looking at the signature.

"Tsara."

"Is that short for something?"

"Tsarina."

"What does he call you?"

"Tsara. Everyone does."

He glanced at Jim and they both shrugged. Mike tore the paper off the pad and folded it. He stood and turned again to face Tsara, his face hard.

"I'm going to give this to Jim," he said, "and he's going to give it to Thornlocke. Before he goes, I'm going to ask you something, and I'm only going to ask it once. You don't have to tell me your full name or how you know that sack of shit in his fancy house. But if you do anything to fuck up the safe return of my son, things are going to get very bad for you very fast. So before I give Jim this letter, is there *anything* in it you want to change?"

Tsara shook her head. The tips of her fingers trembled.

"Anything?" he persisted. His big hand held the folded paper before her. "Last chance."

"I just wrote what you told me—and it's my real name, and that's what I call him, I swear!"

Mike peered at her. She was closer to Thornlocke than she wanted to admit, he thought—and that suited him just fine. It meant the son of a bitch would want her back. Equally important, she'd probably keep quiet about the whole thing afterwards. A man like Castle Thornlocke would have ways of keeping his people in line. He relaxed and passed the note to Jim without looking at him. The little man took it and turned toward the doorway.

"Jim," said Tsara suddenly. Her voice was squeaky, and she cleared her throat. Both men looked at her in surprise. Jim raised an eyebrow. "I'd be careful of Cass if I were you," she went on.

"Yeah? Why?" said Mike.

"Because he likes killing stuff, and he's a really good shot."

The woman looked smug. Like she'd made them blink.

Yeah? Dream on, kid. Mike didn't scare that easy.

Jim dipped his head to Tsara and disappeared through the doorway. Moments later the snort of horsebreath and the thrumming of hooves swept past the cabin. In a few heartbeats the sound was gone, and they were alone.

He sat down again, pulling his chair close to the table.

"Now," he said, "here's what happens when they get back."

Court stepped onto the main terrace off the ballroom, hands stuffed into the pockets of his windbreaker. The October air held a minty chill, and he would have preferred an indoor meal. But the table was set up out here, and no question the view was worth a little frost around the edges. Beyond the flagstone terrace the lawn sloped down to the water. The forest curved around the lake in a stripe of fire-colored maples and oaks that gave way to a dark green band of pines. Above them towered the Silver Mountains in all their granite-boned glory. The lake lay before him as still as ice, and everything, even the pearly clouds, was flawlessly reflected in its surface.

Castle, Alicia, and Hans were already eating, as were the two older kids. Electric warmers surrounded the table, so as soon as Court sat down he felt a glow of heat at his back. "Hey, nice touch," he told Alicia. She smiled at him, pleased.

"Coffee?" asked Castle.

"Cass, no offense, but dumb question," Court said with a smile. Cass gestured, and a magical waiter appeared, carafe in hand. He flipped over Court's cup and filled it. Threads of steam rose from it, blurring the edges of the cup. Court wrapped his hands around it and took a sip. "Thanks," he told the waiter, who nodded and withdrew.

"Colombia's finest," said Cass.

Court squinted at the cup. "Cocaine? Really? In front of the kids and all?" The two boys chuckled and Cass gave a cocky grin.

"Court, would you like some toast?" asked Alicia. "Zaylie and I made the bread, and she's very proud of it."

"Sure, that sounds great." Another magical waiter appeared to saw a thick slice from the crusty loaf that graced the table. He took the slice and departed, assuring Court he would be back as soon as perfection had been achieved in the toast department.

"So where is Zaylie?" asked Court, looking around.

"Still sleeping. Late night," said Alicia.

"Has Tsara already eaten?"

"Haven't seen her," said Zachary, the oldest. "I like your sister, Court. She's a lot of fun."

"I expect she's having a bit of a lie-in," said Castle.

"Youth! It's not what it used to be," said Hans. "She should have been up hours ago, greeting ze dawn with a glad cry. Isn't that how we used to do things, Cass?"

"Speaking of youth, how's yours?" asked Court. "The sick one, I mean."

Hans beamed at him. "How very kind of you to ask. My wife texted me this morning. He's almost entirely better and will be back at school Monday, much to his dismay."

"Poor guy," said Court. "It doesn't seem fair, getting sick on the weekend."

"He's a good student," said Hans. "We love his school. We sent all our boys there."

"So you wouldn't send them to an Austrian school?" said Court.

Hans rolled his eyes. "Never! I wouldn't dream of educating my children in Europe."

"Really?" said Zander. "Why not?"

"Too regimented. Everything is a standard curriculum geared toward standardized tests, without which you can't go to university."

"We get that too," said Zander.

"Yes, but it's worse in Austria," said Hans. "They teach the subject but not the student. Your schools emphasize individuality. Freedom of thought. Very American! I don't want my children emerging from twelve years of education as little robots. They should be able to *use* their learning, think on their feet and come out ahead no matter what the situation."

61

"Like their father," said Castle. Hans smiled.

Court thought back on the previous night's dinner conversation. *Yeah, you guys think on your feet all right.* He took another sip of coffee. *Good thing you're family or I might really feel weird about you.*

As he put down his cup he saw a figure on horseback coming toward them along the margin of the lake. "Who's that?"

Cass squinted. "My gardener," he said, surprised. "But he's not scheduled for today."

The small, dark figure pulled up to the terrace and dismounted, flipping the reins over the railing as though he were outside an Old West saloon. Where he'd been in a brawl the night before, thought Court. The man's face was battered. Walking up to Cass, Jim presented a folded piece of paper.

Cass opened it and read. His face stopped moving.

"Cass, what is it?" asked Alicia. A tang of anxiety made her voice higher than usual.

Too casually he leaned toward her and spoke in a low voice. "You did say Zaylie is still sleeping, right?"

"I checked on her about ten minutes ago. Why?" She leaned over to look at the note.

"Nothing." He re-folded the paper and stuffed it into his jacket pocket before addressing the gardener. "Please wait here. I'll be right back."

The short man nodded curtly as Cass retreated to the house. He stared ahead, avoiding eye contact with the suddenly silent group at the table.

"Jim, would you like some coffee?" offered Alicia weakly. He did not respond.

"I'm going to go help Cass," said Court abruptly. He strode to the door, reaching it just as Cass stormed out, yanking a hunting rifle to his shoulder and drawing a bead on the man with the horse. Alicia screamed.

"Cass—what the hell!" Court slammed his shoulder into his uncle's solid body just as Cass pulled the trigger. The man with the dark eyes had already leapt onto his mount and was tearing back toward the forest, crouched low over the horse's neck.

"Stay away from my family, you animal!" roared Cass.

Court stared from his uncle to the two empty chairs at the table. "Cass. Where's Tsara?"

Castle did not answer. He put the rifle down, leaning it against the wall of the house, and pulled his cell phone from his pocket, stabbing a single number. "Arnie. Get Jordan and come over here now. Something's happened."

Court grabbed Cass by the shoulder and spun him around. "Cass. *Where the hell is my sister?*"

Castle's mouth was a line. He stared through Court and pulled away, but not before the younger man had seen, deep in his uncle's eyes, a flicker of panic.

Court turned and peered down the lawn, following the wing of the house that curved around the lake. There was the terrace outside Tsara's room. And … were the doors open?

She wouldn't have slept with the doors open.

Court ran past the table. His feet pounded on the lawn.

He took the terrace steps three at a time, stopping short at the threshold. His eyes widened, and suddenly he could not breathe.

The long, green curtains were half-torn off the rod and spilled onto the terrace. The bedside table was overturned; Tsara's iPhone dangled in its charger, still plugged in. And the bed—the bed had not been slept in.

Zachary and Zander reached Court's side and stood in the doorway, puffing. Zachary started to step in, but Court threw up an arm before him. "Stay here." The younger man retreated. Court stepped over the threshold, almost tiptoeing.

"Tsara? Sis?"

He walked to the bathroom. Empty. Under the bed, on the far side of the bed, the closet. Empty. Empty. Empty.

As he turned away from the closet door, Alicia appeared in the French windows, breathing heavily and clutching her side. Her eyes swept the room.

"Now, Court, don't let's overreact," she said. "Cass has the whole thing under control."

Court drew a ragged breath and stared at her. Loathing rose in his stomach. Silently he stepped to the iPhone and yanked it out of the charger.

"Court, what are you doing?" said Alicia. "Cass knows these people. We need to let him handle it."

Court turned his back to her, still looking at the phone. He circled the room until bars came up on the screen. He opened the map icon and typed three letters: FBI.

A red pin appeared. He touched it, and the contact screen popped up. Praying they were open on Saturdays, he hit the phone number. It only rang once.

"My name's Court Abrams," he said. "I'm calling from Chateau Thornlocke in Libertyville, and I need to report a kidnapping."

Tsara sat on the bed holding her hands in the shaft of light from the window. She was turning her engagement ring with her right thumb and forefinger, watching colored lights flash inside the diamond. If she tilted it she could make a starburst on the wall. She did so now, watching the dots of light slide over the logs and insulation. Some were white, others tipped with rainbows.

Until now, Tsara would have supposed terror and boredom to be mutually exclusive. She now realized they could coexist quite easily.

Mike had told her the plan. As long as Cass cooperated, Jim and the boy would be back in about an hour. Then Mike would take Tsara to a dirt road not far from the cabin and leave her there. After a few turns the dirt road led to a paved road which led to the highway which led to Libertyville. He made her repeat the directions three times until he was satisfied she had memorized them.

"You won't see us again," he added. He folded the sheet of paper on which he'd drawn a crude map of the roads, and slipped it into his back pocket as he stood up. "We're going to leave town for a while." His hand was on the doorknob, other hand reaching for the key in his back pocket.

"Hey—"

"What?"

"Well ... after this is over ... aren't you afraid Cass might, um, report you? "

He chuckled darkly. "'Hello, proper authorities,'" he intoned, mimicking Cass's patrician cadences perfectly. "'I've kidnapped about half a dozen of the local children, and one of the fathers is getting a bit shirty about it.'" He looked at her. "I'm not worried."

Tsara had to admit he had a good point. Which wasn't to say *she* wouldn't turn him in as soon as possible. But if that hadn't occurred to him, she sure as hell wasn't going to suggest it.

Change the subject.

"Why doesn't Jim ever talk?"

"Maybe he's got nothing to say." Mike turned his back to her and it made her bold.

"Nah," she said. "He has plenty to say. He just does it nonverbally. Signing, whistling—he's not deaf, either."

Mike looked over his shoulder. "Why do you care?"

I like to know every little thing about the people who abduct me. "Just curious."

Mike turned back to the door. "He used to. Till he was four."

"You knew him then?"

"Known him my whole life. We're cousins." Mike opened the door, and grey daylight poured in. He looked at her again and took his hand off the knob. "I guess it doesn't matter if you know." He leaned against the wall, arms folded across his chest. "He was four, like I said. Talked just as much as any kid. Then he got sick, some kind of infection, I don't remember what. His folks decided to take him to the hospital, but there was an ice storm. A semi slid on the ice and rolled onto their car. The two of them died right there. And Jim never spoke again."

"My *God.*" She stared at him, thinking of four-year-old Jim in a crushed car on the highway. There weren't too many things worse than what had happened in her family, but this definitely ranked.

"So—was it the accident?" she said. "Is that why he doesn't talk?"

"The accident, the infection, seeing his mom and dad die like that." Mike shrugged. "They don't know."

"But can he talk if he wants to?"

"I don't know," he said. "I never asked him."

They must be guys, thought Tsara. Aloud she said, "You two sign."

Mike half-grinned. "Yeah. We made that up when we were kids. Drove our teachers crazy."

"Did the other kids—tease him at all?"

Mike's eyes darkened. "Just Jordan and Arnie Stone. Jim was always little," he added. "Maybe it was from being sick that time. Anyway, between that and being mute, yeah, they really ...." He shook his head. "They did all kinds of shit to him. Pushed him around, got him in trouble for stuff he didn't do. I guess they figured he couldn't tell anyone about it."

"But he could tell you," said Tsara.

"He could tell anyone he wanted. He knows regular sign and he can write. But yeah ... mainly he told me."

"So what did you do?"

"I made them stop. "

His tone said he wasn't going to elaborate; but unbidden the image of Arnold's smashed-in nose came to mind. Without wanting to, Tsara glanced at the big man. The black tee shirt did nothing to hide the contours of his chest and shoulders, and with his arms folded like that his biceps looked like footballs. Mike gazed at her steadily until she looked away. Then he left, locking the door from the outside.

That was when the terror started: when she was alone with a thousand ideas of what could go wrong.

What if Cass refused to cooperate? What if he wouldn't turn the boy over to Jim?

Well, that didn't seem likely, she tried to reassure herself. Surely he wouldn't put her in harm's way. Cass loved her. Didn't he?

But Arnold and Jordan might still be on the property. What if they arrested Jim, or beat him senseless? What would Mike to do to her then?

Mike was right about one thing: they would figure out who he was in about five seconds. He had taken no pains at all to hide his identity. Which meant the police would probably come here right away. They would have guns and demands—and she couldn't imagine Mike going down without a fight. Plus, he had a hostage. A vivid image of him using her for a human shield flashed in her mind before she could tamp it down.

It might all work, she thought. He seemed to think so. And then he'd let her go at the dirt road. He said.

But what if she twisted an ankle on the way down to Libertyville? Or took a wrong turn? Tsara had no illusions about her sense of direction, or lack thereof, and the Silver Mountains were no place to be lost without food and proper equipment.

What if Jim and the boy didn't come back?

What if the boy didn't exist?

What if the crazy story about kidnapping all those kids was some delusion Mike had cooked up?

Stop it. *Stop.*

The boredom was easier to tackle, and she found that dealing with it took the edge off the panic that leaped in her stomach every few minutes. She arranged herself on the bed near the light from the opening over her head.

"Okay," she said to the diamond. "Movie titles. One word, alphabetically, beginning with A."

Well, that was easy. *Airport, Airplane, Avatar, An American in Paris.* Oops, too long.

B was harder, until she remembered *Brazil* and *Brigadoon.* C kept trying to be *Charlie and the Chocolate Factory,* but she finally beat it into submission with *Casablanca.*

Dragnet. Enchanted. Fargo. Frankenstein. Gaslight. How about *Ghost?* And *Ghostbusters. Heathers. Harry Potter and the Half-Blood Prince.* Stop it! Stick to the rules. *Hoosiers. Hancock.*

She had just gotten to *Xanadu* and was reflecting that there really is only one one-word movie beginning with X when hooves drummed outside the cabin.

She jumped up on the bed and stared through the gap. Nothing. Jim had pulled up in front.

The bolt jumped in the lock. The door smashed open. Mike filled the doorway, fists clenched.

"I told you not to fuck with me!" He crossed the room in two strides.

Tsara jumped off the bed and tried to dodge past him, but he slammed his hands on either side of her, trapping her with her back to the wall. His rage came off him like heat.

"What?" she cried. "I didn't do anything! I just wrote what you said!"

He leaned in closer, his face clenched tight as a fist. "I told you to tell me everything."

"I did! I told you the truth!"

"Don't lie to me," he shouted. She flinched. "When Jim gave him the note, your Cass shot at him. *Why?*"

"I—" She stared wildly at him. Jim appeared in the doorway, his face shadowed. *Not dead*, she thought. *Okay, good*—. But Mike was at her again.

"Why?" he said again. "Why would he kill for you? What are you, his *kid*? His fuck-buddy?"

"What? *Cass*?" Her fingertips curled in revulsion.

"Then let me ask again." Sarcasm dripped from his voice. "Who is he to you, that he would kill for you? *Answer me.*"

Tsara's eyes thinned. "He's my uncle!" she shouted.

His jaw clenched. "I told you to tell me *everything*."

Furiously, she yelled up at him. "Well, shit, Mike, I thought you might get mad at me!"

His face went slack. A wheezing filled the cabin with soft bursts of *sss* and *fff*. Mike glanced at the doorway, and Tsara looked past him.

Jim was laughing.

"What's so damn funny?" said Mike, but his voice was quieter.

Jim pointed at Mike.

"Me?"

Jim's fingers flew through the air, intricate patterns of dot and dash. Mike opened his mouth to protest but Jim cut him off, slicing with one hand. The big man's shoulders sagged, and he took his hands from the wall. Tsara stared. Jim pointed at her and folded his arms, glaring at Mike. Reluctantly the big man turned to her.

"Jim … says it's not your fault," he said. "He says you warned us Thornlocke would probably shoot, and we didn't take you seriously. He also says he can see why you didn't want to say the man was a blood relation." Jim made a noise with his teeth and lips: *fftt*. Mike sighed. "He says I owe you an apology. He's right." He looked at her. "I'm sorry."

Tsara stared from Jim to Mike and back again. She drew a deep breath.

"You know," she said bitterly, "it is getting fucking hard to know which of you is the good cop."

Jim's face broke open with his sibilant, wheezing laughter. He leaned against the doorframe and his shoulders danced. Mike's were still slumped, but a crooked grin almost lit up his face. Then he became businesslike again.

"C'mon," he said to Jim. "Improvise, adapt, and overcome. Time to work on Plan B." They walked out, and again Tsara heard the lock click in place.

Her knees twitched violently, and she lowered herself onto the bed. It was the one she hadn't slept in the night before, and now she lay down with her head on the pillow, covering her face with her hands. She forced herself to breathe slowly and deeply. *Circular breaths. Circular breaths.*

What the hell was Plan B going to entail?

She wondered why Cass had missed. That wasn't like him. She shifted her head on the pillow. It was damned lumpy. No—there was something under it. Sitting up, she pushed aside the pillow. Her eyes widened.

A small, stuffed turtle with a worn leather shell looked up at her with plastic eyes. Next to it was a wooden box not much larger than her hand.

She picked up the turtle. Its green was mostly brown now. The shell was rubbed shiny in places, cracked in others, and the plush on its feet was worn off in dots. The eyes were so scratched the little creature looked as though it had cataracts. Even so, it gazed at her with a look of silent sagacity, its flat thread mouth neither smiling nor frowning.

Her thoughts darted where she had forbidden them. Josh always carried a stuffed frog he'd had since he was six months old. Abbie couldn't suck her thumb unless she had Mrs. Pinkie, a tattered rag doll that could fit in Tsara's hand. If Abbie couldn't suck her thumb, she couldn't sleep. As a result, everyone in the family cared deeply about Mrs. Pinkie.

Tsara snapped off thoughts of her children. She picked up the box and slid open the lid. Inside were two photos. One was of a woman with brown eyes and long, auburn hair. She was smiling. It was a studio shot, very Sears Family Photo. The second was two figures. Tsara tilted it toward the light.

The bigger one was Mike. On his lap sat a small boy with brown hair and ocean-grey eyes. They both wore firefighter's hats and grinned at the camera. The boy was half-twisted around, holding a toy hatchet in one hand. The walls behind them were cinderblock, painted community-center beige. Halloween party, maybe? Fundraiser for the local firehouse?

The door opened again and Mike stood in the doorway, backpack slung over one shoulder. His jaw tightened and he crossed to the bed, holding out his hand.

"Sorry." Tsara shoved the pictures back in the box and handed it to him with the turtle. He set them on the round wood table and shrugged off his backpack. He unzipped it and placed the turtle and the box at the bottom, reaching in to make room. Then he closed the pack and put it on again, this time using both shoulders. He wore a grey jacket, half-

71

zipped and showing part of the black tee shirt. The jeans were gone, replaced by brown wool hiking pants. His feet wore scarred boots with tire-tread soles.

"Come on," he said. "We're leaving."

The phone rang and David got up from the spirited game of Candyland he was playing with Abbie. She was winning, anyway.

"Hello," he said. "Oh, hi, Court."

Twenty minutes later he was in the car with Josh and Abbie in the back, their hastily packed bags in the trunk. Falstaff was in a neighbor's yard; David had taped a note to the door. Abbie was holding Mrs. Pinkie, and Josh had crammed Froggers into his suitcase as David was zipping it up.

"Why are we going to Grandma's?" asked Josh.

"Because Mommy needs me." David hunched over the steering wheel, gripping it tightly.

"Is she sick?" asked Abbie around her thumb.

"Did she have an accident?" asked Josh.

"Mommy needs me," repeated David. "Here. Listen to your stories." He punched the disk player. Eeyore was reunited with his tail and Winnie the Pooh dropped sticks into a river as David sped to his mother's house.

After he had dropped them off he turned north. As the road whipped under his wheels, he thought about Tsara: how hard and bright she was when she laughed, and the feel of her lips under his.

There could not be a world without her. There could not.

Eyes straight ahead, David drove.

Court sat on the floor, leaning against the doorframe of the French windows in Tsara's room. He was alone. Alicia and the boys were gone, had walked back to the main terrace and into the house on his orders. Tsara's phone was in his back pocket, and he shifted it with one finger so he could sit more comfortably. He didn't want to look into the room any more. He wouldn't look. He had described everything he could see to the FBI, and the phone call spattered through his mind as he wondered if he had left anything out.

"Sir, I'm going to transfer you to the supervisor of the Violent Crimes Unit."

"Don't cut me off!"

"No, sir, I won't. And I have your information so if anything happens I'll call you right back. Here's the supervisor. Sir, we have a complainant reporting a kidnapping …."

"… and you say there was a ransom note?"

"Yes."

"Can you tell me the exact wording?"

"I don't know. I don't know."

"We'll be sending agents from our satellite office in Bedford. In the meantime, here's what we need you to do …."

The entire house was a crime scene, they said. He needed to preserve it. No one must touch the bedroom until the evidence response team got there. No one must leave or enter the house. The kidnappers might be watching. He must not alert the media.

"Has the kidnapper tried to contact you since delivering the note?"

"I don't think so."

"If he calls, ask to talk to your sister. Listen for background noises. But don't antagonize him …."

" … please hurry."

"We'll be there as soon as possible. Try to remain calm."

So Court had tried to remain calm. He had hung up and turned to Alicia, who stood on the terrace clutching her hands together. He wouldn't let her in. He wouldn't let Zachary or Zander in. During the phone call the boys had rubbernecked like motorists at a crash, standing on tiptoe to peer into the room. A couple of times they stopped and looked at each other. Court wondered if they were scared. But he didn't care how they felt. He gave the three of them the instructions he had just received.

"And if you do anything different it's a federal crime," he said. He didn't know if that was true, but it sounded good; and if it made the Thornlockes sick with worry, well, that was something they all had in common now.

Then he sank to the floor of the threshold, his back against the doorway to the lakeside terrace outside Tsara's room, and waited.

"What in God's name do I pay you for?" bellowed Castle Thornlocke. His cheeks were flushed the color of liver, and the tendons on his neck stood out like flying buttresses. "You knew those two were on the property. I told you to keep them out! But they waltzed right back as soon as it suited them—with *horses*, no less. Where the hell were you?"

Jordan kept his eyes down. Arnold's head was up, but he looked past Castle, eyes focused deferentially on an invisible horizon.

Castle leaned over his hulking, dark desk. Behind it was an empty fireplace. To one side a tall window looked out over the lawn and trees. Castle's office at the chateau was isolated from much of the main living area, and the walnut door was solid enough to muffle most conversation. Castle liked it that way generally, and he liked it even more now.

Arnold shifted his weight. "Jordan was at the front gate all night," he said. "I guess they figured that out, so—"

"Oh, shut up." Castle shoved himself off the desk. "My niece is gone," he said quietly. "Bring her back. Do whatever you have to, but bring her back."

The brothers exchanged a look.

"Yes, sir," said Arnold. He rubbed his lumpy nose and sniffed. "Just one question, Mr. Thornlocke?"

"What is it?"

"How much do you value Westbrook's safety?"

76

Castle snorted. "That criminal who stole my sister's child from my house? You be the judge."

"Yes, sir." The brothers turned to go. Castle's voice stopped them.

"One more thing." They faced him again. Jim's note was in his hand. "Suddenly a number of people know about the contents of my wine cellar. Let's try to keep that number to a minimum, shall we?" He picked up a silver lighter from the desk and flicked it open. A blue flame topped with gold appeared, and he held it to the corner of the note. The paper blackened away from the flame in a receding crescent. Castle turned and dropped it in the fireplace, watching as it turned to ash. He stood with his back to them, shoulders squared. "Let there be no misunderstanding," he said softly. "I will keep the secret of your involvement only as long as you do the same for me." He turned to face them again, his face hard. "I can't imagine you would choose to discuss this matter, and especially not with anyone in a position of authority ... but should the temptation arise, ask yourselves whom they would be more likely to believe—you or me."

Jordan dipped his chin and glanced at his brother.

"I think we understand each other, Mr. Thornlocke," said Arnold.

"Your secret is safe with us," added Jordan.

"See that it stays that way," said Castle.

The men left. Castle shut the door. A moment later, a section of the wall paneling opened, and Hans stepped out.

"I don't like hiding," he said, sliding it closed behind him. He and Castle were the only ones who knew about the compartment, excluding the private contractor Castle had hired from out of state to construct it during the final stages of the chateau's renovations. The little room was a closet-sized humidor with soundproof walls and a refrigerator in one corner; and if Alicia ever wondered about where her husband got his Cuban cigars or the Beluga caviar with the Cyrillic writing on the label, she never asked.

"It seemed prudent, under the circumstances." Castle stared out the window. In the fireplace the burnt remains of the paper crinkled in on themselves with a whisper. Castle turned and picked up a poker, stirring them into the mounds of wood ash under the andirons.

"Of course," said Hans. "But I reserve the right to agree without enjoying it." He stepped forward, putting his lumpy, mottled hand on

Castle's shoulder. "Castle, my friend. I am horrified by this turn of events."

"So am I," said Castle. "I wonder now what we were thinking." He shoved the poker at its stand. His hand shook, and he missed the bracket the first time. He dropped it in with a clank. "Why did you change rooms with her?"

Hans started as though slapped. "There was no way to predict this."

"No—I know," he said. "But Tsara—!" He clenched his teeth, staring down at the desktop again.

"I expect it will turn out all right," said Hans. "This man — Westbrook, isn't it? — he has no interest in hurting her. When he sees how hopeless it is he'll probably surrender her without a fuss."

"I hope so." Castle straightened, looking distractedly around the room. "Though what I'm going to say to her I can't imagine." He sighed. "I'm almost glad my sister's gone. If anything happens to Tsara I would never have been able to look her in the face."

"And your brother-in-law?"

"I could never look at his face anyway. Fatuous old gasbag."

"Castle," said Hans, "do you think they will keep their word about being discreet about the children?"

"They'd better," said Castle. "I'm a much better liar than they are."

"But what would you tell—? Court says the FBI is on its way. Do you have a story ready?"

"If need be, yes," said Castle. "The Stone brothers have a long history with this man. They abducted his child to antagonize him, taking the others as cover."

"Elegant," said Hans. "Simple and difficult to disprove. Do you need me to gather evidence against him?"

Cass shook his head. "No need. There's an extensive public record. Arrests ... the man is a criminal. This is the culmination of a long feud. Imagine my shock when I discovered those kids on my property."

Hans's brows drew together in sympathy. "And you, a family man."

"With children of my own. That reminds me," he said abruptly. "Has any food gone down to the wine cellar today?"

"I don't believe so, no."

"Damn!" Castle picked up the phone and jabbed the zero three times. "Have the cook make up a large tray of breakfast food," he said.

"Kid stuff, mainly. Yes, some of the guests ended up staying over unexpectedly. Car trouble. No, don't worry. I'll take it to them myself." He looked up at Hans. "What do your kids eat for breakfast?"

"Mostly that disgusting stuff that looks like pencil shavings with marshmallows in it."

"You'd have them eating bratwurst if you could."

"Absolutely," said Hans. "Wonderful stuff, bratwurst."

Cass turned back to the phone. "Mr. Freihoffer tells me sugary breakfast cereal is very popular with the young set these days. If we don't have any, just do your best and put together a good assortment. Yes, bread and milk and juice—the usual suspects. I'll be by presently." He hung up and looked at Hans. "I'll just have to be careful when I drop it off."

"Speaking of careful."

"Yes?"

Hans chose his words delicately. "The Stone brothers … are they loyal?"

"Trustworthy, clean, and reverent? I doubt it. Why?"

"Zat is how I feel too. Would you like me to find out more about them?"

"Not particularly."

"Just as a backup," said Hans. "It never hurts to, well …."

"Be prepared," finished Castle. "No, Hans, I don't agree. If we go searching for skeletons it would look damned suspicious, don't you think? Looking for dirt on our supposed allies?"

"You are right," sighed Hans.

"Besides, blackmail only works if the other party has been properly informed." Castle shook his head. "I'm afraid we'll have to settle for mutually assured destruction. They know we know and we know they know."

"Right again. I'm sorry, Castle." Hans opened his hands. "I just wish there were something I could do."

Castle glanced at his watch. "You could walk to the kitchen with me while I pick up the provender. You know how I love kids."

"And you know how I have your back," said Hans. He pulled back his jacket to reveal a Browning handgun in a shoulder holster. "In case your meeting had taken an unexpected turn."

Castle appraised the pistol. It was cocked and locked. "Hi-Power?"

"I prefer the French. *Grande Puissance.*"

"Hans," said Castle admiringly as he held open the door to the hallway, "you think of everything."

Outside, Arnold and Jordan buckled their seatbelts and turned their cruiser down the driveway. They had not spoken since leaving the study, and only now did Jordan turn to his older brother.

"Where do you think they are?"

"I'm skipping Mike's place," said Arnold. "No way he'd just stay there. I figure he's gone further up, maybe where him and Jim go hunting in the fall."

"Near the cascades?"

Arnold shook his head. "Nah, I'm thinking Mount Sumner. Better game. We can get a head start by cutting through Idler's Notch. If we're real lucky we'll be waiting for them when they come along the trail. Just gotta pack some gear first."

They passed the iron gates and turned toward town. Jordan's fingers tapped the armrest.

"We could use some backup," he said.

"Nah."

"How 'bout Olsen?" persisted Jordan. "Or maybe Deke."

"Olsen busted his knee last month and Deke's a blabbermouth."

"Well, how bout—"

"*No.*" Arnold stopped at one of the town's three traffic lights then went through before it turned green. "We'll do it by ourselves." His eye twitched and he rubbed it with his knuckle.

"Whatever," said Jordan. "No sweat off my balls."

"Balls don't sweat, moron."

"Yes they do."

"No they don't."

"Bullshit. On a hot day I tell you my balls stick to my legs they sweat so much."

"That's your legs sweating, you dumb fuck."

"So now you're some kind of international expert on ball sweat?"

"Balls are sensitive to temperature," said Arnold. "They don't get hot enough to need to sweat."

"Jesus fucking Christ," said Jordan. "You don't know balls about balls."

"And you don't know shit about shit, asshole. You're such a fuckup those two stole that girl right away from you. Why'n'cha patrol around like I told you to?"

Jordan's jaw tightened. "Why didn't you?"

"Cause I was by the wine cellar, shit for brains. What's your excuse? You're dumber than a dead man's dick, you know that?"

Jordan's fist clenched in the space between his thigh and the door. The smooth rumble of the engine filled the car. *Fucking Mike,* he thought. *Fuck him.*

"Do you think Mike would of told Thornlocke's niece about the kids?" Jordan said. He kept his voice level.

"I would."

Jordan flexed his fingers, feeling the power of his hands. "What do you think Mike's chances are?"

Arnold kept the wheel steady. The twitch under his eye was gone. "I think Mike is going to have a bad accident up there in the woods."

"And the niece?"

"Accidents are contagious sometimes," said Arnold. "Or it could happen that Mike kills her just before he takes a tumble in the wrong place."

"Or drowns."

"They could both drown. We'll figure it out when we catch up with them."

Jordan looked out the window. A small smile lifted his lips.

Once again Tsara sat shoved forward in the saddle, Mike's arm around her waist. Her hands were on the pommel. This time they had used a plastic cable tie to bind her wrists. Mike had been careful to put it well below the scrape marks from the night before. It pushed the bones together and they ached, but it didn't tear at her skin the way the rope had, and she had to check herself from being grateful. He had blindfolded her with the bandana again, but they hadn't bothered with a gag. Jim had wanted to but Mike stopped him when he came at her with the sock. "Don't bother," he said. "She'd just spit it out again." Jim shrugged and returned Abbie's sock to his grimy pocket.

"Don't get any funny ideas, though," Mike warned her. "One sound out of you—"

"Okay, okay." He didn't need explain.

The saddle creaked with the rolling motion of the horse's steps. Their hoof-falls beat steadily, like syncopated metronomes, and periodically one would toss its head and snort. When Mike's horse did this Tsara could feel the motion through its body. She breathed shallowly and tried not to move. Her back was against Mike's chest, and his thighs were around hers. His chin was just above her ear, and she could hear him breathing. He smelled of damp earth and rainwater.

Dear Cass, I am okay, but ...

She yanked her mind away from the words they had made her write on the second note. It leaped back anyway.

Dear Cass, I am okay, but this time ...

The day was getting cooler, and a damp breeze sliced through her worn sweatshirt. Her fingers were chill, and she surreptitiously balled them into fists, trying to warm them in her palms. The thok of the horses' hooves on leaf litter changed to a metallic clang and the saddle abruptly sloped upwards. Tsara gripped the pommel, trying not to slide into Mike.

The ground leveled again and they stopped. Mike dismounted, keeping one hand on top of hers. She could feel his other arm gesturing: the movement flowed through his body. He was talking to Jim.

"I'm going to lift you off the horse," said Mike, and as she realized he was addressing her, his big hands gripped her and she slid off. Her feet pedaled as she tried to find the ground; but to her surprise he scooped her into his arms and began walking. Behind them she heard the rhythm of the horses' feet as they ambled away. Jim must be with the animals, which meant she was alone with Mike. He was holding her like a child, his big hands gripping her arms and legs as her bottom sagged low. Her sweatshirt rode up, and she could feel a breeze on the small of her back. She twisted against his hold.

"Get your hands off me."

"I would," he said cheerfully, "but it'd be awfully hard to carry you with my elbows."

"I can *walk*."

"Not blindfolded across uneven ground you can't."

"Then let me take off the blindfold." She reached for it but his grip on her arms tightened and he yanked her elbows down. He stopped.

"Don't." The voice was grim, the big hands hard on her muscles. She eased her hands down, heart rattling.

"That's better," he said. "Look, there's going to be plenty of walking, I promise you. But for right now, why don't you make things easier on yourself? Relax and let me do the hard work."

Tsara sighed sharply. "Fine."

"Fine?"

"Fine. Whatever." And she forced her body to soften, leaning into his torso and feeling the beat of his heart.

Anyway, it was warmer that way.

Mike walked for several minutes. Presently his steps smoothed and after a few more paces he stopped.

84

"I'm going to put you down," he said. "There's a log behind you, and you're going to sit there. Got it?"

"Yes."

He lowered one arm, letting her feet swing to the ground. "Now sit," he ordered; and gingerly she bent to a seat she couldn't see. It was lower than she expected, between a chair and a stepstool. The log creaked and moved, and she knew he was sitting next to her.

"Give me your hands," he said, and she extended them toward his voice, thinking he was going to cut the plastic cord. Instead, something smooth slid around her left wrist. She pulled back and the thing fell away. He yanked on the cable tie, putting her hands back in position. "And hold still."

"What are you doing?" she said in alarm.

"Just hold still," he repeated. "I'm not going to hurt you." The smooth line went around her wrist again and pulled tight. Something clicked quietly, two or three times. A cold piece of metal slid between her wrists and snipped the cable tie. She felt the brush of his fingers as he pulled the ribbed plastic away. Now her hands were free, but what the hell was this thing on her wrist?

"You can take the blindfold off now," he said. She pulled it over her head, and her eyes teared at the sudden light. She sniffed, hoping the ridiculous hope that he didn't think she was crying, and wiped her eyes with the back of her right hand. He waited, saying nothing.

She looked down at her left wrist. Around it was a loop of thin, metal cable, plastic-coated and held in place with a metal collar. Glittering scratches showed where he had crimped it into place.

She followed the cable with her eyes. It was about six feet long, and ended at a small carabiner hanging from the big man's belt loop.

"We're going to a place up in the mountains," he said. "Do what I say, don't give me any trouble, and I'll take this off when we get there. Understand?"

She nodded, twisting the bandana in her hands. He stood. "And keep up with me," he added. "I'm not going to slow down for you. I've seen what you can do so don't act feeble. Come on."

Looking past him for the first time, Tsara saw they were at the head of a path. It was only about a foot and a half wide, and seemed to blur away into the trees. *Deer trail*, she thought, and turned to see where they had come from. Behind her, great shoulders of granite thrust out of the ground and tumbled down the slope of the mountain. Mike would have left no tracks as he carried her across it. Nothing an ordinary person could find.

"Where's Jim going?" she asked as she stood.

"To get that note to Uncle Cassie. Move." He started walking.

As soon as his back was turned Tsara shoved the bandana into the forked branch of a shrub, then hastened to follow him.

He stopped so abruptly she almost bumped into him. "Give me the bandana." His voice was hard with anger.

"I already gave it to you." Tsara tried desperately to sound confused.

He turned and with one swift move reached past her and plucked it from the branch, stuffing it into his pocket. "Look at me," he said.

She looked up, focusing on his ear, which was much less frightening than the eyes.

"I can feel when you move," he said. The rage in his voice was like metal. "You can't take a fucking step or swing your arms without me knowing it. So I will tell you one last time, *don't fuck with me. Understand?*" She nodded, throat closed. "Answer me!"

"I understand," she said quickly, hating the squeak in her voice. He stepped closer.

"And?"

"And—ah—"

"You'll do what I say and *only* what I say and don't try to pull any more of this half-assed shit."

She jerked her head. "I'll do what you say—"

"—and only what I say—"

"—and not pull any more half-assed shit."

A smile tugged at his lips, but he hid it instantly, scowling again. "Or?"

"Or you'll do something horrible to me."

He folded his arms, looking at her. "I think you've got the picture," he said. "Move." And he set off at a pace that was a little too fast for her to walk but just below a run. She followed him, long steps, doing her best to keep some slack in the line between them.

David stood with Court in the doorway of Tsara's room, their shoulders almost touching. He warmed his hands on a mug of coffee he had no stomach for. Court moved, restless. His eyes were red-rimmed, his jaw tight. They could see men and women with blue-gloved hands combing through Tsara's things. It was high noon but the sun was still cloaked by a dreary sky, and they had turned on all the lights.

"She told you not to overreact?" said David, dumbfounded.

Court snorted. "Said Cass had the whole thing under control."

"What the hell does that mean?"

"Probably that he put his rent-a-cops on the job." He tapped his knuckles with his fingertips. "It took everything I had not to punch her."

David's shoulders bent over his mug. "This whole thing is surreal." He looked into the room. "Thanks for calling them."

"Yeah. Well. With our history, I wasn't going to fuck around."

One of the agents separated from the group in the bedroom and approached Court with a portfolio in hand. She was in her late thirties with straight brown hair that hung down her back like a road. Jeans, green crewneck shirt—she would fit in anywhere, which was probably the idea. Her skin was coarse and unevenly colored. She had seen a lot of sun and rain, he thought. But her brown eyes were calm and practical.

"Mr. Abrams, I'm Erin Spaar," she said. She held out her hand and he shook it mechanically.

"I'm the one who called."

"Yes, sir, my supervisor told me."

"I'm David Adelman," said David, extending his hand. "I'm the husband."

"I need to ask both of you some questions. Can we sit down somewhere?"

"How about right here?" suggested David. The wide hallway outside the bedroom had chairs and occasional tables every few yards. They pulled up a trio of seats, positioning them near the bedroom door. The agent flipped open her portfolio and pulled out a ballpoint pen.

"Mr. Abrams, I understand you were the last person to see your sister."

"She left the party a little early and I came in to say good night," said Court. "We talked for a while, I played a couple of video games on her phone, and then I left."

"About what time was that?"

Court squinted. "Couldn't have been much later than eleven-thirty."

"And how did she seem to you?"

"Fine. She looked great, she seemed happy. She was dancing with everyone at the party."

Spaar scribbled in her notebook. "Can you describe what she was wearing when you left the room?"

"Ah, geeze." Court rubbed one hand over the other. "She was getting ready for bed—I wasn't really—"

"Was she wearing a nightgown?" asked David.

Court blinked. "Ah—"

"Court. Was she wearing a green plaid L.L. Bean nightgown?"

"No."

David turned toward Spaar. "Then she had on a sweatshirt and pajama bottoms. Probably socks."

"Does that sound about right, Mr. Abrams?"

Court looked bewildered. "I guess so."

Spaar scribbled in her notebook. "Anything else?"

"The pajama bottoms were probably blue," said David. "The sweatshirt—I don't know. She has three, and she rotates them."

"That's helpful. Thanks." Spaar turned back to Court. "What was she wearing earlier in the evening, at the party?"

"A dress," said Court promptly. "Long. Formal."

"What color?"

"Red," said David. "It was red."

Spaar looked at Court.

"Everybody was," he said. "I mean, the women mostly wore red. Why do you need to know what she had on before?"

"Fiber sweep," explained Spaar. "We'll be able to get hairs and DNA from it."

"Oh."

"Can you think of anyone who might want to hurt her?" said Spaar. "Had she mentioned anything, or had there been any unusual phone calls or emails?" This question was directed at both of them.

"Not that I know of," said David. "But I don't check her emails."

"She has a separate account?"

"Yes, she—" David pulled himself up sharply. "I didn't bring her laptop. Damn!" He had brought his own computer, pulling up several recent photos of Tsara, which another agent was printing in a nearby room.

"I can have someone retrieve it from your house if you give us the go-ahead."

"Yeah, sure," he said. "But I think if there had been anything she would have said so."

"She's not subtle," said Court.

"And she stinks at keeping secrets," agreed David. He and Court looked at each other and barely smiled.

"So—no strange phone calls?" said the agent. "Can you think of any time you picked up and there was no one there or they just hung up?" David shook his head.

"You can check her cell phone," said Court. He pulled it out of his pocket. "I used it to call you," he said apologetically. "Mine was still charging—and I didn't want anyone listening in on the landline, so—"

"I understand," said Spaar. "Excuse me." She took it with her still-gloved left hand and walked back to the doorway of Tsara's room. "Hey, got a bag for this?"

A second agent joined her, holding out a clear plastic bag. She dropped the iPhone into it and he zipped it shut. "This is Victor Galen," she said over her shoulder to David and Court. Galen curved his lips to show he was pleased to meet them but knew an actual smile would have

89

been out of place. He walked back into the room and Spaar returned to her chair.

"When you were in her room after dinner, what did you talk about?" she asked Court.

"Family stuff."

"Anything specific to your visit here?"

"Yeah. How it was weird being here. What our parents would think."

"Weird?"

"Yeah. There was a lot of bad blood between Cass and our father—Tsara's and mine—and we hadn't seen Cass in a long time. I mean, I'd seen him once or twice, but it was mostly running into him. Tsara I don't think had seen him for about eighteen or twenty years."

"Twenty-five," said David.

"How the hell do you know?" Court hadn't meant to snap but he did. "You hadn't even met her then."

"No, but I can do simple arithmetic," David snapped back. "She just turned forty-three. She was almost eighteen when they fought. That makes it twenty-five years ago."

Court gazed into space for a moment. "Damnit," he said finally.

Voices drifted out of Tsara's room. Spaar looked from David to Court.

"No, wait—she did see him a few times after that." said Court. "The second big blowout was when she was in college. I was still in high school. So let's say," he looked at David, "*almost* twenty-five years."

Spaar picked up her pen and made a notation. "That's a long time to go without seeing your uncle."

"Yes, it is," agreed Court. "But while our dad was alive it was basically a choice between him and Cass."

"So you chose your father."

"Right."

"And your father is deceased?"

"About five years ago."

Spaar tapped her pen on the notebook. "Is Mr. Thornlocke your father's brother?"

"Our mother's."

"And does she get along with him?"

"She died a long time ago. That was when the problems between our father and Cass started." Court grimaced. "The first big blowout."

David spoke. "From what Tsara's told me, that's just when things came to a boiling point."

"Jesus," said Court. "Who made you the family stenographer?"

David pressed his lips together.

"So ... there were tensions between your father and Mr. Thornlocke before your mother died?" Spaar asked Court.

"Yeah," said Court. "Lots."

Spaar wrote in her notebook, and then looked up again. "What was the issue between them?"

"They just never liked each other," said Court. "But after she passed, it was money. Our mom died very unexpectedly, and she left everything to my sister and me. Cass thought he should have gotten it."

The agent's eyes flickered around the vast, high-ceilinged hallway with its scarlet runner, carved mahogany tables, and tapestries. Her face was closed.

"My mom and Cass were really close," said Court. "But yeah—he and my dad really never got along."

"Can you be more specific?" said Spaar.

"What was that story about him?" David said. "You guys got home from the funeral—"

Court rolled his eyes. "Oh, my God, yeah. We got home to set things up for *shiva* and Cass was there. And my father said, 'What are you doing here?' and Cass said, 'Just reviewing the estate.'"

"Reviewing the estate?" repeated Spaar.

"He meant he was there to take inventory of our mom's stuff, since he figured it was his now," said Court.

Spaar blinked at him. "Really?"

"You can't make this stuff up."

"And how did your father react?"

"He threw him out. They never spoke to each other again."

Spaar jotted in the notebook again. "Could there be any connection here?"

"What do you mean?" said Court.

"Well, that's a longstanding feud you're describing. Do you think your uncle would have any reason to want to harm your sister?"

Court rubbed his forehead. "I've been thinking about it," he admitted, "and I can't come up with a single reason why. It doesn't make sense. He wanted her to come up here for the fundraiser ... and she didn't have anything he could possibly want. I don't see how this could benefit him in any way."

David spoke up. "I've never met Castle, but I always got the sense he had nothing against Tsara or Court."

The agent tilted her head toward Court in a *Would you agree?* Court nodded.

"It was a really self-contained feud," he said. "I don't think either of them, I mean my dad or Castle, wanted to involve us in it. Cass always sent us birthday presents and stuff, even—"

"Sparks?" Galen stood in the doorway of the bedroom, looking at them.

"Excuse me." Spaar flipped the portfolio closed and walked into the room. David and Court followed but stopped at the threshold. Galen spoke in a low voice, pointing to a spot on the floor. Spaar squatted for a closer look. She glanced at the brothers-in-law and stood up again. "Let's sit down again," she suggested. Her tone and face were professionally neutral. As soon as they were all seated, she said, "Does either of you know Mrs. Adelman's blood type?"

David gagged. "Oh, God—"

"We've found some blood on the floor. It might not be hers," she pointed out. "If it's not, then we have a good lead on whoever did this."

David's eyes darted around the magnificent hall. "I'm not sure—it's B something. I think. Her doctor would have it, right?"

"What's the name of her doctor?"

David pulled out his phone. "The OB-GYN is probably your best bet." He tried to smile. "They were checking her blood every five minutes when she was pregnant." He pulled up the clinic's contact information and handed her the phone. She copied everything into her notebook and handed it back.

"Can you check it against my blood?" asked Court.

"We can. We'll also run it against her DNA. We can do that pretty quick."

"I thought you didn't have any DNA from her," said Court. "How do you know when you have hers? Plenty of people have been in there."

"We'll get it from her hairbrush."

"Oh." Court was beginning to wish he read more detective novels.

"How long does it take?" asked David. "The analysis, I mean."

"About three days."

"Three *days?*" Court almost screamed.

Spaar let him collect himself before she spoke. "We're doing everything we can as fast as we can, Mr. Abrams."

Court willed himself to behave like an adult. "So how does it look right now?"

"Well. We have fingerprints from the doorknob and various other places, the blood on the floor, and two sets of hoofprints outside the balcony leading into the water."

"Hoofprints?" said Court. "Seriously—hoofprints?"

"Yes. Does Mrs. Adelman ride horses? Particularly at night?"

Court almost laughed. "God, no."

"She doesn't ride," said David.

"Ever?"

"Not unless you count a pony trip into the Grand Canyon about eight years ago."

"Okay, then. If it turns out no one in the family has been riding at this end of the house in the last twenty-four hours, we'll assume the horses belonged to the kidnappers."

"And the tracks go into the water?" said David.

"Right. But they came out somewhere, so we'll bring dogs in to see what we can find."

"And we know it happened some time around midnight or after," said Court. "Could it have been this morning?"

"Probably before. The blood was dry."

"How does eleven forty-seven sound?" It was Galen again. He was holding a clear plastic bag. David stared at it in horror.

"Mr. Adelman," said Galen, "can you identify this?"

"Yes," whispered David. "It's hers."

Tsara's watch. Smashed.

Spaar stood and examined the bag.

"Could have been done on purpose," she said. "Like a heel or something came down on it."

"Could have been an accident too," said Galen. "But it was fresh—glass shards next to it."

"All in the bag?"

He rolled his eyes. "Yes. They're all in the bag." He took it back and returned to the room.

Spaar sat down again. "Just a few more questions. I realize this is a really difficult time for you, but the more information we can get, the better."

"Of course," said David. "Anything. Anything we can do, just ask." Court jerked his head in agreement.

"I need a physical description. Your wife is forty-three years old, is that right?"

"Yeah, but she looks younger. She's five-foot four, blonde hair, green eyes."

Spaar's pen moved over her notebook. "How much younger?"

"She got carded on her fortieth birthday."

"Damn," said Court. "Did she gloat?"

"Endlessly."

Spaar looked up from her notes. "Build?"

"Probably weighs one-fifteen soaking wet."

"Do you know exactly?"

David shook his head. "She doesn't weigh herself. But you could safely say between one-fifteen and one-twenty, I think."

"The doctor would have it. Does she have any medical conditions?"

"No. She's in good shape. Works out at the gym. And we used to go hiking a lot, before the kids."

"Does she take any medications?"

"Not even a multivitamin. She keeps forgetting."

"Okay. And I'm going to need her dentist's contact information."

Court looked at the floor, his fingers gripping the arms of the chair. David swallowed something rancid at the back of his throat and pulled out his phone again. He touched the screen with stiff, unfeeling fingers before handing it to the agent. She took it and balanced it on her knee to copy the screen information.

... in case they ... if they need to identify ...

"This says Mobile," said Spaar. "Is it the office number?"

94

"Huh?" David twisted his head to look at the screen. "Oh, yeah—that's just the default. I forgot to change it to Office."

"Thanks." She copied quickly and handed him back his phone. "Keep it handy. Did she have any appointments in the past few days?"

"Um ... not that I can think of." David's voice was calm. David's voice did not feel the sick fear that was screaming inside him.

They went on like this for a while. Finally, when David had given Spaar the contact information for all of his wife's "known friends and associates" and detailed her movements of the past several days to the best of his ability, Spaar stood up.

"We'll be in touch as soon as we know more," she said as she handed each of them her business card. "If you think of anything else or if you hear from her or the kidnappers, contact me immediately."

"What happens now?" asked Court.

"Now," she said, "I'm going to have a talk with Mr. Thornlocke."

Spaar settled herself into the armchair in Thornlocke's study. It was leather, and soft as talcum powder. The dark grain of the cushions matched the wooden wall paneling and the ceiling with its towering beams. The carpet was dense and burgundy. Thornlocke liked to live well, no question. Spaar opened her portfolio and turned to a new page in her notebook. "So you received the ransom note this morning."

Thornlocke lowered himself into a chair opposite hers. There were lines around his mouth and between his brows. Maybe they were always there, thought Spaar. Or maybe not. She waited for a tremble in his voice, but there was none. He tapped his fingertips together. "Yes," he said, "while we were having breakfast."

"I need to see it."

"The note?" Thornlocke shook his head. "This is going to sound ridiculous, but I'm afraid I threw it away."

"Threw it away where?"

"Burned it, actually."

Spaar put her pen down. "Why?"

"I wasn't thinking clearly. The whole thing was such a shock—I was holding in my hands something from those people, and it felt like poison. All I could think of was getting rid of it, getting it out of my house."

Spaar tapped her pen on her notebook. On a scale of one to quadriplegic, this was one of the lamest excuses she had ever heard.

"Do you realize that destroying evidence is a felony?"

96

"I do now," he said regretfully. "I was distraught."

Spaar waited a moment. "So you were the only person who actually saw the note."

"I suppose so."

"Mr. Thornlocke, this is very important. Could you tell me the exact words?"

"Why the exact words?"

"Because it might link this crime with others, and that would help us track these people down."

"Good heavens, I never thought of that," said Thornlocke admiringly.

"How did it begin?"

Thornlocke frowned. "It started off 'Thornlocke'—then he said he had my niece."

"So he knew your name. What else?"

" 'Thornlocke,'" he recited. " 'I have your girl.' But then the rest was goobledy-gook, you know. It didn't make sense."

"What did it say?"

"Something about 'You have what I want and where it is.' It made no sense."

"The. Exact. Words. Please."

"That's what it said: 'You have what I want and where it is.'"

"Anything else?"

"Yes. The next part was, 'So do what I say. Give it back.'" He frowned. " 'It'?" he repeated. "It might have said 'them.' But in any case, you see what I mean. How can I follow instructions I can't understand?"

"Was that the end of the note?"

"No. After that there was a line from my niece. It said, 'Cass, I am okay but do what they say.'"

"Anything else from her?" said Spaar.

"No, that was it."

"Was it signed?"

"Her part was. I know the signature."

Spaar flipped to an earlier page in her notebook. "Your nephew says you identified the man who delivered the note as your gardener. Is that correct?"

Thornlocke hesitated for a fraction of a second. "Yes."

"What's his name?"

"Montrose," said Thornlocke. "First name James or Jim, I believe."

"Have there been any problems between you and him in the past?"

Thornlocke shook his head. "No, he's always done fine work for us. My wife sends him a bottle of wine every Christmas."

"So you have his address."

"Alicia—my wife—would. It might be an office address."

"It's a start. How about employment records? Logs?"

Castle shook his head. "Nothing so extensive, I'm afraid. He does work for us and we pay him."

"Do you have check stubs?"

"We pay most of our bills online."

"Okay." She would talk to the wife next, thought Spaar, and pull up Montrose's address and dates of employment. Anything the computer didn't have would be on record with the bank. "Do you know any of his associates?"

"He has a number of subcontractors. The one we've seen the most of is a big fellow by the name of Westbrook. I believe they're related." He sat up straight in his chair. "Good heavens. I can't believe this is only just occurring to me."

Spaar couldn't believe it either. "What?"

"We had an incident with Westbrook just last night. He's a local roughneck," he explained. "Been in all sorts of trouble off and on in town. He's never given us any problems, though, until yesterday evening."

"What happened?"

"He forced his way onto the property and wouldn't leave. My security guard had to evict him."

"What did he say?"

"Westbrook? Nothing, really. He was shouting but not making any sense. I assumed he was drunk. I told him to go away and not come back." He paused. "Do you suppose there's a connection?"

"Could be," said Spaar. "We'll talk to him. Does he live in town?"

"I suppose so. He's there often enough."

"Do you have his address?"

"Why would we?"

"From paying him," said Spaar.

Thornlocke opened his hands in apology. "I doubt it. We always paid Mr. Montrose directly and he'd pay his men."

"Getting back to this morning," said Spaar, "how did Montrose know where to find you?"

"We were breakfasting outside. But he's very familiar with the house and grounds. He did most of the landscaping and some of the interior work."

"You read the note," said Spaar. "Then you asked your wife if she knew where your daughter was. Is that correct?"

"Yes, because it said *'girl.'* Both Zaylie and Tsara were sleeping late—I mean, I thought they were. At any rate, they were the only ones not at the table. So I asked Alicia about our own girl."

"And she said she had checked up on her in the past few minutes."

"Yes."

"At which point you asked the gardener to wait, went into the house, and returned with a rifle, which you then fired at him."

"Yes, but that was an accident," said Thornlocke. "I just wanted to hold him until law enforcement could arrive. Unfortunately my nephew interfered and the gun went off. Otherwise I'd have been able to hand Mr. Montrose to you on a silver platter."

"I see." It could happen, thought Spaar. Sometimes guns went off accidentally. In the movies. "So Mr. Montrose fled the scene. Then what did you do?"

"Why, I called the police immediately."

Spaar closed her notebook. So much bullshit, so little time. Thornlocke and his office had the look of a man who would lawyer up if you came down on him too hard, and that she didn't need just yet. Better by far to make him feel important. "Thank you for your help, Mr. Thornlocke. You've given us a number of leads and we'll let you know when we have more information."

"Will you be speaking to Westbrook?"

"It'll be our first stop. Before I leave, though, there's just one more thing." She slid the pen into its holder and shut the portfolio before leaning forward. "I won't lie to you. Your niece's life may be in danger. Sometimes in these cases people are concerned about the appearance of guilt or complicity. They might have reasons for not wanting to tell us everything, or letting one or two facts slip through the cracks."

"I've told you everything I know," said Thornlocke.

"Of course." She stood and handed him her business card. He stood also. "But sometimes after people have some time to think, more details occur to them. So if you remember anything more about that ransom note, please let us know—even if you're worried about how it might look."

Just then the door opened. Galen walked in holding a courier envelope in his blue-gloved hands. "This just came for Mr. Thornlocke."

"Ah, thank you," said Thornlocke absently. He took the envelope and dropped it into a desk drawer before closing it. "Will you be going straight to Westbrook's? And here's my card—it has both numbers on it. I can't tell you how grateful we all are for what you're doing."

Neither agent moved. "Aren't you going to open that?" said Galen.

"At a time like this?" said Thornlocke. "Whatever it is, it can wait."

"It could be from the kidnapper," said Spaar.

"Oh, I doubt it," said Thornlocke. "I've used this courier service any number of times."

Spaar was beginning to wonder if Thornlocke was really stupid or kind of smart. "Open it."

"But—"

"We need your help on this," said Galen. He took a half step closer to Thornlocke. "If that is from the kidnapper, it's our best lead so far."

"But even if it is, I can't open it," protested Thornlocke. "I'd contaminate it with my fingerprints, wouldn't I?"

"Oh, that's no problem," said Galen, producing an extra set of blue gloves. "You had me worried there for a minute, Mr. Thornlocke. I was afraid maybe you weren't going to cooperate with us."

Thornlocke smiled thinly as he pulled on the gloves and took the envelope from the drawer. He tore the plastic strip along the top and pulled out a sheet of paper. The agents moved behind him to read over his shoulders.

Nice try Thornlocke but if you ever want to see your niece alive follow these instructions no second chances

Let the other kids go home but take Aiden Westbrook and do what I say ...

Spaar's eyes flew over the paper. At the bottom, in a shaking hand, was a brief note.

Dear Cass,

I am okay, but this time do what they say or they will kill me.

Tsara

Spaar stared at Thornlocke. "Good God," she whispered. "What have you done?"

Mike was giving them a five-minute rest at a spot where the trail looped out of the woods on a cliff high above the world. Tsara leaned against a tree, water bottle in hand, and ate a granola bar. It was taking the shakes out of her legs, and she wondered if there'd be another one. Mike had unwrapped it before handing it to her, and put the wrapper in his backpack before opening his own. He chewed, looking over the cliff. The Silver Mountain Range spread out before them, its rumpled valleys splashed with orange and russet. The lowest summits were clouded with grey where the trees were already naked, millions of bare branches blurring the outlines of the slopes. Above them the trees gave out. Taller crags were crowned with granite and streaked with frost, and the highest peaks were invisible, pushing into grey mist that swirled around them and tumbled toward the bottomlands in a slow, grey avalanche.

Tsara emptied the water bottle. Mike watched. It made her nervous.

"How did you get past the dogs?" she said.

"Dogs?" Mike swallowed his last bite and put the wrapper in a side pocket of his backpack.

"At my uncle's place. He has three of them."

Mike squinted. "Colt, Buckshot, and … what's the German shepherd's name?"

"Luger."

"Right. Nice dogs." He held out his hand and she passed him the empty bottle. He put it in his backpack and zipped the bag closed. "They like bacon."

Mike jerked his head toward the sky. He grabbed Tsara's arm with one hand and the backpack with the other, pulling them under the pines. A thrumming pulsed in the air and a small airplane flew by, blurring in and out of the mist. Mike's grip tightened and he did not release her till the plane was out of sight and the sound of its engines had faded. Then he let go. Tsara stepped away from him, rubbing her arm and glaring.

"They weren't looking for you," he said.

"How do you know?"

"That was Canadian Border Patrol. They're after drug runners and illegal immigrants."

She looked up at him thinking, *But you're not sure, are you?*

He pulled the backpack onto his shoulders. "Break's over."

He turned into the pathless woods, walking fast. No second granola bar. Tsara gritted her teeth, scrambling the first few steps to keep up. *Sonofabitch. Next time I'll go all loose like water so he can't carry me. Or yank on the belt loop so it tears. Yeah.*

Next time.

Mike stuck to a brisk pace. Presently they hit a trail wider than the others, almost broad enough to walk side by side in places, but Tsara stayed half a step behind Mike, not wanting to encourage him to move any faster. Leaves carpeted the ground in crisp layers. The path led steadily upward through dense stands of beech and maple whose lower leaves were blood-red and gold against the pearly sky. Overhead the canopy was bare, showing the dark clumps of birds' nests that had been hidden all summer.

Presently another sound met them: a low growl that grew to a roar as they approached it. At first Tsara hoped it was machinery—a car, a helicopter—but almost immediately she knew she was wrong. That was water, and lots of it.

The woods stopped as though sheared off with a knife. They stepped out of the forest. To their left a torrent of water crashed from a hulking cliff into a ravine, out of sight. The gorge was narrow here, no more than five or six feet across, but it widened as soon as it passed the cascade.

Mike swore.

"What?" said Tsara. Her voice came out too sharp, and she swallowed. Anything that upset Mike could have serious ramifications for her.

Mike gestured at the gorge. "There used to be a bridge here."

"But there's no road."

"Not that kind," he said. "Natural bridge. Rock." He thought for a moment, and turned right. "Come on." They walked a few yards and he stopped. "Shit."

"What? "

Mike pointed. "There it is."

An egg-shaped boulder as big as a minivan was wedged between the rock walls halfway down the ravine. It had cracked in two, the edges sliding past each other. Chunks of it lay in the river and waves plashed over them. The walls were scraped clear of lichen where the stone had skidded past. It must have been in the past day or so, Tsara thought. She imagined being on it as it slipped loose ....

Mike shook his head and half laughed. "Probably been there a million years, but not today," he said. "Oh, well. Improvise, adapt, overcome." He turned around, returning to the narrow spot where they had first emerged from the woods. Squatting by the edge of the cliff with one hand on a small, twisted tree, he stared at the deep trench. The tree's roots gripped the cliff like arthritic fingers. Tsara stepped forward. Holding the trunk with both hands, she stared down.

The falls pounded into a water-carved basin full of rounded boulders where tongues of foam slapped frantically. The channel narrowed almost immediately, sending the gargling mass through a chute where it leaped in bubbling fans. Mist drifted up the cliffs, dampening the lower roots of the tree. The walls were black and slick with spray, their shiny surfaces streaked with moss, vomit-green, leading to the maw below. A breeze from the waterfall moved her hair and sprinkled her cheek with droplets. She pulled back.

"I need to pee," she said abruptly.

"Fine," said Mike. He stood up, taking a last look at the far side of the gorge before walking her back to the tree line. He stopped by an oak that was wide enough to afford her some privacy and attached the carabiner to a branch over her head, leaving some slack in the cable. "Watch out for poison ivy," he said as he walked back to the ravine.

Oh, piss off, thought Tsara. But she did a quick survey before going as far around the tree as the cable allowed. She pulled down her pajama bottoms with her free hand and squatted. The relief was tremendous, and about the only thing that had felt good all day. She wiped off with leaf litter, doing her best to keep her hand clean.

As she stood and pulled up her pants, she saw what Mike hadn't: a rock about half again the size of a soccer ball, all but buried in leaves and just in reach of her foot.

Tsara's heart hiccupped. She looked over at Mike. His back was to her, and he was pulling a rope out of the backpack. Swiftly he undid it, tossing it so it lay in loose coils at his feet. Still watching him, Tsara stretched out her foot and hooked her heel over the stone, rocking it toward her. It rolled obligingly, showing its damp underside as it flipped through the leaves. She knelt, scraping the fingertips of her free hand over its rough surface to drag it closer.

She glanced at Mike again. He had tied the rope to the base of the tree overlooking the river. The free end was in his hand. There was weight to it; he had tied it to some whatsit from his pack. He threw it across the divide. The rope made a graceful arc through the air and landed noiselessly on the ground next to another tree, bigger than the first.

Tsara wedged the rock between two thick roots and stepped up on it. It wobbled, and she focused her balance as she stretched her hand toward the slender branch where the carabiner dangled.

She unhooked it.

Freedom.

Tsara looped the line into small circles, gripping them with her left hand. Heart pounding, she peered around the trunk again. Mike had backed away from the gorge, and now he ran at it, soaring across the divide and landing several feet in, next to the end of the rope. He was perfect as he leaped, coiled and compact where he landed.

Tsara sprang clear of the tree and onto the trail. Her legs flew in great leaps.

Mike roared. His feet beat on the ground. She heard his breath. Felt his shadow. For the second time in two days his body slammed into hers and they fell to the ground, leaves and dust swirling around them. His arms whipped around hers, pinning them to her sides. His legs crushed her knees together. She jerked helplessly in his grip, almost sobbing.

"I told you before, *don't fuck with me.*" He was breathing hard. "You're going over that gorge."

She clenched her fists. "Oh, that's a great idea. Why don't you just hold your breath till I do that?"

His chest shook, and Tsara knew he was laughing. But when he spoke again his voice was stone-hard. "Don't give me any of your shit." He put his massive hand on her wrist, pulling it behind her back. She reached forward with the other hand, thinking, *Elbow strike!* But he caught it easily and held her that way, letting her feel that he knew her every move before she made it.

"Don't," he breathed.

Don't. Or I will hurt you.

Almost crying, Tsara hung her head and let her arms go loose. He pushed her facedown into the leaf litter, still holding her hands behind her back, and tied her wrists together with the cable. He passed the rest of the line under her waist, and she grunted as his hands pushed the air out of her body. She felt him attach her bound wrists to the loop around her middle before he stood and heaved her to her feet. Dirt tickled her face. She tilted her head to see him.

"Look," she pleaded, "why don't you just let me go? I'll tell them you didn't hurt me."

"You can tell them anything you want," he said grimly. "After I get my kid back."

And with that he spun her around and marched her back up the trail, his grip firm on her arm. Tsara was chagrined to find she had only gone a few yards. It had felt like so much more ....

As they approached the tree with the rope around its base he pushed her to the ground by a sapling and yanked the spare length of cable around it, pulling it tight. Her fingers scraped the bark.

"Stop it," she cried.

"Shut up or I'll hog-tie you." He walked back to the tree by the ravine. Tsara pulled her knees up to her forehead and pressed her head on them, choking on every curse word she knew.

After a few minutes she looked up, wiping her dirty cheek awkwardly on the knee of her pants. Mike had evidently been back and forth over the ravine several times, because now he was putting finishing touches on his project: a rope bridge stretching between two trees.

Well, "bridge" was probably an overstatement. A single strand of rope stretched between the trunks, five or six feet above their bases. It spiraled around the closest tree, all the way down to where the roots bumped through the rocky ground. From there it reached across the narrow ravine to the other tree and back again, a double filament at ground height. Mike was on the far side of the gorge, a fat branch in his hand. He was stripping the twigs off it and letting them fall to the forest floor. Once it was naked, he pushed it between the lower strands of rope, flipping it over and over. The lines twisted together. When the entire length was a single, taut helix, he jammed one end of the branch into the ground against the direction of the twist. That branch wasn't going anywhere, Tsara realized. The two bottom ropes would stay twisted tight.

He came back across the bridge, hands on the upper line. He stepped off lightly and strode to where Tsara sat. Her shoulders ached, and the cord cut into her middle. He sat down next to her. His black tee shirt clung to his back, whether with sweat or river mist she could not be sure. But when he spoke, his voice was even.

"I don't blame you for trying to get away," he said. "But you're going over that gorge."

With that he stood and walked behind her, untying the line from the tree. He scooped her up in his arms, tossing her over his shoulder like a bag of dog food. Her butt was up in the air, head down, hands still tied to her midriff. Tsara grunted as his shoulder dug into her stomach. With his hands around her legs, Mike walked toward the makeshift bridge.

Tsara bucked against his hold. "Stop! *Stop!*"

His grip tightened. "Messing with me right now would be very dangerous for both of us. Just do what I say and don't move." He kept walking. Tsara jerked in his arms again.

"Fuck, no!" she shouted above the roar of the waterfall. "You can't!"

"Watch me."

"I can do it! "

He stopped. "Do what?" He wasn't looking at her—he couldn't—but she felt his head turn towards her. She shrank away from him, but kept her voice steady.

"I can walk across that—bridge you made. By myself. "

His head turned away from her. He shifted his weight.

"C'mon," she said. "It's easier than carrying me, isn't it?" She thought of the wild water and the dark boulders in the river, trying to project the image into his mind.

He set her down. Her sweatshirt rode up as she raked past his shoulder; the cable around her waist kept it in place. "You're not afraid of heights?"

"No. I can do it," she insisted again. "If you don't believe me," *and why should he?* "take my shoes. I wouldn't get far without them."

He looked at her. Tsara was silent. Finally he nodded.

"Keep 'em," he said as he stepped behind her. "You'll need them for walking on that rope."

The cable sprang free from her wrists; his hands grazed her waist as he pulled the cord away. Tsara rubbed her wrists.

"Thank you," she almost whispered.

"Thank me on the other side," he said. "Now listen up, because you only get one chance to do this right. I'm going over first; you'll need help at the end. Keep both hands on the upper rope at all times. Keep both feet on the lower rope at all times. Don't lift your feet to step; just slide them forward so you don't move the structure any more than you have to. Keep moving but don't crowd me." As he spoke he coiled the cable with rapid, efficient motions, tying a final loop around it and tightening it with a jerk. It hung from Tsara's wrist, heavy. "Got all that?" She nodded. "Oh, and one more thing," he added. "Don't look down."

The disgusted look Tsara gave him was lost as he pulled her to the tree, one hand cuffed around her wrist. She looked at the ropes and swallowed. Mike raised his voice over the rush of water. "If you're scared, say so. I won't be mad. But if you freeze half-way across I will kick your ass."

Privately Tsara thought that if she froze halfway across they would both have much bigger problems than whether or not her ass got kicked. But aloud she said only, "No, I'm good."

"You better be."

Mike shoved Tsara next to the bridge and lifted the arm with the cable on it, clipping the carabiner to the higher rope. Then he put both his hands on the rope and squeezed past her, brushing her shoulders with his chest as he stepped onto the twisted lower strands. He placed one hand on the carabiner as he raised his voice over the bellow of the waterfall. "Now." Feet sliding forward on the ropes, he stepped past the cliff's edge and into the air.

Tsara wondered briefly if she could throw Mike off the rope, decided she couldn't, and followed him. Mimicking his actions, she slid her feet over the lower ropes, feeling the twists bumping beneath the soles of her Crocs. Her ribs were bruised from his tackle, and stretching her arms hurt.

Mike looked ahead, moving steadily, keeping his hand on the carabiner. She kept her eyes on his shoulders. Mist caressed her cold cheeks.

Tsara saw why Mike had said she would need help. Near the end the ropes pulled apart, the higher one well above her head. Even now she could feel the span increasing. She stretched to keep her grip.

Through Mike's legs Tsara could see a second reason she would have trouble: a gap in the cliff face next to the tree. It wasn't huge; a big man could clear it with no trouble. Even for someone her size it might be okay—one large stride.

If she could get close enough.

The ropes pulled further apart. Tsara's arms ached. She kept her feet close to Mike's.

A few steps short of the far side of the gorge, Mike stopped. Still looking ahead he undid the carabiner with one hand. It bumped against Tsara's forearm as it fell. Her hands tightened. Her fingernails were jammed with skin from her palms. She focused on a faraway tree.

Mike slid his feet forward. "Hold on," he shouted. He took a big step and let go of the top rope. His body swung forward as his foot landed on the safe side of the gap. He was on firm ground.

The ropes bounced. Tsara's foot slipped. Her body went rigid. The ropes jerked like angry muscles under her feet. Overhead the single strand was slick with mist and sweat. She gasped.

"*Stop.*" He leaned forward. One hand was on the upper rope. The other reached for her. "*Look at me.*"

She did. The mouth was a grim line, but his eyes were calm.

Oh.

He is not going to drop me.

"Give me your hand," he shouted above the waterfall. "On three, you jump. On *three*. Got it?"

Tsara could barely nod. The ropes still spasmed under her feet. Sick with the despair of knowing she needed him, she unclenched one fist and lowered her arm. He grabbed her wrist, his fingers enclosing it. Realizing what he was doing, she grasped his wrist. Even through the haze of panic she felt how warm his skin was ... of course, her fingers were so cold ....

"On three," he roared again. "One—two—*three!*"

Tsara jumped. Mike heaved her arm. Mist on her face, under her feet. Air.

She landed in a crouch, past the cliffs, rocks, water. Mike stumbled, then regained his balance and dropped her hand.

She felt sick.

"You okay?"

"Fucking great," she said blearily. "Let's do it again."

"Take five," he said, and walked back to the bridge.

Tsara parked herself on a rock that was almost big enough to sit on comfortably. Her head swam, and she rubbed her forehead. Something was wrong. All the dark parts of the forest were broadening and waving. The shadows under the branches merged with the black lines on the bark of the trees. This was odd ... and not good ....

Quickly she dropped her head between her knees and breathed deeply into cupped hands. She closed her eyes, making the waving black lines disappear.

When she looked up, the forest was steady again and Mike was standing in front of her. His face was set in silence, and she knew he was waiting for her.

"Are you gonna kick my ass?" she asked.

"Nah," he said, straight-faced. "You were more than half-way across."

"That, and it was your fault."

Mike looked at the sky. "Come on," he said. "It's going to rain." And he unwrapped the cable from its tight coil, reattaching it to his belt loop as they set off again.

24

"And that's what we know so far," said Agent Spaar. She looked at the two men. "This must be a shock. I'm sorry."

They were sitting in one of the living rooms at the chateau where a cluster of furniture hugged an empty fireplace. Court rocked forward in a leather armchair, his head in his hands. David sagged back on the couch, his eyes unfocused, as though he had just been sucker punched.

"He was running a *child kidnapping ring?*" cried Court, not looking up.

"So you had no idea."

"Good God, no."

"None at all?"

Court's hands fell and he stared into space. "I knew some shit—stuff—he did. He used to brag about it. But not this."

"What kinds of things did he brag about?"

"Oh, like cheating on his taxes. Stuff like that. And things from a long time ago. But—*God.*"

"None of the kids was physically harmed as far as we can tell," said Spaar. "And Mr. Thornlocke tells us he was planning on sending them all home Sunday evening." It was one of the few things he had said before realizing he would be wiser to shut up.

"Wait," said Court. "Sunday—no—" He looked at Spaar. "So they wouldn't miss any *school?*"

"You seem to know your uncle well."

"Not as well as I thought."

"But what does this have to do with Tsara?" said David.

113

"We're not sure yet."

He shuddered. "I can't believe I told her to come."

"Dude, I did too," said Court. "And I know him better than you."

Spaar closed the file. "Don't blame yourselves," she said. "If his other crimes were nonviolent, you couldn't have predicted this."

David hoisted himself to a sitting position. "Well, where does this leave us? Where do we go from here?"

"We're taking the kids to the hospital."

"I thought you said they weren't hurt."

"We're not taking any chances. If nothing else, they're going to need psychological support."

"Right. Of course."

"When they're ready we'll question them. In the meantime we've been talking to the parents about their dealings with Mr. Thornlocke." They were also waiting on a translator. The kids spoke perfect English, but the parents were a different story. As far as Spaar could tell, they understood what she said but had trouble finding the right words to answer, especially when they were emotional. Like now.

The door at the end of the room swung open, and Galen held it for an EMT and a short woman in her mid-fifties with an unflattering haircut that was too long for her. She held a small boy by the hand. They stopped just inside the room. Seeing the strangers, the boy ducked behind her legs and peered out from behind them. He smiled cautiously, and his ocean-colored eyes turned into soft crescents.

"Small mix-up," said Galen. "You need to sign off on forms for both families."

Spaar stood and walked to the group by the door. The EMT handed her a clipboard and pen. She glanced at the form. "You're Beth Westbrook?" she said to the woman.

"Yes."

Spaar turned the clipboard so the woman could see. "This your address?"

"Yes."

"And you're responsible for this boy." Spaar smiled at the child, but he turned his head away.

The older woman stroked the child's hair. "He's my grandson. I got here as soon as I could."

"Mrs. Westbrook doesn't drive," said Galen. "We had to send a car for her."

Spaar signed with a quick stroke and flipped to the next page. "And this is this young man's date of birth, yes?"

"Yes—he just turned six."

"Is all the other information correct?" She turned the clipboard towards the other woman again.

"Of course. I already signed it."

"Okay." Spaar jotted a second time and returned the forms to the EMT.

The boy peeked past his grandmother. Court waved gently at him, and he nipped out of sight again. Only his fingers were still visible, clutching the edges of his grandmother's slacks. Spaar turned her back to Court and David and spoke in an undertone. David and Court could hear her voice but the words were too blurred to make out.

"Cute kid," said David quietly.

"Yeah. "

"I wonder how much he knows about what's going on?"

Court shook his head. "What could you tell him? A little guy like that. And after what he's been through."

"How old did she say he was?" said David. "Six?"

"I think so."

"Six," repeated David. They were silent, thinking of Josh and Abbie.

Like Tsara's room, this one had French windows. They overlooked a patio leading to the driveway. As Court and David watched, an ambulance pulled up and parked, engine idling.

Spaar turned her head, and her voice became audible again. "… don't leave town," she said. "We'll be in contact shortly."

"I've tried phoning him," said the woman. "It goes straight to voice mail."

"Just keep trying," said Galen. "We need to talk to him."

"If you reach him, tell him that," said Spaar. "The best thing is for him to turn himself in before anyone gets hurt."

The woman raised her voice slightly, and David was sure she intended him and Court to hear.

"Detective—"

"Agent."

"Sorry. Agent Spaar, I have to tell you just one thing. I already told Mr. Galen." She swallowed. "I don't know what's going on, but—the troubles he's had weren't his fault. He wouldn't hurt anyone. There's been some mistake."

We'll see about that, thought Spaar grimly. Aloud she said, "We just want to make sure everyone gets home safely. But I thank you for your cooperation. As I said, we'll be in touch soon."

"This way, ma'am," said the EMT. "You too, big guy." The boy gripped his grandmother's hand, tugging her through the French windows. Watching from the other end of the room, David wondered vaguely whether the woman had a limp or the boy was pulling her off-balance in his urge to get away.

Galen stood at Spaar's side, watching them go. "So how come you get to be Agent but I'm Mr.?"

"Figure you can fight your own battles, Galen."

"Good point."

"What troubles has her son been in?"

"Has a record." Galen gazed out the window at the glittering mass of FBI vehicles and personnel that seemed to have shot out of the lawn in the past twenty minutes or so. Any time there were children involved, a crime scene started to look like a Cecil B. DeMille production pretty quick. There would be more, too, as soon as the media got hold of this. No way to keep it quiet, not with so many kids at the hospital.

"Okay. Let's check with the local cops on that." Spaar kept her back to David and Court, still using the undertone.

"I did."

"And?"

"No answer. So I asked around. There's two of them, and no one's seen them since this morning. Thornlocke's cook saw them driving away from here. Couldn't tell where they were going, since the end of the driveway's out of sight."

"Thornlocke told me he'd called them."

"Uh huh. They were also here yesterday."

"He said they were doing security for the party."

"I mean before that. In the afternoon."

"Why would they have been here in the afternoon?"

116

Galen gestured to the end of the house he had just left. "From the kitchen the cook has a great view of the driveway. So she saw yesterday afternoon when the cops drove up in their truck and went around the end of the house toward the wine cellar."

"Oh, my God."

"For whatever it's worth, when they left this morning she noticed they looked real nervous."

"Damnit! "

"Anyway, I think we know who the muscle is," said Galen. "And I think we have some idea why our boy didn't go to the cops when his kid disappeared."

Spaar sighed. "I'd run, too, if I had multiple charges of child kidnapping staring me in the face. Get the word out about the cops, and see what you can do about photos and descriptions."

Galen glanced at Court and David, who were still waiting at the other end of the room. "Did Abrams know about his uncle's activities?"

"He seemed shocked."

"How shocked?"

"Just check his phone records, okay? And Thornlocke's emails. I want to see if Abrams had any contact with either of the two families, or anything unusual with Thornlocke. And look into his and Thornlocke's financials. I want to know about gambling, prostitutes, any big debts. "

Galen jotted it down. "Mr. Freihoffer was also shocked."

"Check him out too." She looked again at David and Court. "I'll tell them we're done for now." The agents walked back toward the sofa and chairs by the empty fireplace.

David stood. "I want to thank you both for everything you're doing," he said. Court stood behind him, silent in agreement. "And please, please, if there's anything—" His hands shook, and his palms were damp. He rubbed them together, feeling the moisture slide between them. He looked again at the agents standing in front of him. They were so calm.

"This is normal for you, isn't it?" he said.

Spaar gave her half-smile. "I guess you could say that."

David's voice was low. "How can you stand it?"

Spaar's half-smile vanished. "I like helping people like your wife," she said. "And I like catching the bad guy."

"Do you think you'll catch this one?"

"I think there's a good chance."

"Look at it this way," said Galen. "He has to be lucky all the time. We only have to be lucky once."

David glanced at the door where the little boy and his grandmother had disappeared. "Who was she talking about?"

"We'll be in touch when we know more," said Spaar. "Where are you two staying?"

David waved his hands vaguely. "I just got in—I guess I'll find a hotel in town somewhere."

"I'll come with you," said Court. "Give me a few minutes to pack." He turned away, his shoulders rigid.

"Mr. Abrams." Spaar's voice wasn't loud, but it traveled. Court stopped.

"Yes?"

"We're taking your uncle into custody shortly," she said. "But in the meantime, I suggest you avoid him. Sir."

Court's shoulders drooped, but he nodded and made his way out the door.

"Smooth," said Galen.

"What?" said David.

"I know the look of a man who's going to punch someone's lights out," said Spaar. "Unfortunately, that's illegal."

David snorted. "I wish you hadn't stopped him," he said. "If anything happens to her—"

"I know, sir," said Spaar. Her face had closed like an envelope. "We're doing our best. You and she deserve no less than that." And she and Galen walked out, leaving David sitting alone again, resting his chin on his palm.

Mike hadn't lied. There was plenty of walking. They trod narrow paths that petered out and picked up again. Pine needles brushed Tsara's arms as she walked, and a dense carpet of fallen ones muted her footsteps. At times greenbrier stretched into the pathway. When she couldn't step over it, it gripped her pajama pants with its nasty teeth, leaving little holes as she yanked free.

They skirted marshy areas where prickling clouds of gnats brushed her face and drifted into her mouth, making her spit. Mike kept far enough from the mud that they didn't leave footprints. And whenever they came to an open area, he stopped and looked around—not just at the surrounding woods, but at the sky as well. He was still then, holding up one big hand to silence her, but otherwise moving only his eyes. She breathed quietly, not wanting to risk his wrath. Then his hand curled sharply in a "Come on," and they moved again, through granite outcroppings or old rockslides where chunks of stone the size of closets sat on fields of loose rock that slid under her feet in layers.

These gave way in turn to slopes studded with boulders that were scruffed over with blueberry bushes whose ruddy leaves flickered in the wind. The ribbons of earth between the rocks were narrow and uneven, and the cable around her wrist made maneuvering difficult. Once one of her Crocs got stuck between two boulders and she pulled her stockinged foot clear of it by accident. "Wait," she begged, and squatting down she yanked the shoe free and put it back on her foot.

To her surprise, Mike had been patient, slowing down and holding out his hand to help her over the roughest spots. She took it when she had to, and bit her tongue to keep from thanking him. But when they were back in the woods and the ground leveled off, he yanked her along. "I told you not to play feeble."

So Tsara matched his pace, breathing heavily and strangling the thousand sarcastic remarks that rose to her lips. *Sure, no problem. It's not like you're a foot taller than I am and you know the terrain and have hiking boots. I'm just playing feeble because it's _fun_! This is such a fucking ball for me. Thanks, shithead.*

She caught a small loop of the cable and gripped it in her hand to take the tension off her wrist. It made her think of when they were leash-training Falstaff. The puppy had insisted on carrying the lead in his mouth so they couldn't pull on his collar. It wasn't a flattering analogy, and she shoved it out of her mind.

At first she tried to memorize landmarks. That fallen log was lined with black; it looked fire-blasted. Maybe it had been struck by lighting. This cliff face had brown and orange streaks in it. But eventually all the fallen logs looked the same and all the cliffs were striped. The forest became featureless, punctuated only by occasional clearings that were clones for size and shape and the slant of young trees toward the openings in the canopy. Even the sky was unchanged, solid white smudged with grey that gave forth a bright gloom but cast no shadows. Tsara gave up, keeping her eyes on the backpack in front of her, walking fast so the line between her hand and his waist hung in a curve. They strode on, accompanied only by birdsong and the undulating plainchant of the wind.

Then—a slight shift in his shoulders, a hiccup in the pace. He changed direction, and Tsara followed.

Why had he done that?

She stopped walking, and looked back over her shoulder. The line tightened. He pulled on it sharply but didn't say anything.

He talked before called me feeble why isn't he talking now—?

Tsara spun around. Three large boulders hunched together, blocking her view. But—

Voices. *Voices!*

"Over here!" she shouted. "Help—"

He whipped her off her feet, clamping his hand over her mouth. Tsara thrashed furiously in his arms, yelling through his fingers. Over her own cries she heard someone else bellowing. Feet thudding toward them on the hard dirt.

"*Fuck!*" spat Mike. He dropped her. Tsara jerked away and laughed at him, wild with gloat. But he was looking toward the sounds. His hand went to his waist and he unclipped the line, tossing her the carabiner. She caught it in mechanical astonishment.

"Run," he said.

"Fat chance."

He stepped close, filling the air in front of her. His eyes were hard and dark. "If you want to live another hour, *run.*"

She stared at him.

He wasn't lying.

The footsteps came closer.

Tsara turned and ran.

"Any history of violence?" asked Galen. "Drug use?" He was breathing through his mouth, taking shallow sips of the thick air of the stable.

"You've got the wrong guy," said Soames bluntly. He heaved a hay bale onto the stack and stooped for another while Galen and Spaar watched. Usually stacking the bales was Juan's job; but upon hearing that federal agents were expected at the stable, Juan had developed a migraine of such searing intensity that he had been forced to leave for the afternoon. In a show of solidarity, Carlos and Miguel had taken him home and were not expected to return until tomorrow. Soames's barn manager, Sue, was on the phone with José, explaining to him that he was taking the day off. But it looked like rain, and the hay needed to be off the trailer, inside, and in place. Soames hoisted a fresh bale off the floor. "They aren't heavy," he said over his shoulder, "but at least they're expensive."

"How well do you know him?" asked Spaar.

"Oh, pretty good and for a long time. He's a good guy. I'm telling you, there's been some mistake." Soames shoved the bale into alignment. "No way is he into drugs. I don't think he even drinks coffee. Maybe a beer sometimes. And violent? Nah." Soames shook his head. "He has a temper, I'll admit, but it never lasts. He's in here a lot, and there's never been a problem. Takes good care of his horse." Soames's tone made it clear that proper care of one's horse was a benchmark of civilized behavior.

"Don't most horse owners take good care of their animals?" said Spaar. Her shoe had straw on it. She lifted her foot to let it slide off.

"Yeah, you'd think so, wouldn't you, with an investment like that?" said Soames. "But there's all kinds. Some people are just like, 'See ya,' y'know? They figure they're paying the stable to do all the work. Mike's not like that." He lifted another bale and maneuvered it into place.

"How so?" said Spaar.

"Okay, here's what I'm talking about," said Soames. "I came in here one time, year, might've been two years ago—yeah, two years. We had a really early frost, I remember that. Anyway, I come in and check on Mike's horse 'cause she was sick. You know what colic is with horses?"

"It's a stomach thing, right?" said Spaar. Galen looked blank.

"Sort of," said Soames. "Basically it's gas, a stomach full of gas. Horses can't burp or puke—'scuse me, ma'am, vomit. So if they get overloaded with gas they have to fa—pass wind, but they can't till the pipe gets full of gas. If you don't keep an eye on them they'll lie down or roll to get the gas moving. Then the intestine gets twisted."

"That's bad?" said Galen.

"Horrible," said Soames. "It's just ungodly painful for the animal, you have no idea. Oftentimes you have a horse with bad colic, you shoot it, 'cause it's going to die anyway."

"His horse had colic?" said Spaar.

"Yes she did," said Soames. "And Mike stayed with her for the next three days."

Galen blinked. "You mean twenty-four seven?"

"Twenty-four three," said Soames. "She was okay by the fourth day. But that's what I'm telling you. I came in that day and he'd slept in the stall with her—if he slept at all. And he did the same thing the next two nights running. I said to him, 'Jesus, Mike, get some sleep and I'll have one of the stable hands spell you.' But he wouldn't. That's Mike."

Spaar made notes on her pad. "Anything else you can tell us about him?"

"Couple of times when I've been out of town and my barn manager couldn't be here I left Mike in charge of the place for a few days. I wouldn't do that with anyone else."

"No one?" said Galen.

"I've worked nineteen years to get this place in the kind of shape it's in," said Soames. "As for people I'd trust with it, that's a pretty short list."

"Why does he live in a cabin in the woods?" said Galen.

"If a rich guy lived in a cabin in the woods, would you think there was anything wrong with that?" Soames stooped for another hay bale.

"What else do you know about Mr. Westbrook?" said Spaar. "Do you ever see him outside the stable?"

"He's a good guy, he's good with his kid," he said.

"We think this may have something to do with the boy," said Spaar.

Soames paused, hand against the prickly wall of bales. "Oh. Well, that might be a different conversation."

"What makes you say that?"

"That's his only child, you know. And he's a single parent. Very protective of the kid."

Spaar flipped to a new page in her notebook and jotted rapidly. "Why isn't the boy in school?"

"I think Mike was planning on starting him next year." Soames grinned. "Pretty sure that was a conversation with his mother."

"Are they close? Mr. Westbrook and his mother, I mean?"

"I guess so. He and Aiden lived with her when he was a baby. When Aiden was a baby."

"Why does he have a horse?" asked Galen.

"Lots of people have horses," said Soames. "Besides, he also has a truck. Jesus, he's not the Unabomber, you know."

"Riding," said Spaar, "that's a pretty expensive hobby, isn't it?"

Soames chuckled darkly. "Know how to make a small fortune in horses?"

"Start with a big one?" said Galen.

"You got it."

"So how does he afford it?" asked Spaar.

"He does work for me in exchange for stabling. His horse is only here part-time anyway. And he works for Jim pretty regular. Plus he's not a big spender." Soames brushed off his hands. "Anyway. I can get you descriptions of both horses if that helps."

"It would," said Spaar. "Thanks."

They moved into Soames's office and he sat down at his laptop. "I'll type something up if you like."

"Sure," said Spaar.

Soames's stubby fingers tapped the keys. The door opened and a young woman with a blonde ponytail walked in. "Hey, Sue," said Soames without looking up. "Does Mike drink coffee?"

"I'm not sure," said Sue. "Come to think of it, I don't think I've ever seen him do that."

"Mm," said Soames, still typing. "How tall would you say Chrissy is?"

"Sixteen three," said Sue promptly.

"Chrissy is his horse?" asked Spaar. Her pen hadn't stopped moving since they entered the stable.

"Chrysanthemum. She's a draft cross mare." Sue moved behind Soames to see what he was typing. "'Bay with two white socks in back, medium white star on her face. Black mane and tail.' That sounds about right." She looked up at the two agents. "She's a great horse. Beautiful, crested neck and nice leg action. That's from the Percheron side."

Galen had the uneasy feeling Sue was speaking in code. "So she's a mare."

"Last I checked."

"Is that common, for a guy to have a female horse?"

"Some guys won't," said Sue. "They feel like they have something to prove."

"But Mr. Westbrook doesn't?"

A smile lifted Sue's lips. "Mike has *nothing* to prove."

"Settle down," admonished Soames.

"What about Mr. Montrose?"

Sue was still smiling. "He has a little more to prove." She glanced down at the computer screen again. "Jim's horse's name is Randy. He's a husband horse."

"A what?"

"You know, when a rider comes in with her husband and needs a safe horse for him. Randy's great," she added. "He's tough and smart. Wicked sense of humor."

Soames turned slightly to look up at her as his fingers continued to tap. "Wasn't it Randy that knocked over that wheelbarrow full of manure—"

"—right onto that little snot with the new boots. Yeah, that's our boy." Sue and Soames laughed uproariously before stopping at Spaar and Galen's unsmiling expressions. Soames coughed and turned back to the keyboard. He hit a final key and the paper slid out of the printer. He handed it to Spaar, who added it to her portfolio.

"Thanks," said Spaar. She handed him and Sue business cards. "My number's on that. If you think of anything else, or if Mike contacts you, please call immediately."

"I'll do that," said Soames, and Sue nodded. Soames added the card to a stack in a mug on his desk.

Spaar and Galen paused in the doorway. "One thing I still don't understand," said Spaar. "It sounds like Mike spends a lot of time in Libertyville. Why doesn't he just live here?"

Soames's face clouded. "Have you met his mom?"

"Briefly. We're going to talk to her next."

"Did you notice she walks with a limp?"

"Yes."

"It's pretty bad. She can't even drive anymore."

"Yes, we know. It's a hip injury, isn't it?"

A puff of air escaped Soames's lips. "Yeah. You ask her how she got that hip injury. And then you can ask her why Mike lives out of town."

"Can you tell us?" said Galen.

Soames shook his head. "I'm not going to tell you things I can't prove. You ask her. See what she says."

Tsara ran.

She ran through stands of birches that gave way to pine and back to birch. She ran through piles of oak leaves that whirled up around her feet, and down hills that abruptly turned uphill and had her gasping as she pulled herself up by roots and rocks. She slipped and her knees dug into the ground. She tore past saplings and shrubs whose thin branches sliced at her. Greenbrier ripped the backs of her hands and forearms, leaving them roughed over with flakes of torn skin. A stitch in her side was fire, and each breath cut like a blade in her throat.

She headed downhill again, her legs flying out in front of her. Her foot hit a patch of acorns and they rolled like ball bearings. Her arms flailed and she grabbed a slender tree as the acorns rattled into the dry leaves around them. She held on, gripping the trunk and gasping one tearing breath after another as her heart banged so hard it hurt her bones.

Trying to breathe more quietly, she listened to the woods. The wind blew through the canopy. A few invisible birds sang. Nothing else.

A thin screech made Tsara jump before she remembered what a red-tailed hawk sounded like. *Stop it!* Getting twitchy wasn't going to help. But at least she appeared to be alone. Except for the birds.

Her breathing eased, and she stretched her arms over her head to calm the stitch in her side. She leaned against the tree that way for a moment, and reflected that for the next kidnapping she would definitely wear a bra.

She let down her arms as the pain faded. *Now for that goddamn cable.* Her left hand was cramped around it, her nails digging into her palms. Sitting down, she dropped it and flexed her hand, then pointed her fingers and thumb together to make her hand smaller and pulled the loop down smoothly but firmly.

It didn't budge. Mike had made the ring tight, pressing against the bone of her wrist just above the joint. It wouldn't even fit over the bump there, much less past the splay of her fingers and palm. The coating on the cable was plastic, but she could see the twisted wires inside. The metal collar that held the loop closed was solid. She couldn't even make out a seam where he had crimped it together.

"Fuck," she said out loud. "Fuck, fuck, *fuck!*" She tore rabidly at the cable, yanking and swearing until her wrist turned red. Biting her lip, she leaned against the tree trunk, eyes closed.

Holy shit. Get a grip.

She opened her eyes and pulled the end of the cable toward her, unclipping the carabiner. Then she stood and threw it as far as she could. Which wasn't very. But at least now if she ran into Mike again he'd have trouble binding her to him. Or Jim, or whoever else was out there.

So ... who exactly was after her?

Mike, obviously. But who was after *him*—and why had he let her go?

"If you want to live another hour, run."

As far as she could tell, Mike hadn't lied to her about anything. Not about having a son, not about Cass shooting at Jim. And the look in his eyes when he told her to run had been horrible. Like a man staring at death.

Was Cass after him?

Nah. Even the most agile septuagenarian would have trouble getting around in these mountains. Strip half a century off Cass and sure, he'd have been here in a heartbeat. He could stop the bad guy, rescue the girl, and claim the herohood. But not the Cass of today.

Had her uncle sent someone after them? That seemed more plausible. But who? Arnold? Cass might want to consider an overhaul of his household staff, she thought bitterly, because his security detail didn't seem terrifically reliable. He had doubled it and Mike and Jim had shot right past. Even the damn dogs hadn't stopped them.

Could it be Court? He must know by now she was missing.

No, that didn't make sense either. Her brother wasn't a woodsman. Court was a fan of the great indoors. And if he had somehow tracked her this far, she would have recognized his voice back there. Wouldn't she? Even muffled by the woods?

Besides, Mike wouldn't be that scared of Court.

Mike could be faking it, she thought. Maybe those were her own rescuers she had just run away from. Maybe Mike had told her to flee so he could claim not to be the guy they were looking for, and then track her down later at his leisure. Maybe he had just played her like a cheap fiddle and she was a goddamn fool.

Then she thought of his expression again and shuddered. It would be hard to fake a look like that, and she was pretty sure Mike wasn't that good an actor.

Tsara pulled off her Crocs and tapped them against the heel of her palm. Pebbles putted to the ground, pursued by a flutter of leaf fragments. She put her shoes back on, considering. Where did this leave her?

Well. Various people, or groups of people, might or might not be after her. Cass had apparently greeted the news of her abduction with gunfire, making him at best a shaky ally. He might have alerted the authorities, but he might just as easily prefer to take matters into his own hands. So there was an outside chance he was even now roaming the woods with his favorite blunderbuss, looking for someone to shoot. None of which helped her at all for the moment, because right now she was entirely by herself in parts unknown.

Tsara looked around. The parts were in fact very unknown. She was in the wilds of the Silver Mountains, a place where hikers and hunters died every year. If she didn't intend to join their ranks, she would have to do some planning.

Ordinarily if you were lost in the woods you stayed put so rescuers could find you. This wasn't ordinarily.

"Location, location, location," she said, half-aloud. A chickadee on a low branch flapped away, the twig jumping behind it.

Tsara knew a few things about where she was. She was in the north of the state, spitting distance from the Canadian border. The state capital and most of the major cities were in the south, making that a good direction to walk. Furthermore, all the highways in New Hampshire ran north-south; which meant that if she headed east or west in a straight line for long enough, she would hit one of them. Nowhere in the United States are you ever more than … what, about ten miles from a highway? Something like that. She could do ten miles easy.

Another option was walking till she found a river or stream, and following it downhill. People build by water, and besides, chances were good it would eventually empty into Great Boulder River, which was peppered with campgrounds even before it came to the mills and factories in Saxonville.

So the only direction to avoid was north, which would take her into Canada. She didn't know how far the next Canadian town was, but she was pretty sure there were a lot of trees between her and it.

The only thing was to make sure she was going in a straight line.

Tsara thought of the iPhone, which had a compass app. She had downloaded it for Abbie, who loved the little numbers and the digital needle swinging about.

"Probably no reception here anyway," she said. Damn mountains.

It was early October. They were still in Daylight Savings Time, and it must be after noon. At one o'clock her shadow would be pointing north, or close enough. All she had to do was aim herself away from it, find a landmark, and walk toward that so she wouldn't get confused when the sun started sinking and her shadow swung around to the east.

She squinted at the pearlescent sky.

No sun.

No shadows.

"Well, fuck you, too," she told the sky. She pulled herself up, looking for a landmark to walk towards—a distinctive peak, or a waterfall. That would be especially good, since she was getting thirsty.

The trees pressed in around her, their top branches like dark lace. Midway down they were still full of color, gold and orange and green; and the ground was endless drifts of leaves, brown-edged and dry. She couldn't see more than a few yards in any direction.

So she marked the farthest tree she could see, a broad oak with a broken limb, and started walking toward it. When she got there, she told herself, she would go right around it and look straight ahead to the next furthest thing, tree or rock or whatever, and walk to that. That should keep her going in a straight line.

Stay cool and keep walking, she thought.

Because I'll be goddamned if my kids are going to grow up without a mother.

Spaar and Galen got back in the car and by unspoken agreement drove upwind of the stable and rolled down the windows before talking.

"Jesus," moaned Galen. "How do they *breathe* in there?" He wanted to stick his head out the window and pant like a dog.

"Maybe it smells like roses to them." Spaar pulled over and took out the sheet Soames had given them.

"'Randy is a light rose grey with black points,'" read Galen. "What's rose grey?"

"What are points?"

"Because I have to tell you, never once have I seen a grey rose."

"Mm." Spaar stared at it for a moment. "Well, I think it's safe to say he's grey. And," she glanced further down the page "he has a black mane and tail and a long coat."

"And he's sixteen hh." Galen brightened. "Hands high. And a hand is six inches. I think."

"Four."

"How the hell do you know?"

"I'm a highly trained agent with the Federal Bureau of Investigation."

"I figured a hand would be half a foot. Why would a hand be a third of a foot?"

Spaar handed him the sheet. "No idea. Get this out to the troopers and local town cops. I want a BOLO for two guys with horses matching these descriptions. Add Mrs. Adelman's photo. We'll get pictures of the men soon. Keep it local for now—the horses won't have gone too far. Plus, my guess is he wants to keep close to his kid."

Galen took the paper. "Anyone else?"

"Like who?"

"Rangers, especially in parks with riding trails. Camping grounds. Maybe feed stores." Galen appeared to be thinking deeply. "The local chapter of the Pony Express."

"Funny. Yeah, those first three sound good." She put the car in drive.

"What now?"

"Keep up the investigation while we wait for the warrant on his place."

"Okay," said Galen. "I dibs military records and old girlfriends."

"All yours." Spaar turned the car onto the road and headed toward the center of town. "But first we're going to talk to his mom. "

Not having a watch can really screw with your sense of time, Tsara reflected. Also no shadows, no one to talk to, and no way to figure out how fast you're going. Three miles an hour was slow and six was quick, but what was stepping over logs and half-tripping over roots?

Hungry and thirsty, that's what it was. And tired.

She stepped around her latest landmark tree and saw the little stream before she heard it. It wasn't much, just a ribbon of clear brown water sliding over mossy rocks. She dropped to her knees and drank. The water tasted of stone and bark, and when she sat up it dripped onto her sweatshirt before she could wipe her chin. Her lips were damp, and the jagged feeling in her throat was gone. She stood, feeling stronger.

You and me, dude, she told the stream. *Show me the money.* She followed it downhill so it could merge with a bigger stream and maybe a river or at least a good place to camp that would have a nice family with a Winnebago and a cell phone that actually worked. The streambed widened, leaving a dry stretch on either side. She stepped onto it and walked on the water-smoothed gravel, dusty this late in the season, stubbing her Crocs every now and again. Jewelweed crowded between rocks. Deer tracks gouged into the mud at the water's edge, and once she saw the lacy handprint of a raccoon. Every few minutes she paused to listen, because if she could hear the noise she was making as she walked, someone else could too. But as far as she could tell she was alone. This confirmed her feeling that the stream was her new best friend, and she followed it with increasing confidence.

134

So when it petered out to a scattering of puddles by a fern-drenched boulder, the betrayal felt acute.

"Damnit!"

Tsara rubbed her forehead. She wondered how far astray the traitorous brook had taken her, whether it was worth her while to trace it back upstream and start over again, and whether she would even recognize the place where she'd first started following it. The answers, in reverse order, were no, probably not, and God only knows. Best to start over again: plot a new straight line and this time stick to it. She set her sights on a snaggly limb and walked toward it.

The oaks gave way to pine again. Time was numb. Tsara kept walking.

At first she thought the voices were crows, or running water. Then they spoke again, separate from the murmur of the living forest. She turned her head, straining to pinpoint the source.

To the right?

How far?

She knelt and brushed a clear patch in the pine needles and ground her Crocs into the earth, showing which way she had been headed. Then she jammed four sticks together over the marks, leaning their tips against each other in a skeletal teepee. She walked towards the voices and glanced over her shoulder. Her marker was still visible.

The pine needles made for quiet walking, and she lifted her feet as little as possible. Ahead, a laugh dissolved in the shush of the wind.

One voice or two?

One voice could be Mike talking to Jim.

The sound came from behind a hulking, frost-cleft boulder, taller than Tsara. She looked back. A few more steps and the teepee would be out of sight. She shoved a stick into the ground and broke the top so it pointed towards the marker. Then, walking when the wind masked her steps, she crept toward the sound. It was two voices, she was sure.

Could be Castle and his cops.

Could be a search-and-rescue team.

Could be those guys from Deliverance.

Tsara knelt by the boulder. The speakers were behind it, invisible but clearly audible through the cleft in the granite. It was thin as thread over her head but a good foot wide at the ground where winter and flood had shifted the fractured slabs. She breathed quietly and listened.

A can opened with a pop and a hiss. A wrapper crinkled.

"You should drink." A man's voice, nasal.

I've heard that voice before.

"I hate warm Coke." The second man's voice was higher.

But not that one.

"Have water."

"That's warm too. Warm as piss."

"Jesus, Jordan, just do it."

Tsara heard a swallow and Jordan, he of the high voice, spoke again. "Think he'll talk?"

"If he hasn't by now he's not gonna," said the nasal voice. "You done good, though, Jordie."

Jordan spoke with his mouth full. "Smbitch is giving us a lot of trouble."

"Fuck, yes. Isn't that always the way?"

Tsara frowned. Had he said "son of a bitch"? Or "bitch"?

The nasal voice went on. "Way I figure it she has to be close. He's carrying two water bottles."

"You think he's got her stashed somewhere?"

"Or she's with Dumbo."

"Jimbo the Dumbo," said Jordan, and took another swallow. A wrapper crinkled again.

"Right."

"Arnold. What if she's not?"

"I been right about everything else, haven't I? We'll find her."

"Serve and protect," said Jordan.

"Protect and serve," said Arnold. "Here, gimme that. You eat like a pig, I swear."

Moving slowly, Tsara peered through the crack.

Two men sat on the forest floor, eating. An empty water bottle lay on its side and wrappers gleamed among the pine needles. Both men had short, dark hair and wore jeans and khaki-camouflage shirts. The larger of the two turned his head, revealing a nose worthy of a prizefighter.

Tsara's heart leaped. It was the security guard—and his backup. Castle had sent them to save her!

Probably.

The smaller man crunched two of the several wrappers in his hand and shoved them into his pocket as he stood up. His shoulders slumped even when he was standing. "So now what?" He pointed.

Mike sat on the floor of the clearing, leaning against a young tree, his hands behind it.

Looking at her.

Tsara jerked away from the crack. Her fingertips were cold.

"We'll finish here and find the girl," said Arnold. He sniffed. "There's a good place up-trail, past the turnoff."

"Want me to set it up?"

"I'll do it. I know the place."

"Okay," said Jordan. "I can guard him."

"Yeah, good."

Footsteps. Tsara waited till they died away. Counted to twenty. Then peeked out again.

Mike hadn't moved. The round-shouldered man sat before him on a massive fallen log, his back toward Tsara and well out of reach of Mike's long legs. He was holding a rifle on him.

The huge log had created the clearing years before, taking a crowd of smaller trees with it as it crashed down during some long-ago storm. Now the forest floor was open to the sky, and saplings stretched toward the light. Off to one side were two grey backpacks stained with grime and sweat. One of them was Mike's; the other must belong to Jordan or Arnold. Mike stared straight ahead. Was he looking at her? At the guard? At nothing?

Now he spoke, and she realized he was directing his gaze at Jordan. *Thank God.*

He hadn't seen her.

"I still don't see how this is going to work," said Mike. His tone was casual, except that it wasn't. "You kill me, you still got the problem of half a dozen kids who know what you did. Or are you counting on them being just as scared of you as their folks are?"

The man did not answer, and after a moment Mike went on.

"And then there's Thornlocke's niece. She knows, too. Oh, yeah, I told her all about it. And I don't think you're going to catch her, Jordan."

The man muttered something Tsara couldn't hear.

"Maybe," said Mike, "but even if you do, my guess is Thornlocke won't pay you extra for killing her."

Tsara stopped breathing.

Jordan rested the rifle on his lap. "Nobody cares if *you* croak."

"Yeah," said Mike, "but she's not a nobody like me."

Jordan lifted the rifle and pointed it at Mike. "Bang," he said.

Mike didn't flinch. "He's crazy about her. I was there when she drove in. Lots of family feeling, our buddy Thornlocke. No, I think if you come back and tell him she's dead, he might have a change of heart about covering for you. And then what are you going to do? Kill him? I guess you could," he went on, as though to himself. "But then there's the wife and kids ... and Jim, wherever he is ... and anyone else they might have told." He looked up at the man with an expression of too much earnestness. "Jordie, eventually you two are going to run out of bullets."

Jordan spat. "Who said anything about bullets?"

Mike shrugged. "That's a lot of unfortunate accidents to explain, friend."

Arnold appeared at the far side of the clearing, wiping his hands on his pants.

"Gimme a hand with this, willya?" he said.

"Found a good place?" said Jordan.

"Just hurry up." He disappeared back through the trees.

Jordan stood, shouldering his weapon. "Right there."

He walked to Mike and stood over him. He took his rifle off his shoulder and held it by the forestock, butt down. Then, casually yet deliberately, as though slamming a sticky drawer, he brought it down on Mike's head.

Tsara stifled a shriek, biting her bruised lip. Mike's head lolled grotesquely to one side. He was silent, his mouth slacked open.

Once again Jordan shouldered his rifle. He spoke to Mike, and this time his words carried clearly.

"I never liked you, you son of a bitch."

138

Jordan stumped out of the clearing and disappeared into the woods.

Tsara's breath came in spasms. She stared at the clearing, heart pounding.

The birds started singing again. They had stopped while the men were talking. A breeze combed through the tops of the pines, making the branches hiss. Slowly, Mike raised his head and looked at the spot in the woods where Jordan and Arnold had departed. Then he turned toward Tsara's hiding place.

"He's gone," he said. "You can come out now."

The clock on the mantel read half past three. Galen and Spaar sat on a denim couch in Beth Westbrook's living room where she had led them after explaining that Aiden was asleep upstairs. She was staring at them in disbelief.

"He's not asking for money, but it's still a ransom note," said Spaar. "He really needs to turn himself in before anyone gets hurt."

"Are you sure he wrote it?"

"The DMV is sure," said Galen. "They matched it with the signature on his driver's license. And his fingerprints are all over it."

Beth shook her head as though trying to get a bug off it. "No. That's not who he is."

Spaar leaned forward. "Who is he, then, Mrs. Westbrook?"

Beth stood up. It wasn't Mrs. and it never had been, but she wasn't going to quibble. "Well. He's been in the service, for one thing." She took a framed photograph off the mantelpiece and handed it to the agent. "He signed up on his seventeenth birthday. Oh! Was I mad. I called the recruiter and said, 'How can he do this without asking me?' He said, 'It's legal.' I said, 'Just you wait till you have kids and they do something like this.' Of course he didn't listen to me. I was just the mother."

"But he had a record," said Spaar. She handed the photo to Galen.

Beth flicked her hand. "They gave him a waiver."

"With all those arrests?"

"Doesn't matter," said Galen. He was looking at the photo. It was a kid in dress blues with gold buttons and red piping. No ribbons or medals—he wasn't a Marine, not yet. This boy had just enlisted. "So long as he's not on probation he can still be eligible."

"Exactly," said Beth. "He had to write all these statements—personal statements—about the incidents. You know, to tell them it wouldn't be a problem. I thought he was doing his homework."

"So he enlisted without telling you?" Once again Spaar's pen flew over her notepad.

Beth sat down again. "It worked for him, though. They really teach those guys. When he came home that first Christmas he was *ironing* his jeans and tee shirts. He said, 'Ma, I can't go out looking like a slob.' He wanted to take my iron back with him because it was better than the one they had on the base."

For the next twenty minutes Beth told them about Mike's adventures in uniform, the emails and letters she'd gotten from him, the time he'd been scheduled to be in a convoy that was blown up by insurgents but had escaped only because he'd been reassigned to latrine duty at the last minute. "I don't know why people tell their mothers things like that," she said.

Then he had met Maria, lovely Maria with the long, auburn hair and the smile that lit all his dark corners. They married, and a few years later they had Aiden. And then ....

"Mike called to tell me she was gone," said Beth. "He took it hard. He kept saying, 'Why, Ma? Why?' We never did understand it."

"It must have been a shock," said Spaar.

"She American?" said Galen. He flipped to a new page in his notepad.

"Yes, from Virginia. She was a civilian contractor with the military."

"So then he came back here with Aiden," said Spaar.

"Yes, they lived here with me. That was a wonderful time, you know—having the baby here and all."

"How long was it?"

"About a year and a half."

"Then what happened?"

Beth shifted. "He moved to his own place. We'd had some troubles here in town and he knew it would be better if he left."

"What kind of troubles?"

Beth looked at her hands.

Galen cleared his throat. "Mrs. Westbrook. We just spoke with Mr. Soames at the stables. He said we should ask you how you got your hip injury. He seemed to think it had something to do with why Mike left town."

Reluctantly Beth lifted her head, and her eyes unfocused out the window. "We had a fire," she said. "Not in the house, thank God. It was my garage. Mike woke me up shouting in the middle of the night and it was just shooting flames. We were afraid the house was next. We were trying to put it out but it was winter—really cold—and as soon as we turned on the water there was ice everywhere. And I slipped and I fell and my hip was broke really bad. Mike carried me back into the house and the fire department finally got here and put it out." She looked at Galen. "That's when I told Mike he should leave. He built me a new garage first, though."

Bet the bastard felt bad about torching the first one, thought Galen. At least he had some conscience, though, if he'd rebuilt it.

Spaar frowned. "What was the cause of the fire?"

"It was ... set."

"Were you afraid?" said Galen.

"Wouldn't you be?"

"So that's why you asked him to go?" said Galen. "Because his behavior had become erratic and unpredictable and you feared—"

"What?"

"Well, after he—"

"Is that what you think? *My* son?" Her eyes snapped. "You listen to me, mister. That fire wasn't set by him. It was set *for* him."

After they left Beth's house the two agents sat in the car and looked at each other.

"Why didn't she call someone else?" said Galen. "Like, say, us?"

"She was scared."

"Too scared to get help?"

"Who do you think would have gotten here first, them or us?" said Spaar.

"Us."

"Who do you think would have stayed longer?"

Galen sighed. "You win," he said. As Spaar turned the key in the ignition he added, "Y'know, I'm really starting to not like those guys."

Tsara walked around the boulder into the clearing. She knew she ought to run away, but a hard, angry part of her wanted to gloat.

Besides, she was curious.

She scanned the clearing, and, satisfied the brothers were gone for the moment, she walked to Mike, stopping a safe distance from his unbound legs.

"How does it feel?" she asked coldly.

"Not so great," he said cheerfully. "I have a wicked crick in my neck."

Tsara coughed. "Well," she said, trying to maintain her air of haughty composure, "that's gotta suck. Good luck with that." She turned to leave.

"Which way are you going?" His tone was light, but she stopped anyway.

"Away from you."

"South?" he persisted. "Westbridge is south, and so are Canterbury and Saxonville. South's a good choice. Or maybe you're trying to find Great Boulder River. It's off to the west. That's probably a better bet than a road. They're hard to get to from here unless you know the way."

"Like you fucking care."

"Just wondered which way you're headed."

"Yeah? Why?"

"Because you've been going in a circle. We're about fifty yards from where you started."

She stared at him. "No, we're not."

He tilted his head. "Check over there. Three big boulders where I first heard Jordan and his brother. Trail splits where we went left."

Tsara took a couple of steps and squinted through the trees. Through the trunks three granite mounds rose from the earth.

"Oh, *fucking* hell," she blurted. Her fists clenched, and she wanted to stamp her feet.

"Don't feel bad," he said. "Could happen to anyone."

She ran her hands through her hair. "Oh, thanks—I feel much better now."

"Ease up. I'm trying to help you."

She wanted to scream. "Help someone else. *Please.*"

His jaw tightened. "Were you listening at all? They're going to kill me, and then they're going to kill you too."

"I didn't hear him say that."

"I did."

"Why would he want to kill me?" said Tsara. "I bet my uncle sent him to bring me home."

"He did," said Mike. "And now Arnie and Jordan are going to kill you because they don't want to go to prison." Mike almost raised his voice, but lowered it abruptly. They both glanced at the woods where Jordan had disappeared, but no one came. Mike continued more quietly, his words rushing out. "How many people know about it? Me, Jim, Freihoffer, your uncle, the family that owed him, and their kids. And you. Your uncle and Freihoffer won't talk, and the family is too scared. Always have been. They'll tell the kids to keep quiet, maybe even leave town. That leaves you, me, and Jim." He jerked his head toward Jordan's disappearance. "There's a cliff that way, looks over rapids. Jordie and his brother are over there right now, looking for a spot for me to have an accident. When they're done with that, they'll come for you. And Jim."

The backs of Tsara's hands prickled. "Where's Jim?"

"I'm not worried about him." Mike shifted, trying to straighten his shoulders. "Untie me," he said. "You don't have a chance by yourself."

Tsara backed away. "No."

Mike looked desperately at the woods, then back at her. "I'm not lying to you. They will find you, and they will kill you."

"I've managed so far."

145

"By walking in a circle. While they were busy with me."

"I think you're lying," she said. "I think they want you, not me. And I don't believe that bullshit about killing a dozen people. Sorry, Mike, you're on your own." She turned to go.

"Lift my shirt."

His voice stopped her like a hand. "What? "

"You heard me. Lift my shirt."

"Oh, I get it," she said. "So you can get me close enough, right? What kind of a moron do you think I am?"

"Close enough for what?" he said. "Go on—what can I do to you now?" His voice was rough, yet he pleaded with her.

Tsara hesitated, and then walked back to him, giving the long legs a wide berth. He was as still as the tree at his back as she squatted next to him. His face was striped with dried sweat; it tracked through dirt that hadn't been there before. She could see beadlets of blood at his hairline where the rifle butt had landed, and below that the abrasion from her own roped wrists the night before. She glanced once at the woods that might any minute give forth Jordan and his brother. Then, her hands jumping with anxiety, she reached for Mike's black shirt. Patches of it were shiny. That was odd. Was it wet?

She pulled it up and gasped.

The perfect torso was a field of bruises stretching from the middle of his chest down past his belly. Most were crescent-shaped, and some were bleeding. In places they merged in explosions of red and cobalt edged with black, looking like overlapping smears of jelly.

Tsara realized her fingertips were moist, and she dropped the shirt. Frantically she wiped her hands on her flannel pants, leaving brown streaks on the plaid.

"What the hell happened to you?" she whispered.

Mike stared straight ahead. "One of them held a gun to my head and the other one went to town on me."

"But why?"

He looked at her, not answering.

"Is it—" The taste of metal rose in her throat. "They were looking for *me*?"

Mike dipped his chin once.

"But you—why? But why?"

146

Mike looked away and raised his jaw slightly. "I may not have a lot to be proud of this past day or so, but I was goddamned if I was going to turn you over to those bastards." He paused, and this time his voice was low. "If you believe me, please untie me."

Tsara thought furiously. He couldn't fake those bruises. On the other hand, being with him was no picnic.

"Let's pretend for a second I do believe you," she said. "If I let you go, I'm your prisoner again. Why would I do that?"

He turned to face her, and suddenly the grey eyes were anguished. *"Please,"* he whispered. *"I have a son."*

"So do I," she said. "And a daughter. Did you think of that when you—"

"I'll help you," he said. "I'll get you back to them."

Tsara rocked on her heels, studying him.

"Shit," she said finally. "I hope this doesn't turn out to be the stupidest thing I've ever done."

"Even if it is, you'd better hurry," said Mike. "I hear them coming."

32

"So whatcha got?" said Spaar. She twisted in her seat to see Galen better. It was four-thirty, which made it over sixteen hours since anyone had seen Tsara Adelman. Spaar could feel the time pulse by. The agents were back in their car, a Subaru Outback wagon selected to blend in with the local auto population. They were in the Saturday-empty Libertyville Middle School parking lot. Her partner had an open folder on his lap. He picked up a sheaf of papers and tapped them to line up the pages.

"Her brother's clean as far as I can tell," said Galen. "Divorced about three years ago. No kids. No big debts, no record unless you count traffic violations. He's got family money but his employees say he comes in early and leaves late most days."

"How much family money?"

Galen handed her a sheet. Her eyebrows went up. "Okay, then."

"That's what I thought too."

Spaar handed the paper back. "Any communication between him and Thornlocke?"

"A couple of emails and a phone call in the past week. Not much before that. The emails were about the party last night."

"Okay." Spaar was glad. "What else?"

"Freihoffer." Galen put the first paper behind the stack and started on a new one. "He and Thornlocke go way back. Like, decades. After Thornlocke got out of the army he started backing Freihoffer's business ventures for a share of the profits. It's worked out well for both of them."

"How well?"

"You've seen his house."

"So no debts?" persisted Spaar. "Hookers? Gambling? Anything going up his nose?"

"Nope."

"Anything?"

"I could check for overdue library books."

"So what's he doing loan-sharking for money that wouldn't cover half a semester of college for his kids?"

"Never confuse need and greed, my friend."

They'd get back to Thornlocke later, decided Spaar. "What else you got?"

"Our friend Westbrook does have a record," said Galen. "Just like mama said."

"How bad?"

"All minor, mostly juvenile. And all Libertyville. I can see why they gave him a waiver when he enlisted."

"All Libertyville?"

"Yep."

"Hm."

"Yeah. The town police force is two brothers, Arnold and Jordan Stone. Their father was chief before them, a one-man show."

"What kind of cop was he?"

"The dad? From what I could get, he was against police brutality because it didn't go far enough."

"Cute," said Spaar. "What kind of father was he?"

"Used to beat the boys when they were young. When they got to be older he'd bust the local drunks and let the boys whup the shit out of them while they were in the tank. The injuries were always from resisting arrest."

"Duh. "

"After a while he started hauling in people his boys didn't like so they could do the same thing. Builds character, I guess. Usually it was Westbrook, but not always. The brothers became deputies pretty early on."

149

"Why was it usually Westbrook?" said Spaar.

"The Stone brothers went to school with Westbrook and Montrose. Sounds like the boys never really cottoned to each other."

Tsara scurried behind the tree. Mike's big hands looked damp, the fingers curling toward the palms. She pulled the loops of rope that bit into his wrists, but they did not release.

"These knots—" she said desperately.

"Get my knife," he said. "They put it in my backpack."

Tsara ran to the backpacks, unzipped the first one, and turned it upside down. A cascade of objects fell to the pine-carpeted floor: rope. Binoculars. A bottle of water; power bars. And a gun. Its black grip bounced hard on her knee as it fell.

"Other backpack," urged Mike. "Hurry!"

Tsara dropped the backpack and grabbed the second one. Her damp fingers slipped on the tab and she seized it a second time, yanking it open and upending the bag. Two water bottles and the coil of rope slid out. A small wooden box and a worn, plush turtle. And Mike's knife, still in its sheath. She grabbed it, flinging the cover aside as she ran back to Mike. Again she squatted at his hands, working the blade into the mound of rope. The first loop gave, and he strained against his bonds.

"One more," she told him, and began slicing at it. Again he pulled, and the fibers curled apart at the sharp of the blade. The last tendril snapped and he scrambled to his feet. Tsara stood, knife in hand, just as Jordan and his brother entered the clearing.

"What the *fuck!*" yelled Arnie.

"Get her!" yelled Jordan, almost at the same time. He sprinted toward her.

Tsara ran. Jordan was gaining. His mouth was open in a shout, and he gripped the rifle in one hand. She threw the knife at him. It went wide. Over her shoulder she saw Mike dive for the gun on the ground. Jordan swung his rifle at her legs. It struck her calf. Her knees buckled. She hit the ground on all fours. He grabbed her hair and yanked her upright. She screamed like an animal.

"Gotcha, you little bitch," he snarled.

Tsara spun around, her knees whirling through the pine needles. She balled one fist inside the other and brought them both straight up into his groin.

It lifted him off his feet.

He doubled over with a grunt, his cheeks the color of terra cotta. His hands flopped open. Tsara scrabbled away and kicked his knee. It crunched under her heel. He fell to the other knee, one hand around his groin, the other one stretching for the rifle that lay beside him. Behind him stood Arnie, yanking his pistol out of its holster. He brought it up and aimed at her. Tsara lurched to her feet and ran toward the woods. *Stay low don't look keep moving run run run—*

Shots.

Tsara fell to the ground.

34

"Please," said Spaar, "please tell me this whole thing isn't just some stupid schoolboy grudge."

"Partly," admitted Galen. "But it's a pretty high-octane one. Seems Mike took a lot of crap from the Stones because when they turned their lights on him they left Jim alone."

"Montrose? What were they doing to him?"

"Pretty much everything they could, from the sound of it. They landed him in the hospital once."

"Pick on the mute kid," said Spaar. "Classy."

"They're classy guys."

"You get all this from the NCIC?"

"No, most of it I got from their high school English teacher. She had all of them as students."

"She reliable? This must be a good twenty years ago by my count."

"Oh, hell, yeah. She remembered every grade any of them ever got on a pop quiz. Said Jordan couldn't spell for shit and Arnold called Shakespeare a faggot. I think she's still reeling from that."

"Well, it is pretty heinous."

"She also said Jim was the best writer of the four of them, because he had to do it so much."

"Did she have any particularly vivid memories about Westbrook?" said Spaar.

"Said he was a good kid who wouldn't use punctuation and liked yanking her chain."

"Yanking her chain how?"

"Oh, like, he told her he enlisted to get out of her final exam."

"Anything else?"

"Lots." Oh, she had a fine memory, that one. And opinions.

"So Mike never gave you any trouble, ma'am?"

"Oh, no. I always had a soft spot for those bad boys who weren't really bad."

"And Jim?"

"Jim had potential but he thought he was too good for it. Can you imagine how frustrating that is for a teacher?"

"I guess not," said Galen.

"I outsmarted him, though. I sat him down one day after class and I said, 'Jim, most of us get judged by how we talk. You're going to be judged by how you write, so you might as well learn how to do it.' Do you know, he actually shook my hand, and from then on you never saw anyone work so hard. He jumped three grade levels that semester, and by the time he graduated he was one of the best students I ever had."

"Anything more on Arnold and Jordan? Other than their aversion to Shakespeare?"

"They've been keeping the peace in Libertyville since their old man retired," said Galen. "He had a stroke a few years back; that's when they went full-time."

"Is that when they started in on Westbrook again?"

"No, he was in the Marines by then. But when he came back to town—"

"They picked up where they'd left off." Spaar sighed. "Got anything else?"

"This part I did get from the NCIC," said Galen. "He has guns. Looks to be mostly for hunting."

He showed her the sheet. If Mike's weapons were registered with the National Crime Information Center, they were legal. As soon as the warrant came in for his place they could see if all were accounted for.

Of course, he might have other guns he hadn't told anyone about.

"Can he shoot?" she said.

Galen cleared his throat. "Let me tell you a little about his military record."

Tsara lay facedown on the pine needles, eyes shut, wondering why it didn't hurt to get shot. Footsteps thudded behind her.

"Are you all right?"

She should be in really horrible pain now. There was only one explanation. One of the bullets must have severed her spine.

"Are you all right?"

She was almost certainly paralyzed, at least from the waist down. How the hell was she going to get home now …?

"Answer me!" A hand prodded her shoulder.

Tsara gave a strangled yell and lurched upright, nails digging into the dirt under the pine needles.

Not paralyzed.

She gazed stupidly down at herself. The knees of her pants were muddy, and the left was torn. A glimpse of skin showed through, and it was scraped; but that and the abrasions singing on the palms of her hands seemed to be her only injuries.

Mike squatted next to her. His dirty face sagged with relief.

"Where's the blood?" she asked dazedly.

"Inside you, where it's meant to be."

Tsara sat up. She brushed off her hands and ran them through her hair. Her scalp seethed where Jordan had grabbed her, and she fingered it gingerly. Her neck ached. "I thought I was shot."

"So did I."

She looked up at him. "Why—why—what happened?" she stammered. "They were—where are they?"

Mike's face went blank. He stood, extending his hand to her. She took it, robot-like, and let him help her to her feet.

Two bodies lay in the clearing. Tsara stared from them to Mike. She pulled her hand out of his and walked toward Jordan. As though from a distance she noticed how steady her paces were.

Mike walked beside her. His voice was strangely gentle. "Hey. You don't want to see that."

Jordan was prostrate, his head turned to one side. His hand still reached for the rifle but his eyes stared past it. Tsara squatted by the still form. In his back were two holes, crisp and round and about an inch apart from each other. They oozed, and a dark stain spread across his shirt. As she watched, the threads took up the fluid one fiber at a time.

Arnold was just behind his brother, on his side. His eyes were open and seemed to move, but no—it was the reflection of the boughs shifting in the breeze. One hand clutched uselessly at his ribs; she could see the dusky liquid blushing gently past his fingers. The other hand dug into the dirt, swirls of earth and pine needles flung up around his fingers. His boots had left gouges in the ground, scimitars of clear earth. In the center of his back was a circle about half an inch across. Fluid dripped from it toward the forest floor.

With clinical detachment Tsara noted a boot print-shaped abrasion on the dead man's cheek. And his right hand, the one that had churned into the earth—the knuckles were bloody.

Mike hadn't gone down without a fight.

"Come on," said Mike. "Let's get out of here." His voice was kind, and he put his hand under her elbow and guided her to her feet. They walked out of the clearing, past the two backpacks and the black gun that once again lay on the ground.

The shaking didn't start till they were out of the clearing. Then it came in waves of ice, a cold that had nothing to do with the damp October air but welled up from a dead place deep inside her. Tsara's knees shook and she wobbled, cursing in a whisper.

Mike stopped at the three big rocks. The cable still trailed from her wrist, and he looped it around a branch out of her reach. "I'll be back." He turned and hiked back to the clearing. Tsara gave in to her shaking knees, leaning against the biggest of the three boulders. Different parts of her hurt. Her left arm ached, wrist to shoulder. She peered at her hand, examining the red indentations from her rings where she had pounded Jordan's balls. The diamond of her engagement ring must have been turned to the side when she hit him: it had torn a small divot of skin from the finger next to it.

Mike returned, his knife once more on his belt and his grey bag on his shoulders. He had packed it in a hurry: she could see the butt of the gun poking at the fabric on one side. The shaking was worse, it was in her jaw now, and her teeth were beginning to clack against each other.

"You're in shock," he said, not unkindly. "Take deep, slow breaths if you can." He unlooped the cable from the branch, letting it drop. Tsara hugged her shuddering body with both arms and sank to the ground. Setting the backpack down, Mike shrugged off his jacket and draped it over her hunched shoulders. She flinched at his touch.

"Yeah, I know," she replied as another jerking wave rolled through her. "I recognize it. "

He cocked an eyebrow. "Recognize it?"

"After an accident once." He didn't need to know everything about her. She pulled the jacket around herself, trying to absorb some of its warmth. Her teeth chattered and her fingers were icy. She looked up at him. Dirt still clung to his face in smears, and his hair was wild and sweaty. But the expression was calm.

"Thanks," she said.

"Just a jacket." He looked past her, scanning the area.

"No, I mean—for back there." Her voice stumbled. "Thanks for killing those two guys."

He turned to with a look of bland surprise. "What are you talking about? I didn't kill anyone."

She stared at him. "Those two cops. They were going to—look, I'm *thanking* you for it."

"I can't take credit for that," he replied. His face was serene, nearly expressionless. "Those two were victims of a tragic hunting accident."

"*Hunting* acci—"

"It's deer season, and they weren't wearing their international orange. Happens every year." Mike's voice was tinged with regret.

She felt dizzy and leaned back against the outcropping. "I *know* you shot them." She shook with renewed spasms.

"Really." He peered at her intently. "Did you see them get shot?"

"I—" She hesitated, closing her eyes. She had been running away, then down on the ground. "No. I didn't."

"Did you see me with a gun in my hand?"

"The gun was on the ground, and I saw you go for it."

"But did you see me hold it? Or fire it?"

She rubbed her forehead, rolling her eyes under the cover her fingers provided. "No," she said. "I didn't see the gun in your hand. Counselor."

"And you don't see it now."

This was too much. "It's in your backpack," she almost yelled in outrage.

"Unless you have X-ray vision, you don't know what's in a closed bag," he said, although she saw his eyes flick at the grey pack.

"I know what I saw."

"I understand," he said sympathetically. "You're confused. Temporary amnesia is often a symptom of shock."

"Don't try to gaslight me," she snapped. "You know I don't have amnesia."

She glared at him. He chose his next words carefully. "Why do you need to believe I killed those two men?"

She took a deep breath and let it out slowly, shudderingly. "In a way I'd rather believe you didn't, but I know better." Despite her best efforts, her voice shook. "I mean—thanks for saving my life and all, like I said. I don't feel sorry for them. But …."

"But what? "

It was hard to meet his gaze. "What's to stop me from having a, uh, hunting accident if that's suddenly convenient for you?"

Something like nausea flickered behind his face. He smoothed his features, and when he spoke his voice was level.

"That's fair. First, though, can we agree you never saw me hold a gun, or fire it?"

"Yeah, okay," she said reluctantly.

He gazed at her steadily. "Do you think you can remember that if anyone asks you about it later?"

She stared at him, her heart thrumming. Later meant … later. After all this.

He still planned to let her go. As long as she cooperated, so ….

"Yes," she almost whispered.

"Good," he said briskly. "As for the second thing—well, right now we need each other. You need me to get out of these woods and get home to your husband and kids. I said I'll get you back to them and I will. Meantime, I need you to get my son." He gave a crooked almost-smile, like the one she had seen, briefly, in the cabin that morning. "So I don't think you'll be very accident prone for a while."

She nodded before she remembered how much her neck hurt. "Good to know," she muttered, rubbing it with one hand.

He unzipped the pack, carefully placing himself between her and it, and pulled out a water bottle. "Drink," he said, handing it to her.

"'Kay."

"Just a few sips. If it stays down, have some more. Then we have to move." He reached into the backpack again, pulling out the second

159

bottle for himself. His was battered, with the label torn off. Tsara tipped her bottle and the two drank.

Mike wiped his lips with the back of his hand. "Why did you fall?"

"Fall?"

"Back there in the clearing. For a second—you weren't shot, so what made you go down?"

"I'm not sure." Everything had happened so fast that pieces were already getting lost. Jordan—running—the knife, the ropes, the gun—shouting—what exactly had happened? Remembering it all was like trying to put together a jigsaw puzzle under a strobe light.

Her wrist hurt, and she saw a red line on it where the cable had dug in. She held it up to him. "I think I tripped on this," she said, indicating the trailing line. Which made it his fault.

"Okay." He took another drink. "Makes sense."

Damn right it does, thought Tsara. She took another slug of water, half-emptying the bottle. When she lowered it Mike was looking at her.

"You're a surprise," he said abruptly.

Tsara put the bottle on her lap. "What do you mean?"

"Because you look like a little—" His eyes raked her; she tried not to care. "—bird or something. But you fight like a mountain lion."

Tsara looked down at her water bottle. Her lips moved.

"What?" said Mike.

She looked up at him. "I said, 'A mountain lion who keeps losing.'"

A pause. Mike sat down next to her, wincing as he lowered himself to the ground. "Anyone can lose a fight," he said, stretching one leg out straight.

"So—it's all luck?" That wasn't what the self-defense teachers had said.

"No. It's not all luck." He shifted his shoulders as if getting tightness out of them. "By my count you've won twice."

Tsara felt a smile tug her lips. "Thanks." She rolled the water bottle between her dirty fingers. "How'd they get you?" she asked, looking down at it.

"Who?"

Tsara twitched her head toward the clearing. Mike didn't answer till she looked up at him. His eyes were empty and his mouth was set.

"Taser," he said.

"Oh." She took another sip. He said nothing. "Does that hurt?" she said at last.

"Yep. Had me flopping like a fish." Mike stood and brushed off the seat of his pants. He gave a sharp grunt, and grabbed his ribs.

"Are you okay?" Tsara was aghast to hear herself say.

Mike let out a long, slow breath. "Yeah," he said with the last of it. He moved his hand over his torso, exploring.

"Is it broken?" She didn't know whether to worry about him or exult in his misfortune, so she did both.

Mike shook his head. "Don't think so." He straightened gingerly. "We gotta move now." He gestured at the windbreaker that was still on her shoulders. "You want to keep that?"

Tsara hesitated, then decided the jacket would keep her warmer than her pride. "Yeah." She stood, testing her knees. They would serve. She handed him the bottle.

"Okay." Mike put both bottles in his backpack, still keeping it on the other side of his body. He zipped closed the main compartment and took something out of a side pocket before carefully pulling the bag onto his shoulders. He opened his hand.

A new carabiner.

"Oh, fuck," she sighed.

"I always carry extras."

She looked at him and thought about the blood and bruises under his shirt. She glanced at the woods behind him.

"Don't try it," he said. "I'll still catch up with you if you run."

"You sure of that?"

"Oh, yeah," he said. "Just take a little longer and hurt more. But I'd like to get us out of this alive, so do us both a favor, okay?"

Tsara scowled. "I'm not promising you anything."

"Didn't think you would." He almost smiled.

She held still as he threaded the cable through the sleeve of the jacket then clipped the end to his belt loop. "Come on."

He started walking. Tsara stepped reluctantly, trying to match her strides to his.

She was a prisoner again.

While Galen chased down search warrants, Spaar went to talk to David and Court. She made it a policy to stay in close contact with families during an investigation. The brothers-in-law were staying in a motel barely off the highway and close to Chateau Thornlocke. It was one story, white with a green metal roof slanting down towards the back of the building toward a pool, now empty and covered. Pine-covered mountains crowded behind the motel. David's room was clean but tight enough that Spaar wondered how they'd gotten the double bed in. She and Court sat on opposite corners of the bed, and David pulled up a chair between them. They weren't quite bumping knees, but it was close.

"The boy's father is still missing," said Spaar after she had brought the brothers-in-law up to speed. "We're pretty sure he's the one we want."

"Why?" asked Court.

"Because he's the boy's father, and he's missing," she replied drily. She opened a file and pulled out a thin sheaf of paper. "But there's more to it than that. He's also a known associate of the man who delivered the note this morning. His name is Michael Westbrook; he's in his mid-thirties, goes by Mike. Two years older than James Montrose, the gardener. They're first cousins. James lived with Mike and his mother here in Libertyville from the time he was four until he graduated from high school." She looked at Court. "Did Montrose say anything when he delivered the note?"

"Now that you mention it, no," said Court. "Why?"

"Just checking. Apparently he's mute."

"How does he communicate with the people he works for?" said David.

"They leave voice messages, he texts back. And sends a lot of emails. He also knows sign, which is getting much more popular now that people are using it with their babies."

"We did that with our kids," said David.

"And when all else fails, he pulls out a pad and pen," said Spaar. "Apparently he's made a pretty good business landscaping and gardening in these parts. And he employs Westbrook pretty frequently."

"Does he have a criminal record or anything?" asked Court.

"No. Seems to be a pretty ordinary person, except for the fact that he can't talk. Lives alone in an apartment above his office."

David sat up. "Could Tsara be there?"

"We're getting a warrant now."

Court stood, electric. "Fuck it," he almost shouted. "She's there! Let's just break down the door!"

Spaar didn't move. "Mr. Abrams," she said. "I'm sure I don't have to tell you why that's not a good idea."

"*I* think it's a great idea," snapped Court.

"There's a lot you don't know about Westbrook."

"So what?"

"So if your sister is there with him, breaking down the door could put her in terrible danger. Is that what you want?"

Court's angry face fell. He rubbed his forehead with the back of his hand.

"Sorry," he said, voice low. "I wasn't thinking."

"I get how you feel, and I'm telling you everything I can," said Spaar. "But try to remember, we've done this before."

Court sat down on the bed, drooping. David spoke. "Do we know anything else about this Westbrook guy?"

"Quite a bit, actually." Spaar opened the file and took out several sheets. She put a photo on the bed. It was a copy of the one Beth had shown her and Galen.

"He's a Marine?" said David in disbelief.

"Was. Honorable discharge a few years ago. Do you recognize him?"

David and Court peered at the picture. "No," said David. "I've never seen him before."

"Doesn't look familiar," agreed Court. "But all these dress shots look the same."

"He enlisted as a teenager and did several tours of duty in the Middle East," said Spaar. "Afghanistan mostly, but also Iraq." She glanced at one of the sheets in her hand. Galen had been thorough. "He served with a decorated unit as part of an anti-terrorism detail. Also, he's a pig."

David blinked. "He's a what?"

"Sorry. PIG. It stands for Professionally Instructed Gunman, meaning he has proficiency in firearms over and above what your average Marine would have. The next step is HOG, for Hunter of Gunmen." David and Court glanced at each other. Spaar continued. "He also has a tan belt, that's the first level, in the Marine Corps Martial Arts Program, or MCMAP." She pronounced it "mik-map." "Affectionately known as Semper Fu."

"Those Marines," muttered Court. "What a sense of humor."

"So what does all that mean?" said David. "Are you going to tell us he can eat stuff that would make a goat puke?"

Spaar smiled slightly, then went back to business mode. "This is the information we have on him so far."

"So then what?" said Court.

"Then what?"

"He's in the Marines, he's in Afghanistan. Suddenly he's back in Libertyville. Why? Why is he here?"

Spaar put another photo on the desk. It was an older Mike wearing a beribboned uniform. Behind him an American flag crossed over a red flag with a gold design that was partially hidden in the banner's folds. Mike was hatless, his hair so short his scalp showed through. The gold buttons on his jacket gleamed, and his grin was incandescent. On his arm was a woman in a floor-length gown of forest green trimmed with gold. She wore her auburn hair in a soft up-do that framed her face in waves. She looked at the camera but her head tilted toward Mike's chest.

"While he was still in the Marines he married a woman named Maria Clarke. Six years ago they had a son—you knew that—and then, when the boy was eleven months old, Maria died after a brief illness. Her death more or less coincided with the end of Mike's tour of duty, and he moved back home with his mother."

Court snorted. "Well, that tells you everything you need to know. "

"How so?"

He waved his hand. "First sign of trouble, he goes running to Mommy."

"You don't have kids," said David.

"What's that supposed to mean?"

"Jesus, being a single parent like that? With a baby? Anyone would want help."

"People raise kids all the time without running for help. What a pussy."

"You try it some time!" David raised his voice. "You try to—to look at a baby and wonder what the hell to do with it."

"So, what—it takes a village? Please!"

"Damn right it does, and anyone who says otherwise can afford a nanny."

"Oh, come *on.*"

"Jesus Christ, Court, visiting a few times a year and playing favorite uncle isn't the same thing."

"Why are you standing up for this piece of—?"

"I'm not! I'm just saying it makes sense!"

"Are you done?" Spaar's dry voice brought them back. Half-ashamed, they turned their attention to her. "In any case, he stayed with his mother for about a year and a half. Then he took the boy to a cabin in a somewhat inaccessible part of the woods, but comes in with him pretty often to buy supplies, do contract work for his cousin, and so-forth."

"How inaccessible?" said Court.

"Why did he leave town?" said David.

"Inaccessible enough that there's no road to it. Well, there is one," she amended. "But it stops about half a mile from the cabin. He keeps a truck with a snowplow there. But for the most part he doesn't use it."

Again, David and Court glanced at each other. "Horses," they both said.

"Right," said Spaar. "And he doesn't seem to have a lot of visitors."

"Only Cousin James," guessed David.

"You got it," said Spaar. "He seems to be well-liked enough in town, but not the host with the most. A bit reserved."

Court shuddered slightly. "I'm just wondering if he has heads in his fridge," he said.

"I'm wondering if he *has* a fridge," said David.

"He does," said Spaar. "No heads."

"How do you know?" said Court.

"Galen's there now with a crew." Glancing at the sheet in her hand she went on, "Unlike his cousin, Mike does have a criminal record." David and Court stiffened. "No violence, all very bush league," she hastened to assure them. "But the local cops have had dealings with him, that's for sure."

"So why now?" said David desperately. "Why Tsara?"

"I don't think he was after her specifically," said Spaar. "He wanted a hostage, so he got one. But his history could help us—the Libertyville cops know him, and they're looking for him too."

The fact that the Stone brothers were on the prowl was actually scant comfort for Spaar. She and Galen had stopped by the police station earlier, only to find it locked and empty. A note on the door read, "We know where he is gone and have went to find Westbrook."

It wasn't just the lousy grammar that bothered Spaar. It was the fact that the note made no mention of Tsara. Furthermore, Jordan and Arnold seemed to have notified precisely no one where they were going. No local police, no State Troopers, and certainly no FBI had heard from them. It looked bad and felt worse.

But right now she and Galen had a job to do, and it didn't involve tracking down errant cops who had literally taken a hike.

"Shit," said David. He looked sick, and Spaar ached for him.

She stood to leave. "I'll let you know when we have more."

"Agent Spaar," said David, standing with her. "You're saying he's not a career criminal, right?"

"That's right."

"Well—is that good or bad? For Tsara, I mean?"

Spaar paused. "We have some solid leads," she said. "I think we have a good chance of catching him." She gathered her materials and left the room.

The two men looked at each other. Court broke the silence.

"Don't you hate it when she gets all professional on our asses?"

— ✳ —

After Court went back to his own room, David shot off a quick email to his mother, bringing her up to speed and telling her to hug Josh and Abbie extra tight. He felt guilty not talking to the kids, but he couldn't think of a damn thing to say that wouldn't send them into hysterics. He flopped onto the bed with his hands behind his head and stared at the ceiling.

Westbrook. He wished the bastard had taken someone else. Anyone. Castle, or one of his kids. Then he punched the thought away. He wouldn't want this for anyone. But still ....

Funny thing was, the guy didn't look like a monster. David thought of the picture, and the way the woman had leaned into her husband. He knew without ever having met her that she had always stood that way with him, even if they were apart.

And David felt a reluctant pang for this man who had lost his wife when their child was so young.

Galen scoured the cabin with the evidence team and a canine squad. The four search-and-rescue dogs that had scented on Tsara's red dress whuffed energetically in the corners of the room and both beds before returning to their handlers, heads up and eyes bright.

"What does that mean?" asked Galen.

The head of the SAR team was almost as tall as Galen, and wore hiking boots and a bright orange vest with multiple pockets. The French braid that hung from under her baseball cap was the same butterscotch color as her Golden retriever. "Lots of scent, probably hers. But she's not here now." She pointed to the dog. "See how he's holding his head? He's run out of scent. Can't trace it any further in here."

"How about outside?"

But outside the dogs came up empty, returning once again to the volunteer rescuers. *Sorry. She's gone. Sorry.*

"We'll keep trying," said the tall woman. "But if it rains all bets are off."

"Do what you can," said Galen.

Once the dogs were done with the cabin, the evidence recovery team went in. Soon they had multiple sets of fingerprints and several straight, blonde hairs from the pillows. They found Mike's cell phone and a map of the Silver Mountains on the table in the larger of the two rooms. Galen retrieved a wad of duct tape and a length of rope from the trash, and had them packaged for the lab at Quantico. DNA was wonderful stuff. It got all over everything.

Stepping outside, Galen flipped open his cell phone and found he had no reception. He poked his head back into the cabin. "Gotta go," he said. The team leader gave him a half-wave and went back to work.

Galen walked to the dirt road where he had left the Outback, and drove toward Libertyville. As soon as his phone registered bars he pulled over and called David.

"The dog handlers are sure she was there," he said. "But her scent disappears outside the cabin."

"Why?"

"They left but not walking, so no trail on the ground. I'm guessing horses again, but their scent is all over the place anyway so the dogs got confused. Some dogs can follow a trail through the air, but these aren't trained for that."

Goddamnit, thought David. *So fucking close.* He closed his eyes and rubbed his forehead with his thumb. "Well, how about the gardener?"

"We're looking into him. Mrs. Thornlocke gave us his address and cell phone number."

"You're going to *call* him?"

"Well, we can—"

"What?" said David. "I can't hear you."

Galen glanced at his phone. The bars disappeared, came back, and flickered away again.

"I'll call as soon as I can," he said loudly. "Hang in there, Mr. Adelman,"

David's reply was a faint buzz. Galen put the car in Drive and pulled back onto the road.

"He just turned his phone on," said Galen. It was half an hour later and he and Spaar were in one of the classrooms at Libertyville Middle School. Sleek computers and phones topped half the desks; others held paper, files, and photos. Schools made good mobile command posts.

Spaar rolled her chair over to Galen. He pointed to his computer screen. "Got the lat and long off the GPS," he said. "He's not far away."

"Can you switch to phone towers?"

"Way ahead of you." His fingers tapped on the keys. A satellite image came up. It was mainly trees, and Galen superimposed a schematic of highways and secondary roads. A blue dot bounded along a white strip. "Man, he's really flying. Just passed another tower. Looks like he's doing about ninety."

Spaar frowned. "Why would he call attention to himself that way?"

"Maybe he's stupid."

"He hasn't been so far. There's something else going on. Where is he?"

"I-93 South near Littleton. No, wait. *In* Littleton." With a few clicks Galen zoomed in. "He's in the Wal-Mart parking lot and he's stopped moving."

"Excellent!" said Spaar. "Get the State Troopers in Littleton to bring him in. Tell them it's a hostage situation."

"Extreme caution."

"You might want to mention that, yes."

Galen put in the call and looked at Spaar. "They say there are about forty cars in the Wal-Mart parking lot and do we have a vehicle description?"

"Ah," said Spaar. "No. We don't." They'd already impounded Jim's truck, and it was his only vehicle. He must have stolen another one. "Hold on." She picked up another phone and dialed, then hit the speaker function. After three rings the receiving phone clicked on.

"Hello?" said a male voice.

"Mr. Montrose, this is Agent Spaar of the FBI."

"Oh, shit," said the voice. "Holy *shit.*"

Galen and Spaar looked at each other. Spaar spoke into the phone. "Get out of the car with your hands up. Tell anyone with you to do the same. Now."

In the Wal-Mart parking lot in Littleton, three bewildered and terrified teenagers stepped out of their car with their hands over their heads. Half a dozen State Police cars ringed the parking lot, lights flashing and bullhorns blaring. As the boys stared in shock, four troopers advanced on them with pistols drawn.

In that moment of clarity, the teens wished they had never, ever taken that cell phone from the men's room at that gas station.

"So what do we have?" asked Spaar.

"Lots," said Galen. It was several phone calls later, and the boys had been sent home after explaining that they had been searching for the cell phone's legitimate owner. Two sets of parents had left the State Trooper barracks loudly telling their kids they were grounded until they could no longer use the suffix "teen" to describe their ages. The third dad had been harder to get rid of. He had put a lot of energy, not to say volume, into explaining all the reasons he was going to sue the Troopers, the FBI, and the state of New Hampshire. Galen would have bet even money his was the kid who had actually lifted the phone. But he didn't care, because the thing was a friggin' gold mine. "First off, three Amtrak tickets from Berlin to Manchester for tomorrow. He bought them online. They're waiting for him at the station."

"Smart," said Spaar. Berlin was the northernmost Amtrak station in New Hampshire, and both it and the Manchester stop were unstaffed, cutting way down on potential witnesses. "Anything at Manchester Regional?"

"Three tickets to New York, and he bookmarked Google Maps showing the route from the train station to the airport."

"They don't strike me as city boys."

"No, but from New York you can go anywhere. Or they might have friends there."

"Anything else?"

"A Safari search for stables in the Berlin area. All mom-and-pop operations. He bookmarked Hidden Oaks Stables near Franconia Notch."

"Give me the URL." Spaar typed it into her computer. "Thought so." She pointed at the screen. *We board horses for $450 a month. This includes feed, blankets, and the love your animal deserves.*

"I saved the best for last," said Galen. "Reservations for tonight in a secluded B&B across the street from the stables. He texted them. Says he'll be there at seven."

"So tomorrow they're going to get the kid, ditch the horses, get on the train to the airport, or close enough, and vanish."

"Looks that way."

Spaar glanced at her watch. Six-thirty, and the sun was setting. "If he hasn't checked in yet, let's see who we can get down to the B&B to be innocent tourists. Tell them to drive a Subaru or a Prius. And let's get passengers at both those stations."

"How long before he notices his cell phone's missing, you think?" said Galen as he picked up the phone.

"If we're really lucky we'll get him before he puts in his breakfast order."

Rain sluiced down in sheets and spewed up from the ground in a grey mist. They were out of the trees and among low shrubs and slabs of rock that covered the earth like sloppy paving stones. Tsara's hair dripped water onto her cheeks; Mike's jacket slicked to her back. It was far too big on her, and the neck opening might as well have been a storm drain. An icy stream poured down her back and soaked her pants. The jacket's hem flapped mid-thigh, and her pajama bottoms wrapped wetly around her legs. Her toes curled in her waterlogged socks, and her Crocs sloshed with every step. She quaked with cold.

Mike tramped through the hazy torrents. He hadn't looked at her since the storm began. Tsara didn't care. He had said they were going to a place up in the mountains, and presumably this place had a roof. Very little else mattered at the moment.

Mike stopped under a tree by an outcropping. Manila-colored leaves clung to the tree's branches, and streamlets coursed down its smooth, grey bark. He turned to face her. His hair was plastered to his head and rain dripped off his jawline. He unclipped the cable from his belt loop and twisted it into a figure eight, cinched in the middle. He grabbed her wrist and shoved the looped cable over it. "Follow me," he shouted, and hoisted himself into the tree like a gymnast onto a horse.

You are shitting me, she thought; but he gestured impatiently and she followed, her feet slipping inside the Crocs.

Tsara went slowly. The tree was ancient, its trunk as broad as a sidewalk, and chunky branches spread out on all sides. About four feet

173

up, one broad limb extended to the nearby rock face, resting on a ledge. Mike was waiting for her. "Come on."

Then he was gone.

Tsara blinked and shook her head, scattering rainwater that was immediately replaced by more. *What the hell?*

Hesitantly, she stepped onto the large limb. This wasn't a repeat of the ravine, she reassured herself. One step, two, and she was standing on the rain-slicked ledge.

Her foot slipped.

A hand yanked her through a triangle in the rock. Her head banged on the edge, and she clenched her teeth to keep from crying out.

Inside it was black as velvet, and Mike's big hand was on her arm. She pulled away, but his fingers only tightened.

"Let go of me," she protested.

"Not a chance. You take one wrong turn in here and nobody'll ever find you, including me. There's pools in these caves no one's ever found the bottom of, and tunnels that end at fifty-foot drop-offs. So just hold still and let your eyes adjust."

As usual, he was hard to argue with. Tsara stood, feeling droplets tickle down her back and chest. She knew he must be able to feel her shivering. She shook harder, hoping it would make him feel guilty.

"Do you see where it's a little lighter?" said Mike. "Don't lie to me."

"No."

"Look ahead."

"Which way's ahead?"

His free hand landed on her far shoulder and shoved it. "The way I'm pointing you. Look again."

She stretched her eyes to their useless widest. At first only clouds of red and purple floated before her, thumbprints of light from outside. Then a greying opened to one side.

"I think I see it," she said. "Off to the right?"

"Yep. Start walking. "

With his hand still firmly on her arm, they stepped forward. Tsara kept her free arm arched over her head for protection, her eyes fixed on the blur of not-quite darkness. Her feet were hesitant but Mike kept a steady pace. "Keep going."

They rounded a bend into a vapor of grey light. A cavern opened before them. The ceiling soared overhead, twenty feet or more, and the walls receded on either side. Underfoot was sand, mostly dry and scattered with loose stones; and directly ahead was the mouth of the cave, a crescent-shaped opening laid flat on its side through which curtains of graphite-colored rain needles undulated with the wind. A breeze cut through Tsara's sodden clothes, and her shudders intensified.

"This way," said Mike, and turned left. They walked toward a dark spot knee-high on the cavern wall. In the vague light Tsara took a moment to realize it was an alcove off the main chamber. Mike stepped up onto the ledge and half-pulled her with him. It was dark, and Tsara looked over her shoulder at the scant illumination from the larger room.

"I'll get a light," Mike said. "Stay here." He dropped her arm and moved into the darkness, leaving Tsara with the realization that wherever they were, he could literally get around it with his eyes shut.

One click and then another. The glowing bars of two Coleman lanterns lit the room. Tsara barely looked up. She was wet to the bone, and her mind was fogged with cold.

"Sit," she heard Mike say. "I'll get you a towel."

Sit on what? she wondered, glancing around. Deciding he must mean one of the boulders that jutted out of the sandy floor, she perched herself on the closest, her feet wide for balance.

A towel landed on her lap, and Mike stood before her with one of his own draped across his neck. Numbly she took the oblong of terry cloth and rubbed her dripping hair, then circled her neck and under her jaw.

Mike squatted in front of her and took her left hand in his. He slid a small tool under the loop of cable. It pinched; the opening was tight. He snipped once. The cable parted and he pulled it free. Tsara withdrew her hand and continued scrubbing. *He kept his word,* she thought. *Good to know.*

Mike sat down on another boulder, larger than hers but seat-high for him, and watched as she wiped her shoulders front and back. He rolled the tool gently in his hand. It was a vise grip. She recognized it from installing car seats for Josh and Abbie. A sob ached in her chest. She shoved it down.

I will get through this.

175

"I'll be letting you go tomorrow," he said.

She wiped her hands on the rough cloth. "Yeah, I know. When you get your kid back."

"Even if I don't."

Tsara's eyes flew to his face. Her fingers dug into the towel. "Why?" she almost whispered.

His wet hair was dark and his eyes were in shadow. "You don't deserve this," he said.

Tsara buried her face in the towel. She rocked back and forth.

"That would be good," she said through the towel, though she wasn't sure he could hear.

When she lifted her head he had his back to her and was rummaging through a row of plastic bins at the wall. There were a dozen or more, some on a natural rock ledge, others stacked neatly on a wooden shelf she assumed he had built himself. The bins were in shadow, front ends gleaming in the light from the lanterns.

"We gotta get you out of those clothes," he said as he reached into one and pulled out a plaid shirt. Tsara felt her face stiffen. Glancing over his shoulder at her he added in disgust, "Don't flatter yourself. You're no good to me with hypothermia."

Tsara went back to drying off as well as she could, quickly wiping under her sweatshirt while his back was turned. Her face felt wet again, and warm; it stung as she dabbed it. She glanced at the towel and her eyes widened.

"Shit. I'm bleeding."

Jim's apartment had been a bust. It was utterly ordinary, in a bachelor pad kind of way. Unmade bed, a John Deere calendar on the wall by the phone with appointments written on it in Sharpie, kitchen and bathroom mostly clean. A frying pan sat on the stove, lined with a beige crust of bacon grease. A few clothes were draped around, but nothing gave the impression Montrose had left in a hurry, or that there had been any sort of struggle. Or that Tsara had been there. And the dogs found nothing.

"So, total dead end?" said David. It was an hour past sunset. They were back in his motel room; Court's was across the hallway. The agents perched awkwardly on the bed. David had the sole chair, and Court was leaning against the wall.

"It was just one lead," said Spaar. "There are others."

"Like what?" said Court.

"We're staking out a place where he has reservations for tonight," said Galen. They had a guy and girl agent posing as a married couple hanging out at the B&B, and others within driving distance. The lobby also had a new trainee behind the desk, complete with nametag. Galen thought that was a nice touch. The owners, a gay couple, were frankly enthralled. It was hands down the most exciting thing ever to have happened at their establishment. They had recent photos of Mike and Jim, and had programmed Galen's number into their phones.

"Remember to act natural," he begged them as they leaped to the window for the hundredth time that minute; and they assured him they would.

Galen had also put an agent across the street as a stable hand. In the interests of verisimilitude they set him to work mucking out stalls. Galen tried not to cackle on his way out.

"When's he supposed to get there?" said Court.

"Actually, he's late," admitted Galen. "But we'll keep people there till midnight anyway."

"Well—if he doesn't show, then what?" said David.

"We'll keep asking questions in town," said Galen. "Something new may come up."

David pounded the arm of his chair. "Why?" he almost shouted. "It sounds like what you're saying is, 'We'll just keep doing what hasn't worked!'"

"Sir," said Spaar mildly.

"Don't call him sir!" shouted Court. There was silence, and suddenly David gave a snort of laughter.

"Thanks," he said. "I needed that." He turned back to Spaar, who was smiling faintly. "What did the second note say?"

"Essentially they want a prisoner exchange," she said. "Of course, Westbrook doesn't know his son is at his mother's house. He thinks the boy's still locked up at Thornlocke's."

"In the wine cellar," said David.

"Right," said Spaar. "He's thought it out pretty well. The place he chose backs up to the mountains with just one road running past. Good view in most directions."

David frowned. "He told you where to go? Why?"

"What do you mean?"

"I mean why telegraph it? Why not phone ten minutes before and keep us all scrambling?"

"We think he's in the back country," said Spaar.

"So, no phones?" said Court.

"Exactly," said Galen. "He might also figure the landlines at the chateau are tapped, or that we could trace him through his cell phone." Mike would have been right about both those things. "He says he already has people there. He's probably lying."

"So ... what?" said David. "He says to go to this place and when he gets his kid back he'll let my wife go?"

"That's it," said Spaar.

"Well, hell!" blurted David. "Give him his kid and get my wife back!"

"Mr. Adelman," said Spaar, "that's not how we do things. A ransom—"

"This isn't a ransom. It's his son."

"If we acquiesce to demands from people like this, it would just—"

"No, it wouldn't," interrupted David.

"You don't know what I was going to say."

"Yes, I do. You were going to say that if you cooperate with kidnappers it creates a market for kidnapping. You were going to tell me about some Podunk fifth-world nation with no toilets where someone paid a million-dollar ransom to get someone back, and now the going rate for ransoms over there is a million dollars and kidnapping has spiked a gazillion percent and all because someone caved to criminals."

The faint smile returned to Spaar's lips. "Actually, it was three million dollars, and the spike was sixteen percent. But that's not really the point."

"Yes, it is, because whatever those statistics are they have nothing to do with this situation," said David. He was out of the chair, pacing as well as he could in the crowded room. "This guy Westbrook isn't a drug cartel or a terrorist or whatever. It sounds like he's not even a criminal except for some piss-ante stuff that doesn't seem to have anything to do with what's happening right now." He stopped and looked at them. "Do you have kids?"

"No," admitted Spaar.

"Nieces and nephews," said Galen. "But—"

David cut him off. "Then I'm the only one in this room who's a parent. Am I the only one who's married?" The silence said yes. "For God's sake!" His voice rose almost to a shout. "His wife's dead. His *six-year-old* is stolen from him and the only law enforcement around is the people who have been kicking his ass his whole life? And you wonder why he didn't go to the cops?" He stood over the two agents. "That wasn't a ransom note. He's not asking for money."

"Mr. Adelman," said Galen, "there's something you're not seeing here. It would have been easier if he were asking for an ordinary ransom."

"Why?"

"Because we'll let money walk. But we don't let people walk."

"Especially not when one of them is six years old," said Spaar.

"But it's *his* six-year-old."

"And the father is a fugitive and suspected kidnapper with a criminal history."

"Only because he's trying to save his son."

"Maybe. But in the past couple of days he's made it clear he's capable of violence. No judge would put a minor in that situation."

"Look," said David. "Are you willing to concede the *possibility* that he's telling the truth and just wants his kid back?"

"Sure," said Spaar.

"Well then," he said triumphantly.

"I'm also willing to concede the possibility that he has a long-simmering psychosis and snapped under the stress of his son's abduction. Or that he has a violent past we know nothing about. I'm willing to concede any number of possibilities, but I'm not willing to bet a six-year-old's life on any of them, or a woman with kids of her own."

David hesitated. "Just give him his son back," he said finally. "I'm betting he'll return my wife. Track him down later if you want to. I don't care." He sat down heavily in the chair. "If you have a better idea, I'm all ears."

Spaar and Galen exchanged a look. Spaar stood up. "I'll call later," she said. "Stay by the phone. Cell reception here is pretty bad."

The agents left, closing the door behind them. Court and David looked at each other.

"Well, I thought you made a hell of a case," said Court quietly.

"Thanks." David stood and looked out the window at Galen and Spaar as they got into their car. "I hope they think so."

In the foothills across the road, columns of mist drifted through the trees like hunchbacked ghosts. Higher on the slopes clouds tumbled, their edges trailing like long fibers.

"It's raining up there," he said.

Court joined him at the window, gazing at the hills. "Mountain weather." They were both silent, thinking the same thing.

"I hope she's not out in that," said David. "Just somewhere, you know … warm and dry …." He clenched his teeth, staring at the mountains. Court said nothing, but his eyes, too, were fixed straight ahead.

— ❋ —

In the car, Spaar and Galen were going through their notes. Galen drummed on his portfolio. "Wish Montrose had showed."

"Would have been nice."

He drummed some more. "What did you think of Adelman's suggestion?"

"I think he wants his wife back and doesn't know what he's talking about." Spaar checked the map showing the drop site. "We need to know more about the topography behind this road."

"Still," said Galen. "She's an adult."

"What's your point?"

"Maybe if they signed, like, a b'jillion consent forms—"

Spaar stared at him. "Are you nuts?"

"Just trying to think outside the box."

"The box is there for a reason."

"I know."

"The other vic's not yet in kindergarten."

"I know."

"We'd never get legal authority for a trade. Not to mention the part about leaving a young child in a place like that, for crying out loud."

"Yeah. I know."

Spaar returned to her map. "So we'll stick to Plan A."

"Didn't say that."

Spaar slapped the map on her knees and glared. "If we do *anything* that guy says, a woman could die, a kid could die, and we could be letting a violent psycho run free."

"I never said anything about kowtowing to Westbrook, Sparks. And I've been doing this as long as you."

"Hell, the *horses* could die. Wouldn't the animal rights groups love that?"

181

Galen stared ahead. Grey mist gathered on the windshield, a harbinger of the storm rolling down the mountains. Spaar turned back to the map, tracing the contours of the mountains with her fingertip, imagining the likeliest places for unmarked trails.

"All I'm saying is, let's color outside the lines," said Galen.

Spaar didn't look up. "Like handing over a kid to that guy? Brilliant."

"Let's talk to his mother again."

Spaar rubbed her eyes. Visions of her career flushing down a large toilet flashed before her. "Why?"

"Because she knows him better than anyone else we've talked to."

"So?"

"This isn't a typical case."

"You had a typical case once? What was that like?"

"All I'm saying," said Galen, "is no matter how we pull this off, I want to know more about him."

Spaar said nothing. Mist gathered into droplets on the windshield and coursed down, leaving clear, wavy lines behind them.

Jim led the horses under a rock shelf and clipped lead lines onto their halters. He tied a knot on the end of each line and wedged them securely between large rocks. The animals shifted so their hindquarters faced the wind and rain, clamping their tails to their buttocks and hunching their backs. Jim wasn't worried. The overhang mostly sheltered them, and anyway, these horses were tough. They would have been okay outside, even in a pretty vicious downpour.

He loosened the girths a notch but left the saddles on to keep the horses' backs warm, then stretched nosebags over their heads. They crunched on the grain mix, giving occasional grunts of satisfaction. Jim unrolled his sleeping bag behind the rocks holding the lead lines, and sat down. He unwrapped an energy bar and took a bite.

He felt bad about the phone. The damn thing was almost new. But if anyone smart were after them—like, smarter than Jordan and Arnold—it would give them plenty of reasons to look in a bunch of wrong places while he and Mike got Aiden and themselves to safety.

He could always get another phone.

Mike whipped around and Tsara shrank from him, holding up the stained terry cloth like a shield. Instantly he was at her side, cat-fast and graceful, lantern in one hand. "Bleeding? Show me. Where's it coming from?"

"I don't know! "

He lifted the lantern and his fingers touched her jaw, gently turning it to one side. His shoulders relaxed.

"Okay."

"Okay *what?*"

"It's your head, but it's not bad," he said, setting down the lantern. "Just a scrape. When did it happen?"

Their faces were closer than she liked. "Um … coming into the cave, I think," she said. *When you dragged me in here and bashed my head on the rocks.*

He went back to the stack of bins and opened a new one. "Let's fix it up and get you some dry clothes. Here we go." Returning, he sat down again. On his lap was a white box with a red cross. Glancing in, Tsara snorted and clapped her hand over her mouth. He looked at her quizzically.

"Sorry," she said through her fingers. "I just wasn't expecting Curious George bandages."

"My kid likes them." He grinned sheepishly.

Aghast she blurted, "You take a six-year-old here?"

183

"Figured I'd start this fall," said Mike. "Hunting season." He was all business again as he tore open an alcohol pad and wiped his hands with it. Next he took out a fat, square bottle of clear plastic and snapped off the top. "This is just sterile water. I'm gonna flush out the wound. Scrape." He put a new towel in her hand and pressed it to her cheek, below the warm trickle of blood. "Here. So we don't get you any wetter."

As if, thought Tsara. But she held still as Mike squeezed the bottle, and a cool stream moved around a spot at her hairline. It stung. She flinched as tears came to her nose, and marveled at the dots of warmth along her cheek where his fingers steadied her head.

Mike put down the empty bottle and reached into the first aid kit again. He tore open a sterile gauze pad and handed it to her. "Press this." He took the sodden towel from her cheek and guided her hand to the stinging spot. "It should stop in a few minutes. Head wounds bleed like crazy, but this one's nothing to worry about."

"Okay." She pressed the gauze to the side of her forehead. In the ensuing silence she could hear the hiss of the rainfall outside the cave. Her free hand relaxed in her lap, and she let out a breath she hadn't known she was holding.

"That should do it," said Mike presently. "Get changed and I'll take another look to make sure the bleeding's really stopped."

"Changed into what?" She wanted to point out that tragically she had left her uncle's house without dry clothes, but it seemed unwise.

"Let me see what I got." He returned to the boxes, half-talking to himself. "Of course, nothing's going to fit ... Jim's stuff isn't clean ... maybe this will work ...." He pulled several items out, neatly folded, and handed them to her with the plaid shirt on top. Standing up, she took the stack and looked around.

"Ah ..."

"Come on." He took both lanterns and walked to the entrance to the alcove. "Big step here."

Tsara followed him, carrying the towel and clothing. He half-jumped to the floor of the larger chamber and held out his hand to her, but she ignored it, jumping down by herself. To their right was the tunnel where they had entered; immediately before it was an enormous boulder, dropped by some ancient flood aeons ago. It was at least seven feet high and about the same across, and it half-blocked the mouth of the tunnel. It had been on Mike's side when they walked in. He must have put her opposite it on purpose. That was why she hadn't smacked into it.

He handed her a lantern. "You can get changed back there." She took the lantern, shifting the towel awkwardly to the same hand as the clothing. As she walked toward it he added, "Just keep talking so I know where you are."

Talk. "Ah ... okay. Four score and seven years ago, our fathers brought forth on this continent a new nation, conceived in liberty and dedicated—"

"Louder."

"—to the proposition that all men are created equal," she bellowed, ducking around the boulder. She and her mother used to memorize and recite their favorite texts for fun, sometimes having contests with each other. Tsara was willing to bet her mom had never envisioned that skill coming in handy in this situation. She set the lantern on the ground. "Now we are engaged in a great civil war—" She pulled off his jacket and draped it on the rock, where it clung damply. Next she peeled off her sweatshirt and the plaid pajama bottoms, twisting them with both hands as water splatted onto her feet and the sandy floor. She plastered them next to the jacket and rubbed her goose-pimpled skin with the bloodstained towel. A flush of magnificent warmth glowed through her as she assured Mike at the top of her lungs that government of the people, by the people, for the people would not perish from the Earth.

He had given her a white undershirt that hung midway down her thighs. It was spotlessly clean and smelled of Tide. She wondered if he did his laundry at his mother's house. The shirt was much more transparent than she would have liked, and she crouched to see what else was in the stack.

"Keep talking." His voice was close, and her hands jumped.

"Okay, okay. Um—She should have died hereafter. There would have been a time for such a word—tomorrow and tomorrow and tomorrow—"

The flannel shirt was next in the pile, and while Macbeth came to grips with the sudden death of his wife Tsara triple-cuffed the sleeves and shrugged it on over the tee shirt, buttoning it closed. The red plaid hem reached almost to her knees. Very fashionable, if a bit drafty. What else had he given her—?

"In Xanadu did Kubla Khan a stately pleasure dome decree, where Alph the sacred river ran, through caverns measureless to man, down to a sunless sea." Well, that was appropriate. She pulled out a pair of long underwear bottoms and stared at them, aghast. Wearing this—? Lifting the lantern, she inspected them closely. "Um … 'enfolding sunny spots of greenery ….' Lucky guy …." The thermals were as clean as the two shirts; and, well, it beat wandering around bare-assed. She leaned against the rock to roll up the legs while she cast about for more on-demand poetry. Frankly, the one she was on got a little too hot and heavy for her present taste.

"If it were done when 'tis done, then 'twere well it were done quickly," she opined. "If th' assassination could trammel up the consequence and catch with his surcease success—that but this blow might be the be-all and the end-all—" She paused for a moment, wondering if she had ever memorized anything that didn't have to do with sex or killing people.

"Keep going." Mike's voice was further away, but she twitched anyway. The son of a bitch sounded amused. Well, screw it—she had to say something.

"We the People of the United States, in Order to form a more perfect Union," she recited loudly as she pulled on the newly shortened long underwear, "establish Justice, insure domestic Tranquility, provide for the common defence, promote the general Welfare—" The thermals had a drawstring waist, and she yanked on the cords, scrunching the waistband into a miniature mountain range.

Nice of him to think of socks, she thought, picking up the thick, brown tubes that were all that remained of the pile he had given her. She wrung her own out and stuck them to the slope of the boulder along with the rest of her wardrobe while trying to keep her voice up. "—do ordain and establish this Constitution for the United States of America."

She brushed the damp sand from her soles with the towel, trying uselessly to get her feet clean. His socks were huge; she could have fit both feet into either of them. Leaning against the rock she pulled each one high on her calves, and then rolled the long underwear over it to keep it anchored. The heels stuck out behind her ankles, but her feet were warm and dry. A very welcome change.

Tsara hastily finger-combed her hair and then peeled her wet clothes and Mike's jacket from the sloping face of the boulder. She rolled them into a bundle in the towel and picked up her Crocs and the lantern before shuffling back around the big rock.

"When in the Course of human events it becomes necessary for one people to dissolve the political bands which have connected them with another, and to assume among the powers of the Earth, the separate and equal station to which the Laws of Nature and of Nature's God entitle them, a decent respect to the opinions of mankind requires that they should declare the causes that impel them to the separation," she said loudly. Her voice was getting tired. "We hold these truths to be self-evident: that all men are created equal, that they are endowed by their Creator with certain unalienable Rights, that among these are Life, *Liberty*—" she gave that one special emphasis, because Mike was in sight now, sitting at the entrance to the alcove waiting for her. His hair was rubbed dry and the dirt was gone from his face. The black tee shirt and hiking pants were gone too, replaced by a sweatshirt and dark jeans. New boots too: dry ones. Lucky bastard.

His eyes flicked over her and his mouth twitched, but he said nothing. Tsara had a brief image of herself swimming in his too-big clothes. Damn, she must look stupid.

"Yeah, I clean up good." She held up the bundle. "What do you want me to do with this stuff?"

"Over there." Mike pointed, and Tsara scrambled onto the ledge, following him as he stood and walked into the alcove. A spindly-looking drying rack was set up next to a blackened fire ring. Mike's wet clothes and towel weighed down one side, but the rungs facing her were bare. She hooked the Crocs over the jutting ends of the top rods, hoping the fleece lining would dry, and undid the bundle. She put Mike's jacket with the rest of his things before hanging out her own clothes. She felt her cheeks redden. If he chose to inspect what she was laying on the rack he would know she didn't have any underwear. If he cared.

"Want a Band Aid?" he said.

Tsara's head throbbed. "You tell me."

187

"Probably wouldn't hurt." He inspected the first aid kid, which lay open on the rock he had been sitting on. "The Curious George ones are spoken for, but ... here we go." He tore open a small oblong and held up a flat, flesh-colored oval. "Sit. And hold still." She lowered herself to the large stone in front of him. He reached up and lifted her hair out of the way before pressing the bandage to her forehead. Tsara barely breathed until he leaned back, satisfied.

"Hungry?" he said.

"Yes." She was sick with hunger.

Mike reached into one of the plastic bins and pulled out a large bow. It was black, and a rubber cog above the grip held dark arrows whose tips glowed fluorescent: green, yellow, orange. "Come on," he said. "But be quiet and stay back when I tell you."

Tsara dipped her chin, thinking she might as well show how quiet she could be right away. Mike hopped down into the large antechamber and paced quickly toward the mouth of the cave, this time not stopping to offer her his hand. Oddly annoyed, she followed him.

At the crescent-shaped opening Mike stopped, holding up his hand without looking back. Tsara froze. Mike stood at the wall, scanning outside. The rain had stopped, and smudgy clouds scudded across the sky. Mike's profile was limned with the watery light as he held perfectly, unnaturally still. Only his eyes moved.

Tsara craned her neck. Beyond the mouth of the cave was a field, shaggy with green and sere stalks bent nearly double by the force of the recent rain. Mountains encircled the view. Some were almost cliffs, steep spills of granite and rubble. A few trees and some low shrubbery dotted the level ground, but mainly it was open: a mountain meadow, almost perfectly round and secret in the embrace of the peaks. A breeze pulled at the leaves of a nearby sycamore, and she could hear the splat of rain droplets as they shook to the ground.

Still looking out at the meadow, Mike pulled a red-tipped arrow from the cog. With a smooth motion he pointed the weapon down and loaded it. He raised the bow to eye height, pulling back on the string. Small wheels on the top spun silently as the cord ran through them. He held the bowstring at his cheek for five seconds ... seven ... then released it with a *thack*.

188

Tsara exhaled, realizing for the first time that she had stopped breathing. Mike leaped fluidly into the tall grasses and disappeared. Cautiously Tsara edged toward the opening. Was it okay to move now?

Mike was back, bow in one hand. In the other he held a massive, floppy wild turkey. Its wings waved with his every step, and its red wattles lay to one side of its neck. He carried it by its feet. He had to. The head was gone.

"Damn," said Tsara. "Do you ever miss?"

"No." He kept walking.

Back at the alcove Mike put the turkey aside and set about making a fire in an ashy circle on the cave floor. As Tsara looked at the fire pit a few drops of water patted into it. She squinted at the ceiling. There must be a crack there, to let rain in and smoke out.

Mike took pinecones out of a small box. The tips of their scales glittered with crystallized sap. He made a small pile of them, tenting kindling over them in a teepee shape. The larger logs he balanced on char-blackened rocks. One touch of flame from his lighter and the pinecones burst into a profusion of yellow light, sending blazes flapping toward the kindling and filling the little rock chamber with glow and shadow.

Mike picked up the turkey and yanked off enough feathers to expose the breast. Then he pulled out his knife and cut the skin in a straight line down the center of the breast. He flipped the blade over, loosening the skin with the blunt edge. Soon he had removed the breast meat, which he set on a clean, plastic plate. A thigh soon followed, and he cut everything into small chunks.

Tsara watched the knife whip through the bird's flesh. She rubbed her neck.

Mike produced an iron skillet to which he added a glunk of oil from a bottle. Tsara inched closer, holding her stiff fingers to the flames. It was a young fire, and didn't throw out much heat yet; but it would soon.

"Can I do anything?" she asked.

Mike didn't look up. "How are you with a can opener?"

"I manage."

He pointed with his elbow as he screwed the cap back on the bottle of oil. "Third box from the left. You can pull out two cans of beans and get the lids off."

The can opener was the kind with little wheels and no sharp bits, which probably explained why he trusted her with it. It was nestled in among cans of soup, B&M brown bread, and beans. More precisely they were beans and bacon, she saw from the label. Tsara made a swift decision not to tell him she didn't eat pork. A temporary suspension of kosher law seemed expedient under the circumstances. She selected two cans and carried them back to the fire where she sat again, twirling the stubby handle of the can opener until she heard the soft click that meant the lids were off.

Now he wasn't doing everything for her.

As soon as there were embers Mike set the skillet on a grate over the coals. When the oil had heated he added the turkey. It crackled and spat, and he moved the pieces with a fork. Tsara once again crept close to the fire, stretching her fingers and toes to its warmth. Hunger curled like nausea in her gut, and she swallowed. She glanced at Mike. He said nothing, focusing on the food; so she relaxed and they sat together in weirdly companionable silence as their dinner sizzled.

Mike loaded a plate with turkey meat and a lumpy pool of beans and handed it to her, holding down the fork with his thumb. "Eat."

She didn't have to be told twice. Even knowing there was pork in the beans wasn't enough to make her hesitate. The food was savory and hot. She alternated forkfuls of beans dripping in brown sauce with meat and swigs of water. Mike had filled their bottles from a stream outside, and from the tang in every gulp she knew he'd added iodine. After the first few mouthfuls she slowed, eating steadily but not rushing. No one was chasing them. The rain might come again but it would not come in here. Warmth surged to the tips of her fingers and toes, and Tsara felt saturated with a delicious sensation of tranquility.

"So I'm curious about something," said Mike.

Tsara swallowed. "What?"

"Tsara." He pronounced it Sah-rah. Most people did. "Why spell it with a T?"

"It's short for Tsarina. I told you." Tsara put her bottle aside and wiped her lips.

"Oh. Right." He chewed for a moment. "What's that—Spanish?"

"Russian. It's, like, the wife of the Tsar. Empress."

"Are you Russian?"

"No."

"So why'd they call you that?"

191

Because my mom was totally stoked to have a girl but she thought Princess would be a stupid name. "They liked it, I guess." She went back to her plate, stabbing a shred of meat and combining it with beans before popping it in her mouth.

Mike took a pull on his bottle. "And another thing," he said, setting it down. "You say Thornlocke's your uncle, but you haven't seen him for twenty years."

"About that, yeah. A little more."

"How does that work?"

"How does what work?"

"How is it that you don't see him for that long? He was real happy when you drove in."

Tsara put her fork down. How much should she tell him? "Well, he's definitely my uncle," she said. "Mother's brother. "

"I thought he didn't have any family. Outside his wife and kids, I mean."

"He doesn't. She died a long time ago."

"How?"

Tsara's stomach clenched. "In an accident."

"Car accident?"

"No."

"Then how?"

Jesus, he was persistent. "It was …."

This wasn't her favorite topic. But Mike had soft spots, and if he knew this about her … if he knew that she, too, had suffered ….

She studied his face, wondering how it would hit him. That always told her a lot about people.

"She was visiting a neighbor," she said. "She—the neighbor—had just had babies … twins … and she'd also just separated from her husband. Because he was an abusive bastard." The plate was burning a spot on her knee, and she shifted it to the other leg. "He thought the babies weren't his … so on this particular day he decided … he broke into the house to kill her and the kids. But she ran away. So he killed my mom instead."

Mike's eyes widened. "God Almighty."

Tsara said nothing. Most people stopped asking questions once they got that far. She never told anyone what happened afterwards. The phone call from her father, telling her … the way she couldn't stop screaming ….

"Did they catch the sonofabitch?"

"They didn't have to. He shot himself."

Mike shook his head. "Coward."

"No shit."

"How old were you?"

"Seventeen."

He was silent for a moment. "Is that what makes you so tough?"

She glanced at him sharply. He was serious.

Despite all the shrinks and counselors and well-intentioned meddlers who had tried to talk to her about the incident over the past quarter century, no one had ever asked her that question. But she knew the answer.

"I guess so," she said. "There's not much that could happen to me that's worse than that." *Including you.*

"Were they his? The kids?"

"They were hers."

"So—"

Tsara shoved her water bottle into the sandy floor. Her fingers dented the plastic. "Look. I don't blame her for marrying the wrong guy. Happens every day. And I sure don't blame her for throwing him out. *But she ran away.*" Her voice rose. "It wasn't my mom's job to die protecting those babies. It was *her* job." She glared, daring him to deny it.

Mike was silent for a moment. "You wouldn't have run," he said.

"No." She picked up her fork and jabbed at the turkey and beans. "And neither would you."

They ate in silence until Mike spoke again.

"So Uncle Castle wasn't a rally-round kinda guy?"

"What do you mean?"

"I mean I don't see the connection. His sister—only sister?" Tsara nodded. "—only sister dies suddenly. Then you don't talk to him for twenty years?"

"You ask a lot of questions."

"Yeah, and you're going to answer them. Uncle Cassie has my kid, and I need to know what I'm up against."

Tsara put another forkful in her mouth and chewed, stalling for time. Mike didn't seem to be after cash, but she didn't want to put ideas into his head. She swallowed. "Well—my mother's estate was considerable."

"Meaning she had a lot of money," translated Mike.

Tsara tipped her head in agreement. "And Cass—well, he's never held a job."

Mike's eyebrows went up. "Never?"

"Not really. He was in the Army in the fifties, but that was because he was drafted. Other than that he's lived on, um, family income."

"Meaning what?"

Oh, hell. "Meaning he waits around for rich relatives to die," she said bluntly. "And yeah, he was really torn up about my mother's dying—and—we all were—" An image flashed into her mind. The day of the murder, Cass had slumped on her, weeping. She hadn't known he could cry. It was like seeing a tree in tears, or a painting. But that day she couldn't cry, nor for many months afterwards. Years, actually....

"And?" prompted Mike.

She put down her plate. "I don't talk about this," she said softly.

There was a silence. "You don't have to," he said finally. His voice was low. "Just tell me about Thornlocke."

She wasn't fooled by the gentle tone. He wasn't going to quit till she told him the whole story. Or at least the parts that mattered to him.

"What do you want to know about him?" she said.

"What kind of man he is."

"You've worked for him."

"Yeah, I cut brush on his property. You grew up with him."

"That was a long time ago. I can't help what he's like now."

"I'm not going to blame you for anything he did," said Mike. "Just tell me what he was like back then."

Tsara drank some more. *Okay, fine.* "Well, after the funeral we came home and Cass was in our house."

"Your house?"

"My mom had given him a key, so it wasn't totally shocking." She set the bottle down. "But when my dad asked what he was doing there, he said—he said he was—I think he said 'taking stock.' Maybe 'inventory.' And he actually had a little pad and pen, and he was walking around—"

Mike's brows drew together. "What the hell was he doing?"

Tsara sighed. "He figured my mom's inheritance should come to him, so he was looking around to see what he was going to get and he said he was taking notes so my dad wouldn't switch anything out for cheap imitations."

Mike made a choking noise. Tsara opened her hands in silent agreement.

"So what did your dad do?"

"He got nervous."

"Why?"

"Cass is the kind of guy who gets away with stuff."

"I've noticed. Go on."

"And because of the way my mom's will was written my dad was afraid Cass might actually get the inheritance."

"So then what happened?"

"My dad threw Cass out, changed the locks, and donated my mom's estate to charity."

"No shit." Mike was impressed. "All of it?"

"Most of it," said Tsara. "Ever heard of the Christina Abrams Cancer Center? It's at Mass General Hospital."

"I've heard of it." Mike looked down at his plate, piling meat and beans together.

"Well, that was my mom. Christina Abrams. And the cancer center was what my dad did with her estate."

Mike shook his head, almost smiling. "Okay. So how did Uncle Castle respond?"

"He was pissed."

"I bet."

Mike frowned. "You're not thirty-seven."

"I never said I was."

"Your father and Castle had their big fight when you were seventeen. That's more than twenty years ago. You're forty-five anyway."

"Forty-three." That was annoying. People usually guessed low. "Well, I used to still see Cass every now and again, you know, at family

195

things, and he'd send me birthday presents and stuff. Then when I was in college—um, he, um—"

Mike waited.

"He and my dad had another fight."

"About what? "

She was silent.

"About *what?* "

"Well," she sighed, "you've met Cass."

And there it was again, that lopsided grin that lit up his face. His shoulders shook briefly.

"Yeah," he said dryly, regaining his composure. "I've met Cass." He glanced at the frying pan, where some of the meal remained. "Want more?"

"Hell, yeah." She held up her plate and he tilted the skillet over it, spilling the contents in a gentle cascade. He put the pan down, whipping the drips off the edge with the side of his knife. Tsara set to work on her newly heaped plate.

"So what was this fight about?" he persisted.

"Money," she said vaguely.

Mike frowned and slowly shook his head. "No. They'd already fought about money."

She looked at him, not answering.

"So what was it?"

Tsara stared at the fire. The center of a log gave way and the ends collapsed in a soft shower of sparks.

"What *was* it?"

No. He'd have to beat it out of her. And that wasn't his style.

Mike leaned back, looking at her. "Did he ever hurt you when you were a kid?"

"Who?"

"Don't be cute. Thornlocke."

She shook her head. "He was my favorite uncle," she said softly. "I loved him." Choosing between Castle and her father—it had hurt like hell. Like losing the last part of her mom. She rested her chin on her hands and stared past Mike.

Mike nodded. "Okay."

"Okay what?"

196

"Okay. You don't have to tell me what it was about." And he poured the last of the beans and turkey onto his own plate.

Tsara felt a wave of gratitude and spoke in a rush. "Castle found out about a check my dad had written to the husband, the psycho who killed my mom. And he said my dad had paid him to kill her. For her money." There, it was out—the thing only she and Court and David knew.

Mike looked at her. "A check. Was it real?"

"The guy had done yard work for us. Yes, it was real."

"Jesus." Mike shook his head. "So that was when you stopped talking to your uncle."

"That's when."

Mike let out a slow breath. He ate some more beans and turkey. Tsara felt strangely off-balance.

"He didn't do it," she said loudly.

"I believe you."

Her shoulders sagged and she took a long drink. When she could look at him again he was eating, giving his food every iota of his concentration. She followed his example, and the only sounds in the cave were those of eating and the occasional pop from the fire.

Mike heard the click when Tsara set her fork down on her plate. "So tell me about your son," she said.

A corner of his mouth tightened. "You're trying to keep me talking, aren't you?"

She grinned, eyes dancing. "How'm I doing?"

Mike hadn't seen her really smile before, and suddenly he realized she must do that a lot. Ordinarily. It made her cheeks lift in little curves, and her teeth sparkled in the firelight. He felt himself smile back at her. "Not bad."

And hell, he thought. *She told me all her shit.*

So he talked about Aiden. How an early love for Bob the Builder had yielded to Curious George, though Mike suspected Spider-Man was making inroads. How the boy would recite the names of dinosaurs to waitresses when they went out for lunch. His favorites were the flying ones. How he wanted a horse when he grew up, which for him meant when he turned eight. How he had spontaneously started reading on his fourth birthday—"His grandmother was reading him a new book and he all of a sudden starts going along with it. We still don't know how."

Mike looked at the fire while he talked. Everyone in his life already knew about Aiden. He wasn't used to bragging about him to a stranger and he felt a little goofy, like some grandma pulling pictures out of her purse. But when he turned at Tsara she was resting her chin in the cup of her hand and smiling at his anecdotes.

Kids.

He wished she hadn't told him about her uncle's finger-pointing after her mom died. He'd just gotten hopeful that the kids would be okay, that Thornlocke wouldn't hurt them. But anyone who would accuse a man of offing his wife like that—well, it showed the way his mind worked, and Mike didn't like it.

And Jesus, what a story she had to tell, poor kid. He had a sudden flash of what it must have been like for her when he and Jim—

But that was different.

"Why is it you and he live in a one-room cabin in the woods?" said Tsara.

"It's a two-room cabin," he corrected her mildly.

"Did you build it?"

He arched an eyebrow. "What makes you think that?"

"It's not prefab and it's in the middle of nowhere. Seems like your style to build it yourself."

"You're smart. Yeah, I built it. About three years ago."

"Why?" she said. "Why not live in town? You said your mom was there, and Jim."

"Geeze, you're nosy." She did not reply and finally he said, "I did live in town. I was born in Libertyville, and I came back there when Aiden was one. We lived with my mom, and I worked for Jim. After a while we moved out."

"Why?"

"Because no man wants to live with his mother forever."

The set of his mouth said he wasn't going to elaborate, so Tsara didn't try. "And ... the boy's mother?"

Mike looked at her from under lowered brows. "My *wife*," he said, "died when Aiden was one."

Silence filled the cave. "I'm sorry," said Tsara at last. "And ... no disrespect intended."

Mike shrugged. "Cancer," he said, though she didn't ask. He straightened up, looking at her strangely. "Wanna know something weird? We went to your mom's center."

"You did?"

"Yeah. We did. The doctors were really nice," he said almost apologetically. "Nicer than most of the others ... but it had spread by then. There wasn't much they could do."

"I'm sorry," repeated Tsara. She could see why people never knew what to say when she told them about her mother. Which was as seldom as she could manage. Usually she said her mom had died a long time ago, and anyone asking generally thought it was an illness, especially if they knew about the cancer center. If they asked for details she said it was an accident, which for most people meant a car crash. And they were very sorry.

"I got her home before she passed," said Mike. He looked past her again. It was a flood of relief, telling the story to someone who hadn't suffered it with him. "I had a little place in town by then. Made up a bed for her in the living room. She was tough. Everyone keeps telling her I'll be okay, right? Finally she pulls me over and says, '*You're* going to be okay? Hell, I'm the one who's dying here.'" He tried to laugh but couldn't.

Tsara said nothing, and presently Mike went on. "She hated to die." He almost seemed to be talking to himself. "She said to do everything … chemo, everything. Didn't want to leave me … we were going to be together forever. And Aiden …. God, she loved him." He stared at the cave wall.

Tsara was silent. His grief and hers seemed to hang in the smoky air of the cave. If he had been anyone else in the world, she would have touched him on the shoulder or wrapped her arms around him. She would have told him what it had taken her decades to work out: that even after you lose your reason for living, a different life can emerge. She would have said to him, *You never get over it. But you can get through it.*

But he was Mike, so she sat still, listening to the embers settle in the fire pit.

"Done with that?" said Mike, indicating her plate. She scooped up the last shred of turkey and the three beans that clung to the rim and handed him the plate.

"You're probably used to fancier food," he said.

Tsara swallowed. Mike stood up. "Come on." And gathering the remains of their dinner and the deflated-looking turkey carcass, he led her to the half-moon opening of the big cave. One of the lanterns swung from his thumb, making shadows splash in waves along the floor and walls of the rock chamber.

Tsara hadn't been past the opening before. It was slightly above the meadow, so one would have to step down as Mike had when he retrieved the turkey. The sky had cleared, and a football-shaped moon a few days short of full glowed in the purple clouds. To the left of the cave a stream flowed from the rock wall and into a shallow pool before undulating through the meadow in a thread of mercury. The grasses still curved with the weight of rain, beaded over with black droplets of water, each dotted with a circle of moonshine. Mike dunked the dishes into the pool, scrubbing them with sand and rinsing them off again.

"I gotta pee," said Tsara.

"Do you ever not gotta pee? "

Tsara felt her face grow hot. "It was better before I gave birth to two ten-pound babies," she snapped as Mike climbed back up the ledge. In the darkness she couldn't be sure, but—had he just flinched?

"Yeah," she went on heartlessly. "There wasn't time for an epidural with the second one. She came barreling out like a cannon ball through a toothpaste tube, if you know what I mean, so there was all this tearing—"

Mike cut her off. "If you gotta go, go."

Tsara wondered if her smirk were visible. She jumped down to the meadow, heading for the sycamore tree she had seen earlier. Its jigsaw-puzzle bark looked grey and white in the moonglow. Water squished through her socks and instantly her feet were sodden again. *Shit,* she thought. She slid them forward in a glide, flattening the spiky layer of dead grasses underfoot so the stalks wouldn't stab her soles.

When she trailed back again Mike was sitting at the entrance to the cave with the plates and forks damp and stacked neatly at his side. She knew he had been watching the tree while she was behind it. This had made it damn difficult to urinate.

"Just a sec," she said, and squatted by the pool where he had washed the plates. She could see the crisp indentations of his boots in the sand as she swished her hands in the water. The air was cold and the water was colder, and she flapped her fingers before wiping them on the long hem of the plaid shirt. Mike's eyes were still on her. He could afford to be patient. She wondered about his plans for the next day.

He stood as she approached, and silently they went back to the campfire. Tsara sat on what she had come to think of as her rock while Mike put everything away. She took off the heavy wool socks and twisted the rough material in her hands, trying to wring them out; but they were thick and released little moisture. She stood and put them on the rack by the fire, touching the worn sweatshirt and the plaid pajama bottoms. They were dry in patches. She turned the shirt over and adjusted the pants to shift them closer to the heat.

Behind her one of the bins opened with a snap. "Heads up." Mike tossed her something. A new pair of socks landed softly in her hands.

"Thanks," she said in surprise, and sat to put them on.

"You're welcome." He reached further into the bin and produced two bedrolls which he unfurled a safe distance from the fire. Each had a small, flat pillow and a fleece blanket. "Get some sleep. We're getting up in a few hours."

His heart sank as Tsara looked from the side-by-side mats to him and shook her head, face frozen. *Goddamn it*, he thought. She was doing that thing where she tried not to look scared shitless.

He wasn't used to a woman being afraid of him. It wasn't a great feeling.

"Just lie down."

"No."

He sighed. "I can get laid when I want to," he said. "It's not about that."

"Then let me sleep somewhere else."

"I need to know where you are. Relax. I know you're married and all."

"Like that ever stopped any man from doing anything."

With effort he kept his voice neutral. "You are a means to an end for me," he said. "I have no interest in you physically. I promise you will be absolutely safe with me tonight."

He hoped that would work. She seemed to respond well to logic. But his stomach grew heavy as she glanced again from the bedrolls to him and then at the entrance to the alcove.

"Are you weighing your options?" he asked. When she nodded he said matter-of-factly, "You don't have any."

"Yeah, I know." She ran her fingers through her hair. They got stuck in a tangle and she pulled them out abruptly, looking up at him. "Do you mean that?" she demanded. "About ....." Her voice trailed off.

"That's what I said."

She snorted. "You also *said* I'd be sleeping in my own bed tonight."

He almost smiled. "Yeah, I did. Okay, then. I promise."

Tsara wiped her hands on her legs. Like maybe they were sweaty or something. "You have to swear."

"You think you can tell me what to do?"

"Humor me. "

Damn, she had balls. Her voice barely shook. "Okay," he said. "I swear to God—"

Again she shook her head. "Swear on your kid."

His eyebrow went up and for a moment there was no sound in the cave. When he finally spoke his voice was slow and careful. "On the life of my son, I swear I won't touch you tonight." He paused, and the silence was tight between them. "Good enough?"

She shrugged sharply. "Like you said, I don't have any options." She lay down on the bedroll and pulled up the blanket, turning her back on him.

The blanket smelled of Tide. *His mom's washing machine must get a lot of traffic,* Tsara thought bitterly. Shoulders clenched, she stared at the garnet embers of the fire. Electricity sparkled along her spine as she waited for Mike to stretch out behind her. She didn't want to face him and she wasn't going to lie on her back, so this was the least worst option.

This was horrible, she thought. She hadn't lain next to anyone but David in twelve years. It felt like adultery.

She heard Mike take off his boots and put them to one side. He sat down on his bedroll.

"I want to thank you," he said unexpectedly.

"For what?" she snapped. "Being a compliant victim?"

He ignored the sarcasm. "For untying me this afternoon," he said. "You had every reason not to, but if you hadn't I'd be dead and my son would be an orphan." He cleared his throat. "So. I thank you."

Tsara's thoughts banged into each other like a murder of drunken crows. What the hell was he expecting—"You're welcome"? But clearly he was expecting something because he was still sitting up. Waiting. So finally she spoke.

"I'm going home tomorrow."

"That's right."

"Okay then."

Mike lay down next to her. She made her breaths even and regular, letting her stomach rise and fall. It probably wasn't fooling him, but she didn't care.

The fire dimmed and the cave grew dark. Neither of the two figures lying side by side moved. Night sounds came in from the meadow, wind and crickets and the occasional bird, but inside the little chamber all was silent except for two sets of deep, slow breaths.

Tsara woke up because Mike was gone. She knew before she sat up and saw his empty bedroll, barely visible by the red smudge of the dying fire. Leaning over, she put her hand on it. The pillow was cool, but further down the blanket still held some warmth.

A white light swung at the entrance to the alcove, making the opening lurch in the shadows. Mike stepped up onto the ledge, Coleman lantern in his hand and backpack on his shoulders. He leaned on the larger of the two boulders and pulled off his boots. Tsara sat cross-legged with the blanket still pulled to her waist, and waited for him to say something. When he didn't, she blurted, "Where did you go?"

He lowered himself to the bedroll, carefully placing the backpack under his pillow. "You aren't the only one who needs to take a leak every now and again."

Tsara lay down again, letting her eyes unfocus at the bed of embers glowing pomegranate red and black. Exhaustion pressed down on her like a heavy blanket and she slept.

46

David blinked. He had been half-dreaming of Tsara, half-remembering. How she looked first thing in the morning, with her hair sleep-lumpy and eyes puffed with slumber. It was his favorite look for her. She'd have killed him if he'd ever taken a picture of her that way.

He got up and went to the laptop charging on the wobbly motel desk, opening it and clicking on the file labeled TSARA. There she was when they were dating. Her hair had been longer then. The night he'd given her the engagement ring. She said she spent the first few weeks walking into doors because she was always holding up her hand to look at it. Their wedding—not his favorite pictures, actually, because they were all formal. Then a few years later, a posed shot captioned, "Barefoot, Pregnant, and in the Kitchen!" She was holding one hand under her beachball abs and proudly displaying one puffy and distinctly unshod foot. The other hand held her master's diploma and a letter of acceptance for her most recent teaching position. She hadn't stopped working till after the second baby was born. He skimmed ahead, looking for something more recent.

That was more like it. There she was with the kids in a neighbor's swimming pool a few weeks ago. And this one, probably his favorite: Tsara in a green turtleneck that precisely matched her eyes. The shirt was shot through with gold threads, and they glittered. She was sitting in a shaft of sunlight at the dining room table, Sunday comics in one hand, half-laughing in exasperation because Josh was taking picture after picture after picture of her. Good photographer, that kid.

David's cell phone burbled and he grabbed it, glancing at the name that came up on the screen.

"Did I wake you?" It was Court.

"Didn't sleep. Much." David stood to push aside the curtains at the window. It was still dark. He could barely make out the hunkering mass of mountains across the street. "Anything new?"

"Nah. They'd probably tell you before me anyway."

"Maybe."

"Want some coffee?"

"Sure."

"I'll be over in a few minutes."

David got dressed and brushed his teeth. He was shrugging on a sweatshirt when he heard a tap at the door. He opened it and Court came in carrying two paper cups from the motel lobby. They sat in silence, sipping. Court gestured at the laptop, still open. "Got any new pictures of the kids?"

"What did she send you most recently?"

"Abbie's birthday, I think."

"Oh, we've got stuff since then." David put the cup down and opened the folder marked KIDS. Josh on a pony at the petting zoo. Abbie giving a big thumbs-up as she stood on the edge of the pool at the JCC, about to jump in. That kid was fearless. And a really nice close-up of Josh holding Froggers up for a portrait. The boy's dark hair was rumpled, and a grin split his face in delight.

"He looks just like you," said Court.

"All but the eyes. Those are Tsara's."

"I dig the scar on his chin," said Court. "It adds to his rugged handsomeness."

David almost smiled. "Do you know why Tsara quit working?"

"Because you had the second kid."

"Yeah, but that wasn't it. She was going to be supermom, you know? Work all day and cook five-star meals all night and never get tired. So she was running herself ragged to prove she was perfect. Then one day she's getting ready to go to work and the babysitter shows up stoned."

"Oh, shit."

"Tsara fired her on the spot. So when Josh found out they were getting a new sitter he was so upset he ran into the telephone table and cut his chin open. He needed stitches and she was driving to the hospital with the kids during rush hour and the car broke down and Abbie started projectile vomiting."

"Oh, God." Court laughed softly.

"She called me but I was in a meeting and they wouldn't give me the message. While she was waiting for Triple A—who never got there, by the way—she phoned her department secretary to say why she'd be late. Her boss came on the line and told her if she got pregnant again the college would cut her salary in half."

"That's not legal!"

"Turns out it is if you're part-time. Anyway, after she got home and washed the vomit out of her hair she decided, screw it, no salary is worth this." He looked at the picture of his perfect, happy little boy with the big grin and the stuffed frog. "It's not easy," he said softly.

They finished their coffees. They looked at the phone. The phone kept not ringing.

"It could be good news," said Court.

"Like, no news is?"

"Yeah."

"Could be," said David. The agents had told them they would most emphatically not be in touch during the operational phase of the rescue. So that could mean his wife was being rescued right now.

David looked out the window. Somewhere out there Cass's sedan was making its way to the rendezvous point. It might be there already.

David imagined the child in the car. Was he sleepy? It was so early. Was he leaning back against the car seat with his eyes closed? Maybe some loved object, like a teddy bear, in his loosely curled fingers.

No, surely not. He couldn't be tired now. He must be staring out the window at the ink-black trees and the flash of stripes on the road. He must be leaving smudges on the glass, fingers and nose and chin.

Who else was out there? The Stone brothers were still AWOL, thought David, and wondered what that meant for Tsara. "Could mean something, could mean nothing," Spaar had said. "The likeliest scenario is they're in the mountains out of cell phone range. It's been less than twenty-four hours."

For her maybe, he thought. For him it had been endless, time stretched thin and painful as a needle. David rubbed his forehead and sighed.

The phone didn't ring.

"It's time."

Tsara lay with her eyes closed. David was trying to wake her up. He wanted her to go to the hospital so she could have the babies.

"C'mon. Get up."

But she didn't want to wake up. She was tired, tired as lead. And besides, she'd already had the babies, so doing it again seemed silly ....

A hand landed on her shoulder. She gasped, whirling out of sleep. Mike was squatting beside her, his face lit by the lantern at his feet. His jaw was dark with a night's stubble. She wondered if it felt rough, like David's.

"I was dreaming," she mumbled.

"It's time to go," said Mike. He handed her the sweatshirt and pants, warm and wood-smoky from the fire. "Get changed. Bring me back my clothes."

Tsara staggered to her feet, limbs still sleep-clogged, and headed off to her rocky changing room. When she got back Mike had cleared the small cave. The bedrolls were put away and all evidence of their meal was gone as well. Except for the warm embers and the marks in the sand, it could have been empty for months. She handed him his clothes, hoping he liked the way she had folded them, embarrassed that she cared. He just seemed particular about so many things ....

Mike shoved the clothes into one of the plastic bins and tossed her a granola bar still in its wrapper. It was sweet but dry in her mouth, and she gulped as much water with it as she could. Sand gritted between her toes. Her socks were dry but dampness still clung to the fleece inside the Crocs.

Ugh.

Putting the bottle down she stood up. Mike was in front of her, grey jacket zipped and backpack on his shoulders. In his hand was the cable, already looped over. The other hand held the vise grip and a small metal collar the size of a knuckle.

"Give me your— "

"No." Tsara snatched her hand away and clenched her jaw.

He blinked at her before becoming businesslike. "We don't have time to waste, and we both want out of here. Just do what I say and make it easy on yourself."

"Easy on you, you mean."

Some of the coldness came back to Mike's eyes. "I can make you do it."

"Anyone can lose a fight," she said.

"Not this one."

"Yeah? Maybe you'd win," she said. "But we'd waste *valuable* minutes."

Mike dropped the vise grip and metal collar. He grabbed her arm. With his free hand he shoved the cable onto her wrist. She twisted, pulling and writhing.

"I untied *you*," she shouted. "I let *you* go, you *bastard!*"

Mike stopped.

"Shit," he said, and dropped her arm.

Tsara backed away from him. Her heart was pounding.

"You trying to mess with me?" he said. "Because if you have any cute ideas about running away—"

Tsara shook her head. "Look," she said. "You said you wouldn't touch me last night, and you didn't. So when you say you're going to let me go today I believe you. I have no reason to try to get away this time. I'll stick close; I'll do whatever you say. But I'm not wearing *that.*"

It was a good speech. She'd rehearsed it in her head the night before. Mike looked at her, the cable hanging from his hand.

"Compliant victim, my ass," he muttered.

He coiled up the cable and scooped the vise grip and metal collar from the cave floor. With a swift motion he shrugged off the backpack and shoved everything in before zipping it closed again and replacing it on his shoulders. "Come on."

He set the lantern back on the rock shelf and turned it off. In the sudden darkness he grasped her wrist with his big hand. His fingers stung in the rope abrasions, but she said nothing. They stepped off the ledge and made their way to the half-moon opening of the main cavern. Mike paused at the still-dark entrance and yanked her close to him. His grip tightened. "You even breathe funny and I'll tie you up and carry you the whole way if I have to. Got it?"

Tsara jerked her head, her throat tight. "Yes," she forced herself to say, in case he hadn't seen her nod.

"Same goes if you don't keep up with me."

"I'll keep up."

Mike stepped off the ledge into the meadow and Tsara half-jumped with him. She wondered if he wanted to prove she couldn't keep up. It would give him an excuse to make good on his threat. But then they were moving briskly though the dripping grasses and she had no time for any thought beyond matching her pace to his as the rain-soaked blades whipped her flannel pants, leaving them sticking to her legs.

At the edge of the meadow a wall of rock plunged to meet the ground. Mike turned sideways, pulling her with him. Her eyes adjusting to the darkness, Tsara saw that what had seemed to be a shadow was a passageway through the cliff face. Mike's hand tightened on her wrist as they bent to avoid the granite wall that tilted over their heads. He moved fluidly with the twists of the channel, once pushing her shoulder down to avoid an outcropping she had missed in the darkness.

They emerged into boulderous mountain territory. She glanced back at the crack they had just come through. It was a dark wrinkle, a shadow of shadows. The animals knew it was there. And Mike did. Maybe Jim. But no one else would ever find it except by accident.

The sky was black and powdered with silver stars. Today would be bright and clear. Then Tsara was too busy to think, stepping rapidly to keep up. Soon she was puffing, her breaths occasionally visible in the starlight. But Mike kept a quick, steady pace and his breathing was even.

Presently they came to a cliff with a path at its base. Her eyes now accustomed to the darkness, Tsara could see that the trail broadened before them, becoming almost wide. Mike grasped her shoulders and turned her so she faced the rock wall.

"Don't move," he said.

A bandana went over her eyes, tightening at the back of her head. The blackness took away the stars and the cliff, and the ground seemed to shift under her feet. She swayed, and was instantly afraid he would be angry with her.

His hand went under her elbow. "You're okay."

The world righted itself and she stayed still, knowing once again he would not let her fall.

Presently a sound drifted out of the silence: the clop of horses' feet and the snort of their breath. They stopped and Mike guided her toward the noise. He still did not speak, and she had the sudden feeling that she was a thing for him. An object.

You are a means to an end for me ....

She did not resist as he lifted her into the saddle and wedged himself behind her. She gripped the pommel, her fingers cooling in the chilly air. The reins lifted, pressing against her arm as he took them in his hands. The horses walked forward in the darkness.

Tsara was counting again, trying to estimate the time on horseback. They were walking this time, not trotting or galloping. The horses' hooves had clumped on what must be pine needles, crunched through leaves, and clanged on bare rock. As far as she could tell, the ride took about an hour. Not that that really mattered. If she were Mike, she'd have the horses go in circles for a while to disguise their location. But counting was all she could do right now, so she did it, adding up seconds in her head and minutes on her fingers, curled out of his sight on the pommel.

The horses stopped and Mike dismounted. He pulled her off the saddle, his big hands under her arms. This time she only stumbled a little as her feet hit the ground. He pulled the bandana off, taking a couple of hairs with it. She blinked.

The sky was still mostly black but held fewer stars at its whitening eastern base. The trees stopped before her. They were atop a slope studded with short, rounded lumps. She squinted, trying to make sense of them.

Jim was with them. He had dismounted and was tying both sets of reins to a branch. He was wearing a dark knit cap, and slung over one shoulder like a bandolier was a coil of rope.

"Over here." Mike kept one hand on her upper arm as he led her forward, stopping in the shadow of the tree line. He pointed. "Do you see the road?"

Tsara stared. Now that he had shown her, she did: a dark strip curving past the bottom of the slope and out of sight. "Yes."

"It goes to Libertyville," said Mike. His voice was soft, almost in her ear. "If anything goes wrong, turn right at the base of the hill and stay on that road. It's a long walk but not hard. You'll be fine. Got it?"

"Turn right and stay on the road."

"Good."

"Can I go now?"

She felt Mike shake his head. "Hell, no. We're waiting for Uncle Cassie." And so they stood, his hand still firm on her arm, while Tsara watched their breaths smoke past their mouths in luminous puffs.

A lone car drew up and stopped at the base of the hill. The engine kept running, and mist curled in the white cones of its headlights.

"That's it," said Mike eagerly. He reached around her with his free arm, bringing up a flashlight. He clicked it on and off twice.

The headlights of the car flashed twice in response.

"Come on," said Mike. He pushed her forward till she stood on a small rise overlooking the slope. They were among the dark structures, and now she could see they were gravestones. It was an old cemetery—old enough that no one was going to be paying predawn respects of a Sunday morning. "Stand there," he ordered. "Look straight ahead and don't move." He let go of her arm, moving to one side and ducking behind one of the markers before turning on the flashlight once again. This time he trained it on her, starting with her face and moving it down her body to her feet and up again. Then he turned it off. Bright streaks floated before her eyes, and she tried to blink them away.

Tsara heard a click as a car door opened. A light jumped out and began moving up the hill. The motion was jerky, but it came steadily closer.

Mike exhaled. "Go with Jim," he said. "Do what he says." He reached around the edge of the gravestone and turned the flashlight on again, leaving it on the ground. But he stayed crouched behind the marker, waiting.

Jim had tied a bandana around the lower part of his face, like a character in an old Western. Only his dark eyes and the bridge of his nose were visible. He yanked her hands behind her, and she heard the zip of a cable tie as it tightened on her wrists. He drew her forward by

215

one arm and she followed him, stumbling in her new night blindness. Stopping at one of the gravestones, he pulled her arm down. Tsara lowered herself awkwardly to the dew-sodden ground, thinking, *I will just do this, I will get through this and then I can go home.* The cold and wet splashed through her pajama pants. At her back was a granite slab with rough edges, and Jim tugged her towards it until her spine touched the cold stone. Then he ducked behind the marker, pulling the rope off his shoulders. Swiftly two lengths went around her torso. He pulled them tight and a series of quick jerks told her he was knotting them on the other side of the granite slab. He reappeared with the depleted rope coil back in place across his chest. He squatted next to her and she could see a bandana in his hand. In the other was something small and dark.

"No—" she protested, but he shoved it into her mouth, keeping his hand on her face. Abbie's sock. It was warm and gritty from his pocket. He twirled the bandana into a line and passed it through her mouth, tying it tightly. She wrenched her head away as soon as he finished. The knot pulled her hair. "Asshole," she said through the gag.

Even in the darkness she saw him stiffen. She glared at him, almost wishing he would try it. But he wouldn't hit her, would he? Not with Mike right there.

Jim stood up and walked back to the horses at the tree line.

Mike kept his eyes on the light as it lurched up the hill. Something was wrong. That jerky motion wasn't a young child stumbling in the dark. The light was too high, the steps too long. This was an adult. He switched off the flashlight. "Stop right there," he barked.

"Mike, don't shoot. It's me."

What the hell? "Stay there," he ordered. "I'm coming down."

He scrambled down the slope and stopped in front of the woman with the flashlight. "Hi, sweetheart," said Beth softly.

"Where's Aiden?" He glanced down the hill. "Is he—Oh, God, he's not—"

"He's fine," said Beth quickly. "He's asleep in his own bed at my place."

Mike drew a breath. He felt a lightness in his chest he hadn't known for the past few days. He closed his eyes for a moment. "Thank God." He opened them, peering at her in the darkness. "Who drove you here? Was it Thornlocke?"

Beth shook her head. "He's in jail."

Mike felt like shouting and jumping. Aiden safe—Thornlocke in jail—the day couldn't get much better. "Can you wait here for a moment, Ma? I gotta do something." He turned up the hill. No fair leaving Tsara trussed up like that anymore. Maybe they could even give her a lift into town.

"Mike, wait."

Something in her voice made him stop. A sudden, dreadful suspicion curled into his mind like mist floating off a lake. He turned to face her again. "How did you know where I was?" he demanded. "And who did drive you?"

She stepped close to him. Her voice was pleading. "Mike. The whole area is surrounded. You can't get away."

"No, it's not. I didn't see anyone."

"They said you wouldn't."

Mike looked around. The woods were motionless. "Who's out there?"

"Federal agents and—they wouldn't tell me much."

He felt sick. "So why are you here, Ma?"

"I told them you'd listen to me. I just want you to be safe." She put her hand on his arm. "You don't have to do everything the hard way, Mikey."

He laughed, a single bark. "Is that right? I guess we all make mistakes."

"Sweetheart, let that poor woman go. If you feel like you need someone, take me with you."

So she knew about that, too. He looked at her, wishing he could see her face. "You wouldn't happen to be wired for sound, would you, Ma? And you probably have what, about a thousand tracking devices on you?"

"Mike—they think you're armed and dangerous—"

"Maybe I am." He raised his voice slightly. "Maybe I have a gun—and a hostage—and maybe if anyone comes near me I'll blow her head off." He turned, running up the hill. "Go," he shouted over his shoulder.

He scooped up the flashlight from the ground next to the grave marker and sprinted toward Jim. With one hand he made a slashing motion. Jim's eyes widened. He jerked the reins loose from the branch and leaped onto his horse. Mike grabbed the saddle of the larger animal. Then he stopped and looked back at the figure in the shadow of the gravestone.

— ✳ —

Tsara's eyes were wide. What the hell was going on now? She'd heard voices but hadn't been able to make out the words until Mike shouted, "Go." They didn't have the boy. Something had gone wrong— so where did that leave her? Her face was damp with mist and sweat, and a tendril of hair tickled where it clung to her cheek. Tight behind her back, her fingers pressed against the icy granite. Droplets of dew and yesterday's rain crept up her pants, and her legs shook with cold.

Were they going to leave her here to die?

Mike tossed the reins to Jim. The little man stared at him. Even with his face in shadow, Tsara could see his bewilderment. He yanked down the bandana that covered his jaw. *"Ffft!"* He made an impatient noise with his lips and gestured frantically at the enticing darkness of the woods.

Ignoring him, Mike hiked rapidly toward Tsara. He squatted next to her, and in the crepuscular light she could see his face almost clearly. His eyes seemed translucent, and the scruff on his jaw was darker than the shadows. He reached out one hand and gently pushed the stray lock of hair behind her ear.

"They'll be here in a few minutes," he said softly. "You'll be fine."

He stood and half-ran back to his horse. In seconds they were gone, even the hoof-falls absorbed by the dense stand of trees.

Chill shook in Tsara's legs and back, and her wrists stung. Her jaw hurt from the gag, and the ropes cut into her chest when she breathed. She wanted to hurt Mike.

He had left her.

"Pilot says he can see her," said Galen. "She's behind one of the tombstones." They were sitting in Castle's old Volvo at the base of the hill. It was loaded with more equipment than any car had a right to dream of.

"Good, 'cause I can't," said Spaar. Her heart had jumped at the sight of the hostage in the beam of Westbrook's flashlight. But then she had disappeared. Spaar scanned the hillside with night vision goggles. The view was perfect, if green. "She blew it. Why do I listen to you?"

"Worth a try," said Galen. He had really hoped Beth would be able to talk her son down. Failing that, he'd been hoping to get something incriminating on the audio. That had been a bit more of a success.

"He was going to get the hostage," said Spaar.

"Yeah."

"She should have let him."

"Yeah."

"Air cover still sees her?"

"Yep." The Cessna was flying high, out of hearing range. As the sun rose, the pilot had the best view in the house.

The agents watched the light make its uneven way down the slope. "We'll wait a minute till Mrs. Westbrook's out of the way," said Spaar. "I wish she could limp faster."

— ✳ —

At the top of the graveyard, Tsara worked at the gag, moving her jaw against it till it dropped under her chin. She spat out the sock. Now what?

If she yelled, she might just be alerting Mike or Jim. Although she was pretty sure they were intent on putting miles between themselves and her, it wasn't worth the risk. Jim especially might figure it was worthwhile to come back and clock her.

Tsara pulled against the ropes, yanking forward. There was almost no give, and she stamped her foot in frustration. *I'm like a thing.* Like a bag of groceries waiting to be picked up. The idea of being found this way was almost too much to bear.

Worse yet was the thought of not being found. *Does anyone know where I am?* The zip cord was tight, cutting into her wrists. She moved her hands behind her back.

There had to be a way out of this.

She glanced at the edge of the monument at her back, and—

There *was* a way out.

She shoved herself to one side with her feet. Although the ropes had refused to yield when she pulled forward, she could move laterally with little problem. Reaching the side of the grave marker, she jammed her bound wrists at its edge and rubbed the cable tie up and down. The stone scraped the edges of her palms, missing most of the plastic and peeling off skin. Cursing, she repositioned her hands and scraped the cord again as hard as she could. The granite still rasped her hands, but she didn't care. The cable tie would give. She would make it give. She pushed fiercely against it. Finally it parted with a soft *tic* and fell to the wet grass.

Quickly she pulled her hands from behind her back. The ropes went slack, and she grabbed the top loop and shoved it over her head. It slid easily past, as did the second one. Tsara lurched to her feet and heaved a breath of dawnshine. Air sparkled in her lungs and tingled to the tips of her fingers, bright and alive. She glowed as if awake for the first time, and a newborn vigor blazed in her veins. She was free!

A movement in the woods caught her eye. A figure—no, two—

Shit!

She turned and ran down the slope, toward the road.

—If anything goes wrong—you'll be fine—

Could she make it? Would they dare follow her? What were they afraid of down there? Was it after her too?

Three figures stepped in front of her. She threw her hands up and shrieked before she dimly saw they wore jeans and crumpled hats. Two of them had binoculars around their necks. The third had a multi-pocketed vest and carried a rifle.

… Birders and hunters … ?

Several more figures stepped out of the woods behind her. They were similarly attired. Overhead a small plane clattered. The man with the rifle spoke. "Mrs. Adelman?"

Tsara stared at him with a feeling of utter unreality. "Yes?"

"We're with the FBI." He stepped close, rifle pointed at the ground, and put a hand on her shoulder. "Are you all right?"

Tsara stared at the circle of concerned faces. "I—" She stopped, stomach lurching.

"Can you make it the rest of the way down the hill?" He pointed. The dark stripe of road was seething with cars and vans and a big black Suburban. Doors clicked open and people swarmed, their faces turned toward her.

"Mrs. Adelman?" he repeated.

She stared at him.

"I think I'm going to throw up," she said.

And then she did.

— ✳ —

The phone rang. David leaped for it. Court jerked upright, fists clenched.

"Yes?" said David. "Is she—oh, my God. Where? We're coming. Thanks. Oh, my God." He hung up. When he turned around his face was summer and fireworks.

"She's alive," he shouted. "She's okay, she's fine, she's—"

"Where?"

"A graveyard a few miles past Libertyville."

"I'm driving."

"The hell you are."

222

The sun was up and as David drove them north light flooded the road. His car roared through puddles, and water rose on either side in glittering white waves like seagulls' wings.

At the graveyard David slammed the car into Park. The road and hillside were full, teeming with surprisingly brawny hunters and birders and about a thousand different cars and vans and SUVs and station wagons such as innocent nature-lovers might use. As David stepped out of the car, Tsara hurtled into his arms, burying her head in his neck. She smelled like rain and smoke and mud and horses. He flung his arms around her. They cried, saying each other's names and sobbing. Court stepped out of the passenger's side and stood awkwardly next to them until Tsara pulled him into the embrace. The three of them stood wrapped together, rocking back and forth.

Tsara hadn't known there were such things as SWAT medics. She was sitting with a cohort of them in their black Suburban with a blanket over her shoulders, her stiff and dirty fingers around a mug of coffee whose warmth she gratefully absorbed. David was with her, and she smiled at him over the head of the nice guy with the short hair who was asking her if that hurt. No? How about that? He seemed genuinely pleased when nothing did, at least not much.

"They'll give you a more thorough examination at the hospital," he said.

"I don't need to go to a hospital," she said. "I'm fine. This is just a few scrapes."

David's hand was on her leg, above the scratches that showed through the ripped pajama bottoms. "Sweetie, it's probably best to have a doctor check you out. Just in case."

"In case what? There's nothing wrong with me."

"Mrs. Adelman," the medic said, "have you seen a mirror in the past couple of days?"

She cackled. "I haven't seen an indoor toilet in the past couple of days. Why?"

The young man handed her a small mirror. The face that looked back at her was smeared with dirt and layered with shades of dark purple, black, and even green along the left side. Her left eye was open, but not as much as the right, and the whole mess was crowned with twig-tangled hair.

224

Tsara handed back the mirror. "Maybe I should go to a hospital," she suggested. "Just to be on the safe side." As the SUV started she leaned her right cheek on David's shoulder. "I thought my eye felt a little funny," she murmured. David stroked her hair. The Suburban bumped down the road with Court following in David's car.

The regional hospital near Libertyville was a mid-sixties pink brick monstrosity, its harsh lines barely softened by a scattering of maples that punctuated its gently sloping lawn. The agents had called ahead, and the emergency room staff popped Tsara into a wheelchair and whizzed her past the admitting office and into the hospital proper. The hallways were painted in pastel colors, and inspirational posters dotted the walls. *Climb Every Mountain*, urged one with a photo of Mt. Washington. Tsara fought back a hysterical giggle. Check that off the list.

A few minutes later Tsara sat with David in an examination room, waiting for someone to salve and catalogue her injuries. Every scrape and bruise was evidence. She was wearing only a hospital johnny, since in the most tactful way imaginable the agents had explained that they would need her shoes and clothes as evidence. Tsara had surrendered the bundle with no regret. "It's not like I'll ever be wearing them again," she said when they apologized.

"I phoned Adara," said David. "She's going to do a *Mi Sheberakh* for you, and the blessing for when you've been through danger."

"*Birkat HaGomel*," said Tsara absently.

"Yeah, that."

"Do you need a *minyan* for those?"

"I think Adara can scare up a *minyan* if she needs to."

"Oh. Right." Tsara shifted on the examination table. The paper crinkled under her bare bottom. "What did you tell her?"

"I said you'd been in an accident and you were in the hospital but okay and you'd probably call her later to tell her all about it."

"Thanks. "

The door opened and a chesty nurse with tight, grey curls bustled in carrying a white cardboard box. "There you are, you poor dear," she exclaimed. "Goodness gracious, what you've been through!" She set the box down on the counter and opened it, removing several blue-capped jars and long cotton swabs. Black letters on the side of the box read

EVIDENCE COLLECTION KIT. "You'll have to leave now, Mr. Heydleman," she said over her shoulder.

"Why?" said Tsara and David at the same time.

"For a rape test the victims usually like some privacy and you know it makes the husband feel very violated too, especially if he's a sensitive man. You are, aren't you?" She turned around, snapping on latex gloves. "I can just tell. When a woman is raped the man who loves her is a victim too. That's what they told us in the sensitivity workshop."

Tsara stared at her. "That won't be necessary. I already told them that."

"Of course it is, dear." She reached into the box and pulled out a sheet, reading aloud from it. "'A sexual assault kit is the victim's best way to document the attack and help ensure prosecution of the attacker.'" She put the sheet down. "When you've been doing this as long as I have you already know *that*. The DNA evidence can be *instrumental* in a conviction. Why, just last week one of the girls I swabbed went to court and in the end it was the rape test that convicted that animal. She didn't want to do the test either, so just imagine how she felt after the trial. I said to her, 'Aren't you glad now?'" She jerked the stirrups into place. "So come on, now, put your feet up."

Tsara clamped her knees together. "No."

"Now, honey, this is hospital policy. Last year one of the girls who works here wouldn't do it and she was *reprimanded.*"

"Gosh," said Tsara. "How very awful for her."

"Yes," said the nurse solemnly. "That's why we have to talk to the rape victims about how important it is. Often they're in shock after their violation."

"That didn't happen."

The nurse picked up a swab. "Dear, most rapists—"

"He wasn't a rapist."

The nurse smiled gently. "Well, dear, if that's what you need to tell yourself, that's all right for *now*. But don't be selfish. Think of his future victims."

"But—"

"It won't hurt a bit, and we can get evidence from your body, which is a crime scene right now, and it could put someone behind bars before he can attack another girl." She paused as she took in the bruises on

Tsara's face and the scrapes on her knees and arms. "Was it *terribly* painful?" she whispered.

Tsara began to look around for something to throw. David spoke first.

"Get out."

The nurse stared at him. "Mr. Heydleman—"

"Get out. Send another nurse." He picked up the rape kit and handed it to her. "This doesn't come back to the room. My wife has been through enough."

She took the box. "The other nurses are all busy," she said with dignity.

"Then I guess we're leaving."

"Sounds good to me." Tsara slid off the table. "I'll shower at the motel."

The nurse shifted in front of the door for a moment. "I'll see if I can find someone," she said as she reached for the doorknob.

"You do that," agreed David. "If no one's here in five minutes, we're gone."

"This is a very busy hosp—"

"Then I guess you're really in a hurry," said Tsara. "Goodbye."

The nurse opened and shut her mouth like a thwarted cod. She backed out the door, closing it behind her. Tsara snorted.

"Fucking cow," she said.

"No shit."

They were silent for a moment until David said, "Did you notice her name?"

"Nurse Ratched?"

"Betty Cohen," he said. "Don't you hate it when it's one of ours?" And suddenly he grinned and even though her face hurt she grinned back and they were both laughing when the next nurse walked in four and a half minutes later without a rape kit.

A change of clothes and a long, hot shower later, Tsara sat with Spaar and Galen. She liked them right away, mainly because they acted as though there were nothing at all weird about having been kidnapped and held hostage for a weekend. The three of them were at the FBI's mobile command post, which to Tsara's trained eye looked a lot like a middle school. Dimly she wondered when the kids would get back to classes. Probably when the agents were good and ready.

It felt strange and ordinary to be in a classroom. She glanced around. On the blackboard in perfect teacher-cursive were the words, *"We read everyday!"* Tsara grimaced. *And maybe some day we'll learn how to write,* she thought.

David and Court had sprinted to the hospital Starbucks while she cleaned up, and she held a Signature Hot Chocolate, made with milk. The way God intended. She shifted her fingers, noting with pleasure how clean they were. Yes indeed, every nick and scrape stood out in perfect bas-relief against her lovely, dirt-free skin.

"How are you feeling?" Galen asked as he pulled out a chair for her.

Tsara sat down and tried to make a gesture that would encompass "Relieved, exhausted, still a little jumpy, but a hell of a lot better than a few hours ago." They smiled back at her when she settled on, "Kind of tired. It's been a long weekend."

"We realize you must be exhausted, but we do have some questions."

"Sure," said Tsara. "And can I just say—back at the graveyard—I mean, oh my God. I couldn't believe all those people were there just for me."

"It's what we're for."

Tsara took a sip. "How's the guy I threw up on?"

"Anderson's tough. He'll pull through."

"Could you tell him I'm so, so sorry about that?"

"Sure. And when you're ready we can begin." Spaar put a manila file on the table in front of her.

Tsara glanced at the blackboard. "Just a sec." She got up and erased the sentence, rewriting it in her own teacher-cursive: *We read every day.*

"Thanks," said Spaar. "That was driving me crazy."

"What?" said Galen.

"Why didn't you change it?" asked Tsara.

"It's not my classroom."

Tsara sat down. "Can't help myself. It's a sickness."

Spaar smiled and took a photo from the file. It was more recent than the one she'd shown David and Court the day before. "Do you recognize this man?"

Tsara set her drink on the table and put on the extra pair of reading glasses David had brought her. God love that man, he had thought of everything—glasses, her favorite green turtleneck, even a jar of moisturizer. The organic stuff that smelled like lemongrass. Gently spreading it over her skin and taking in the familiar scent had felt like a touch of heaven.

She looked at the picture, now pleasantly in focus. It looked like a DMV photo, just a head shot with a plain white background. A man, staring straight ahead with no particular expression on his face.

Wavy hair. Grey-green eyes with a dark circle around the iris.

"Yeah," she said. "That's—yeah. His name's Mike."

"This is the man who abducted you?"

Tsara rubbed her forehead. "One of them."

Spaar slid a second photo across the table. They'd gotten it off the security cameras at the courier's. It was blurry and taken from a high angle near the ceiling, and she hoped it was clear enough for an ID. "And this?"

"Jim," said Tsara. "He doesn't talk."

229

"Are you sure of both of them?" said Spaar.

"Yes."

"Was there anyone else?"

Tsara shook her head. "Just those two. It was enough."

Galen spoke. "Were they holding anyone else that you were aware of?"

"No."

"Did they threaten you?"

"Mike did. And then in between he kept saying he wouldn't hurt me." She took a sip of her hot chocolate. "So he was a tad inconsistent."

Galen made some notes. "What exactly did he say?"

"With the threats? It was usually pretty non-specific, like, 'Don't fuck with me' and stuff like that. Though one time he said he'd tie me to a chair and ... put a knife to my throat if I screamed." She swallowed.

"Did he say anything about why he abducted you?"

"He said my uncle—" She stopped. "Where's my uncle? "

Cass should have been with her at the hospital, exulting over her escape. Giving the doctors hell. Where was he?

"Mr. Thornlocke is in jail in Madison," said Spaar. "He's scheduled to appear before a federal magistrate tomorrow regarding his involvement in this matter."

Tsara looked at the agents, hoping they were talking about two different things. That maybe Cass was a material witness or something. Anything.

But she knew better. "So it's true?" she said finally. "About the kids—and the ... there was a loan to a family .... Is it all true?"

"Yes," said Spaar. "I'm afraid it is."

Tsara stared at the tabletop. "Could you give me a minute?"

"Sure." Spaar picked up the file and the agents walked out of the room. When they came back a few minutes later Tsara was standing in an oblong of sunlight by the window, looking at the swings hanging straight as pencils in the playground.

"Are you all right?"

She didn't look at them; her voice held no tears. "Yeah. I just feel like I need to have my DNA fumigated."

Galen cleared his throat. "When you're ready?"

"Okay." She walked back to the table and sat down again.

230

Spaar sat down and another photo came out of the folder. This one was of two men in uniform, posing with their hands on their guns. One was slightly taller than the other, and his nose was a mass of bulges and flat bits where there oughtn't to be any. "These are Arnold and Jordan Stone, the town police in Libertyville. They did security work for your uncle on an occasional basis, and he sent them to look for you. They've been missing since Saturday morning. Do you know where they might be?"

Tsara sat still, eyes on the picture. "Yes," she said quietly.

As she told her story, Galen took notes, his hand skimming over his notebook. "And you saw the gun?" he asked.

"I saw it on the ground. I never saw it in his hand. And I know it was in the backpack, but I never saw it there either. He was really careful not to let me see into it."

"So he still has it?"

"I guess so."

"Could he have disposed of it during the time you two were together?"

"I don't see how."

"Not a chance, eh?" said Spaar.

"I don't think—wait." Tsara rubbed her forehead with her thumb. Something was niggling at the edges of her mind.

Not a chance.

When had he said that?

Not a chance. There's pools in these caves no one's ever found the bottom of, and tunnels that end at fifty-foot drop-offs ....

Mike had been wearing the backpack when he came back to bed the night in the cave. At the time she had assumed he didn't want her to open it and get the gun while he was away. Now another thought presented itself.

"Well," she said, "I know a really good place for you to look."

The entire story, from the first time she'd seen Mike in the driveway to when he and Jim galloped into the woods above the cemetery, took a long time. She told them everything she could about him: his height and his eyes and his mannerisms, and how he was always dressed in colors of smoke and earth.

— ✳ —

After Tsara left, Spaar and Galen looked at each other in abject frustration.

"Double homicide," said Galen.

"Can't prove it."

"He had motive and opportunity."

"And we don't have a witness or a weapon."

"We can find it."

"At the bottom of a pool in a cave no one's ever heard of."

"Come on," said Galen. "How many caves like that can there be?"

Spaar stood and collected everything from the folder, tapping it together neatly. "I guess we'll find out."

It was late afternoon when Tsara and David said goodbye to Court and climbed into David's car. The minivan was part of the crime scene, which meant it was still being scoured for evidence; a rather officious tech had assured Tsara it would be returned to her in a few days. As they turned onto the highway David clicked on the radio. Music filled the car, heavy on the strings.

"What is this piece?" said Tsara, reclining her seatback.

"Well," said David, "what's Bugs Bunny doing now?"

"Putting Figaro Fertilizer on Elmer Fudd's head," she yawned, "and patting it with his ears."

"Then it's *The Barber of Seville*." Keeping his eyes on the road, David reached over and put his hand over hers. "Hey, babe. Why don't you try to get some sleep? Just let me drive—you don't have to talk."

She did not answer. Glancing over, David saw that her head was turned toward the window and her eyes were already shut.

"Are you asleep?"

"Yes."

He smiled and put his hand back on the wheel and flipped on his lights so he wouldn't forget later. They drove south through mountain shadows that lay across the road in dusky pools.

It was dark when they pulled into their driveway. Tsara gave a small shake and sat up straight when the car stopped. "Thanks for letting me sleep," she said, her voice thick.

"No worries." David turned off the car. The house was dark except for the living room, whose curtains glowed. "My mom," he said. "I called from the road."

"The kids are probably asleep," said Tsara, opening her door and stepping out onto the driveway. "I'll just peek in on them when—"

The outside light came on and the front door opened. Josh and Abbie rocketed down the stairs and across the lawn in their striped pajamas and fuzzy slippers, shrieking at the top of their lungs. "Mommy Mommy Mommy Mommy! Mommy's home! Daddy *saved* her!"

Tsara dropped to her knees and flung her arms around the kids, frantically kissing their cheeks and the tops of their shampoo-scented heads as they tried their hardest to scrabble onto her lap. In a distant part of her mind she wondered how she could ever have been such an ass as to think of not waking them.

Her chest shook. The quiver turned into a quake that bloomed into a sob, and then another one; and she didn't want to cry in front of the kids, really she didn't, but suddenly she was safe and home and she *could* cry, clutching Abbie and Josh as they leaped and writhed and clung to her neck and her chest and her arms and her stomach, and really, how many places could a kid grab at the same time? She wept deep, satisfying tears that would not stop, crying more desperately even than she had with David and Court at the cemetery.

David's mother stood in the doorway, silhouetted in the bright light behind her. "I let them stay up," she said.

David looked at Tsara and the kids, all but rolling on the lawn in a ball of arms and legs.

"Good," he said.

The next afternoon Spaar stopped by David and Tsara's house to update them. It was a postcard day, the sky sapphire blue and the trees tricked out in orange and green and burgundy. Falstaff barked with indignation until David told him to stop. Spaar scratched the dog behind the ears, and he leaned his hundred pounds against her and rolled his eyes up as his tongue dropped halfway to his knees.

"We ignore him," said Tsara. "That's why he turns to strangers for affection."

Spaar switched her scratching to under Falstaff's chin, and he grumbled with pleasure. "I can see how abused and neglected he is."

"Shameful," agreed Tsara. "Can I get you a cup of coffee or tea or anything?"

"No, thanks," said Spaar. "I have some stuff to share with you, though. Can we sit down anywhere?"

"I expect so," said David. He glanced at the dining room table, which still held the detritus of an exuberant pancake brunch they had shared with the kids. "Living room is probably best."

They sat on the big red sectional sofa that formed the heart of the living room, and Spaar put her folder on the mahogany coffee table in front of it. It had belonged to Tsara's mother and was almost the only item of furniture in the house that wasn't kid-proof.

Spaar took in the pictures on the walls: a flotilla of sailboats on the Charles, a pencil sketch of Mrs. Mallard and her ducklings, a framed plaster print of Josh's feet when he was a baby, and Abbie's handprint on her third birthday. "So the kids are in school?"

Tsara bobbed her head. "We let them sleep late—"

"—and feed the dog pancakes—" said David.

"—but we thought it was probably a good idea to keep to their normal schedule as much as possible," said Tsara. "Josh just started kindergarten and Abbie's in nursery school a couple days a week. They're very serious about it."

"But we are *so* skipping Hebrew school today," said David.

"Rabbi's orders."

"How much have you told them?" said Spaar.

"Some," said Tsara. "They know there was a bad man involved, and that the good guys are looking for him."

"That sounds about right."

"So how's the search going?" asked David. "Do you have him yet?"

"We have some solid leads," said Spaar. "But no, we don't have him yet."

Tsara half smiled. "I'm not surprised."

"You don't sound worried," said David.

"I'm not," said Spaar. "Once we know who he is, his days are pretty much numbered. But we think we found the cave where he took you, Mrs. Adelman." She opened her folder and passed her a couple of pictures. "Does this look like the place?"

Tsara looked at the photos. The first one had been taken in the meadow. There was the crescent-shaped opening, with the small waterfall and sandy basin off to the right. The second photo showed the alcove where she and Mike had slept. It was lit white by the photographer's flash, and she could clearly see the fire pit, the two boulders where they had sat, and the stacks of waterproof bins on the ledge behind them. "You guys are quick."

"Are you sure that's it?"

Tsara handed back the pictures. "Just past the alcove further into the main cave, was there a big boulder half-blocking the tunnel?"

"Yes." The treads of the footprints behind the boulder matched Tsara's Crocs. They'd taken plaster casts. Between that and the other physical evidence that was even now shuffling down the mountain on its way to Quantico, they had plenty of data. Case file 7A-BS-090201 was getting plump. But hearing it from an eyewitness was always nice.

"Okay, then," said Tsara. "That's the place."

"Good," said Spaar briskly, returning the photos to their folder. "Then we can start looking for that murder weapon. By the way," she added, "there's a much easier access than the one you described."

"I figured there had to be," said Tsara.

"Why's that?"

"He said he was taking his son up there. I couldn't imagine a six-year-old making that trip without a lot of help. Besides, everything smelled like laundry detergent, so he had to be packing stuff in and out."

"Well, you were right. The slope on the other side is much gentler. I expect he was trying to confuse you about finding it again."

"He didn't have to try that hard," said Tsara. "I can get lost climbing out of a bathtub."

"Oh, I'm sure you're exaggerating," said Spaar.

"Not by much," said Tsara. David gave a quick nod, thinking of the days before they had put a GPS in Tsara's car, and the number of times she had called him from the road demanding to know where the hell Boston had drifted off to.

Spaar smiled and pulled out another folder. She hesitated for a moment. "This isn't directly relevant … but I thought you might be interested." This photo showed a vertical cliff soaring high above rapids studded with boulders. "Look familiar?"

Tsara shook her head. "It's not where we crossed the river. "

"I know. It's just beyond the clearing where we found the Stone brothers." She pulled out another eight-by-ten color glossy. This was a close-up of a cliffside path. Tsara could see gaps along the edge, air where there shouldn't be.

"What's this?"

"It's the trail above the river. It looks like they shoved a few rocks out of the way at the perimeter." She paused. "It would be a very convenient place for someone to slip. There's no riverbank for at least half a mile of rapids … and then the whole thing goes underground." A third photo showed the end of the river, a white mass of foam surging into a crack in the rocks.

David stared at the photos. His gut clenched like a fist, and he looked away.

Spaar left with promises to be in touch as soon as they had anything new. David let her out and sat back on the sofa where his wife waited. Tsara leaned her head on David's shoulder and closed her eyes. The night before she had slept like deep-sea diving, but she was still tired. "Will you stay with me while I rest for a minute?" she asked softly. David's hand closed around hers in response. She leaned against him, feeling his warmth and the scritch of his sweater.

"Sweetie?" he said.

"What?" she barely murmured.

"Why did you say you weren't surprised?"

"Surprised about what?"

"Just now. That they haven't found him yet."

"Oh, that …. Just because he's very resourceful. Always had a Plan B." She twisted around so she was looking up at the ceiling. "A couple of times he said something about adapt and improvise …. I don't remember. Anyway, that's why." She turned around again, head once more on the shoulder. "I was surprised to find out he was a Marine, though," she added. "He never called me ma'am even once."

David did not respond. She poked him. "Oh, c'mon," she said. "That was funny."

"Yes, it was," he said absently. "Sweetie, can I ask you one more thing?"

"Mm-hm."

"Well." He hesitated. "Why were you so insistent about not having a rape test?"

"Because I object to foreign objects being shoved up my hoo-ha unnecessarily."

"Well, sure," he said. "But ...."

"But what?"

David did not answer. Tsara sat up, pulling away to see him fully. "But *what?*"

David looked down. "I just wondered if there was anything else you wanted to tell me. If you wanted to."

Tsara stiffened. "What are you saying?"

"Well, if—if something happened like that."

Tsara shook her head and backed away from him on the sofa. David spoke in a rush to fill the horrible silence. "I mean, I understand if—"

"Wait a minute." Tsara buried her face in her hands and spoke through her fingers. "Are you suggesting he raped me and I forgot to mention it? Or that—he didn't—and I was—I did—" Her hands flew from her face. She shouted. "What do you think this was for me? *Fun?*"

"I—"

She yanked up the sleeves of her sweater. Her wrists were still encircled with angry red dots where the skin had torn loose. *"Does this look like fun to you?"*

They stared at each other. The air was tight.

"I had to ask permission to *piss,*" she said finally.

David waited. When he spoke, his words came slowly. "I'm sorry, honey. I didn't know how to say it."

"How to say *what?*"

"I just wanted to say ... not that he ... attacked you. You would have said. But if ... if anything else had happened ... if you felt like you needed to—go along with him ... I would understand. You wouldn't have to be afraid to tell me." He touched her hand with his fingertips. "I'm sorry, sweetie," he whispered. "I'm an idiot." He blinked rapidly, his eyes suddenly too shiny.

"Oh, God," said Tsara. The rage slipped away like a handful of sand underwater. "Oh, Davey." She reached out with her free hand and stroked his jawline. "Honey, I'm sorry." She sighed, wondering how to explain and loving him for the tears. "You are just the dearest, sweetest man in the whole world. But … it wasn't like that."

Outside a squirrel chattered. When David spoke, his voice was barely a whisper. "I just didn't want you to think there was ever anything you couldn't tell me."

Tsara flung her arms around him and buried her head in his shoulder. His hands went on her back, and he shook silently.

"I'm back and I'm okay," she whispered when he was still. She drew a tissue from a box on the coffee table and wiped his damp cheeks as though he were Josh or Abbie. "Dearest, sweetest man," she repeated.

"No, I'm not," said David indignantly. His voice was cloudy. "I'm a moron."

"But in a nice way." Tsara put the tissue aside and waited until his face had relaxed. Then she lay down with her head on his leg. Fatigue whispered at the edges of her mind. "Stay with me while I nap?"

"Want the dog too?"

"Yeah."

So David clicked his tongue and Falstaff lumbered from the other room like a happy sofa. He licked Tsara's face, giving her a look of molten adoration, and at David's gesture clambered up next to them on the big red sectional. Tsara buried her feet in the dense fur of his sides and pushed her shoulder into David's leg. She closed her eyes, and she and Falstaff slept while David watched a baseball game with the sound off.

That night Tsara lay in bed staring at the darkness. The blankets were heavy, the comforter warm and thick. Beside her David was still, a peaceful lump under the covers. She pressed her spine against his. He rolled over and pulled her close, his arm around her chest.

"David?"

"Whha?" David jerked, his arm jumping. "Are you okay? Bad dream?"

"Sorry," she whispered. "I thought you were awake."

"Ah." David lay back against his pillow. She could imagine his heart thudding. "Yes. I'm awake."

"Sorry," she said again. "You moved when I snuggled up to you so I thought—"

"I'm awake," he repeated. "It's fine. What's up?"

Tsara rolled onto her back, looking up. The darkness of the room gave anonymity, and she could say everything lying down that she might not say standing up. "I was thinking about what you asked me this afternoon."

David groaned. "Honey, I'm so sorry. I should never have said anything."

"No, it's okay—I'm not mad. I was just thinking about it ... and I was thinking ...."

David turned his head toward her.

"I mean, what I said is true," said Tsara earnestly. "But I started thinking, after you asked me .... I just ... honestly, if ... if it had been that kind of situation ..." She hesitated, wondering how to say it, or even if she should. "I—kept trying to get away and it never worked. So if I'd thought for one second there was ... another way ... to get back to you and the kids ... well, maybe I'd have done it. Probably, even." She paused in the heavy darkness. "But it wasn't like that."

David did not move. When he spoke his voice was husky. "I'm afraid to touch you."

Tsara was silent. Slowly she reached out and traced his hand with one finger. David went on, each word painful. "I've been afraid I might hurt you—or scare you—or—"

"Oh, *God*," cried Tsara. Her voice was rough with tears and her hand clenched his. "I *need* you to touch me. I need you to love me. I need to feel you holding me like you love me. That's what I need."

David turned his hand over so his palm faced Tsara's. He laced his fingers through hers and slowly, gently pulled her toward him in the warm bed. His lips slid over hers, barely moving, and he could taste the salt from her cheeks.

"My God," he whispered. "I love you so much."

They caught him the next day. It was almost an accident. He walked into a convenience store near the Canadian border to buy postage stamps. He paid for the stamps, agreed with the clerk about the weather, and left. Seconds later the little TV behind the counter flashed a news story about the manhunt, showing pictures of Mike and Jim. Even though Mike was wearing his baseball cap pulled down low, something about the curve of his jaw caught the clerk's eye. The announcer stressed "presumed armed and dangerous," and the clerk had family nearby. He grabbed the phone to call the number at the bottom of the screen. He could see Mike through the window, dropping something in the mailbox. The lid swung closed and Mike started to walk away.

In a fluke of timing that later made reporters and true crime writers wet themselves with joy, the town's only cruiser happened to pull into the parking lot while the clerk was still dialing. Dropping the phone, the clerk ran outside, shouting and pointing. Two cops leaped out of their car with weapons drawn. They had seen enough pictures of Mike in the past forty-eight hours to know exactly who he was.

"On your knees," shouted one of the cops. "*On your knees!*"

And Mike crashed to his knees, face stony in defeat.

Mike chose to exercise his right to remain silent, and he wouldn't tell the cops where Jim was; but finding him didn't take long. Jim told him about it afterwards: how the helicopters roared up one side of the mountain and the dogs came yelling and barking from below. Between them they herded him to the road where the local cops and the State Police were waiting, knowing they'd won.

Mike was still in the cell at the back of the police station when they brought Jim in, his hands cuffed behind him. Jim lifted his head and looked at Mike, his eyes black.

"I'm sorry," whispered Mike. "Oh, God, Jim, I'm sorry."

"Now remember," said Galen, "he can't see or hear you."

"Okay," said Tsara. It was the next day, and they were in the lockup in Madison, the same place Castle had been taken when he was arrested. A large window filled most of the wall in front of them, showing an empty room with a small platform and height markers on either side. Tsara could see her reflection in the glass. Her face was calm. Only David, holding her hand, knew her fingers were icy.

Half a dozen men walked into the room and arranged themselves in a line on the platform. They shuffled their feet and faced forward, eyes focused on nothing.

"Take your time," said Galen.

"Number three," said Tsara.

"Are you sure?"

"Have him look to the left."

Galen pushed a button next to the big sheet of glass. "Have Number Three face left."

The big man stepped forward and turned his head in profile, looking far away. Tsara pointed.

"That big bruise up by his hairline is from where Jordan clocked him with the butt of his rifle," she said. "The abrasion below that is from where I hit him while he was trying to get me onto his horse at my uncle's house. If you tell him to pull up his shirt, you'll see a bunch of bruises from where the Stone brothers beat him up."

Galen spoke into the microphone again. The officer inside the room repeated the command. The prisoner nodded and faced the glass. His eyes unfocused again. He untucked his shirt and with a fluid motion pulled it up to his chin. The muscular chest and narrow waist had healed somewhat in the days since the beating, but they were still painted with overlapping clouds of purple and black. David caught his breath.

"That'll do," said Galen into the microphone.

At a word from the officer Mike dropped his shirt. But he stayed where he was, facing the glass, and his mile-long stare suddenly focused, hard and precise, on Tsara.

Abruptly she turned away, pulling David's hand as they moved toward the exit. Galen hurried after them.

"Mrs. Adelman, I need you to—"

"Not now," said David firmly. "We'll be back in a minute."

Tsara could only look her thanks at him as they walked out into the cold air. Leaning against the railings outside the police station, she drew a breath and rubbed her damp hands together.

"Did you see the way he looked at me?" she whispered.

David moved to stand beside her. His hands were thrust into the pockets of his jacket. "Sweetie, he couldn't see you."

"I know," she said. "But he knew I was there."

David rocked on the balls of his feet. "I guess he did," he admitted. He drew a deep breath and blew it out in a stream that was almost visible in the chill. "I don't suppose I have to tell you he's locked up and you don't have to worry about him ever again?"

Tsara shoved her jacketed shoulder against his. "You could tell me you love me."

"'Course I love you," he chided. His arms went around her and he drew her close. "Did getting kidnapped make you stupid or something?"

She nodded gravely. "The IQ points are just draining away. I'm barely eligible to vote right now."

"I guess so," he said, shaking his head in disgust. "Do I still love you? What kind of crazy talk is that?"

And they stood together like that on the stoop until Galen opened the door for them.

From his car in the jail's parking lot, Hans released his breath. There was no reason he shouldn't be visiting Cass, after all; but meeting Tsara and David would be—well, awkward. So he counted to twenty to give them enough time to get to wherever they needed to go in the building, then turned up his collar and headed inside.

Minutes later Hans was sitting with Cass in the visiting room, a vast, tan rectangle with a long table down the middle. Inmates sat on one side, a row of orange uniforms. Visitors were on the other. Physical contact was forbidden, and a corrections officer stood by the door to make sure all rules were strictly observed. He looked bored, but Hans noticed his eyes made a sweep of the room every few seconds.

Alicia had been there earlier. But they were keeping the kids away, at least for now.

"Has anyone asked you about this Cretan Labyrinth we've pulled ourselves into?" asked Castle.

"The two agents, briefly. They assured me they would be back to chat again."

"How very thoughtful of them."

Hans cut to the chase. "Castle, my friend, I think we need to discuss plausible deniability."

"There are any number of things we need to discuss," said Castle. He kept his voice low to blend with the blur of sound around them. Other inmates talked to visitors, laughed or coughed, tapped the table for emphasis; chairs scraped as people got up or down. It was good cover. "But we can start there. What did you have in mind?"

"Well, I wonder how much of this we can attribute to the sociopathic Stone brothers. They were the ones who took the children, after all. How likely is it that you knew they were in your wine cellar?"

"How likely is it I didn't?" said Cass. His fingers tapped restlessly.

"Castle, think! It was to say the least a busy weekend. You were running a charitable event with over a hundred attendees, and you were looking forward to a reunion with your niece. Why would you have been inspecting the outbuildings?"

"True," said Cass. "You raise a good point. One my lawyer was curious about."

"And as for that unpleasantness up in the mountains, they did have a longstanding feud with Westbrook."

"Yes. That's right." Castle leaned forward, eager but cautious. "I called them in to find my niece and the man who abducted her. They took it upon themselves to kill him—"

"—and Tsara—forgive me—"

"Not at all. Of their own initiative, while hiding the truth from me." He thought for a moment then sighed and shook his head. "No, it doesn't work. I asked Cook for food for the kids, remember?"

"Of course you did," agreed Hans. "But it was really for Tsara. You concocted the story about hungry children so as to keep secret her abduction, but you wanted to make sure she would have food when Jordan and Arnold found her."

"That's not bad." Castle stroked his jaw. "But why did I ask for enough for half a dozen kids?"

"In addition to providing sustenance for your niece, you wanted to be sure the Messrs. Stone would be well-provisioned for their arduous journey into the back country."

Castle considered, tapping one foot under the table. "That might work …. But Cook saw them leaving before I called for the food. My lawyer was asking about it."

"A fine woman, your cook, and no one can surpass her in the kitchen," said Hans. "However, it's easy enough to get confused about little details like that. She actually saw them leaving *after* you ordered the tray." Castle was silent, and Hans prompted him. "They left with all the necessary provender. You were taking no chances in the rescue of your niece."

Castle shifted around in his chair so his voice came from a new direction. None of the other inmates seemed interested in his conversation, but he wanted to be careful anyway. "I've been wondering why I didn't call the FBI the way Court did. Considering my Galahad-like innocence."

For a moment Hans was silent. Then his face brightened. "First and foremost, you knew the Stone brothers were more familiar with the mountains than any outsider could be. Second, by the time it became an issue, the agents were already on their way."

"That has a certain elegance," agreed Castle thoughtfully. "Especially when you consider the Stones did catch up with Westbrook almost immediately."

"Exactly. They knew right where to go."

"Unlike the well-intentioned but essentially bewildered G-men."

"Good heavens, Cass, I don't think this has to be a *film noir*," protested Hans.

A faint smile came to Castle's lips. "Do you have anything else for me, Hans?"

"Not at the moment, but I'll be in touch." He pushed his chair back and stood. "Can I bring you anything? I assume the food is atrocious."

"Ghastly," agreed Cass. "And it's all the same color, too. One big gelatinous pile of monochromatic slop. And no knives, of course."

"Why—oh." Hans smiled apologetically at his own slowness. "Of course."

"I'm far too dangerous," said Castle. "Which also explains the absence of bail. Peril to the community and so-forth."

"In our younger days, perhaps." Hans was trying to be jolly, but it fell flat.

"The lawyers are working on it," said Castle.

"Working on ...."

"Getting me out before the trial."

"I expect they'll succeed."

"Perhaps. Hans," said Castle quietly. "There is one favor you can do for me. It's the only thing I'll ask of you."

Hans sat down quickly and dropped his voice. "What is it?"

Castle looked at him for a moment without answering. "Go away," he said softly.

Hans blinked. "Excuse me?"

"Go away," repeated Castle. His voice was barely a breath of sound. "As far as you can. Take the family. And stay away."

"Castle," protested Hans. He leaned forward. "After all we've been through—do you really think I'd desert you at such a time?"

"Of course not, you damn fool," replied Castle with a touch of his old flair. He kept his voice low and urgent. "That's why I'm telling you to go. Be reasonable. This thing is ugly and it's going to get downright hideous. If you stay, you'll end up getting sucked into it. How does that help anyone?"

Hans looked around the room. All the other visitors were hip-deep in conversation, talking or listening or gesturing to paint their stories more brightly. No one else seemed at a loss for words.

"If I were to go, I'd look guilty," he said.

"If you stay you'll look guilty too, but you'll be close enough to arrest," said Castle. "Hans, listen to me. I will assert your innocence if it comes up, and I'll keep asserting it. But there is absolutely no point in your getting tarred with this brush." He smiled grimly. "Besides, you'd look positively foul in orange scrubs."

"They are fairly repugnant," conceded Hans, eyeing his friend's attire. "You look as though you're about to perform surgery on a giant pumpkin." He leaned forward, serious. "Castle, I cannot fault your logic. But there is such a thing as loyalty." He glanced at the officer by the door and his voice dipped. "It was my idea, Cass. How can I abandon you now?"

"Jesus Christ, you ass!" Castle's voice was a hiss. "You're not abandoning me—I'm telling you to go. If you can come up with one good reason for staying that doesn't involve some misguided Teutonic notion about fidelity, I'll listen. But for God's sake, this isn't an opera. There's no dramatic final act and you won't get extra points for clinging to the spars of a sinking ship like some brain-damaged rodent. You have a wife and children, and their lives will become very difficult if you are behind bars. Believe me," he added heavily.

Hans viewed him with pursed lips. "Exactly what Teutonic opera has someone giving extra points to rats clinging to the spars of sinking ships in the final act?"

"Oh, hell, I don't know. Probably something by Wagner."

Hans folded his arms. "You've said your piece, and I appreciate the sentiment," he said. "But I'm not leaving."

Castle shrugged his boxy shoulders. Something ancient and weary clouded his face. "Suit yourself." He stood and the two men walked to the door.

"Done?" said the guard.

"Yes, thank you," said Castle. "Mr. Freihoffer needs to leave." He looked significantly at Hans. The other man clasped his friend's hand.

"I will visit again, Castle."

The guard opened the door. Hans turned and walked down the hall.

Two days later Aiden got a postcard at his grandmother's address. His grandmother read it to him because handwriting was still too tricky.

> *Hey Aiden I cant come home for a while and neither can Uncle Jim but I'll explain everything when I can so for now be a good boy and do what Grandma tells you Love ya buddy Dad*

It was postmarked in a small town near the Canadian border.

That night Tsara got into bed and promptly fell wide awake. When Mike was on the run he had begun to feel vaguely fictional. Now he had morphed back from phantasm to fact, and he and the machine of justice were gearing up to drag her away from her family again.

Tsara stared into the darkness. She thought about Mike. The Stone brothers. The kids in the wine cellar. Castle.

Her heart thumped hard and fast, and she couldn't breathe evenly. Everything was wrong and broken and lost, and she didn't know how to get home again.

The next day Tsara lay on the red sofa and pulled a throw over her shoulders. It smelled comfortingly of dog, and she closed her eyes.

"Mommy," said Josh, "will you draw with me?"

Tsara cracked one eye. Josh stood in front of her with crayons in one hand and construction paper in the other.

"Oh, sweetie," she murmured. "Later. Right now I'm very tired."

Josh scowled. "You say that a lot now."

"Well, that's because it's true. I didn't sleep well last night, so I need a little rest." She shut the eye. "Later, okay, honey?"

Josh didn't answer but she heard his footsteps as he walked away. She felt a spasm of guilt. But it was true—the night had been wretched. When she finally got to sleep the nightmares started.

251

She wandered through her house until she came to a clearing in the woods where two bodies lay in the dirt. They rose as though pulled on marionette strings and shambled after her, their faces slack. When she ran they grabbed the cord around her wrist. As they leaned in to kill her, she could see sky through the holes in their bodies.

Her cry had awakened David, and he held her while she choked out the dream. He kept holding her until he fell asleep again. But Tsara did not sleep that night.

Josh's footsteps came back. He shoved something soft under Tsara's chin. She twisted her head away. "Not *now*, honey. I said I'd play with you later."

Josh walked away.

Twenty minutes later Tsara opened her eyes, pleased with the nap. Then she glanced down in surprise. "Josh?" she called.

"What?" Josh was in the playroom with Abbie.

"Can you come in here, please?"

Josh shuffled in, his green eyes anxious. Tsara held up a stuffed wolf. "Is this what you brought me?"

Josh nodded.

She smiled. "You thought I'd sleep better with Wolfson?"

"Not *exactly*," said Josh.

"Then why did you give him to me?"

"So you wouldn't be scared any more."

Tsara pulled her feet away from the far end of the sofa to make room for her little boy. "Sit. Now, sweetie—scared of what?"

Josh bounced on the sofa cushions. "The thing you were scared of last night. I heard you telling Daddy about it when I got up to go to the bathroom."

Shit shit shit shit. "I didn't know you were awake, love."

Josh crawled over her knees and flung his arms awkwardly around her. "The point is, Mommy, you don't have to be scared any more."

Tsara hugged him, blinking hard. "Because I have Wolfson."

"Well, that's *part* of it." Josh was still clinging to her. "Me and Daddy and Abbie will take care of you too. Sorry—Daddy and Abbie and I."

"But Josh, you don't have to. They caught the bad men, remember?"

Josh didn't answer. Tsara sighed. She still held Wolfson in one hand. "This helps a lot, honey. Thanks."

Josh's head popped up. "Feel better, Mommy?"

"I sure do, buddy."

Josh slid off the sofa and went back to the playroom. The door was open and Tsara could hear him talking.

"Why did you give Wolfson to Mommy?" asked Abbie.

"For protection," said Josh solemnly. "She has bad dreams, and I get worried." He sighed deeply. "Hey, Abbie, how do you spell 'February'?"

Abbie, who was three years old and knew only that A was for Abbie, mulled this over. "I don't know," she said at last. Her tone indicated that she had given the matter great thought. "You should copy it off the callingder. "

"That's a good idea, Abbie. Thanks."

Tsara went to the phone. The hospital near Libertyville had recommended a shrink near her, and she had put the number on the table as soon as she got home. Every day she had intended to call. But then they caught Mike and they caught Jim and she'd had to go to New Hampshire a few times and she was busy with the kids and had things to do and God damnit she didn't want to go back into therapy.

She'd been shrunk for years after her mother's death. It helped. But no matter its efficacy, therapy was expensive, inconvenient, and time-consuming. She had thought she was done with that part of her life. And she had young children—she needed to be here for them.

But she wasn't. Not if her five-year-old thought he had to rescue her.

She picked up the phone and dialed.

"**N**o trial."

Castle looked at his wife. Right now everything about her was hard—her hair, her mouth, the skin around her eyes. "What makes you say that?"

"You don't have a prayer."

Castle was silent. Around them the visiting room mumbled with its usual activity. A few kids were visiting, and the littlest ones were allowed on their fathers' laps. It had been seven days since his arrest, and apparently a hell of a week for Alicia. Castle kept his eyes on her. There was more coming, he knew. After a moment she went on. Her words were hard and clipped. She had clearly thought this out before their meeting.

"More to the point, I'm not enjoying my new status as pariah. The way everyone looks at me whenever I go outside the house."

"Tell them it was all my doing and you had no idea." Castle turned sideways to his wife. He stared past the walls. "It has the advantage of being true."

"The ones who would believe that already pity me." Her fingers tightened in disgust. "The fascination—in any case, Castle, I have no intention of sticking around for the public humiliation of a trial you're sure to lose."

Castle looked up. "Are you going somewhere?"

"I'm thinking of taking Zaylie to Europe until this dies down. She's hoping the late-night comedians over there aren't quite as delighted with you as the American ones."

"For long?" Castle swung to face her and his hands gripped the edge of the table.

"Until this dies down," repeated Alicia. "Six months ... a year or so."

Castle sagged in his chair, suddenly feeling every one of his years. He did not speak.

"It's easier for the boys," went on Alicia. "They're older ... and college students aren't quite as cruel. But Zaylie has been ...." She let her voice trail off.

Castle stared down at his hands. When he spoke his voice was low. "Are you going to divorce me?"

"I haven't decided yet."

He looked up. "I suppose you could take me for every nickel I ever squeezed."

"I suppose I could, too. If this were about money." She shook her head. "Oh, God, Cass, why did you do it?" He did not answer and she went on. "That loan—good God, why? And the children—*why would you do such a thing?*" Her face crumbled and she turned aside. Castle reached out to touch her, but she jerked away.

"Don't."

He waited until she had composed herself, the tightness back in place.

"Why," she said. It sounded like a statement, not a question.

He sighed deeply. "Honestly, love, right now I have no idea."

"Is that what you're going to tell the jury?"

"No, because apparently there isn't going to be a trial."

"It's not as though we even needed the money, for God's sake."

"I know."

"Did you think we did?"

"No."

"Did you think it was all right to treat those people that way? Did you think it was legal or defensible in any way?"

Castle winced. "Please," he whispered. "Please."

She was silent, looking at him. She stood. "I'll let you know before we leave. And I'll make sure Zaylie writes."

He nodded. As she moved to the door he spoke.

"Alicia."

She turned to look at him. She had never seen his eyes so naked.

"Do you still love me?"

Alicia paused for a long moment. "I love the man I married," she said.

The guard opened the door for her. Alicia did not look back.

"Your cousin's decided to plea bargain," said the public defender. He was average height and a little too heavy; his hair was hair-colored, light brown, and his suit fit reasonably well. His name was Jerome Traveler, and he was Mike's lawyer.

"I know," said Mike. "He told me."

The prison library was a strange place, thought Mike. Much bigger than his cell. Books on two walls, a TV in the cabinet—it looked a lot like a regular library, except lots of the books were law and the TV was actually a video arraignment system. No Monday night football on that sucker.

Mike and his lawyer were alone, and a radio sat on the table between them. When they were finished Traveler would call the guard with it.

"I really think it's the best thing to do," said Traveler.

Mike barely nodded. "Do I have to sign stuff, or what?"

"I'll bring in the paperwork after we've settled the terms."

"Okay."

The public defender stood, briefcase in hand. "I'll be in touch."

Mike was looking at the wall. He'd been looking at a lot of walls lately. "Thanks."

"Well, that's three for three then," said Traveler. He reached for the radio.

Mike's head snapped up. "Thornlocke's going to plea bargain?"

"Yes."

"I changed my mind," said Mike. "I want a trial."

257

"You want—" Traveler stopped, his hand on the radio. "Why?"

"I have a right to a trial."

"Yes, you do. But as your lawyer, I have to tell you I don't think that's the best approach."

"How come?"

Traveler wondered whether or not to laugh. "Because you're guilty."

"And I might end up in prison?"

"Another prison, and for a much longer time."

Mike snorted. "From what you tell me I'm never seeing the light of day again anyway. At least this way I get to say what that son of a bitch did."

Traveler let go of the radio and straightened up. "Mr. Westbrook, a trial isn't about revenge. It's about a jury deciding what happens to you, maybe for the rest of your life."

"I know my rights."

"You could *die*," he said. "You killed two cops during the commission of a felony. That's firing squad material in most states."

"Nobody gets executed in this state any more."

"Really." Traveler tightened his lips. "There's one guy on Death Row in New Hampshire. Know what he's there for?"

Mike was silent.

"Killing a cop," said Traveler. "Still want a trial?"

"Yes."

Dear God, he was stubborn. Traveler sighed and thought of the rest of his caseload. He had about a hundred other clients. Drug addicts, wife beaters, petty thieves … most of them were guilty. But he was paid to give a rat's ass, and most days he tried. He leaned forward, hands on the table.

"Okay, look," he said. "I'm not going to bullshit you. If we go to trial, they can execute you. That's a fact. And they're going to want to, because when the jury looks at you they're going to see a crazy vet who snapped and went on a violent crime rampage that ended with the double murder of two officers of the law. So give me one reason why an uncooperative, uncommunicative, cop-killing kidnapper needs a trial to save his miserable life when I can do the same thing with a plea bargain."

Mike's eyes were still and clear. "Because if I don't," he said, "that's the story my kid is going to hear for the rest of his life."

Traveler glanced at the ceiling. "And you have a better story?"

"Yeah," said Mike. "I've got what actually happened."

He didn't look away, and Traveler felt something shift inside him. "How different is that?"

"Different enough."

"And you think telling the world is going to do what for you?"

"It'll make Thornlocke testify," said Mike. "He'd lie for a plea bargain."

"But he'll tell the truth in court and you'll tell the truth and we'll all be up to our eyeballs in truth. Is that the idea?"

"That's the idea."

No, thought Traveler. *Don't do it. Talk him out of it. He has some grand, romantic dream about redeeming himself but it doesn't work that way. He's going to be the DA's piñata.*

"You'd be taking a hell of a risk," he said quietly.

"Yeah," said Mike. "I know."

Traveler sighed and sat down. He opened his briefcase and took out a new legal pad and a pen.

"In that case," he said, "we have a lot of work to do."

61

The phone on Tsara's desk rang and she reached over the mouse pad to get it. "Hello?"

"Mrs. Adelman? This is Lawson."

The DA who was handling the case. They had met a few times in the week and a half since her abduction, and she liked him. In addition to his obvious intelligence, he radiated sympathetic warmth. He looked about her age but was old-fashioned enough to insist on calling her "Mrs." It was hard to imagine not liking him, and harder still not to trust him.

"Call me Tsara," she said. "How are you?"

"Just fine, got some news I wanted to share with you. Keep it quiet because it's not official yet, but Mr. Thornlocke has decided to plea bargain."

Tsara sucked in a breath. "What does that mean?"

"It means he's going to plead guilty to a lesser charge to—"

"No, no." She spoke more forcefully than she had intended. "What does it *mean?* What's he going to admit to, and what's going to happen to him?"

"Don't know yet," said Lawson. "He's still working out details with the Feds, and it's all confidential. But I thought you'd want to know before it's announced in open court."

"So he'll cooperate with them and get some lenient sentence?"

Lawson hooted. "'Scuse my language, but hell no. It'll be less than if he were found guilty, but don't worry—he's not going to be terrorizing the countryside again any time soon."

Tsara's hand ached, and she realized she was gripping the phone tightly. She shifted it to the other ear and pinned it in place with her shoulder while she opened and closed her fingers.

"I see," she said, because Lawson wasn't talking.

"You okay?"

"It's a lot to take in."

"For us too," he said.

"Really?"

"Sure. Believe me, I don't feel lenient. But no matter what kind of deal he cuts he's going away for a long time, and this way it spares you having to testify at his trial."

"True," said Tsara. "That *is* a relief."

"Thought it would be. Well, look, I'll be in touch as things develop. Say hello to Mr. Adelman for me."

Tsara was still sitting at her desk and staring through the window at the filigree of maple branches in the back yard when David walked in a few minutes later carrying his closed laptop. Falstaff followed him and flopped down in the corner.

"What was the phone call?"

"Lawson," she said. "Cass is going to plea bargain."

"Thought he would," said David cheerfully. He put his laptop on his desk and plugged it in. Tsara's silence grew heavy and he glanced at her. She was rubbing her lip with her thumbnail. "You okay?"

"He's an old man," she whispered. "He's going to die in jail."

"Well … no …." David was suddenly uncertain. "They'll probably let him out when he's dying."

Tsara's face shuddered and she collapsed on her desk, head in the crook of her elbow, crying savagely. Again. Everything was dead, all over again.

Falstaff padded over to her and thrust his muzzle under her free hand, chucking it to the top of his head with a series of brisk jerks. He mashed against her, and the gentle waving of his tail made his entire body sway. His fur was warm under her fingers, and he stayed with her until she ran out of sobs.

"I don't understand," said David. He was still standing on the other side of the room by his computer. A little orange light on the plug said it was charging. "Why aren't you glad?"

"Please stop talking," she said, so softly she didn't know if he could hear her. Her fingers rubbed mechanically behind the dog's ears, and he smiled at her with his big brown eyes and his grinny mouth. The tail plumed back and forth in a gentle arc.

Falstaff always knew just what to say.

In his role as public defender, Jerome Traveler had long practice in talking to people who maintained their innocence despite mountains of evidence to the contrary. Most of them became downright garrulous as they explained the extraordinary series of coincidences that had led to the erroneous appearance of their guilt. What he wasn't used to was someone who just wouldn't talk. He sighed inwardly as he looked at his client. When Westbrook chose to be silent he put the local mollusks to shame.

"Have you thought about what I said?" asked Traveler.

"Yes."

Traveler waited a few seconds. When no more syllables were forthcoming he said, "No jury is going to buy the hunting accident. The bullets came from a handgun."

"Yep."

"What does that mean, *Yep?*"

"Means I read the report. You gave it to me last time."

"Did anything else in the report jump out at you? Ballistics-wise?"

"Like what?"

"Like the shots were fired from a few yards away."

Mike said nothing. Traveler felt a quick tide of impatience rising in his chest. "Mike. If you want anything other than a paint-by-numbers defense from me, you have to give me all you've got. Understand?"

"Yep."

Traveler grimaced. He hadn't said *firing squad* or *you can swing for this* yet today, but they were among his current favorites. Along with *Throw me a bone here, Mike.* He tapped the clicker end of his pen on the table. "Okay. So let me just ask you this. Is there any chance at all that a gun might turn up with your prints on it?"

"Sure," said Mike. "I own guns."

"For God's sake. The gun that killed Arnold and Jordan Stone."

Again Mike was silent.

"I'm asking for a reason," said Traveler. "If you're not going to answer, I can spend some of my underpaid time with clients who are actually innocent. "

He let the silence fill the room, willing it to sound like a lawyer who was about to walk out on his client.

"What's the reason? "

Yes! thought Traveler, and he resisted the impulse to punch the air. Instead he leaned forward, palms flat on the tabletop. "If that gun *happens* to turn up with your prints on it and you stick to the hunting accident story, you'll have committed perjury as well as double murder. That's not a good way to get a jury to like you."

"Yeah?" said Mike. "Which one carries a longer sentence, perjury or murder?"

Traveler chose his next words carefully. This was as close as Mike had ever come to admitting anything about the Stone brothers. "Legally speaking, killing in defense of others can be valid, just like self-defense. Both you and Tsara Adelman say those men were drawing on her when they were shot. She was in mortal danger, and so were you." He paused. "Saving that woman's life could get you a lot of sympathy with the jury—especially considering that these particular cops had a sideline kidnapping children. Spinning fantastic tales you couldn't beg them to believe will only squander that."

Mike rubbed his chin with a slow, circular motion. Finally he said, "I had a long history with those two. What if the jury decides I took the opportunity to pop 'em?"

"I don't think that would be a problem," said Traveler. He kept his voice neutral, but excitement unfurled within him. "I've been looking into them—it would be pretty easy to paint an accurate and very unflattering picture of them."

"More sympathy from the jury, you mean."

"That's right."

Mike did not answer, and Traveler knew better than to press him. He stood up, briefcase in hand. "Think it over," he said. "I'll be back tomorrow."

As he turned toward the door Mike said, "Got a piece of paper?"

Traveler sat down again and unlocked the briefcase. He slid a legal pad and pen over to Mike, who began to draw with sharp strokes. He turned the pad back toward his lawyer.

"Check there," he said, tapping a circle at the end of a line. "Big pool at the end of that offshoot tunnel. It's small at first but it widens up after the first few yards. They'll need divers. Tell them to be careful. There's a ledge about six feet under, and the current gets pretty tricky."

Traveler put the pad into his briefcase, locking it again. "I'll tell them." He stood up. "Thanks, Mike. I'll see you tomorrow."

Mike nodded. He was silent again as the guard walked him back to his cell.

One evening a few weeks later when the nights had gotten longer and colder and cider doughnuts were already out of season, the phone rang as Tsara and David unpacked groceries in their kitchen.

"Got it," said David. "Hello? Who? Yeah, hold on a second—I'm putting you on speaker phone." He hit the orange button on the handset and put it on the counter before leaning over his shopping bag.

"—John Baxter," said an unfamiliar voice. "We went to law school together."

"So we did," said David. "John, you old bastard, this is a fundraising call, isn't it?"

Baxter laughed. "No, I swear. I haven't sunk that low. But I see the grand jury indicted your boy."

"Without breaking a sweat," agreed David.

"Surprised?"

"Any reasonably competent DA could get a grand jury to indict a cactus," said David.

"I thought the accepted metaphor was a ham sandwich," called Tsara from across the room. She opened the freezer and put in a bag of peas.

"Just keepin' it kosher, babe." David put two loaves of bread on the counter: one whole wheat, one raisin for Abbie.

"Hey, is that your lovely wife?" said Baxter.

"That's my beautiful wife," said David.

"The ugly wife is on vacation," said Tsara. "Luckily I was available."

266

Baxter laughed again. "Hey, nice to meet you. So what do you think of the defense?"

"Ugh," said Tsara.

"Well, it's certainly novel," said David.

"What do you mean?"

"I mean the PD is either going to throw the ball a hundred yards for a touchdown or fall flat on his ass," said David. "It's a Hail Mary pass."

"Do you think he has a prayer?"

"Westbrook? I think he's a selfish bastard who could save us all a lot of time, money, and trauma by copping a plea instead of showboating on the witness stand."

"Daaay-vid," said Baxter reproachfully. "He's an American citizen, and he has a right to a trial."

"Hooray for him," muttered David. He opened a drawer and dropped in aluminum foil and a box of parchment paper.

"Plus, he's got the necessity doctrine going for him," went on Baxter, who appeared not to have heard.

"What's that?" said Tsara. To her now-practiced ear, Baxter sounded like a reporter. The fourth estate had lately provided her with endless hours of entertainment, although coverage had been surprisingly mixed. Some of the papers and bloggers had painted her as a hapless victim and suggested Mike had horns and a tail. Others, which David dubbed the "Knuckle-Dragger News Crews," blamed the whole mess on her: for not knowing about Cass's activities ("claiming not to know," said one story), for not locking her door, for not screaming loudly enough. Others were quixotic: one TV piece had all but excluded Tsara to focus on Mike, the tragic superdad on a doomed quest. They didn't actually call his son Tiny Tim, but it was close.

At the other end of the spectrum, the Women's Center had found in her a new cynosure. She was a survivor, and they were all about survivors. Her picture wallpapered their website, along with quotations and a link to The Full Story, As Told To. Similarly, *The Jewish Advocate* had published a three-part series called "A Woman of Valor," in which Mike had only a cameo appearance. It implied that Tsara had survived her ordeal by being acutely Jewish. The series ended with her apple crisp recipe and a picture of her and Abbie lighting Shabbat candles.

"'My heinous actions were justified' kind of thing," said David. "I think that's going to be a hard sell for the jury."

"He did what he did to save his kid," said Baxter. "And he wants a trial so he can tell the truth to America."

"He could have saved his kid by calling the Staties or the Feds, the way my brother-in-law did," said David. "And if he's so hell-bent on telling the truth, he can plea bargain and make a statement at his sentencing, which wouldn't involve dragging my wife and family back through this nightmare he dreamed up for us."

Parry. Thrust. Tsara loved it when David went into attack mode.

"You must know the jury is going to love him," said Baxter. "He's an American hero. He's literally battled terrorists on their own soil. He's *literally* chased the devil to the gates of Hell and stared him in the eye."

"Actually, that's a metaphor," said Tsara.

"And all to save his kid," went on Baxter. "It doesn't get any more basic than family, David. This is a father who'll risk everything for a return to our traditional values. I have to tell you, some people really don't understand why you want to attack his greatness. The man is a champion."

"He's a whacko who kidnapped my wife and shot two cops. If he cares so much about his son, why is he risking a trial on capital charges?"

In the silence that followed, the phone emitted a faint click.

"John," said David, and there was steel in his voice, "are you *recording* this?"

"Yes."

"Why?"

"Because I represent the Stamp Act, David."

"And that would be?"

"I'm surprised you haven't heard of us. We're the new voice of reason in American politics. We believe that small government and a return to traditional values are the only way to restore the nation's moral and fiscal health. See, this is an exceptional nation and it's organized around principles of freedom and responsibility. So the only real question is, how long can we continue to be exceptional when, no offense, people like you stand in the way of—"

David smashed the receiver back into the phone. His back was to Tsara.

"Okay," he said in a strangled voice, "just tell me. Did you see that coming?"

"About halfway through," she said.

"When?"

"Telling the truth to America was a dead giveaway." She put a bag of grapes in the fridge and closed the door. "Don't feel too bad. One guy yesterday called me a sugar-coated Satan Twinkie."

"Oy," said David.

"Vey," she agreed. "Do you think your buddy John knows the Stamp Act was British? And that the Colonists didn't, y'know, *like* it?"

David shuddered and shook his head. "I think he's full of—" They both glanced reflexively in the direction of the playroom; David lowered his voice. "—fecal matter. I think this trial is a farce, during the course of which I think the DA will shred Westbrook and feed him to the jury on crackers. I think he's guilty as goddamn, and the only things he has going for him are outsized balls and a smart lawyer."

"Tsk, tsk, Mr. Used To Be a Smart Lawyer Yourself."

"Why do you think I stopped? I got tired of being smart at someone else's expense."

Tsara gazed at him admiringly. "How did I get so lucky with you?"

"*You* lucky with *me*?" David sighed in disbelief. "Sometimes I think you're just simple in the head."

"You dummy." Tsara stuffed the canvas shopping bags together and put her apron on. "Want to put a DVD in? It's Abbie's turn to choose." The kids were allowed to watch TV while the designated parent made dinner. Tonight it was her turn to chop and sauté while David suffered through twenty minutes of talking trains with ethical conundrums.

While her husband and kids settled themselves on the squooshy red sofa in front of the television, Tsara got out the cutting board and put a slippery pile of chicken thighs on a plate next to it. She picked up the first one and cut through it with the carving knife.

And then it happened. A rush of terror. She was about to die. Tsara dropped the knife and gave a choked cry.

Instantly David was at her side. "What?" But she could only stare at him, eyes wide and unblinking. He looked from her to the cutting board and back again. "Did you cut yourself?" He picked up her hands, but they were unharmed. She shook her head, still not speaking.

"Come on." David led her gently to the sofa. The kids were still glued to the screen, oblivious. Tsara made her knees bend and sat stiffly down. She yanked at the apron, and David pulled it off for her as she leaned back, staring at the ceiling. "Breathe," he said, and she breathed.

"Sorry." She rubbed her hand against her forehead before she remembered it was sticky with chicken juice. "Ugh."

"I'll get you a damp cloth. What happened? "

"I don't know." She licked her dry lips. The panic was ebbing. "I felt like a truck was about to hit me."

"Are you going to be okay?"

"I think so."

David folded the apron over his arm. "Why don't you stay here with the kids? I'll make dinner."

"I can do it."

"Of course you can. But why don't you let me make it tonight?" David picked up the remote and hit pause.

"Hey! No fair!" yelled Josh.

"Whoa, whoa," David admonished. "Listen to me for a minute. Mommy is not feeling well, so she needs some hugs and kisses, yes?" Tsara nodded. "And the best behavior from both of you for the rest of the night. Got it?"

The kids got it. And while Abbie covered Tsara's cheek and nose with her special, petal-soft kisses and Josh asked David when he could be naughty again, Tsara hugged her children loosely and grappled with the fact that she, the most multi of taskers, was suddenly unable to chop a chicken thigh, for God's sake.

After the kids were in bed Tsara and David cleaned up the kitchen.

"Has that ever happened before?" asked David.

"Never."

"I was thinking you probably want to tell the shrink about it."

"No kidding," she snapped. "What, did you think that was the kind of thing I might neglect to mention?"

270

David didn't answer. He dropped the utensils into the silverware rack in the dishwasher, pointy ends up, the way he liked it.

"Sorry," she said presently.

"'Sokay."

Tsara set the kids' plates in the dish drain. "You know what I was thinking?" she continued as she wiped her hands on a towel.

"What?"

"I was thinking Thanatos would be a great name for a rock band."

"I guess it would at that," he agreed. And they finished the rest of the cleanup in silence.

"Want me to make dinner for a few days?" he asked as they walked into the living room.

She hesitated. "Probably smart for a while anyway."

So David took over dinner, and the kids reveled in the parade of chicken nuggets, hot dogs, and mac 'n' cheese until Tsara took over again out of fear they would develop scurvy.

Cooking again made her feel better, even if sometimes it was all she could manage. Because as the weeks went by her reality had taken to shifting, sometimes so sharply she gasped.

Good days were almost normal. But on bad days she was paralyzed in secret darkness, bound so tightly she could barely breathe.

"Panic attacks," said the shrink. "It's a stress response."

"Well, what good does it do me to panic *now?*" said Tsara. It was mid-November, a good month and a half after the abduction, and by her count she was supposed to be getting better, not worse.

The shrink's office was in a yellow and coral Victorian not far from Tsara's house. The room was an artful meld of homey and professional designed to put visitors at ease. It was carpeted in dark green, and potted plants graced the bookshelves and windowsills. The books were mostly psychiatry journals, but the doctor also had *Water for Elephants* and *The Night Circus*. Framed diplomas on the wall explained that Irena Zaslavsky had been to Yale twice and now had lots of initials after her name. There was a flat couch with a pillow on one end, presumably in case anyone wanted to go full Freud. Tsara had taken an armchair. It faced another one in which Irena sat with her legs tucked under her. She wore her hair in a strawberry blonde bob, and a navy cashmere sweater made her blue eyes very bright.

"Did you experience anything like this after your mother died?" asked Irena.

Tsara sighed. "No ... I just stopped eating and I couldn't think. I didn't notice I was losing weight till my dad showed me the bones in my arms were poking out. He made me drink frappes for a few weeks. And I used to—shake all over. They said it was shock. And my grades went in the crapper."

"But no panic attacks?"

"Not like this, anyway."

"What about your brother? He was younger than you."

"Three years. He got into a lot of trouble in middle school."

"What kind of trouble?"

"He was really mad for a long time," said Tsara. "You can't imagine—and there's nowhere to put it. So he'd yell at his teachers and a couple of times he broke stuff."

"Do you know if he experienced anything like what you're going through now?"

"I can ask him. Why?"

"Just let me know if it happens again," said Irena. With a name like hers Tsara had half expected her to talk like a villain in a Bullwinkle cartoon, but Dr. Zaslavsky spoke with the most ordinary of American accents.

"Will it?"

"It might."

"Is it likely to?"

"Everyone's different."

This was part of how you could tell she was a shrink. She had special training in not actually saying anything.

"Well, what's typical?" said Tsara.

Irena smiled, knowing she was trapped. "It might happen again; it might not. Either way let me know."

"And then what?"

"And then we can address it." She glanced at the clock on the wall behind Tsara. "Well, our time is up. Can you come again next week?"

"Sure." Tsara stood up. "Do I have homework?"

"Write down panic attacks," said Irena. "See if there's any pattern to them, or if you can isolate what triggers them. It can be any number of things after an experience like yours, and the more we know about it the better." She smiled and held open the door.

"The other family's gone," said Traveler. They were back in the prison library and his mouth was a tight line.

Mike blinked at him. "Gone?"

"Disappeared. Took the kids and the car and all their cash and left in the middle of the night. Didn't tell anyone where they were going, but I don't think they're coming back." He shook his head in a sharp movement. "They were scared, I guess."

"Of what?" said Mike. "Thornlocke?"

"Partly."

"He's in jail."

"Yeah, well, they're also scared because they're illegal immigrants involved with illegal activities regarding an illegal loan. The police snatched their kids and suddenly they're talking to the Feds about all kinds of shit they'd rather not discuss. They come from a country where people who talk to government agents usually disappear. Or maybe they were afraid they'd be deported or sent to Guantanamo. Hell, I don't know. But they're gone."

Mike ran his hands through his hair. "Is anyone looking for them?"

"Yes."

There was silence. *Damn them*, thought Mike. Aloud he said, "How bad is this?"

Traveler drummed his fingers briefly on the tabletop. "The Feds interviewed them at the hospital, so we have their report. But Thornlocke says he didn't know the kids were there and that's why he didn't respond to the notes you sent. He says he figures the Stones were after Aiden to antagonize you, and the other kids were collateral damage."

"And Jordan and Arnold just happened to stash everyone at his place."

"He says they probably did it so they could keep an eye on them. They were going to be on the estate for the party that night anyway."

Mike's chest tightened. "He told the Feds he was going to let the kids go Sunday."

"He says they misunderstood him, and what he really said was that he would have *discovered* the kids in the wine cellar Sunday evening anyway because he always got a fresh bottle for dinner at the end of the weekend."

"And he would have let them go then," said Mike dully. "Cuz he's such a good guy."

"Right."

"Shit," said Mike. "How bad is this?"

Traveler's lips twisted into a distant cousin of a smile. "Ready for the good news-bad news? The other family weren't going to be great witnesses anyway."

"What are you talking about?"

"They didn't know if Thornlocke was behind it."

"What the f—" Mike swallowed hard. "They were the ones who *told* me about it. I went to their place to pick up Aiden and they said—"

"They said Jordan and Arnold grabbed their kids and drove away with them. They told the FBI and their lawyer that they *assumed* it had to do with the non-repayment of the loan, but they were scared and it all happened really fast and there was a lot of shouting and their English isn't so good. So they couldn't swear to it."

"I went to Thornlocke—"

"He says you didn't."

"Jim knows about it," said Mike desperately.

"Jim knows what you told him."

Mike clenched his fists under the table. "Shit. Shit."

"We've got character witnesses, Mike," said Traveler. "We have people who will say great things about you and how you saved their asses in Iraq and Afghanistan. We have our shrink who'll say you're not

275

delusional. But as for someone to back you up for what was going on that weekend—damn."

There was a long pause, and presently Mike lifted his eyes. "So it's just her. That's what you're saying."

Traveler nodded. "Yeah. And you better pray she remembers the Stone brothers the way you do and isn't inclined toward perjury, because right now that woman's your best friend."

David was teaching when the call came in. The phone was on vibrate and he glanced down, prepared to ignore it, but the number was Tsara's.

"Summarize the key points of this case and show how lawyers for both sides used the same amendment to support their arguments," he said, thinking fast. "See how much you can come up with in five minutes." He walked out of the classroom, grateful this was a senior elective and thus full of students he could trust on their own for a few minutes.

The phone had stopped ringing. He hit Recents, and in a moment his wife's voice sounded in his ear.

"What's wrong?" he asked. Something had to be wrong. She knew he was teaching.

She sounded distant and preternaturally calm. "I don't think I should be driving right now."

"Where are you?"

"Driving."

"Can you pull over?"

"I did."

"Okay. So you're not driving."

"I was, but I pulled over."

"Are you all right?"

"No."

"What's wrong, and do you need me to come get you?"

He heard her draw a slow breath. "Sorry, babe. I panicked. I think I can make it home now."

"Sweetie." David's heart was speeding up. "Can you tell me what happened?"

"Um ... not really."

David ground his teeth. Tsara was never at a loss for words. "Why did you call me?"

"Don't be mad at me."

"I'm not mad at you. I can come get you."

Silence. "Just for a second ... everything seemed all wrong and unreal. Like I was driving through a watercolor. So I freaked out and pulled over." Her voice got stronger. "But it's better now. I'll just go straight home. It's okay. I'm sorry I bothered you."

"Are you sure?"

"I'm sure. I'll see you at home."

David pulled the phone away from his ear to check the time. "Look. This is my last class of the day. I'll skip the staff meeting and come home early."

"You don't have to."

"I'm going to. I'll see you in about forty-five minutes."

Silence. "Okay, babe," she said finally. "That's probably a good idea."

"See you soon, sweetie."

"Bye."

David hung up and walked back into the classroom. "So how's our good friend the First Amendment holding up?" he asked. A dozen hands shot into the air, and David spent the rest of the period inciting riot among proponents of passionately held positions.

When he got home Tsara was waiting for him. She looked absolutely normal, except maybe a little embarrassed. She opened her mouth to speak, but he cut her off.

"Don't," he said. "I hate staff meetings anyway." And they both smiled.

But when she woke up that night in a cold sweat and couldn't say why, he made a decision.

"I'm going to get medical leave for the rest of the semester," he said.

"Oh, no, don't do that." Tsara was genuinely horrified.

David was glad the lights were out. Darkness made honesty easier. "Honey. You are the world's most competent person. But right now I think you need to look on this like … like you got an infection."

"But I didn't get an infection. I got a kidnapped."

"And it's making you a little bit ill." She was silent. He hoped this wasn't humiliating for her. "Look. You're doing everything right, right? You're seeing the shrink and doing the group thing and everything else everyone's said you should do, right?"

"Right," she said reluctantly.

"And everyone says there's a way through this, right?" He didn't wait for her to answer. "Look. If you had some disease that kept you bedridden I'd take leave for a few weeks and I bet you wouldn't think twice about it and neither would anyone else. So why not take the same approach here? I bet the faster we can nail this thing, and the earlier on, the better you'll be."

She sighed in the darkness. "So you think … we should treat it sort of like a project?"

"Exactly."

"Okay." She turned over, pulling away. "I guess it beats treating it like I'm an emotional cripple."

"You're not—"

"Whatever."

David was silent. He wondered if he had shamed her. But damnit, this really was the best thing to do. Probably.

Presently she slid close to him. "Davey?"

"What?"

"Thanks."

He put his arm around her and they fell asleep.

— ✳ —

The next day Tsara came home from grocery shopping and found David in the living room reading the previous week's *Parade* magazine. She glanced at the clock. Well before the end of the school day.

"So I take it they said yes," she said, putting down the shopping bags and shrugging off her jacket.

"Not at first."

279

"What changed their minds?"

"His," said David. "I was dumb enough to go to Jeffrey first, as a courtesy. He said no."

Jeffrey was the principal. "What happened?"

"He came around when I explained I was willing to advocate parthenogenesis."

Tsara stopped, one arm still in the sleeve of the jacket. "You told him to go fuck himself?"

"Of course not. That would be rude."

"David—"

"I said I had a health situation at home which he was damn well aware of since everyone knows or thinks they know what happened to you, and that I needed to cut down on my hours for the sake of my family. Then we had a little chat with HR. By the time I left they had shoved him into a corner and were reading him the fine print of the Family Medical Leave Act while explaining that they would prefer not to be sued off the face of the planet." He picked up the magazine, which he had laid down on his lap to talk to her. "Told him I'd go part-time for the rest of the semester and we can revisit the situation come January."

"So what's part-time?"

"Just the law class. They don't have anyone else who can do it, and it's my fave anyway."

Tsara leaned forward and hugged him, the jacket still on her arm. "You're my superhero." She glanced at the grocery bags. "Oh, God— ice cream's melting." She grabbed them and hurried into the kitchen.

So David took over. He got the kids up in the morning and packed their lunches and drove them to school so Tsara could sleep in whenever she had had a rough night. He picked them up from school and took them to the playground with all the cool climbing structures so they would be flop-tired by the time they got home for dinner. Sometimes this actually worked. He signed them up for gymnastics and swimming and tap dance at the JCC so they could continue to be tired when the weather got too nasty for reliable outdoor fun. And he made dinner for them whenever Tsara's therapy sessions conflicted with the evening meal.

While the kids were at school Tsara hit the gym. She had always tried to go once a week; now she made it twice or three times. She left damp fingerprints on the free weights and sweat angels on the mats. Sometimes she walked out of the gym drippy but elated. Other times she drooped like a comma. But always she was better.

She started working with trainers. The first ones were too nice to her so she asked for the former Navy Seal with muscles on his tattoos. He called her Moose and had a way of making her laugh right before she lifted more than she had thought she could. It helped chase the demons away. "I exorcise while I exercise," she told David.

One dark morning after a night hacked with nightmares she couldn't do it. "I'm too tired," she almost whined.

"So don't," said David.

"But—"

"What are you, Linda Hamilton from *Terminator II?* If you feel like you need exercise, why not walk the dog? He'd like that."

Falstaff's ears perked up and his mouth dropped open. He clearly thought this was a sterling idea. So Tsara took him to a dog park with a pond full of Labradors, and let him run. She took him often after that. Sometimes Adara joined them with her own dog, an exuberant boxer named Barbara. (Adara tended to vote Democratic.) The two women would walk in the woods behind the pond and talk about their kids and sushi and Jewish philosophy and the latest offering from Pixar while the dogs bounded ahead of them. Then usually Adara went to work and Tsara ran errands or went to therapy.

But no matter what else was going on, Tsara always put the kids to bed. She gave them their baths, marveling at the perfection of their soapy bodies; she brushed their teeth and wiped the toothpaste off their lips, combed their hair, and shoved sometimes-uncooperative feet into footie pajamas. She dealt with the meltdown when it turned out that Abbie's favorite towel, the one with the rabbit ears, was in the wash; and she found Froggers hiding in Josh's lunch box when no one else could.

And when everyone was warm and dry, they would cram themselves together on the sofa for story time. Those evenings when Tsara lost herself in Little Bear's gentle adventures or the cheerful grotesqueries of Dr. Seuss were the best part of any day. Her voice was accompanied by the syncopated slurps of her children sucking their thumbs, and the warmth of their little bodies shoved into her ribs was a sweetness so intense it was almost pain.

"I have great news," said Traveler. They were at their table in the prison library, and Mike had barely sat down. "Your cousin's dropped the plea bargain. He's not going to testify against you."

Mike looked startled. Then his face lit up with a smile. "That's great."

"It's more than great. A huge chunk of damaging evidence against you is off the table." He opened his briefcase and took out his files and a legal pad. Finally, a break in this goddamn case. "He's doing you a hell of a favor."

"He's a good guy."

"He'd have to be." Traveler took a pen out and put it on the pad before shutting his briefcase and putting it on the floor.

"What do you mean?"

Traveler clicked the pen. "That's his problem. Don't worry about it."

Mike frowned. "Why did Jim change his mind?"

"Well, I guess he finally figured out that if he went with a plea bargain he'd have to testify against you, so—"

"What happens to him now?" interrupted Mike.

"Oh, he's facing the same capital murder charges you are," said Traveler breezily.

"What?"

"That's the deal. He understands it. I met with his lawyer yesterday."

"But he didn't do it!"

"In the eyes of the law he did."

"Bullshit," said Mike. "He wasn't even there."

"He doesn't have to be."

"But—"

Traveler put down the pen. "Mike. Listen to me. This is law school 101, so pay attention. Felony murder rule says if you are part of a felony which leads to a murder, you are equally culpable of the murder whether or not you actually committed it."

Mike's eyes widened with horror. "He could die?"

"You could die," said Traveler. "Remember?"

Mike did not answer, and after a moment Traveler went on. He was trying to be patient without sounding like he was trying to be patient. "Jim has a lawyer and she's very good. He understands the risks, and nobody pressured him into anything."

"Did he say he was doing it for me?"

"I can't answer that."

"Look, if he— "

"Mike. Right now my job is saving your butt, and even though this is all good news it means we have a lot of work to do in terms of restructuring our strategy. So let's focus, okay?"

"Okay," said Mike. "I'll focus." He yanked the legal pad over to his side of the table, picked up the pen, and began to scribble.

"Make yourself at home, Mike," said Traveler. "I think it's great you feel so comfortable that you can take my stuff without asking."

Mike tore off the piece of paper and folded it over. He shoved the pad and pen back to Traveler and handed him the sheet. "Can you get this to Jim?"

Traveler did not take the paper. "You're not going off on me again, are you?"

"Can you?"

"You're not supposed to communicate with him."

"I'm not. You are."

"No, I'm not."

Mike half-stood and ran his hand through his hair. "You said he could die."

"So could you. And you have a kid."

284

"But—"

"Mike, let Jim worry about Jim. Believe me, you've got enough on your own plate. And mine."

"But he's guilty."

"So are you."

Mike sat and stared at Traveler in desperation. "He's not going to swing for me. You can't let that happen. It's not right."

Traveler counted to five in his head. Then he added another three because five wasn't enough. He pointed to a spot on the table. "Mike. You see that?"

"Uh huh."

"Know what it is?"

Mike shook his head.

"That," said Traveler, "is where I want to bang my head every time you start telling me what's right."

Mike slid the note across the table to his lawyer. When he let go of it his hand shook.

"Please," he whispered. "Please."

— ✳ —

That afternoon Jim's lawyer paid an unexpected visit to him and handed him a folded piece of yellow legal paper.

Jim dont do it
Ill find some way out of this mess
My life is not worth your life to me

Mike

Hans drove steadily, keeping up with the stream of cars around him. No hurry—he was just another tourist heading to the border crossing at Stanstead. He'd selected it carefully. Comins Mills was too small. He might be one of three cars to go over that day. The guard might be bored and chatty. It wasn't worth the risk. By contrast, the one at Lewiston was too busy; there was usually a line, often a long one, and sitting in a traffic jam waiting for someone to recognize him did not suit his purposes. So he'd chosen Stanstead, hoping it was the sort of medium-sized crossing that would combine anonymity with ease of— for lack of a better term—escape.

Hans had plenty of experience with border crossings. At one time he'd been an expert. In the fifties the Bloc states had been hemorrhaging refugees, and anyone with a car and the right attitude could make a fortune. The roads, the forests, the porous segments of state lines— Hans had known them by heart.

A young woman drifted to mind. Probably in her mid-twenties and still beautiful, though war and hunger had aged her. She had walked to the Austrian border from Budapest with only the clothes she wore and a homemade sack full of bread. When Hans asked for payment, she grinned like a rat and broke open one of the loaves. It held a roll of American dollars—magic money in that economy. She was a millionaire with bloody feet. Hans had laughed out loud. He drove her all the way to Salzburg, where she had people. The original agreement was only as far as Graz, but her audacity and uncombed loveliness had captured him. They sped past ruined houses and bomb craters with the car top down and the wind in their hair, because Hans knew bombast was the best camouflage.

He wondered what had become of her.

Hans thought about Castle. He had meant what he'd said about sticking by him. He really had. But then those wretched agents had come around, asking all those questions—often the same one phrased slightly different ways, he noticed. It was unnerving.

It was frightening.

They had come to his house in Connecticut one day when the autumn sun streamed through the big windows that looked out over the swimming pool. "How long have you known Mr. Thornlocke?" the one named Spaar had asked.

"Decades," replied Hans. "We have been friends and business partners for many years. I have always known him to be scrupulously honest."

Spaar glanced at her notes. "We're getting a very mixed picture of him. Not everyone agrees with you."

"Who would disagree?" asked Hans indignantly.

The agent named Galen spoke up. "A number of people in Libertyville felt otherwise."

Hans tensed the corners of his mouth. "Libertyville is an economically polarized community. The Thornlockes are quite wealthy, and I'm not surprised there's a certain amount of jealousy from some less fortunate quarters."

"What makes you think it comes from less fortunate quarters?" asked Galen.

"Does it?"

Spaar stepped in. "Have you ever known Mr. Thornlocke to engage in illegal activities?"

Hans smiled, partly because he knew he'd been right, which was why Galen couldn't answer. "He is incapable of anything dishonorable."

"Did you know he was extending illegal loans to families in Libertyville?"

"Certainly not."

"He says you did," said Galen.

A staccato burst of German oaths detonated in Hans's mind. He and Castle really needed to get their stories straight. But there hadn't been time ....

"He told me about it after he was arrested," he said. "If he mentioned it to me before, I forgot. Senior moment, you know." He smiled sadly.

Spaar and Galen so carefully avoided looking at each other that he knew they didn't believe him.

"Did you know anything about the children being kept in Mr. Thornlocke's wine cellar?" said Galen.

"I was as shocked as anyone else when they were discovered." Hans hoped they noticed all the pictures of him and his wife and kids on the walls and shelves of his living room. He was a nice family man. As was Castle.

"Are you sure?"

"Of course."

"The reason I ask is that Mr. Westbrook says you were aware they were there," said Galen.

"Who?"

"Michael Westbrook. The man who—"

"Oh, him. Really now." Hans shook his head in disbelief. "Why would you take his word on anything having to do with that weekend?"

"Because we don't see how implicating you helps his cause," said Spaar. "He's not saying he didn't abduct Mrs. Adelman; he's saying you knew the kids were being kept on the property."

"I most certainly didn't."

"When did you first realize they were?"

"When everyone else did. My understanding is this was primarily a matter between the local police and Westbrook."

"What makes you say that?" asked Spaar.

"Castle suggested it, and it makes the most sense to me. Occam's razor, you know."

"When did Mr. Thornlocke suggest that to you?" asked Galen.

"I don't recall precisely. Why?"

"Was it before or after Mrs. Adelman's abduction?"

"I'm not really ...."

"When did you discuss this with him?" said Spaar.

"There was so much confusion—I couldn't say exactly."

"Did you talk to him about it more than once?"

"I may have."

"When was the second time?"

And so it had gone on. Finally Hans pleaded fatigue and saw them to the door. They weren't smiling when they left.

Now he leaned out the car window and dropped a handful of coins into the toll basket. He had been careful to pay in cash at every one of these, even when the long lines made his fingers clench the steering wheel. But he didn't dare use EZ-Pass. There was no point in announcing his location via a series of credit card hits along the highway. A roll of quarters purchased his invisibility at what struck him as a bargain price.

The rental car had been a bit more of a challenge. At first he had thought he could simply pay with a check. Lovely things, checks. They took several days to clear. But it turned out that these days rental companies required a credit card, which Hans thought showed a disturbing lack of faith on their part. It wasn't as though he planned to steal the thing, after all.

His wife had surprised him. "My car's in the shop," she said when he got home.

"Why?"

"Funny noise when I accelerate. I had to get a loaner." She put a set of keys in his hand and folded his fingers over them. "Don't tell me where you're going," she said softly. "But call me when you get there."

Hans stared at the highway. Once he was safely on a plane—or better yet, on the ground in Europe—she could join him with the boys. In four weeks it would be Christmas. Who wouldn't want to spend Christmas in Austria? The Christmas market in Vienna, those elegant lamps bedecking Graben, the food, the music! No one did Yuletide better. That was what they would say if anyone asked.

Hans hadn't bothered to get a ticket for himself in the United States. He didn't want to inconvenience Spaar and Galen like that— have them galloping off to the airport to intercept him when it really wasn't necessary. And explaining everything to them would be frightfully awkward. So he had tried to put himself in their place. He imagined they would call the State Department, get the name on his

American passport, and put him on the No-Fly List. If that were indeed the case, Hans reasoned, he could spare everyone a lot of trouble by taking a quick trip up to Canada. Happily, the weather was just right for driving.

The border crossing was in sight. Hans was pleased to see the traffic flowing past the guards at a slow but steady rate. Perfect camouflage. He pulled up to a booth and handed over his passport. The guard opened it and smiled. "That's kind of a mouthful, isn't it?"

Hans smiled back in agreement. The guard laid the open passport on his desk, stamp in hand.

"Business or pleasure?"

"Pleasure."

"How long do you intend to stay?"

"A few days." Actually, it was only a few hours—the airport in Montreal wasn't that far.

The guard stamped the Austrian passport and handed it back. "Enjoy your stay."

"Thank you." And Karl Friedrich Johannes ("Hans") Freihoffer drove into Canada, adhering strictly to the speed limit. Caution was the word of the day.

Hans wasn't a young man any more. He wasn't a buccaneer in a red convertible.

Mass General Hospital wasn't the most convenient place to get to, especially at rush hour; but sometimes, Tsara reasoned, you had to do inconvenient things and go to inconvenient places, especially if some of the people there can help you. So she'd parked the car at Alewife and was taking the Red Line in and remembering that she used to do this a lot, back in grad school.

Irena hadn't insisted—shrinks never did—but she was pretty clear in her recommendation. "How often does this happen?" she had asked.

Tsara thought. They had been seeing each other for several weeks now, and she felt comfortable in the green, book-lined room. "The dreams are a couple times a week, I guess. Never two nights in a row."

"Is a couple two?"

"Two or three."

"Okay. And the panic attacks?"

"They're a lot more random."

"But if you had to guess."

"Once—twice a week, maybe. Maybe three. Sometimes one. Or none." She smiled at how not useful this must sound. "I haven't been keeping track."

"Right now I'm more interested in frequency."

"In between I'm fine," said Tsara.

This was true. On an ordinary day preceded by an ordinary night she was her usual self—getting the kids dressed and brushed, putting together lunches with an emphasis on organic and whole-grain, getting everyone out the door in time, keeping up with friends and paying bills on time. The beds were made and Falstaff's bowl was clean and life felt almost as good as it had before she'd decided to visit her uncle.

"Two or three nights a week is a lot of sleep to miss," said Irena. "I think we need to address this medically."

"Meaning … ?"

"With medication."

"I'm not taking sleeping pills," said Tsara. The idea of being doped up in case of an emergency was not something she was willing to contemplate.

"I was thinking of anxiety medication."

"But I'm already anxious."

Irena smiled. "Anti-anxiety. I'm going to send you to a colleague at Mass General. He's very good, and I'd feel better having you visit a specialist instead of just having your PCP prescribe whatever's popular right now."

Tsara shifted in her seat. "What do they do? I mean the meds."

"He can explain it to you better than I can." Irena reached behind herself for a small, grey pad and scribbled on it. She ripped off the top sheet and handed it to Tsara.

Tsara took the piece of stationery with the new doctor's name on it. She hesitated. "Look—I'm not opposed to this, but I wonder how important it is to go on medication. I feel like the therapy is really helping."

"We'll continue to meet," said Irena. "But if you don't sleep, and I mean regularly, there's no way you can climb out of this hole."

The heat of the crowded bodies on the T made Tsara sleepy, and she leaned against the pole with her eyes shut, head cushioned on her arm so in case they stopped abruptly she wouldn't arrive at the doctor's office with a black eye. The night before had been one of the grim ones. Her scant sleep had been alive with terrors, and when—mercifully—she had woken up, there was no getting back to anything like the silken oblivion she craved. She spent the rest of the night wide-eyed, listening to the drumming of her heart until the windows turned grey.

She thought about stopping in at the Christina Abrams Cancer Center when she got to Mass General. The staff might remember her from when she was a teenager cutting the ribbon on opening day with her father and Court at her side. Then again, they might not. She hadn't been there in years, even though she was religious about sending a donation every year on her mom's birthday.

Commuters held Starbuck's cups and Kindles and Nooks, and others turned the pages of their magazines. Students read textbooks and fat novels for Victorian Lit classes. And Tsara slept a little, just from the neck up, as the train lurched along like a drunken grizzly.

District Attorney Lawson pressed the intercom on his desk. "Jeanine," he said, "what's my afternoon look like?"

"You have a meeting in ten minutes. After that you're clear."

Lawson's intercom looked like an old Ma Bell rotary phone, but the dial had buttons and a speaker in the center. It was bright red and very quasi-retro. His wife had given it to him after watching the first four seasons of *Mad Men* in a back-to-back DVD marathon. He pressed the button again. "Can you push the meeting? I want to mull."

"Sure thing."

"And cancel my three-martini lunches," he said. "All of them."

Jeanine giggled. She knew he didn't drink.

Lawson turned off the intercom and leaned back in his chair. It was December, two months since Libertyville's crime wave, and Montrose's plea bargain was already in the works. His lawyer had just left, and Lawson needed a few minutes to decompress.

The lawyer looked about twelve and wore a curly blonde ponytail pulled Gidget-high on her head. All of her sentences? Ended with questions? As she burbled through her client's conditions. No, he wouldn't cop to the two homicides; felony murder rule notwithstanding, he had, she pointed out, been oh her gosh *miles* away at the time of these alleged acts. Now, the other charges, those were up for discussion.

Discuss they did. At the end of the meeting, Lawson was dazed to find that the State of New Hampshire had agreed that Jim would plead guilty only to the kidnapping. All other charges would be dropped, and

Jim would cooperate with the prosecution in all details pertaining to nailing Mike's hide to the wall. On behalf of her client, Gidget accepted twelve years, out in eight. It wasn't nothing, but it was a long way from the death penalty.

Gidget was a hell of a horse trader.

Tsara squeezed off the childproof cap and peered inside the amber bottle. Miniscule white pills rolled against each other as she tilted it. She poured a few into her hand. They were tiny, maybe half a millimeter across. Stack five of them together and you'd have a grain of rice. She looked at the label. How many were there?

Ninety, it assured her. *Two refills.*

Good God, how anxious did they think she was?

David came into the living room. "Meds?"

She poured them back into the bottle and screwed the top on. "Yeah."

"Taken any yet?"

"I just got them." She handed him the pillowcase-sized information sheet that had come with them. "You can read up if you want." David liked to know about side effects; Tsara didn't. They had long ago decided he would do the research so if one of them, say, broke out in purple pustules then he at least would know why.

He took the sheet and folded it up. "Looked them up when you called me. As long as you don't take them when you're drunk, obese, or pregnant, you're probably okay."

"It says I shouldn't drive till I know how they affect me."

"Why not take one now? You don't have to drive for a few hours, so if it puts you in a coma—"

"Does it do that?"

"No. But if it does, I can pick up the kids."

"Your reasoning is sound," she said gravely, and opened the bottle again.

Half an hour later David walked back into the living room, having finished reading the information sheet. Tsara was flopped back against the cushions on the sofa, eyes closed.

"You awake?"

Tsara sighed deeply and opened her eyes. A mischievous smile played on her lips. "These things are *great.*"

"Not so anxious?"

"Know what I feel like doing?" she said dreamily.

"What?"

"Issuing presidential pardons."

David sat down next to her. "Are you gonna let Manson out? Because I gotta tell you, guys with swastika tattoos make me antsy."

"I was thinking more like Thanksgiving turkeys and stuff." She frowned. "What time is it?"

David glanced at the clock on the DVD player. "Time for *me* to get the kids," he said. "Why don't you take a nap?"

"Okey-dokey," she said brightly, and burrowed into the cushions.

One day in early winter when the sky looked like flannel and the air was sharp with cold, Tsara and her rabbi walked through the woods with their dogs while Adara did her best to argue that Yoda was a short, Jewish sage.

"Exhibit A," said Adara as Barbara the Boxer stopped to whuffle at a small hole under a root. "What does Yoda say about his height?"

"'Size matters not. Look at me. Judge me by my size, do you?'" Tsara shuddered. "Pity me."

"Never. Now, listen to this: 'Do not look at the container, rather what is inside of it.'" She spoke in her best Frank Oz.

"That's not in the movie."

"That's right."

"So you're quoting …."

"*Pirkei Avot*," said Adara in triumph. "Ethics of the Fathers."

"Gaak." Tsara shook her head. "Next you'll be telling me what *yeshiva* he attended."

"Beit Hillel," replied Adara without hesitation. "Nurtured talent among all the people, rich or poor, learned or not."

Tsara grinned. "Could explain the complexion."

"What do you mean?"

"That library tan. I've seen *yeshiva* boys looking not dissimilar."

Falstaff gave a booming bark. Barbara flicked her head up from the ground, scattering pine needles and clumplets of dirt as she and the bigger dog took after a squirrel. It twitched up a tree with yards to spare before the dogs gathered at its base, barking wildly. The squirrel clung to a branch well out of their range, shrieking threats and imprecations as its tail jerked in rage.

"A hound's reach should exceed its grasp," said Adara.

"Or what's a squirrel for?" agreed Tsara. They stood in silence as the dogs made useless attempts to down their prey.

"Can you look after Falstaff next month?" said Tsara.

"For how long?"

"Few days."

"I expect so. Going out of town?"

"The trial starts in January," said Tsara. "We're staying overnight."

"What about the kids?"

"Grandma's."

"She won't take the dog?"

"Allergic. She loves him—it's the tragedy of her life."

"That would be tragic," said Adara. "How's he pleading?"

Tsara almost laughed. "For a second I thought you meant Falstaff. Um—he's pleading not guilty."

"To what?"

"To everything. B and E, murder, kidnapping, assault. The whole ball of wax."

Adara took a sharp breath and decided that "You are shitting me" might not be considered a proper rabbinical response in some circles. "But he's guilty."

"Yes," said Tsara. "Yes, he is."

Adara looked at her friend. Tsara had lines around her mouth, and her shoulders were hunched. She clearly wasn't sleeping well—her eyes looked like two burnt holes in a blanket.

"Oh, and trespassing," said Tsara. "Don't forget the trespassing."

"I'll bet you're looking forward to seeing him squashed like a bug," said Adara. She would have done the squashing herself if she could.

"Not as much as you might think."

"Why not?"

"Because," said Tsara, "if killing those two guys was murder, then saving my life was a crime."

They watched the dogs circle the tree. Barbara stood on her hind legs with her forepaws on the trunk. Falstaff sat and scratched his ear with his hind foot, keeping his eye on the last place he had seen the squirrel.

"How long is the trial?" said Adara.

"Few weeks. But not every day."

"We'll be happy to take Falstaff," she said.

— ✳ —

Tsara dropped the dog off at home before driving to therapy. When she got back, the kids were upstairs in their rooms, howling. Falstaff lay on the floor and David stood in the front hall and sorted the day's mail onto a side table with grim savagery.

"Wow," said Tsara. "What happened?"

David did not look up. "I grilled the asparagus instead of steaming it," he said through clenched teeth.

"Uh-oh."

"Abbie liked it just fine," said David. "She snargled it down and asked for more. Josh acted like I'd made him put a live scorpion in his mouth."

Josh was their fussy eater. "And then?"

"I told him to eat three pieces. Then I went into the kitchen to get their milk and he *screamed*—I mean, my God, I thought he put a fork in his eye. So I come tearing out and I'm like, 'What? What?' and he screams, 'Falstaff is licking my pants!'"

Tsara coughed violently. "Oh, Falstaff," she said with reproach.

Falstaff studied the far wall, but the tip of his tail twitched in a nervous giggle.

"So I yelled at him and told him not to do that any more. Then Abbie goes, 'Stop it! You're just mean!' At which point I'm *so* pissed I yell at them both and they start crying so I sent them to their rooms."

"And then?"

"And then you came home."

Tsara glanced up the stairs. "Think I'll have a little chat with them."

David tossed an envelope into the recycling pile. Tsara went upstairs. The crying stopped, started again, and dissolved into damp giggles. A few minutes later she reappeared.

"The kids are making an I'm Sorry Daddy card for you," she said. "Abbie is drawing the pictures."

David did not look up from the neat stacks of envelopes. Bills, To Do, and File Pile. "How do you do that?"

"Do what?"

"Just—walk in and make everything perfect."

"I don't," she said, thinking of all the times David had come home to find the kitchen looking like a Superfund site.

"They think you do," said David. "I'm busting my ass trying to stay on top of everything, and all I hear is, 'Mommy does it this way. Mommy does it better than you.'"

Tsara flinched. "Oh, honey." She shoved herself under his arm so it draped over her shoulder. "Would it help if we made love like crazed weasels?"

"It might," muttered David. He pulled a flyer out of the File Pile. "Women's Center. It's a self-defense course on multiple armed assailants."

"Now that," said Tsara solemnly, "would have been very useful a few weeks ago."

"Do you want to do it? It could be therapeutic."

She shook her head and pulled back to give herself a little room. "I'm not ready." She flipped open the flyer. "But this course on Japanese flower arranging looks *awesome*."

"So how are the meds working?" asked the psychopharmacologist. He seemed like a nice guy, all curly brown hair and glasses. His face was young and round. He looked like the head of the high school science club.

"Great," said Tsara. It was a few weeks after their initial consult, and she'd used the pills several times. "I can totally see why people get addicted to them." Nowadays when she woke up at four in the morning for no reason other than that her heart thought she had been running a marathon in her sleep, she could do something about it. Those little white disks packed a kick like a mule—but a benevolent mule, one with her best interests at heart. Within a few minutes of taking the dose she could feel a gentle warmth creep up her legs. After that she was always able to get back to sleep. This really beat lying in bed trying to reason with the monster pounding her chest. The monster didn't care about reason. The monster was fear itself, and she feared it.

From the window in this Spartan office she could see one corner of her mother's cancer center. That was a funny feeling, like maybe her mom wanted her to be here. Or that the window happened to face that way.

"Any questions?"

"Yeah. Am I going to get addicted to them?"

The doctor smiled. "To get dependent on this class of drugs you'd have to take increasing amounts daily over a long period of time, well in excess of what I would prescribe for you." He checked his notes. "And you say you've never been addicted to anything."

"Maybe Godiva. But I didn't have to go to rehab or anything."

"I see you're still seeing Dr. Zaslavsky, and the weekly group."

"I'm a tough nut to crack."

"How often are you taking the meds? And how much?"

"A few times a week. Only one a day."

He checked his notes again. "You can take up to three daily."

"No, I can't," she said firmly. "I'd be catatonic."

"Meaning what?"

"If I take one in the morning I need a nap that afternoon and I sleep like a rock that night. I can't imagine what three would do, never mind every day."

The doctor swiveled his chair toward her. "I'm thinking that upping the dose might help it work as a preventative. You've been taking them after the attacks, right?"

"Right. But like I said."

"After six hours it's out of your system," he said.

She pursed her lips. "Maybe it's out of *your* system."

He smiled again. "Of course, everyone metabolizes it differently." He closed the folder. "Well. It sounds like it's helping and you've found a level you're comfortable with, or at least a trade-off that works for you. So let's keep going as is. If you have any questions or concerns, give me a call and we'll set up an appointment."

"Thanks." She pulled her purse onto her shoulder and walked to the door, then turned and faced him. "I've never—I never thought I would be the kind of person who needs this kind of thing."

He shrugged. "You can always go back to being the kind of person who needs it and isn't taking it."

"No, thanks." She turned the knob. "Better living through chemistry," she said over her shoulder.

"Live long and prosper," he replied as the door shut.

Tsara chuckled. That was a pretty good comeback, especially for someone in his profession. Maybe lots of shrinks were wiseasses in their spare time. Or maybe this one was a shrink weirdo and none of the other shrinks would let him join in all their shrinky games.

She came out of the building and onto the sidewalk. On impulse she turned and walked briskly toward the Christina Abrams Cancer Center.

— ✳ —

"Don't tell me that's Tsarina Abrams!"

Tsara grinned and put out her hand. "Hi, Dr. Grace. It's Adelman now."

The old man in the white lab coat shook her hand vigorously. "And when did that happen?"

She blushed. "About ten years ago."

"So I'm off the hook for a wedding present. Splendid!"

Tsara looked around the foyer of the cancer center. Windows looked out over the sidewalk, spider plants on iron stands dotted the room, and Ansel Adams prints hung on the walls. "The place looks great."

"Thanks to you and your family," he said. "What brings you here?"

"I was in the neighborhood."

"Can I give you the quick tour? We have some really exciting plans in the works."

"Sure. I have time."

For the next twenty minutes she followed Dr. Grace through the center as he waved grandly at walls that would come down and rooms that didn't yet exist. "This is my favorite part," he said, opening a door to an empty space. "This is going to be the Children and Family Center. We'll have a gym, playroom, art therapy, and three guest rooms for overnight stays."

"That sounds fabulous."

"It's what your father always envisioned, you know—a place the whole family could come." He turned and looked at her, his face serious. "We can't cure everyone. But we do our best to make sure they're healed."

"That's a lovely goal."

"We couldn't do it without the Red Dress Brigade," said Dr. Grace. "With the check your uncle sent, we'll be able to break ground in the spring."

Tsara blinked. "My uncle?"

"Oh, didn't he tell you? It was back in the fall—October, I think. Just over a million dollars. And he sent a lovely note with it. Of course."

Tsara looked at Dr. Grace. He was such a thoroughly classy guy that it was impossible to tell if he hadn't heard about the maelstrom surrounding Castle, or just didn't want to make her unhappy.

"He didn't mention it," she said.

Somehow, despite everything, Castle had remembered to send the check.

"It's Court," hollered David.

Tsara was upstairs combing Abbie's wet hair. "Tell him I have acute stress disorder and I can't come to the phone right now."

There was a pause while David relayed the information. The comb wiggled in a tangle, and Abbie yelped and clutched Mrs. Pinkie. "Sorry, babe," whispered Tsara.

"I hate it when you comb my hair," grumbled Abbie.

"You'd hate it worse if I didn't."

Abbie spoke with the careful enunciation of a three-year-old. "I am looking forward to the day when no one will comb my hair."

David called up the stairs. "He wants to know if it's causal and if not why aren't you talking to him?"

Tsara put the comb in its drawer and fluffed Abbie's hair with her fingertips. "Tell him both statements are true but there is no causality and I'll give him a ring when the kids are in bed."

"I'll read to them if you want."

"No, I'm good."

Twenty minutes later when both children were tucked in, David found Tsara sitting at the dining room table sniffling into a tissue with the lights off.

"What is it?" he said in alarm.

"Abbie doesn't want me to comb her hair," she sobbed. "And soon she's going to be a teenager—and then she won't—love me any more."

"Holy cats," moaned David. "Just call your brother, okay?"

"Okay." She blew her nose, abashed. "Hey."

"What?"

"Do you ever miss your old wife? The one who doesn't cry at cotton commercials?"

"God, yes."

"Ouch, you meanie. Where's the phone?" David handed it to her and she dialed Court's number.

"Acute what what?" he said as soon as he picked up.

"Stress disorder." Tsara dropped the tissue into the wastebasket and walked into the living room, settling on the sofa with her feet under a cushion. "Or so they tell me."

"Is it as much fun as it sounds like?"

"Very nearly." She was delighted her problem had a name. "My favorite dwarves right now are Grumpy, Weepy, and Scaredy."

"Geeze, I'm sorry, sis," he said. "I'd like to kill that sonofabitch. "

"Mm."

"Anyway, look, I'm going to be late getting in."

"How late?"

"I'm not sure. It's this stupid back order thing—anyway, I just need to be here for it. Wednesday night, maybe. I'm really sorry."

Tsara and David were going to New Hampshire in the morning for the trial. This had required finding a hotel, buying court-appropriate clothes, meeting repeatedly with Lawson and his crew, and, of course, nailing down childcare.

"Does Wednesday night mean Thursday?" she said.

"It might," he admitted.

"Don't worry about it. David's mom is coming tomorrow before we head out. You're basically our Plan B in case she gets grandma fatigue."

"She's okay if I pull in late?"

"I'll call her and make sure. Oh, and the extra car seats are in the garage, but you can just use the minivan if you need to drive them anywhere."

"And I get to give them chocolate cake for breakfast."

"Deal. Just destroy the evidence so I don't have to kill you."

"How are they holding up?" said Court. "Seriously."

Tsara glanced at the hallway to be sure no one in fleece pajamas was padding downstairs. She lowered her voice. "Honestly, I'm not sure.

Most of the time we just make out like we've got nothing to worry about."

"How?"

"The bad men are in jail and can't get out. The good guys won. That kind of thing."

"I guess that works." Court hesitated. "Did you know they were investigating me for a while?"

"Yeah, they told me."

"Pisses me off."

"Well. You can see why they did it."

"No, I can't. I was the one who called them in the first place."

"And Cass sent the cops to find me, and look how that turned out."

"Cass … yeah …." Court's voice trailed off. "Felons in the family. God, I'm glad Mom never saw this."

Tsara sighed. Thinking of her mom hurt. Thinking of Cass hurt.

"I'm so fucking sick of people," went on Court. "I finally went apeshit at this one FedEx guy who kept making Castle Thornlocke jokes."

"Did he know you were related?"

"No, he was just quoting Leno. But he kept getting the punch lines wrong. Geeze, if you're going to be an asshole at least do it right."

Tsara briefly wondered what anatomical improbability Court had countenanced for the hapless FedEx guy. "At least our name isn't Thornlocke."

"Isn't Cass in the same jail as that guy?" He meant Mike.

"They were for a while, at first."

"Don't you think that's kind of stupid? I mean, what if they meet up with each other in the prison yard or whatever? Geeze, there must be more than one jail in New Hampshire."

"When they were in the county jail they were in different wings and there was a separation order keeping them apart." Tsara was learning a lot about procedure. "And the trial's in Madison so I suppose, uh, *he's* somewhere close to there." She never knew how to refer to Mike. Usually it was just "he" or "the guy."

"Anything else I can do?" said Court.

"You're doing a lot, honestly. Knowing I don't have to worry about the kids is huge."

"I'd do more if I could," he said.

"I know. And thanks."

They hung up. The phone rang again.

"One more thing," said Court. "And you really pushed me into it by not doing the chick thing and sharing your feelings. How are you?"

"I have a shrink for my chick feelings."

"How are you with the trial starting?"

"Oh, hell. You really want to know?"

"I called back."

Tsara rubbed her forehead. "You're not going to believe this."

"Yeah, probably not."

"I—" she took a breath. "I miss Cass."

Court's roar rattled the receiver. "You are fucking *kidding* me."

"I'll see him when he testifies. I can't help being in the same room with him."

"How—can you—*miss* him?"

"Because I do." Tsara's voice felt hoarse. "He raised all that money for the Red Dress Brigade. He made sure they got it before he—I never asked him to do that, did you?"

"He's rich and she was his sister. He's *supposed* to do stuff like that."

"He was so happy to see me," she said miserably.

"So happy he goddamn near got you killed. And those kids—and the cops—" Court gargled into incoherence.

"Court, will you listen to me? I don't miss him—the way he is now. I was thinking about that weekend, before everything started. He put stuff in my room that he knew I'd like. He even found some old letters of Mom's for me. It was so sweet. It made me think of when we were kids and he used to help us climb trees and go fishing. And stuff." She cleared her throat. Hell and damnit, she was sick of almost crying. "I miss the old Castle."

Summertime Castle. Ice cream when Mom was away Castle, and sparkling presents and surprise visits Castle.

When Court spoke, his voice was heavy. "Tsara. The new Castle is the old one. We just didn't know it back then."

"Yikes," said David as he pulled into the Madison courthouse parking lot. Onlookers crowded the steps of the handsome, red-brick building. Several of the more blow-dried spectators held microphones, and Tsara could see TV cameras on the shoulders of shaggy-haired guys in down vests and fingerless gloves. As David cut the engine the crowd swayed and a murmur went up. Tsara had a flicker of sympathy for celebrities with stalkerazzi.

"Are you ready for this?" said David.

"Absolutely." Tsara paused to place an invisible diadem on her head. It was a lot like the one Kate Middleton had worn when she married Prince William, but Tsara had added emeralds to bring out the green of her eyes. "Let's roll."

They stepped out of the car. The January air gleamed with winter's thin light, and her nose instantly grew damp from the cold. Tsara held David's hand. The air was frigid, and she curled her thumb in the hollow of his palm. The microphone gang flooded toward her, shouting and jabbing. Because of the diadem, Tsara held her back straight and her head high. She smiled regally at everyone while serenely avoiding eye contact.

"Tara, what's it like confronting the man who attacked you?"

Spiffy! Positively corking!

"How do you feel?"

Like I've been to hell and back so many times I'm on the frequent flyer plan!

"Ma'am! Over here!"

"Tara!"

"Sarah!"

"Zaharah!"

It's Mrs. Adelman, schmuck! "No comment. Excuse me, please."

David moved half a step ahead of her and opened the door. Tsara walked through with measured paces. The hallway was warm and dark after the bright light outside. As soon as the door shut they broke down laughing.

"Okay, this really isn't funny," said David, pulling himself together with effort.

"Sez you." Tsara wiped carefully under her eyes. "How do I look? Did I smudge anything?"

"You look great," said David. "You always look great."

Tsara looked down at the soft teal sheath that skimmed her body, ending at mid-calf. It had a matching jacket with a shawl collar, and the waist was cinched with a broad, oxblood belt with a bronze buckle. Around her neck was a double strand of freshwater pearls dyed multiple pastels so as to go with any outfit in the world. Gold and pearl earrings, a gift from David, provided the finishing touch. "I'm trying to look petite and vulnerable."

David looked at her appraisingly. "I'll give you petite," he said. Tsara smiled and they walked toward the courtroom.

"Did you take your meds?" asked David in a low voice.

She shook her head. "Didn't think it would look good if I nodded off on the witness stand."

They walked through the double doors into the courtroom. A strange emotion rippled through her like a snake and vanished. It wasn't terror but it was like terror. Everything would be decided here, but she didn't get to decide any of it.

One side of the room was picture windows that looked out over the parking lot. The walls were beige and the carpet was one shade darker. Rows of bare wooden benches like old church pews filled the spectators' section, and every one was jammed with onlookers trying to keep their elbows to themselves. Some were press. Others were involved with the case. The rest were just gawkers.

David and Tsara seated themselves behind the plaintiff's table where the District Attorney was seated. Mike was a few feet away. He and the public defender were at a large table covered with a cloth that hung to the floor. Mike wore a dark blue suit and navy tie with red dots. If it was something his lawyer had bought for the occasion, he had done a good job. The suit fit well, and the collar wasn't too tight. Mike was clean-shaven, his wavy hair combed neatly and his hands on the table. Tsara was weirdly relieved to see they weren't cuffed.

David nudged her. "That's his mom," he said, barely moving his lips. "Behind him. Long hair."

Mike's mother was expressionless, or nearly so, and wearing what must have been her best outfit: a dark sweater over a white blouse and a simple gold chain. She held a burgundy clutch purse in her lap, and her fingers tapped on the clasp.

The jurors were in the jury box. It was a mix of men and women. Several held notepads and pens. The foreman, a woman with a steel-grey perm and reading glasses halfway down her nose, glanced at Tsara and David then looked past them at the tall windows.

"All rise for the Honorable Judge Magnus Nordlander," said the bailiff.

A stocky figure in black robes came in from a door behind the judge's bench. His thick hair was white and his face was craggy, and he wore a button-down collar and tie under his robe. The court rose *en masse*, sat down when the judge did, and the trial began. Tsara was the first witness, and she felt her shoulders tingle as she walked past Mike toward the front of the room. He looked straight ahead. She placed her hand on the court's Bible and repeated the oath the bailiff pronounced for her, swearing to tell the truth to the best of her ability. *And to keep breathing*, she reminded herself as she settled in the chair.

Lawson walked over to her, radiating calm. "Mrs. Adelman," he began. "Could you tell us briefly what happened to you the night of Friday, October third of last year?"

"Yes," she said, impressed at how calmly and clearly this person on the witness stand spoke. "I was visiting my uncle and his family in Libertyville when two men came into my room and kidnapped me at knifepoint."

"How long were you in captivity?"

"Until that Sunday morning."

"And do you see one of those men here today?"

"Yes."

"Could you identify him for the court, please?"

Lawson moved to one side and Tsara pointed to Mike. "There he is."

Mike looked up and their eyes met. Tsara kept breathing, but it seemed as though someone else were doing it. The courtroom was a movie set, and it slowly fell away from her, walls receding, people in the jury box drifting away. Only with great effort did she pull her attention back to the District Attorney's voice.

"Let the record show the witness has identified Michael Westbrook as the defendant charged in the indictment," said the DA. He turned back to Tsara and continued questioning her, gently guiding her through the events of the night and the next two days; and again she was amazed at the composure his witness exhibited. She sat up straight, her still hands folded in her lap; her voice was steady, and she gave the necessary information with almost clinical detachment. Only her left foot, crossed elegantly over the right, twitched rhythmically as she spoke.

"So he told you no one would hurt you," said Lawson.

"That's right."

"Did you believe him?"

Tsara felt her lips curve up. "Not for one second."

"Why not?"

"Because he already had hurt me. So I knew he'd do it again if he found it expedient."

"Thank you, Mrs. Adelman," said Lawson. "I apologize for having to ask this next question." His voice dropped and slowed. "I realize this may be very difficult for you. Can you tell us what you were thinking— what was going through your mind—during this dreadful episode?"

"Objection," said the public defender. "The term 'dreadful' is prejudicial to my client."

"Overruled," said the judge. The set of his mouth indicated that he would brook no nonsense in his courtroom. "You may answer the question, Mrs. Adelman."

"Do you mean ... during the abduction?" Tsara asked Lawson.

"Yes."

Tsara's hands that had been so still and obedient in her lap suddenly writhed. "You can't imagine." She wondered if she were speaking loudly enough, and paused to clear her throat. "You just can't imagine the terror. I couldn't—nothing I did mattered, I couldn't stop them. They just … did whatever they wanted … and I thought, 'Oh, God, I'm not a person any more, I'm a thing.' I was just this *thing* they were taking. Nothing about me mattered—not that I had kids, not whether I was a good person, not what I had for breakfast that morning—I wasn't me anymore, I wasn't me, I was just this object they were throwing around." She drew a deep breath. Several jurors leaned forward, staring at her intently.

"And then?" prompted Lawson.

"Well … he started shoving me through the door, and I was thinking, *'Don't let him take you anywhere!'* But I couldn't stop him. I tried."

"And why were you thinking that?" Lawson's voice was low and gentle, and his eyes were liquid compassion.

"Because … I thought they were going to take me somewhere and kill me, and my family would never even find my body." She clenched her teeth and blinked.

"Just one more question, Mrs. Adelman." Lawson appeared to be gathering his thoughts, finding just the right phrase for her. "During the next day and a half, did you think about your family a great deal?"

"No." One of the jurors pulled back in surprise, glancing from her to David.

"And why is that?"

"Because I knew if I thought about them I would lose it. And I couldn't afford to lose it." Her voice caught and she wiped under one eye with the knuckle of her forefinger. "I'm sorry," she whispered.

"Your Honor?" said Lawson.

"Ten-minute recess," said the judge. His gavel chunked down on his desk and everyone stood as he left the room.

Tsara rose and scanned the milling crowd. *Where's David?* she thought. And then he was in front of the witness stand, waiting just for her. She stepped down and buried her head in his shoulder, willing herself to stop those idiot tears.

David's chest stiffened and Tsara looked up. He was glaring at the defendant's table. Abruptly Mike stood, staring at them. David stepped forward. The bailiff yanked on Mike's arm. Traveler jumped to his feet and muttered something in his client's ear. Mike's shoulders sagged and he sat down again, unresisting. As everyone else flowed toward the doors, a second bailiff strode over to the table.

Tsara put her hand on David's. It was a fist, and it shook under her touch. "Come on," she said softly. "Let's go out in the hall for a minute."

Once in the hallway Tsara ducked into the ladies' room, leaving David waiting for her on a bench outside. She emerged with makeup freshly applied. "These crying jags have got to stop," she said grimly. "I don't care if I have to swallow silica gel packets." David looked at her, saying nothing.

Traveler stood outside the holding cell, looking in at his client. "Are you okay?"

Mike passed his hand over his eyes. "It won't happen again."

"What was that?" Because it was sure as hell something. Mike never slipped.

Mike put his hand down and stared straight ahead. "She never cried," he said. "The whole time ... she never cried."

Traveler looked at him. *Please,* he thought. *Please show this side of yourself to the jury. Let them see this. Let them see the guy who comes unglued at the sight of a woman crying.*

David gave Tsara's hand a squeeze as they reentered the courtroom. He sat down in the spectator area while she went back on the witness stand. Lawson reminded her she was still under oath. The DA had one more line of inquiry he wanted to pursue.

"Mrs. Adelman," he said, "could you please tell us what your life has been like since these events?"

Tsara drew a deep breath. "Not too great, actually," she admitted. "I have a lot of nightmares. Other times I'm afraid to go to sleep."

At first she had told David about the dreams. She was trapped— something was about to kill her. Or she was lost in a cave. She didn't have any meds to keep the dreams from happening.

Eventually she stopped telling him. "Wake me up," he told her, but she didn't want to disturb him. Usually nowadays she crept out of bed and went down to the living room to watch reruns of *I Love Lucy* and old screwball comedies on Turner Classic Movies. They were so jolly, those movies. Even the kidnappings turned out all right.

As often as not he would join her. The first few times he had chastised her for not waking him. She hadn't answered, just pulled the fleece throw higher over her shoulders and kept watching. These days he usually just sat with her till the kids woke up. Sometimes he slept.

"But you haven't taken sleep aids," said Lawson.

Tsara shook her head, half-smiling. "Not crazy about the side effects, and most of them are addictive."

"And during the day? "

"Little things set me off," she said, and guided him through the panic attacks.

"Does the medication help you sleep?"

"Yes, but that's more of a side effect. It makes me sleepy but I take it to make the panic stop."

Lawson folded his hands. "Have you ever used this sort of medication before?"

"No. I never needed to."

Lawson turned to the judge. "No further questions, Your Honor."

They broke for lunch, Judge Nordlander reminding them they would reconvene that afternoon. As the crowd stood up Tsara noticed three reporters headed toward them, their press badges flapping as they elbowed through the spectators. "Let's get out of here," she said in David's ear.

They drove to the outskirts of town and settled into a booth in the Big Band Café, a mom-and-pop coffee shop whose splintery walls were almost entirely covered with photos and record jackets from the 1930s through the fifties. Over the speakers Doris Day crooned that whatever would be would be. Tsara adjusted her skirt, pleased. The restaurant was a big trivia game that could take them all through lunch.

"Tommy Dorsey," she said, pointing. "And look—Benny Goodman."

"The Andrews Sisters," said David, looking past her shoulder. "Count Basie. And Ava Gardner."

Tsara twisted to see. "She wasn't a singer."

"No," said David dreamily. "But she was Ava Gardner." And he gazed adoringly at her while Tsara scanned the room for pictures of Gene Kelley or Cary Grant.

The waitress appeared with menus. Her nametag read *Annette.* "Can I get you drinks to start with?"

"Just water for me," said Tsara. "With lemon, please."

"Same," said David. He picked up the menu and they read.

The waitress came back, drinks on a tray and a folded newspaper tucked under one arm. She put the glasses down and took their orders before setting the newspaper on the table between them. "Thought you folks might be interested," she said, and walked back to the kitchen.

David picked up the paper. It was that day's *Madison Telegram-Gazette* and the headline took up much of the first page. *KIDNAPPING TRIAL BEGINS TODAY,* it read; and in smaller letters the sub-header noted, *Bizarre Case of Marine, Housewife, and Rogue Cops Rivets Madison, Region.* Below it was Mike's military portrait and a picture of Judge Nordlander.

"What, nothing of me?" said Tsara. She had scooted in next to David and was leaning over his elbow. "I'm twice as photogenic as he is."

"They talk about you," said David, skimming the columns. "Apparently you have a Ph.D. Did you know that?"

"No idea." She reached across the table for her reading glasses, which she had laid down beside the menu. "My gosh, I'm an accomplished person."

"Also, we've been married fifteen years," said David.

"Yeah? How many kids do we have?"

David angled the paper so they could both read. Most of the article was accurate, or nearly so.

"Oh, look," said Tsara. "Here's the spin on Hans."

Hans Freihoffer, a close friend of Thornlocke and his family, remains in Austria where he traveled with his wife and children shortly after the conclusion of the hostage drama. Agent Spaar of the FBI has described Mr. Freihoffer as a material witness in the case, adding, "We're very disappointed that he chose this time to leave the country, and have been making every effort to contact him."

Reached at her rented home in Switzerland, Alicia Thornlocke, the wife of Castle Thornlocke, stated, "Hans is an Austrian citizen and has often said he wanted to spend more time there and expose his children to his native land and culture. My understanding is the Freihoffers had longstanding plans to be there at this time." Mrs. Thornlocke could not say when, if ever, the family planned to return.

"Slick as a stick of butter, isn't she?" said David. "You notice she doesn't use the word 'extradite.'"

"Spaar and Galen do," said Tsara.

"So what's the holdup?"

"Hans has a lot of friends. And unless the other country agrees to grab him, our guys can't make a move. So zippy quick is like, six months."

"Mph," said David.

> Through his attorney, Mr. Freihoffer has indicated his willingness to cooperate in the investigation. "My client is eager to discuss this matter with the FBI at their convenience," stated the attorney. "He asks only that they phone him. This they have not done."

> Agent Spaar responded, "We have tried repeatedly to contact Mr. Freihoffer at his residence in Austria, but to no avail. Furthermore, if he really wanted to cooperate he'd be here talking to us."

They were almost done when the waitress reappeared with their food, and David held the newspaper out of her way so she could set the plates down.

"Careful, they're hot," she said automatically.

Tsara indicated the newspaper. "Thanks. We hadn't seen that one."

The waitress beamed. "You're welcome to keep it."

David folded the paper and put it on the bench next to his coat while Tsara went back to her own seat. "How did you know it was us?" he asked.

The waitress shrugged, still smiling. "Madison's a small town," she said. "Anything else I can get for you folks?"

"No, I think we're all set," said Tsara.

"In that case, the manager asked me to tell you lunch is on the house. Including dessert, if you want it." She leaned forward conspiratorially. "If you like pie, I recommend the apple. We make it from scratch. Lots of brown sugar and cinnamon with a streusel topping. You won't regret it."

"That's very kind of you," said Tsara. "But we're happy to pay."

Annette shook her head emphatically. "The manager is my husband Kevin," she said. "I told him if even half of what the papers say is true, you deserve at least a decent meal and some good wishes from the folks around here considering what you've been through."

Tsara's cheeks warmed with happiness. "When you put it that way, I guess we accept. Thanks."

"And apple pie sounds great," said David. "Two?" Tsara grinned, and the waitress once again withdrew. Tsara picked up her fork, thinking about warm apples with brown sugar and a streusel topping. Ella Fitzgerald's elegant voice filled the room, assuring them she loved Paris in the summer when it sizzled and in the winter when it drizzled.

On their way out of the restaurant David stopped suddenly. "I have an idea," he said, and turned into the Walgreen's next door. Tsara followed him and watched as he purchased a dozen large manila mailers and then wrote his name and work address on each.

"Curious?" he asked.

"A bit."

"Patience, wife, and all will be revealed." He zipped up his jacket again and they returned to the coffee shop where Annette was wiping down their table. David approached her holding the envelopes and a twenty-dollar bill. "I wonder if you could do us a favor," he said.

"Seems likely," she said, glancing at the twenty. "But if you're paying me it's not really a favor, is it?"

"I guess not."

"Nah, I'm just messin' with ya," said Annette. "What can I help you with?"

"We're not always in town," explained David, "and the *Madison Telegram-Gazette's* website keeps crashing on me. Would you mind mailing us the news stories?"

Annette grinned broadly as she took the envelopes and the twenty. "I'd be happy to, Mr. Adelman." She turned and hollered over her shoulder. "Hey, Kevin, you hear that? Start saving the newspapers."

"Save the newspapers. Got it." Through the window to the kitchen Kevin winked and touched his paper chef's hat in mock salute.

"Thanks," said Tsara. "Just promise me you won't believe everything you read."

"Hey, no problem." She hesitated, then blurted, "You mind if I ask you something, Mrs. Adelman?"

"Sure. And call me Tsara."

"Oh, is that what you go by?" Her cousin had told her it was Sarita. "Anyway, is it true you knocked that guy unconscious?"

"One of them, yeah." She couldn't help smiling just a little.

Annette raised her hand for a high five, which Tsara cheerfully gave. "Rock on! I like women who can kick a little ass."

"It's true, she does," called Kevin from the kitchen.

"We have to go now," said David, glancing at the time on his cell phone.

"Sure. You two have a good rest of the day now."

Tsara half-smiled. "Well."

"Yeah, I guess that was a dumb thing to say," conceded Annette. "Sorry."

"Don't worry about it." Tsara stepped toward the door David held open for her. "Thanks again for the paper."

After lunch Tsara went back on the stand for Traveler's cross-examination. He approached her with legal pad in his hand, flipping the pages as he walked. David shifted forward on the wooden bench, his shoulders tight. He did not want Tsara to be cross-examined. She'd been through enough. And if that goddamn PD even hinted that any of this was her fault, he, David, was going to vault the barrier between the spectators and the courtroom and punch the guy in the neck.

"Mrs. Adelman," Traveler began, "I'd like to ask you a few more questions about the information you've already presented to the court. I understand that during the weekend in question you sustained a number of superficial injuries. Is that right?"

"Objection," said Lawson. "The nature and extent of Mrs. Adelman's injuries has been well established." The jury had been given a sheaf of eight-by-ten color glossies to peruse, and, lest they should miss the point, several poster-sized photos of her more exciting lacerations stood next to the jury box. They made David ill. He hated the photos and he hated Westbrook.

"Overruled," said the judge.

"Mrs. Adelman?" prompted Traveler.

"Yes, I sustained a number of injuries."

"Could you describe them, please?"

"Well, I had some pretty severe bruises, especially on my face and legs. I needed PT for my neck," that had been courtesy of Jordan Stone, "and besides that I had a lot of abrasions and lacerations, mostly on my knees and hands."

Traveler bowed his head. Like Lawson, he was all sympathy. *That must have been awful*, said his demeanor. "These lacerations," he said. "Did any of them require stitches?"

"No."

"Any broken bones? "

"Objection," said Lawson. "This is not in evidence."

"Your honor," said Traveler, "the nature and extent of the injuries Mrs. Adelman sustained at the time of the alleged incidents needs to be clearly defined."

"Overruled," said the judge. "You may continue, Mr. Traveler."

Traveler turned back to Tsara. "Were any of your bones broken?"

"No."

"Internal bleeding?"

"Oh, no. Nothing like that."

"I see." Traveler turned back to his legal pad. "Mrs. Adelman, you were with the defendant almost the entire weekend. Is that correct?"

"Yes."

"During that time, did he ever hurt you with malice?"

"He certainly hurt me when he felt like it."

Traveler nodded, as if this were exactly what he himself would have said under the same circumstances. "Yes. But did you ever get the sense that he was doing it, well, just to be mean?"

Tsara's hands made a small gesture of defeat. "No."

"Did he torment you verbally?"

"Objection."

"Call you names or use crude language to describe you?"

"Objection!"

"Did he ever try to make you cry?"

"*Objection!*" Lawson was standing at his desk. "We're not interested in what the defendant didn't do. The evidence for what he did do speaks for itself."

"Your honor," said Traveler, "I'm laying a foundation for a line of questioning that is relevant to establishing my client's mental state at the time of these alleged acts. I'm entitled to question the witness as to what she knew about my client's mental state at that time."

"Overruled," said the judge. "Please answer the questions, Mrs. Adelman."

Lawson sat down, scowling. David knew how he felt.

Tsara looked at Traveler. "No," she said calmly. "He never did any of those things."

Traveler tapped his legal pad. "Mrs. Adelman, I see you refused to have a rape test when you were taken to the hospital after these events. Is that correct?"

"Yes."

"Why is that?"

"Because he didn't rape me."

"Did he ever try to rape you?"

"Objection."

"Overruled."

"No," she said. "He didn't."

"Thank you, Mrs. Adelman," said Traveler. "During the time you were with the defendant, did he ever exhibit concern for your well-being?"

"Objection!" exploded Lawson as he pulled himself to his feet again. His chair scraped the floor. "Your Honor, my colleague is trying to make a violent abduction sound like a picnic with Dudley Do-Right."

"Your Honor," said Traveler, "as I stated earlier, this line of questioning is directly relevant to establishing my client's mental state during that weekend. Mrs. Adelman was the sole witness for most of these events—I would be negligent not to question her about them."

"Overruled," said Nordlander. "But Mr. Traveler, be sure to confine yourself to those lines of questioning relevant to the case at hand."

"Thank you, Your Honor. I will." He turned back to Tsara. "Mrs. Adelman?"

"Yes," said Tsara. "There were times ...."

David relaxed and leaned back. God, she was good. She spoke clearly and without ums and uhs. She sat up straight. No self-pity and no bullshit. No wonder so many of her pupils had fallen in love with her. David had, too, when she was just a pretty, smart grad student at the desk next to his. And he still felt that way, still fell in love with her, still wondered what the hell she saw in him. Every day. That was the magic of Tsara.

When she was done, Traveler said, "Thank you." He paused and turned a page before looking up again. "Mrs. Adelman, what happened to you was terrible. It was frightening and unfair. No one denies that. But did my client ever tell you why he abducted you?"

Here we go, thought David. *Sympathy for the devil.*

"He said his son had been kidnapped and he wanted to do a prisoner exchange to get him back," said Tsara.

"Did he tell you who had taken the child from him?"

"He said it was my uncle."

"Did you believe him?"

"I had just been kidnapped at knifepoint," she protested. "I didn't know what to believe."

"Of course," agreed Traveler. "But knowing your uncle as you do, did you think it was possible he might do such a thing?"

"Objection," said Lawson. "Speculation."

"Sustained," said Judge Nordlander.

Traveler put his notepad down. "Mrs. Adelman," he said. "You've told us my client was not wantonly cruel to you. You've given us several instances when he went to effort on behalf of your comfort and safety. It seems pretty clear he wasn't out to hurt you, kill you, or attack you sexually. Would you agree?"

"Yes."

"So is it possible he had a reason for what he did that weekend?"

"I'm sure he thought he did."

"Did he ever lie to you?" pressed Traveler.

"About what?"

"About his son. About your uncle. About anything."

David felt a zing from the jury box. All eyes were on Tsara. By God, they wanted an answer.

"I don't know," she said.

"Did you know that your uncle employed the Libertyville police as his private security force?" said Traveler.

"I found out on Friday evening, when I arrived at his house."

"Did you know he also paid them to abduct the children of local families who owed him money?"

"Objection!" If Lawson hadn't said it, David would have. "This is speculation."

"Your honor," said Traveler, "reviewing the actions of the Stone brothers is essential in the establishment of mitigating circumstances."

"Overruled," said the judge.

"Did you know that?"

"Mi—the defendant told me," said Tsara.

"Did you believe him?"

She almost threw her hands in the air. "I didn't know what was true or what wasn't. I didn't even know for sure if he had a son, or if he did whether the kid was alive or dead. And it's not like I could ask anyone else to find out."

Traveler waited for her to compose herself. "Was there a point at which you began to believe what my client had told you?"

Tsara sighed. "Yes."

"And when was that?"

The jurors were all turned toward her. Tsara kept her eyes on Traveler. "When we met Jordan and Arnold Stone in the woods."

Once again calm and collected, Tsara described the scene. Watching her, David seethed. At that moment he hated due process. David didn't want to see Mike found guilty. He wanted to strangle him.

He turned to glare at the defendant's table, hoping to catch the criminal's eye. Let him see how much he hated him. Tried to put into a single look the loathing he felt.

Mike was watching Tsara. His brows drew together and he rubbed his forehead with his thumb and forefinger. His eyes were anxious.

After Tsara's testimony the judge declared a ten-minute recess, which Tsara had begun to realize were glorified potty breaks. The jury filed out of its box in one direction and the courtroom spectators exited the big doors in another.

"How you feeling?" asked David.

"Fine," she said, smiling. Her part of the trial had gone well, and it was over.

"The jury loved you," he said.

"Oh, good for them."

As she stepped through the doors Tsara pulled her purse onto her shoulder. It felt light, and she patted the side pocket.

"Damn."

"What's wrong?" asked David.

"My cell phone—it must have fallen out. Hold on a sec." As the last person came through the door, Tsara ducked into the courtroom and strode to her seat. The phone was on the floor, and she picked it up and slid it back into her purse.

As she straightened up she realized the room wasn't empty. Mike was still sitting at the table, his lawyer standing a few feet away. Armed bailiffs stood on either side of him. A third crouched at Mike's feet. He pulled his arm back and a chain clunked onto the floor. Mike stared ahead, as if a doctor were taking his blood. The bailiffs put their hands under his arms and he stood. They walked him forward. The third bailiff watched, one hand on his gun, the other holding the chain. Mike shuffled around the table. As he passed it Tsara saw the manacles on his ankles. They clinked as he took low, mincing steps.

The bailiffs led Mike out through a back door. It swung shut behind him, and Tsara was alone.

— ✳ —

That evening after dinner Tsara and David retired to their hotel. It was generic and affordable, with white walls and brown carpet. Tsara lay in bed, her limbs heavy.

"You okay?" said David.

"Tired." She looked up at the ceiling.

"Me, too."

"He was chained," she burst out. "His legs were chained. I saw it when I went back for my phone."

"Yes."

"You knew?" she said.

"Mm-hm."

"Why?"

"Because he's a violent, dangerous criminal," said David.

"No, I mean—"

"Oh. Well, I didn't know for sure. I just figured he would be, especially when I saw the tablecloth."

"It goes all the way to the floor," said Tsara.

"Yeah."

"Hides everything."

"The judge is a good guy," said David. "He doesn't want the jury to see the leg irons. Neither does the PD."

Tsara sighed and rolled over. David rubbed her back.

"What do you think so far?" she asked presently.

"I feel sorry for him."

Tsara lifted her head. "You do?"

"God, yes. The poor guy's running through hell wearing gasoline underwear. All he's got is, 'My client is a kinder, gentler kidnapping psycho.' I don't know why this ever went to trial—his client's guilty."

"Oh," said Tsara. She had thought he was talking about Mike.

In the woods he had moved like a panther. He wasn't poetry in motion—he was perfection. And he had said she was like a mountain lion.

She couldn't tell David that.

The next day Lawson called in a stupefying number of forensic witnesses to testify about every bit of nit or grit related to the case. Had that been Jim's blood on the floor of Tsara's room? It was. And was the splatter pattern consistent with someone's having shaken his head after receiving a bloody nose? Why, yes, it was. Was Mike's DNA on the rope? And did highly scientific ballistics testing confirm that the gun retrieved from the hidden pool at the cave was in fact the very same weapon that had killed the Stone brothers? Certainly. Each witness trumpeted his or her qualifications prior to testimony (not one but two degrees in criminology! Years in the forensics lab!).

After each had said his or her piece, Traveler cross-examined. Politely, as though he just wanted to be sure he understood what they were saying, he did his best to make them look like drooling Neanderthals. Wasn't it true that the lab where this witness worked had misplaced several DNA samples the year before? And did that particular master's degree *really* qualify this witness to make these statements? They responded with theatrical indignation. Tsara got the sense that sometimes Traveler had inflicted damage, but more often not.

She snuck a look at Mike. He appeared to be listening, but she couldn't read his face.

He and she were unique in the courtroom, she thought. They were the only ones who really knew what had happened up in the mountains that weekend.

The courtroom was stuffy. Tsara's purse slipped from her lap to the floor, and she nudged it under the bench with one foot. A small noise caught her attention: *tink*. *Tink*. She glanced around the room. The bailiff was clipping his fingernails.

"Is this why you left legal practice?" she said in an undertone.

"You bet," said David. "The adrenaline got to be too much."

"The prosecution rests," said Lawson finally. As indeed it had a right to: every iota of evidence had reinforced the defendant's guilt. Mike was in deep.

Two days later David brought home a chubby envelope from Annette. He and Tsara disemboweled it while the kids were at school. Along with several newspaper articles, Annette had included a Post-It with a smiley face done in Sharpie and a coupon for a free salad at the restaurant. Tsara and David sat in a block of sunshine on the couch in the TV room and read the first story.

TWO BODIES, NO KILLER

That brothers Arnold and Jordan Stone are dead is not in dispute: their bullet-riddled bodies were found in a remote area of the Silver Mountain range in early October. Prosecutors have a weapon. They don't have a witness—even though two other people were present when the brothers died.

They also lack a consistent picture of the victims.

The brothers comprised the police force of Libertyville, NH. Whether their tenure was a rule of law or a reign of terror is widely and passionately disputed.

"'Rule of law or a reign of terror,'" repeated Tsara admiringly. "I think the writers are having fun with this."

"You're ahead of me." David read more slowly than Tsara.

Some citizens recall them as exemplary peace officers. Others have asserted that the Stone brothers were often brutal. Even before the now notorious October weekend during which the

333

hamlet witnessed multiple abductions, including several involving children, and a bizarre, under-the-radar flight from justice by a former Marine and his housewife hostage, the Stone brothers were said to have been involved in an astonishing panoply of crimes both major and minor.

"I hate it when they say 'housewife,'" said Tsara. "It sounds so frumpy."

"What would you prefer?"

"Um … overeducated domestic executrix?"

"They'd vandalize your property if they didn't care for you," said Christopher Sweet, a lifelong resident of Libertyville. "Sometimes it was harmless, like keying your car, but sometimes it was much more than that. "

Other Libertyville citizens point to instances when people in custody at the local jail emerged battered and bruised but unwilling to lodge formal protests. "Everyone was scared to death of them," said Sweet.

When asked why no one had ever reported Arnold and Jordan Stone for their brutality, Sweet said simply, "This is New Hampshire. People don't like to ask for help."

But another picture is also in the frame. "We got the lowest crime rate of any town in New Hampshire," said resident Nils Olson. "That's because of Jordie and Arnold. Around here you never had to worry about your kids no matter what."

Mr. Olson spoke without apparent irony.

Absent either a witness or a straightforward motive for the shootings—Westbrook is claiming he acted in defense of his hostage, whom the brothers were threatening—other Libertyville denizens have rallied to the defense of someone they see as one of their own.

Bob Soames, owner and manager of Cliffside Lea Stables and a longtime friend of former Marine turned alleged kidnapper Michael Westbrook, expressed sympathy for the accused man. "If he did it, then he must have thought he had a good reason. That's all I can figure."

His opinion was echoed by retired English teacher Honoria Saxon, who taught the Stone brothers as well as Westbrook and his co-defendant, James Montrose, in high school. "Mike and Jim never gave a minute of trouble to anyone who didn't ask for it," she said. "Jordan and Arnold were schoolyard bullies."

When asked if the Stone brothers had changed as they grew into adulthood, she replied, "Yes. They put on uniforms."

Her stance is not unique. The defense has a long roster of witnesses slated to testify about their experiences with the Stone brothers.

"If Mike really did kill them, I say slap a medal on him," said one witnesses, who spoke on condition of anonymity. "They did terrible things. I went to the funeral just to make sure they were really dead."

Legal experts have pointed out that such testimony might backfire, as long-term abuse might easily present itself as a motive for murder ....

"Is it upsetting for you, reading this stuff?" asked David.

"No."

"Because I would think it would be."

"I would think it would be too," said Tsara. "But that's the hell of it. I never know what's going to set me off." David looked so sad that she added, "Endless hours of entertainment," and folded up the newspaper article.

As she handed it to him, the red number on the answering machine caught her eye. New message. She got up and hit play.

"Hi, it's Adara. Listen, my mom took a turn for the worse. It's not a panic situation, but I can't take Falstaff next week. I'm really sorry. Give me a call so I know you got this."

"Oh, I forgot," said David. "Adara called."

"Did she?"

"I told her to call back and leave a message so I wouldn't forget to tell you."

"Thanks," said Tsara drily. She picked up the phone. "Mind picking up the kids so I can figure out doggie care?"

"Don't I always?"

"You do," she said. "It's one of the reasons I love you."

"Hm." David pursed his lips. "Guess I better keep doing it." He went back to the papers as Tsara dialed.

82

Three days later, Tsara and David were back in Madison for Jim's testimony. The sky was steel-grey, and the clouds spat a mix of rain and slush. Jim looked about as cheerful as the day. He wore what Tsara guessed was his first suit. It looked like a Men's Wearhouse special, wool charcoal with a subtle stripe in the slacks and matching blazer; but no man had legs as short as Jim's and no boy had shoulders so wide. The pants legs and sleeves were actually rolled up, and the jacket hung a good two inches too long. But his hair was cut short and tidy, and his beard was trimmed. He looked as presentable as his lawyer could make him.

From Tsara's point of view, the most exciting part was the court interpreter who stood by the witness stand and articulated Jim's signs. She wore pearl earrings and a dark suit with three-quarter length sleeves, and her nametag read *Sara Sullivan*.

Jim took the witness stand and Lawson approached him. After establishing the basics—he was James Montrose, of Libertyville, New Hampshire; he, too, was involved with the case at hand—the prosecutor got down to business.

"Mr. Montrose, how do you know the defendant?"

Jim's hands flew through the air. "He's my cousin. His mother raised me after my parents died." When Jim's gestures were small and hesitant, the interpreter spoke softly; when they were large and agitated, her words were loud and emotional.

"How old were you then?"

Jim held up the fingers of one hand. "Four," said Sullivan.

"So you and the defendant, Michael Westbrook, were raised by the same person, grew up in the same house, and attended school together. Is that correct?"

Jim nodded. "Yes," said Sullivan.

"Was he your childhood protector?"

"He was and is my best friend."

David leaned closer to Tsara. "There's not going to be anything new here," he said in an undertone.

"Mm-hm." Tsara kept her eyes on the witness stand as Lawson droned on and Jim answered with his hands.

"They've already established his testimony. This is going to be as exciting as watching oatmeal coagulate."

"I know." She pulled away, intent on the questions.

"We don't have to stay."

"I *get* it," she said. "Can I please just listen now?"

David shifted away from her. After a moment she put her hand on his knee.

"What were you doing the night of Friday, October third?"

"We went to Chateau Thornlocke to kidnap a hostage," said Jim's hands and Sullivan's voice. Several jury members jotted on their notepads.

Well, that was direct.

"And did you succeed?"

"Yes, sir, we did." Jim described entering the house and going to Tsara's room, and deciding to take her.

"During the course of this abduction, did Mr. Westbrook assault Mrs. Adelman?"

"I—did that—no." The interpreter's voice faltered as Jim's hands thumped on the arms of the chair. "Hold, please," she said, and turned toward him. He flicked his hands.

"Ms. Sullivan?" said the judge.

"Interpreter error on the statement concerning Mr. Westbrook's assaulting Mrs. Adelman," said Sullivan. "The correct statement is, 'I did not see that. I was unconscious.'"

"And why were you unconscious?" said Lawson.

"She knocked me out," said Sullivan with surprising gusto. "She's fast as a snake." Jim looked at Tsara, and his eyes glittered with a wicked expression of delight. It was as if he had pumped her hand and bellowed, "Well played, madam!" She smiled inwardly.

Jim hadn't been present at the Stone brother's demise, so Lawson focused exclusively on Tsara's kidnapping. Jim answered all queries in meticulous detail. They hadn't wanted Tsara; they had wanted Hans. Hans was evil. The children had been kidnapped because of a loan. ("All this over a loan, Mr. Montrose?") The Stone brothers and Thornlocke were part of a conspiracy. ("I see.") Castle had laughed when Mike had begged for Aiden's release. The more questions Jim answered, the more fantastic it sounded.

Tsara snuck a glance at the defendant's table. Mike was so still his face looked as if it were carved of wood. This must be hell for him.

"Did you witness the abductions of the children, Mr. Montrose?" said Lawson.

"No."

"Did you speak to the parents of the other children?"

"No."

"So did you have any first-hand or second-hand information that Jordan and Arnold Stone were responsible for these acts?"

"No."

"Were you present when Mr. Westbrook allegedly spoke to Mr. Thornlocke on behalf of his son?"

"No."

"Mr. Montrose," said Lawson, "over the course of the weekend in question, did you have any reason for your actions other than what the defendant told you?"

"No."

"Then why," said Lawson, "should the jury believe any of it was true?"

Jim clenched and unclenched his fists. The interpreter cleared her throat. Jim pointed to Mike and made two quick gestures close to his own face.

"Mike doesn't lie."

Tim was the prosecution's last witness. Aiden was the defense's first. After Lawson wrapped up his closing arguments and sat down, Nordlander banged twice with his gavel.

"As I believe everyone here knows," he said, "our next witness is Aiden Westbrook, the six-year-old son of the defendant." He paused to let that sink in. "As always, the job of this court is to arrive collectively at the truth, and that extends to respecting the witness and the process." He banged again. "Will Aiden Westbrook please enter the courtroom?"

The doors at the back of the room opened and a court-appointed social worker in a navy skirt and jacket walked in, leading a little boy with brown hair. His face was solemn, his ocean-grey eyes wide. In one hand he clutched a barely green stuffed turtle with a brown leather shell.

That poor baby, thought Tsara. He was the only kid in the room, and hundreds of grown-up eyes were going to be on him while he described the worst thing that had ever happened to him. He couldn't even get a hug from his dad first.

She looked over at the defendant's table. Mike was leaning forward in his chair, drinking in the little boy with an expression of unguarded longing so excruciating that Tsara had to turn her head.

The social worker stood with Aiden while the child placed his hand on the court's Bible and took his oath. As the gate to the witness stand swung open Tsara saw a booster seat on the chair. Aiden climbed into it and sat very still as the gate clicked shut.

Traveler approached the stand. "Hello, Aiden," he said. "We're glad you could be here today to help us out."

Aiden's voice carried with surprising clarity. "Okay, sir."

Through gentle questioning, Aiden explained that he was Mike's son; that he was an only child ("My dad says I'm his main man"); and that he had always lived with Mike but now he lived with his grandmother. Then Traveler asked him about the weekend of the kidnappings.

"Two men came to my friends' house where we were playing," said Aiden. "I knew they were bad because they were shouting at us."

Traveler produced a photograph and handed it to the boy. "Are these the men?"

"Yes, sir."

"Let the record show that the witness has identified Jordan and Arnold Stone as the men in question," said Traveler. "Go on, Aiden. Then what happened?"

"They put us in the truck."

"Did you want to go?"

Aiden shook his head vigorously. "No, sir. I kept saying, 'Please, please stop.' But they wouldn't listen."

"I see," said Traveler. "Now, Aiden, this is important. You say they *put* you in the truck. How did they do that?"

"They lifted us off the ground and threw us into the back and then they locked the doors. It hurt my arms. My friend was crying."

Tsara shuddered. The air in the room felt tight.

"Then they drove away," went on Aiden. "I thought I was going to be carsick, but I wasn't."

A few jurors smiled. Tsara relaxed, though her fingers were cold.

"Where did these men take you?" said Traveler.

"A bad place," said Aiden. "It was a *very* bad place, if you know what I mean."

Traveler's face was serious. "No, I don't know. Can you describe it for us?"

"Okay." Aiden sighed. "It was cold, like a basement. There were windows, but they were high up and we couldn't see out of them."

"Did you want to go there?"

"No, sir. They pushed us in."

340

"How long were you there?"

"We thought it was a week, approximately."

"Objection," said Lawson. "The witness is in no position to judge the time elapsed."

The witness probably couldn't even tell time yet, thought Tsara.

"Sustained," said the judge.

"Our information, based on interviews with the families in question and the FBI agents who later found the children, indicates they were imprisoned in Mr. Thornlocke's wine cellar, which is detached from the main house, for roughly twenty-four hours, from mid-morning Friday to midday Saturday," said Traveler. "But I can see how it would have seemed like a lot longer."

"Objection!"

"Sustained. Mr. Traveler, you will abstain from further speculative comments."

"Yes, Your Honor."

He speculated on purpose, thought Tsara. Just in case the jury missed the point that being kidnapped and tossed into a stone outbuilding overnight might really suck.

"Aiden," said Traveler, "were the other kids scared?"

"Yes, sir."

"Were you scared?"

"No, sir."

Traveler let his hands hang at his side. "Why not, Aiden? That all sounds pretty scary to me. I bet I'd be scared."

"Well, I was at first," conceded Aiden. "But I knew my dad would come get me."

"I see," said Traveler. He took a beat to let the jury think about that. "And the other kids?"

"I didn't know if their dad would help them," said Aiden. "I felt sorry for them."

Tsara and David looked at each other. David's eyebrow was up, a sure sign he was puzzling something out.

The other kids' dad hadn't come for them.

84

"Did you see Nancy Grace last night?" said Galen. He kept his hands on the wheel as they sped through the winter vista. Mid-January made the Silver Mountains white and savagely beautiful.

"No," said Spaar.

"She was talking about Thornlocke."

"They'll run it again," said Spaar. "Was it the one where she interrupts everybody, or the one where she wears too much eye makeup?"

"Watch what you say about my girl Nancy."

"Sorry," said Spaar. "Turn here."

"The GPS says go another three miles."

"It also says we're driving on a lake. Turn here."

Galen turned. The road was freshly cleared, the right shoulder covered with a long mound of snow indented at regular intervals by the blade of a snowplow.

"So Nancy's all upset about Thornlocke," said Galen.

"Lots of people are upset about Thornlocke."

"And the kids. Says he's a pathological liar and abuser, and why should she believe anything he says."

"Is this about the plea bargain?" said Spaar.

"And then, so this guy phones in," said Galen. "Starts complaining about how he's sick of rich bastards like Thornlocke getting off easy just because they cooperate."

"Does he mind when poor people get off because they cooperate?"

"So then—she's got a panel of lawyers, right?—one of them starts in about how in a lot of countries they don't even have plea bargaining but it's to make sure the defendant's not coerced. And then the phone-in guy starts yelling—"

"Did they say Thornlocke's being coerced?"

"No. He's yelling that a lot of states don't even have plea bargains and this is what happens when East Coast liberals are in charge. So Nancy, she's all, 'There are *children* involved here, people,' and—"

"Liberals in charge of what?" said Spaar. "Child kidnapping rings?"

"The government, I think."

"What states don't have plea bargaining?"

"Alaska outlawed it in the seventies."

"There are only about three people in Alaska."

"Some days I'm with Nancy, you know?"

"No, you're not. You're just pissed about Thornlocke."

Galen scowled. "Damn right. He used kids as a crowbar to get money."

"We'll nail him," said Spaar. "Today, if we're lucky." Castle would talk, but only in exchange for a reduced sentence.

"He could lie. He probably *will* lie."

"If he does, we'll catch him."

"No plea, no one takes any shortcuts. Defendant goes to trial; justice gets its day."

"Did Nancy Grace say that?"

"One of the other lawyers did."

"Why do you watch that crap?"

"It's a popular show."

"So Nancy Grace is telling the nation that Thornlocke doesn't deserve a plea bargain," said Spaar. "Was that before or after she said something like, 'Somewhere in New Hampshire, the devil is doing his happy dance'?"

"You can see her point."

"No, Galen, I don't," said Spaar. "Is your girl Nancy saying the prosecutor's lazy? That Thornlocke's being squeezed? Or that you and I built a shit case and don't know what we're doing?"

Galen followed the curve of the road. Pines grew thickly on either side, and the snow beneath them was speckled with flecks of dirt and camel-colored pine needles. "Oh, hell, Sparks. The caller guy was an idiot, but I feel for him. He wants to nail Thornlocke's balls to the floor."

"If we go to trial we could lose."

"Not likely."

"Yeah?" said Spaar. "His two underlings are dead. His co-conspirator skipped town. The other family is MIA."

"Kidnapping," said Galen almost musically. "Conspiracy, racketeering, child endangerment—"

"The kids never saw him."

"—bribery of public officials, destroying evidence, multiple charges of aggravated assault, unlawful use of a firearm—"

"That one's a bullshit charge and you know it."

"Bet we could get him for wire fraud. He used a phone."

"No witnesses and no physical evidence," said Spaar. "He could walk. I don't want to be the agent who made this guy into New Hampshire's Casey Anthony. This way he'll talk."

"Ten years," said Galen. "It's not enough."

"At his age it's plenty."

Galen tightened his hands on the wheel. "I want to drop him down a very deep hole."

"And I want to find out exactly what happened that weekend," said Spaar. "When we hit the highway, hang a right. And get your nail gun ready," she added. "We should be there in about fifteen minutes."

Castle was glad to be home, even if the place was too full of empty with Alicia and the kids gone. The lawyers had done what he paid them for, and convinced the judge that bail was in order while they worked out the details of his plea bargain. Now all he had to deal with was his shattered family, the devastation to his reputation and finances, and the two FBI agents in his living room.

He just wished he didn't feel so tired. Tired and brittle.

"May I get you some coffee?" He kept his voice pleasant.

"We need to talk to you about Hans Freihoffer and the extent of his involvement in this matter," said Spaar.

"Well, that's easy," said Castle. "He hasn't any."

"That's what he said, too," said Spaar.

"There we are, then," said Castle.

"We know he's lying," said the agent. "We'll get the truth eventually, but if you want to help yourself it'll come from you."

"I've told you already," said Castle. He hoped the weariness in his voice would sound like that of an innocent man clinging to the truth. "None of us here knew about the children until you discovered them. Good lord, Agent Spaar, just think—even if I were going to commit a crime of that magnitude, why would I choose a night when I had scores of people on the property? Any one of them might have turned out to be a wine aficionado and gone to the cellar to look around. My own son was talking to my niece about it during dinner that night. He wanted to show her the stock."

In point of fact, he and Hans had only realized this weakness in the plan afterwards, when the whole thing had gone to Hades and news crews were crowding the iron gates at the foot of the driveway. Poor strategy on their part, no question—but now it made a damn fine cover story.

"Uh huh," said Spaar.

"Why did you burn the first ransom note?" said Galen.

"Heavens, I wish now I hadn't."

"If Jordan and Arnold Stone were behind all this, why were both notes addressed to you?" said Spaar.

"Well, clearly Westbrook thought I was the guilty party. I can see why," added Castle generously. "Unfortunately his son and the others were on my property. The man just put two and two together wrong."

"Did he talk to you that day?"

"Westbrook? No, not at all."

"He says he did."

"He's lying."

"You threw him off your property that evening."

"Well, yes—that was the first time I saw him that day."

"So you did talk to him."

"That evening. I told you about it at the time." Castle hoped that was different enough.

"Mr. Thornlocke," said Galen, "whose idea was it to abduct those kids—yours or Mr. Freihoffer's?"

"The Stone brothers'," said Castle. "They hated Westbrook and wanted to antagonize him. The other kids just got caught in the same net."

"Forget Westbrook for a minute," said Spaar. "The other family was in debt to you. They couldn't pay. And they told us a very different story. We have the statement they gave us at the hospital."

"I see," said Castle. "Was that before or after the interpreter arrived?"

"After."

Castle tapped his fingers together.

"Mr. Freihoffer skipped town," said Galen. "He left you to take the blame. You don't owe him anything."

Castle looked out the window and thought of Alicia.

346

"Freihoffer didn't leave because he's innocent," said Spaar. "He left to make you look guilty."

She and Galen leaned back in their chairs, saying nothing. Castle sighed. A kind of dullness descended on him, a deep and stupefying weariness. Something was crumbling away from him, and he couldn't stop it.

Alicia was gone.

The silence was crushing him.

His children despised him. Hans might as well be dead.

No one was with him, to stand with him; so Castle was no one. He had lost his self. It was with everyone who used to love him. He was nowhere now. His house was like a museum piece, something to observe, not a place to live in and love in and gather his family in. It was not real. It was a painting by a stranger.

Castle felt something shatter deep inside of him, something he had always thought was hard as sharks' teeth. He wasn't hard. He was soft and wounded and somehow foul. The pain was almost physical.

And so it was that the moment of Castle's surrender was not a cataclysm, but the soft implosion of his world.

Castle lifted his eyes. He cleared his throat. "Hypothetically speaking," he said, "how culpable would someone be for an idea—a concept?"

"We don't deal in hypotheticals," said Spaar. "You agreed to cooperate with us, Mr. Thornlocke."

Castle sighed. Many years ago he had been a smoker, had quit for Alicia. Usually he didn't think about it, but right now he wished he could pick up a pipe, fill it, and tamp down the tobacco before lighting it. His hands wanted badly to have something to do. Instead he clasped them in his lap and ordered them to be still.

"I've known Hans a great many years," he said. "Most of my life and most of his, in fact. We met shortly after the war, in Germany. I was in the military then. I think in a way Hans rather envied me that, because he hadn't been."

"Hadn't been what?" said Spaar.

"In the military. He was too young during the war, and of course he couldn't enlist afterwards. But he always wanted to. If the conflict had gone on another six months I understand he'd have gotten his chance. But no, he never served in uniform."

"Was he in Hitler Youth?" asked Galen.

"Of course he was," said Cass irritably. "If you weren't in Hitler Youth your parents could be arrested. Where was I?"

"Never served in uniform," prompted Spaar.

"Oh—yes. Thank you. Hans had a brother, Klaus, who was stationed in Norway during the Occupation. He was older by a few years—Hans idolized him. I only met him once. A god of a man, tall, broad-shouldered. Extraordinarily handsome."

Cass fell silent, remembering. They had all been gods then, or at least so it seemed now. Joyful and fearless ....

"And?" said Spaar.

"Oh. Forgive me." Cass smiled apologetically. "Klaus died about ten years ago—I was just thinking about him. In any case, he was an army engineer, and his job was to get the trains through. And it was a hellacious job, because the Norwegian Resistance blew up the tracks every night. The Germans rebuilt them every day and they'd be blown up again that night and the Army and the Resistance kept each other engaged in a symbiotic cycle of mutually assured employment." He chuckled. "Then the Resistance blew up a few trains along with the tracks, and that was when Klaus felt he had to take steps. He decided the best way to assure the safety of the trains was to put something on them none of the natives would want to destroy—something they would do their best to protect, in fact. So the next time he needed to get a shipment through he sent soldiers to get some of the local children and he chained them to the front and sides of the train. He had a soldier with a bullhorn on top announcing the new policy as the train rolled along, and it worked like a charm that time and each time subsequently. The Resistance was thoroughly cowed, the trains got through, and the children were always released unharmed afterwards."

Galen hoped his face was blank. He wondered how many of those unharmed children still woke up screaming decades later.

"Go on," said Spaar. She had her notepad out and was writing fluidly as Castle spoke.

"So Hans suggested we do something similar. On a much smaller scale, of course," added Castle. "The kids would never have come to any harm, you know."

"So it was Mr. Freihoffer's idea," said Spaar.

"Yes."

"But you implemented it."

"Yes." Castle looked at the floor.

"It wasn't a vendetta between the Stone brothers and Westbrook."

"No."

Spaar flipped to a blank page in her notepad. "Let's go over some of this again. When did Westbrook come to you about his son? And what did that first ransom note really say?"

The day of Mike's testimony was hideous with sleet. Rawness crept into the courtroom and up Tsara's legs even when she kept her knees pressed together. David sat next to her, his dark hair flecked with ice from their dash into the building.

Tsara knew she was supposed to hate Mike, but she couldn't help but admire his composure—especially since she knew he must be chained to the floor of the witness stand. He was already in place when the jury filed into the box and spectators took their seats. But Tsara knew.

Mike sat up straight, made eye contact with his lawyer. As Traveler led him through the events leading up to that Friday night, Mike's answers were simple and straightforward. His only child had been abducted. He had tried every legitimate means he could think of to retrieve the boy. The police were the criminals, and because of his record he thought he couldn't go to anyone else for help.

"And do you still believe that?" asked Traveler.

Mike shook his head. "No. I see now I was wrong."

"No shit," muttered David. Tsara poked him.

Traveler continued. "Mr. Westbrook, throughout the time you were with her, did you ever deliberately hurt Mrs. Adelman?"

"I know she got hurt," he said. "But I never set out to do that. I just wanted my son back."

"You threatened her with a knife."

"I did. But I would have never used it."

Tsara leaned over to David. "Oh, now he tells me," she whispered. David grimaced.

Traveler led Mike through a detailed description of the next day and a half. He had lit a fire in the cabin so Tsara would not be cold. He had slept with the horses instead of in the room so she would not be frightened. He had brought her food and drink the next day so she would not be hungry. And so-on.

Tsara gritted her teeth, fury rising with each statement. "It wasn't goddamn Club Med," she hissed to David.

He turned toward her, his lips almost at her ear. "He's a self-righteous son of a bitch. We can leave if you want."

Tsara shook her head. "News would say I had a breakdown and stormed out." She took a soothing breath and settled herself for the long haul, holding David's hand on her knee.

She wanted to stay. The trial was as much about her as it was about Mike.

Next Traveler turned to the subject of the Stone brothers. He gave the jury photos of Mike's battered torso while his witness told the story. He set up posters, close-ups of deep purple marks and scrolls of skin hanging from dark red streaks dotted with crimson. Tsara could see eyebrows go up, and the foreman looked nauseated as she shoved her eight-by-ten to the next person.

And finally, Traveler and Mike concluded, Mike had been as good as his word, letting Tsara go even though he hadn't gotten his son back. If "letting go" could be considered synonymous with "bound and gagged and tied to a gravestone," thought Tsara.

"No further questions, Your Honor," said Traveler.

Now it was Lawson's turn to cross-examine. Before the trial he had told Tsara he was surprised the public defender was putting Mike on the witness stand. It was a risky move that worked in Lawson's favor. During Traveler's lengthy questioning the DA had watched, leaning back in his chair in an attitude of supreme boredom. Now he strolled to the front of the room, serene as a morning in May.

"Mr. Westbrook," he said, "on the night in question did you break into the house of Castle Thornlocke?"

"The door wasn't locked," protested Mike. A couple of jurors smiled.

"But you had been evicted from the premises earlier, is that not the case?"

"Yes."

"And told not to return?"

"Yes."

"So you entered the house. Did you then go into the room where Mrs. Adelman was staying?"

"I didn't know—"

"Just answer the question, please."

"Yes," said Mike. "I did."

"Did you and your associate attack Mrs. Adelman?"

"Yes."

"Two of you against one of her. Is that right?"

"Yes."

Lawson looked at Mike as though sizing him up. "How tall are you, Mr. Westbrook?"

Mike shifted in his chair. "About six-three or four."

Lawson looked at his notes. "My information states you are six feet, four inches tall and weigh two hundred and twenty pounds. Does that sound about right?"

"Yes, sir."

"Tsarina Adelman is five feet, four inches tall and weighs one hundred and seventeen pounds," said Lawson. "Did you threaten her with a knife?"

"Yes."

Lawson picked the knife up from the evidence table. He turned it, and the long blade flashed. "This knife?"

"Yes."

Lawson put down the knife and picked up a length of rope. "Did you and your associate then proceed to bind Mrs. Adelman's hands with this rope?"

"Yes."

"And did you drag her out of the room and abduct her to a remote cabin in the woods?"

"Yes."

"Even though she fought you every inch of the way."

Mike looked at him steadily. "Yes. We did."

"And the next day," said Lawson, "did you abduct her a second time, to an even more remote and primitive location—a cave known only to you and your associate?"

Tsara sat very still. The swimming, unreal feeling was coming over her again. She would tell the shrink about it when she got home.

"Yes," said Mike.

Lawson put down the rope and held up the cable, its snipped loop clearly visible at one end. "During the majority of that time, I understand you restrained Mrs. Adelman with this cable."

Tsara rubbed her wrist and wondered why Mike hadn't ditched the cord. He must have been distracted. Oddly, the thought focused her, and the courtroom settled back into reality.

"Yes," said Mike.

"I see." Lawson checked his legal pad. "I understand you are an ex-Marine."

"Former Marine," said Mike.

"You were on an anti-terrorism detail in Iraq, weren't you?"

"Yes, sir, I was."

"Could you explain to the jury what you did during that time?"

"We arrested suspected terrorists," said Mike.

"Did they go quietly?"

"Not usually."

"So when you were in the Marines and you had to arrest someone who resisted, what would you do?"

Mike shifted slightly. "We used appropriate force."

"Could you explain exactly what that means?"

Tsara could see *Oh, shit* in Mike's eyes. "Usually we would throw the suspect to the ground and handcuff him. It was to keep everyone safe," he added. "We couldn't ever tell if someone had a bomb on him or what, so—"

"Where did these arrests take place?"

"Wherever the terrorist suspect was."

"And where was that usually?"

Mike paused. "Usually in the guy's home," he said finally.

"I see," said Lawson again. "So you're experienced at entering people's houses, capturing them and binding them, and transporting them against their will."

"I—"

"You're used to using these techniques to get your own way, aren't you?" said Lawson.

"Objection," said Traveler. "Leading question and prejudicial."

"Your Honor," said Lawson, "I am pursuing this line of questioning to establish that the defendant is an experienced abductor."

"Overruled," said Judge Nordlander.

"Thank you, Your Honor." Lawson turned back to Mike. "I'll repeat the question. You're used to using these techniques to get your own way, aren't you?"

"No."

"Really." Lawson glanced again at his pad. "Then why did you say to Mrs. Adelman, 'You are a means to an end for me'?"

That was unfair, thought Tsara. He had only said that because she was afraid.

Mike's back was mast-straight and tall. "When I was in uniform I followed orders and served my country in wartime."

"When in wartime you were acting under the lawful orders of your government. What are you acting under now?"

"Objection," said Traveler. "My client's military record is exemplary and I see no foundation for the remainder of this question."

"Sustained," said the judge. "The jury is instructed to disregard this remark."

"Then let me rephrase," said Lawson. "Mr. Westbrook. You have special training in abducting dangerous men. You broke into a bedroom and applied all your force and all your skills against a woman half your size. Do you really expect the jury to believe you didn't intended to harm her?"

"I was wrong," cried Mike. "Everything I did then was wrong. If I could do it over again—" He swallowed. "But I never wanted to hurt her. And all I want the jury to know is that anything I did that weekend was to save the life of my son."

Lawson was unmoved. "Does that include shooting Jordan and Arnold Stone?"

"Yes!"

The foreman jerked upright. Several other jurors bent to scribble on their pads. Someone from the seats yelled, "Murderer!" Judge Nordlander gaveled for order.

For the next fifteen minutes, Lawson picked apart Mike's previous testimony with Traveler. He established that Mike and the Stone brothers had a long and violent history. That Mike resented Castle. That Mike had not seen the children being abducted. That he never actually saw Aiden on Castle's property. By the time Lawson was done, the heroic father who would risk all for his son was obliterated. In his place sat a deluded brute.

"No further questions, Your Honor," said Lawson.

David grinned in grim satisfaction, and squeezed Tsara's hand. "Score," he whispered.

The door at the back of the courtroom opened and a woman in a beige suit and pink blouse strode in, followed by Spaar and Galen. She marched to the judge and held out a laminated card like a driver's license.

"Your Honor, please forgive this highly unusual interruption. I am Frieda Smith, U.S. Attorney for the state of New Hampshire. I need to address the court in chambers on an urgent matter pertaining to this case."

Nordlander's mouth tightened. He banged the gavel. "Twenty-minute recess. And this better be good."

As everyone stood, David touched Tsara on the arm. "Let's get out of here."

"Okay, but not too far," said Tsara. "We only have a few minutes."

"We have hours," said David. "Trust me. Whatever just happened isn't going to be resolved in twenty minutes."

Spaar followed Judge Nordlander into his chambers. Galen was at her side, closely followed by Lawson and Traveler. Smith hurried through the door after presenting her license to the court stenographer.

The judge's office held a spacious, almost bare desk of tiger maple. Behind it, a large window looked out into the sleet that slid past in grey sheets, like rice paper screens. In front of the desk stood three chairs. The walls were lined with shelves full of fat books bound in burgundy leather with faded gold letters on the spines.

As they stepped over the threshold, a Norwegian elkhound with a white muzzle lifted himself stiffly from a round bed next to the desk. He walked to Spaar, wagging his tail gently. She scratched his ears without thinking.

"Pay no attention to Tiki," said Judge Nordlander as he settled himself at his desk. "He was toothless even when he had all his teeth. Now, please be seated and explain this disruption of my court."

"Your Honor," said Smith, "I believe you know Agents Spaar and Galen of the Federal Bureau of Investigation. They have just shared with me information they have obtained in a related investigation that may have material impact on the current case."

"Proceed," said the judge. "And sit down."

Smith and the agents sat in the chairs before the desk. The lawyers stood behind them. Spaar spoke. "Your Honor, someone we are investigating in a child kidnap-for-profit ring has told us that the two police officers the defendant is charged with murdering were hired to be kidnappers for this ring, and that one of their victims was the defendant's child."

"That's what my client's been saying from day one," said Traveler.

"How credible is this information?" said Nordlander.

"We're trying to corroborate it," said Spaar. "Unfortunately, our material witness has skipped town."

Sleet hissed on the window.

"My, my, my," said Nordlander. "This is an unholy bucket of eels, isn't it?"

"Well, it's not murder one, Your Honor," said Galen.

"It's not even manslaughter," said Traveler. "You're going to have to drop all those charges, Your Honor. It was killing in defense of another, pure and simple."

"That woman wasn't in any danger until your client put her there," said Lawson.

"Your Honor, I move for an immediate mistrial," said Traveler. "There's no way my client can get a fair trial with this jury. They've been poisoned against him with information we now know to be false and prejudicial. Also known as bullshit," he added under his breath, but Spaar heard him.

"The state objects," said Lawson. "The best anyone can say about the defendant is that he's a homicidal vigilante."

"Enough," said Judge Nordlander. "We're going to continue with the trial and let the jury decide. However, Agent Spaar and Agent Galen, this mysterious witness from your investigation is going to testify or I'll throw the whole thing out of court."

"Good news, Your Honor," said Spaar. "He's scheduled for tomorrow afternoon."

"It's a game-changer," said Traveler. He looked excited, and that was new.

"It's what I've been telling you all along," said Mike. They were back in the prison library. Mike had started to kind of like this room. It was so much bigger than his cell.

"Yeah, but now it's coming from Thornlocke. He hates you but he's backing your story anyway. This is huge, Mike."

"Think he'll tell the truth on the stand?"

"He has to. We have signed statements from him, and he spilled his guts to two FBI agents." Traveler rubbed his hands together. "This will be great drama. Juries love drama."

"Other than the drama," said Mike, "how does it help?"

Traveler ticked off the reasons. "First and foremost, it shows you had reasons for your otherwise illegal actions. You actually *were* saving your son and a pile of other kids. That takes you from deranged to heroic in one step. Second, once we convince the jury you were telling the truth about that, they're more likely to believe you about why you killed two cops."

"But she backed me up on that already," said Mike.

"Who—Adelman? Yeah, sure. But hell—before this we had, 'They followed you into the woods and beat the shit out of you because they were on a mission to rescue an innocent woman you abducted.' Now we have, 'They followed you into the woods and beat the shit out of you and were going to kill you *and* her because the FBI was hot on their tail and they needed to cover up their own felonious acts involving minors.'"

Mike frowned thoughtfully. "Yeah. That plays better."

Traveler almost laughed. Mike gave a half-grin.

"Thanks for everything you're doing for me," said Mike. "I know I haven't always made it easy."

"Ah, hell," said Traveler. "That's why they pay me the big bucks."

Mike guessed Thornlocke's suit cost a couple grand. Probably custom tailored, some Italian designer. But he was pleased to see the old man had lost weight, and as Thornlocke walked to the witness stand he leaned more heavily on the cane than he used to.

Lawson went first. The best he could do was go over old ground: he and Thornlocke agreed that on the night in question Mike had broken into the chateau, abducted Tsara, and sent two ransom notes. The second one had threatened her death. Mike flinched inwardly. Why the hell had he made her write that?

"How did you respond to the first note?" said Lawson.

"I panicked," said Thornlocke. "My sister, Tsara's mother, was murdered. The idea of losing her daughter to another violent crime—I stopped thinking. I only knew I had to act."

"So what did you do?"

"First I tried to hold the man who delivered the note."

"And that was?"

"The defendant's associate, Mr. Montrose."

"And how did you do that?"

"I grabbed a rifle. Unfortunately, with what I'm sure were the best intentions, my nephew blocked me. The gun went off accidentally and Mr. Montrose made good his escape."

Liar, thought Mike. Thornlocke had wanted Jim dead.

"And then?"

"I called the Libertyville police, Jordan and Arnold Stone, and sent them to find my niece."

"Given the gravity of the situation, why not call federal agents or state police?"

"First and foremost, I knew the Stone brothers were more familiar with the mountains than any outsider could be," said Thornlocke. "Second, in fairly short order my nephew had called the FBI, so the agents were already on their way."

"Do you still feel you made the best choice?"

"Certainly," said Thornlocke. "Especially when you consider the Stones caught up with Westbrook almost immediately. The federal agents weren't able to do that."

"Thank you, Mr. Thornlocke," said Lawson. "No further questions, Your Honor."

Traveler approached the witness stand.

"Mr. Thornlocke," he said, "isn't it true that you yourself are materially involved in this case?"

"Very much so, I'm afraid."

"And isn't it true that you are getting a reduced sentence in exchange for today's testimony?"

"Yes."

"Mm-hm. Mr. Thornlocke, do you recall the original charges against you?"

"They were quite extensive. I'm sure I couldn't recite the entire litany."

Traveler produced a sheet of paper. "I can understand that, Mr. Thornlocke, as it's in the dozens. Your Honor, I would like the jury to see the complete list of original charges."

"Proceed," said the judge. Traveler handed the list to the foreman. Her eyebrows went up.

"And what was it reduced to?"

Thornlocke didn't balk. "Kidnapping, conspiracy, and racketeering."

"And your sentence?"

"Ten years. I am scheduled to begin it in three weeks' time." His voice was flat. Like reading from a phone book, thought Mike.

Traveler picked up another sheet of paper. "Mr. Thornlocke, you gave a detailed confession to the FBI. Would you share some of it with the court? Start right there, please."

Thornlocke reached into a breast pocket and pulled out reading glasses, which he didn't manage to get on properly the first time. He cleared his throat and read aloud. "'Together with my accomplice, Mr. Hans Freihoffer, and two subordinates, Jordan and Arnold Stone, we abducted and held on my property, with my knowledge and my consent, multiple minors.'" He adjusted his spectacles. "'This was done for the purposes of financial gain.'"

Mike tried not to smile. He didn't want the jury to think he was gloating.

"Thank you, Mr. Thornlocke," said Traveler. "Now, is it true that one of the children in question was Aiden Westbrook, the six-year-old son of my client?"

"I found out after the fact that that was the case."

"Yes or no, please."

"Yes."

"And is it true that Mr. Westbrook, upon hearing that his child had been abducted, came to you and, in a completely nonviolent manner, requested the child's return?"

"Yes."

"Where did this conversation take place?"

"At my house, in my study."

"Who was present, other than you and Mr. Westbrook?"

"Mr. Freihoffer and the Stone brothers."

"And when Mr. Westbrook asked you to return his son to him, what did you say?"

"I refused."

"What did the Stone brothers say?"

Thornlocke hesitated so long that Traveler said, "Mr. Thornlocke? Did you hear the question?"

"Well, yes I did, but ...." He turned toward the judge. "Your Honor, am I to repeat what was said verbatim? They employed some rather salty language, and there are ladies present."

"Verbatim will do just fine," said Nordlander. "Proceed."

Thornlocke turned back toward Traveler. "Jordan—I believe it was Jordan—said, 'Better not make waves, Mikey. Hate to see any more shit happen to that kid of yours. He's already spending the night with rats big enough to fuck a turkey.' Then Arnold said, 'Remember the good old days in the drunk tank, Mike? You got your balls in a hell of a twist a few times back then.'"

The stillness in the room felt brittle as glass. Mike could feel his breath heaving in and out, like he'd been running.

"Go on," said Traveler.

"Then Westbrook said, 'You ain't the only cops around. Just let 'em all go or I'll call someone.'"

Mike frowned. He hadn't said "ain't." But the rest of it was right, so okay. He forced his breathing back to a normal rate.

"And then?"

"Arnold told him he was a—I'm not sure exactly—I believe it was 'a maggot-sack of goat shit,' excuse me, Your Honor, ladies, and told him that since he was a known criminal the police would treat his phone call as a prank and he would be arrested."

"Did he say 'arrested'?"

"No. He said 'bust your sick ass and beat the shit out of you till you cry like your kid.'"

Mike clenched his jaw so hard it hurt. His stomach twisted just like it had that day in Thornlocke's fancy study. He could see the men standing around him, grinning. It was almost like a flashback, like some guys had after combat. He could feel terrible forces welling up within him, rage and fury and a lust to hurt and kill.

"And how did you respond?" said Traveler. God, how could he be so calm?

"Me personally?"

"You, your associates."

Thornlocke bowed his head. "I am ashamed to say we laughed."

"Laughed," repeated Traveler.

"Yes."

"So," said Traveler, "on the afternoon of October third, upon hearing that his only child had been forcibly abducted and was being kept against his will, the defendant came to you in a nonviolent, nonthreatening fashion and begged for his son's release. At that time you refused to release him, and your associates indicated that the child was in danger from them. When my client attempted to turn the matter over to law enforcement authorities, as would have been proper, they told him that his own life would be in danger and suggested that his son might further suffer as a result of any such actions. Is that correct?"

Thornlocke stared far away. "Yes."

"No further questions, Your Honor," said Traveler.

In the crystalline silence that pervaded the room, Mike snuck a look at Tsara. His stomach flipped. Her face was the color of smoke. She looked like she was about to be sick.

This must be hell for her.

The jury deliberated for ten days. They emerged from their seclusion at the end of the day, so Judge Nordlander told them to come back in the morning to deliver the verdict. Lawson called Tsara immediately, and she was grateful. She needed to be there, even though the last few weeks had been hard—hard emotionally, hard logistically while she and David scrambled for childcare and puppy sitting, and hard as hell when Abbie clung to her legs, screaming, "Why do you have to go *again?*" and Josh, as befitted a manly five-year-old, ran into the house and hid under the coffee table.

So the next day Tsara held Abbie and wiped her tears one soggy tissue after another; and when the storm was largely spent she handed her baby girl to Court and they got into the car and drove away.

There was no way to make her kids understand that this was the culmination of a process that was largely about her but entirely beyond her control.

Now they stood in the familiar courtroom with its white walls and big picture windows. Mike was at his table, and his mother leaned forward and gave his shoulder a squeeze. He put his hand over hers, covering it completely, and smiled at her. A bailiff stepped forward with a frown, and Beth withdrew her hand and sat back.

Crews from the local TV stations hoisted their cameras to their shoulders as the jury filed in. Several jurors focused on Mike as they sat down. Others seemed to be avoiding looking at him. Tsara wondered what that meant.

"Has the jury arrived at a verdict?" said Judge Nordlander.

The forewoman stood. "Yes, Your Honor, we have."

"Continue," said the judge.

The forewoman unfolded a sheet of paper. "In the matter of the first-degree murder of Jordan Stone, we find the defendant, Michael Westbrook, not guilty. In the matter of the first-degree murder of Arnold Stone, we find the defendant, Michael Westbrook, not guilty."

Screams of outrage came from the pro-Stone section of the public area. Cheers blossomed behind the defendant's table. Mike's mother gasped and covered her mouth with her hands. Her eyes were shot through with tears. Nordlander banged for order. Only Mike was still, still as granite.

Tsara felt as though she were somewhere else.

"Proceed, Madame Foreman," said Nordlander.

"Thank you, Your Honor. In the matter of aggravated kidnapping, we find the defendant guilty. In the matter of breaking and entering, we find the defendant guilty. And in the matter of trespassing, we find the defendant guilty."

She sat down.

"Madame Foreman, members of the jury, I thank you for your service to this court," said the judge. "The details of this case have been extraordinarily complex, and the nuanced nature of your verdict indicates to me that you have taken that into account. Sentencing will be in three weeks' time."

He banged the gavel again and left the room. Tsara bumped into David as they stood.

"Are you okay?"

She shook her head. "Let's get out of here."

Three weeks went by fast. The kids, initially suspicious of Tsara's assurances that the trial was over, gradually relaxed. Court went back to Baltimore, and David's mother retreated to her own house while reminding them she was only a phone call away. Eventually Adara came home from taking care of her mother, and one day after an ice storm that would have made walking the dogs a peril rather than a pleasure, suggested they get together at their favorite coffee shop. Tsara drove to meet her, leaving the kids baking cookies with David.

She pulled into the parking lot and cut the engine. Adara's banana-yellow hybrid was parked next to her. The bumper sticker read, "It's an Election Year. *Expecto Patronum!*"

It made her smile, which was good because last night had been one of the rough ones. The dreams were so vivid.

She could see Mike and this time she was strong and he was helpless. As she closed in on him and saw the terror in his face her joy was hard as diamonds because she knew as soon as she killed him she would never have to be afraid ever again. He slipped under the wheels of her machine like a piece of paper, and she laughed out loud.

Until she looked behind her and saw the body on the ground and she ran to it because it wasn't Mike, it wasn't even a man ... it was a little boy ....

Why had she killed a child?

Tsara stepped out and made her way to the door. Frozen slush crunched under her Uggs.

— ✳ —

Adara sat at her favorite booth, cell phone in one hand and coffee in the other. The establishment was Mel's Coffee Shop, but she and Tsara usually called it Mel's House of Carbs. The pancakes were legendary. It was a popular place, full of clinking flatware and steam from hot drinks. The warmth from all the bodies fogged the narrow windows on either side of the door, but Adara was pretty sure the smudge with the long scarf was Tsara.

The rabbi waved as her friend came through the door and wove through the waitresses to get to the booth. They hadn't seen each other for weeks—Tsara and David had been spending so much time in New Hampshire, and then Adara had been out of town because of her mother. Tsara looked better, thought Adara as they hugged. The smile lines around her mouth were back.

"Checking email?" Tsara indicated the cell phone.

The rabbi shook her head. "Know what this phone does? It's a phone. It doesn't even have a camera."

Tsara gazed at it admiringly. "Now, that's just *adorable*."

"I want something no twenty-year-old kid is going to want to steal."

"That's probably smart. I heard about three teenagers who got into a peck of trouble that way."

"Had breakfast yet?"

"I just need a drink. No, I'll get it."

Tsara stuffed the scarf into the sleeve of her jacket and hung it on the coat tree. As she strode to the counter, Adara could see tightness in her shoulders. But when she returned moments later the smile lines were out in force as the cumulus cloud of whipped cream on her hot chocolate tilted regally to one side.

"Eep!" Tsara licked an errant blob from the rim, eyes laughing. "Abbie has this new thing," she said as they sat down. "Every time she takes a sip of milk now she says, 'Wipe off your mustache, Abbie!' and she does it."

"My daughter was a fanatic about not getting her fingers sticky at that age," said Adara. "We had to set a damp washcloth beside her plate at every meal."

"Josh's the exact opposite," said Tsara. "You could dunk him in hot fudge and roll him in sprinkles and I don't think he'd notice."

"So the kids are good?" said Adara.

"The kids are great. They like taking care of me, and sometimes I even let them."

"How's their mommy? You're looking fabulous, by the way." Tsara wore a purple sweater that clung in all the right ways before skimming over the hips of her jeans.

"Yeah, but there's a picture of me in the attic that looks like crap."

Adara laughed. "What's your secret method?"

"Very mysterious. I spend a lot of time at the gym. I told David I'm gunning for the 'Most Buff Former Hostage Award.'"

"Well, it's paying all kinds of dividends."

"I think the word you're groping for is 'supermodelicious.'"

"No, that's how I describe myself."

"Ah, so that one's taken."

"You know, I really admire you," said Adara. "You're just so positive."

"Don't overestimate me," said Tsara through the whipped cream. She took a sip. "There are reasons I'm keeping the therapist community in clover."

"Sure. But you're not deep in a bottle or having manic rages or—or abusing prescription drugs. That kind of thing." Adara thought of her congregation. People sometimes went to dark places when their world came apart.

"There's a lot you don't see," said Tsara.

"Of course." Adara took a sip of her drink. "How are the nightmares?"

"Oh, hell, I don't know." Adara was the kind of rabbi you could say "hell" in front of. "I think they're getting a little less frequent, but—" She gestured with one hand. "My shrink says I have acute stress disorder."

"What's that?"

"Post-traumatic stress lite."

"Really." Adara put down her mug. "How so?"

"Fewer calories," she replied, deadpan. "No, kidding. It's pretty much the same thing, just not as nasty."

"In what ways?"

"Well, for starters, it goes away."

"And the other one doesn't?"

"It keeps coming back. Sort of like emotional malaria. But acute stress disorder lasts a few months and then you're done. Or anyway, that's the plan." Her smile disappeared. "And that would be nice, because I really, really don't want to keep freaking out whenever I see a gun in a movie, or jumping like a spawning salmon every time someone taps me on the shoulder."

Adara wished she could hug across the table. That this should have happened to Tsara, of all people. "It's so unfair."

Tsara shrugged. "I had one very bad weekend."

"Don't downplay it. What that man did to you was horrible."

"Yes, I know. I was there at the time."

"And you're still suffering from it. That's what I'm trying to say."

"I don't know how much of it was him and how much was the two guys he shot."

Adara frowned. "There's really no way to parse that out, is there?"

"Aah, that's a lawyer's job, not a rabbi's." Tsara smiled. "He kidnapped me; they tried to kill me. The public defender made much of this distinction."

"I saw the verdict on TV in my mom's hospital room," said Adara.

"How is she, by the way?"

"Much better, thanks. She's back home now. I couldn't believe it when they acquitted him of the homicides."

"Well, the PD did a pretty good job of showing those two guys weren't worth the dirt they died in. I mean, my God, the parade of witnesses who had to stop themselves from doing the Highland fling when they heard the lads were not coming home again."

Adara tilted her head. "But he was guilty of ... aggravated kidnapping?"

"And B and E. "

"So that's something."

Tsara's smile glinted back. "And trespassing."

"Naturally," said Adara. "Do you think it was fair?" *Justice, justice shall you pursue.*

370

Tsara's smile flattened as she looked past her friend. "I was relieved. Which—I don't know if I should be."

"Because?"

"I'm okay that he got off on the homicides. But I can't figure out if that's because I think … he did it for me."

Adara could feel a pulse in her chest. "You think he killed two men for your sake?"

"He only fired when they were drawing on me," said Tsara. "And I expect he could have gotten away if he'd wanted to. So … yeah." She looked into her mug.

Oh, no, thought Adara. *You are not going to carry that around.*

"Put someone else in the story," she said. "If he had done the same thing but with another person there, how would you feel?"

Tsara lifted her head. Her gaze returned from far away. "I'd think he'd saved her life and the jury would have been stupid to find otherwise." The smile was surprised. "You're *good* at this."

"Did you ever ask him about it?"

"At the time he kept insisting they had died in a hunting accident. You know, the special kind with perfect aim and timing."

"You can almost see the machinations of God." Adara was not above sarcasm.

"Except that unlike God, this particular miracle worker is in a cell awaiting sentencing."

"And how does that make you feel?" Adara liked to trot out the counseling courses she had taken in rabbinical school.

"Like I already have a phalanx of shrinks to ask me questions like that. "

"Sorry." Adara gave a rueful smile. "I'm the kind of person—when I see a problem, I want to fix it."

"Hey, me too. Do you think we might secretly be guys?"

Adara laughed and they busied themselves with their drinks. Tsara drained her mug.

"Actually," she said, "I did want to ask you something."

Adara waited.

"Okay, so—reverence for human life and all that—*nefesh* whatever it is—"

"*Pikuach nefesh?*"

"I think so. How many *nefeshes* are there?"

"*Pikuach nefesh* is the idea that the preservation of human life overrides almost everything else," said Adara.

"Yeah, that's the one."

"What about it?"

"Best *nefesh* ever."

"What about it? You're stalling."

"Okay, okay. So—two men died on my account, and I'm not sorry about it. I'm not." Her eyes were large, the glint of laughter doused in their darkness. "Does that make me a bad Jew?"

Adara shook her head. "No. It might make you a bad Quaker, but we have a little more leeway than that."

"Good. Because I'm really not."

"No reason to be."

"Okay, next thing." Tsara hesitated. "Okay. It's almost a year till Yom Kippur. So looking ahead to forgiving everyone—not that I always do," she admitted. "Sometimes at the end I'm like, 'Okay, God, I hereby forgive everyone except those below; see appended list.'"

"Or 'I'm still working on these three over here; can I get back to you?'"

It was a struggle, thought Adara. No, more than that. Yom Kippur was the Mount Everest of Jewish faith and practice. Genuinely to absolve all the fallible people in one's life—not easy. She remembered one year she had managed to exculpate someone in the last moments of the service, as the windows darkened and stars signaled the end of the best and hardest day of the year. She had felt like doing a victory lap around the synagogue.

"Yeah, exactly. So. This year's going to be hard." Tsara's eyes were full of memories. "That night at my uncle's place ... I really thought I was going to die, that my kids would have to grow up without a mother." Her voice cracked and her fingers twisted together. "Shit."

"Take your time," said Adara softly.

Tsara wiped her eyes with her napkin. When she spoke her voice was thick. "Even later, when I'd figured out he wasn't interested in hurting me, I couldn't get away from him. I tried." She twitched. "Forgiving him's going to be a bitch. I don't know if I can do it."

"Nobody says you have to," said Adara.

"I checked the *machzor* last night," said Tsara. "It says—"

"I know what it says." Adara could picture the holiday prayer book with its gold Hebrew lettering along the spine, and she was pretty sure she knew the passage Tsara had read.

"Well, it's pretty unambiguous."

"Forgiveness is the goal," said Adara. "But look: certain categories of offenses—of sins—fall outside that purview. They're considered unforgiveable."

"Okay." Tsara ran her finger around the handle of her mug. "Which ones and why?"

"Well, murder is one."

"Doesn't apply. Obviously."

"And rape."

"Same. But my God, people keep saying, 'Well, he didn't rape you,' like *that* makes everything okay—"

"Who says?" demanded Adara. "What kind of idiot would say something like that?"

"A certain head of the worship committee, since you asked."

Adara's lips tightened. "I'll have a word with her."

"Tell her she's an ass."

"I'll have a word with her," repeated the rabbi. "But getting back to the point at hand—essentially, anything that kills the divine within you is considered unforgiveable. So murder and rape fall into that category."

"He didn't do those. But, God, sometimes I—last night I dreamed I ran over him, and I was glad."

"It was a dream."

"It was a rush. But then I felt like shit."

Adara put her chin in her hand. "Okay. So why do you feel you need to forgive him?"

Tsara goggled at her. "I thought I was supposed to."

"No one says it has to be instantaneous." Adara took a sip of her drink and wrinkled her nose before putting it down. "Cold," she explained. "Let me ask you this: is there any other reason you think you should forgive him?"

Tsara continued running her finger around the mug handle. "I think it's partly because what he could have done was so much worse. I mean, the two cops were homicidal. Sadistic. But this guy—" She stopped.

"What?"

Tsara sighed. "I don't know what to call him."

"How badly did he hurt you?"

Tsara shrugged. "Bumps. Scrapes."

"Well, that makes a difference, of course."

"Yeah, well, that's part of what I'm struggling with. He never intentionally injured me. Although I do think there was a certain level of collateral damage he found acceptable."

"I remember," said Adara. After the abduction Tsara's face had been a sunset of bruises.

"And he thought he had a really good reason. I'm not saying I agree—but it wasn't about me. He just wanted his kid back and thought this was the only way."

"Do you believe him?"

"As far as I can tell, he never lied to me. Oh, wait." She held her hand to her forehead. "Except about killing the two cops, and getting rid of the gun. But I can let that go."

Adara tapped her fingertips against her cheekbone. "How does not forgiving him make you feel?"

"Like there's a fire I can't put out."

A waitress walked past, her apron clinking with forks. Across the room someone laughed at someone else's laughter.

Adara put her hands down. "Here is what I suggest you do. And at the moment I'm speaking as your rabbi in addition to as your friend. Don't try to forgive him right now. Don't," she repeated as Tsara began to speak. "It's too much to ask of yourself. But be aware that forgiving him is as much for your own benefit as it is for his. Holding onto your anger is natural, but I can see it's affecting you in a negative way. Forgiving him—when the time is right—will have a positive effect on your life."

"How?" protested Tsara. "Honest to God, I don't even know where the switch is. How can I make it like this never happened?"

"Oh, you can't," said Adara. "Don't even try. Forgiving isn't forgetting. But what you can do is set the memory aside so it's not a stumbling block you've set before yourself. Put it aside," she repeated. "Take it out again in six months and see where you are. Maybe you can forgive him then. If not, you can always put it away again."

Tsara drummed her fingers on the table. "What if I'm not done by High Holy Days?"

Adara smiled. "The great thing about Yom Kippur is it comes around again. You can try for next year if this time isn't a hundred per cent."

"I'll have to think about all this," said Tsara. She stood up. "Ethical questions make me thirsty. Can I get you a refill?"

"I'll join you."

One coffee and one hot chocolate later they were back at the table.

"One more thing," said Adara. "You're not required to do anything unless he repents."

"No kidding," said Tsara. She licked the spoon she had seized to subdue the whipped cream. "God, I love being Jewish. How does he do that, and how can I tell?"

"He has to recognize that he has done a wrong. Has he done that?"

Tsara frowned and pulled in a corner of her mouth. "I think so, yeah. A couple of things he's said …."

"At the trial?"

"Before." Tsara busied herself with her drink.

"Second, he has to show true remorse and regret."

"Mm."

"And he has to make a sincere attempt to right the wrong."

"How? He's in prison." She shook her head in desperation. "I don't see the happy ending here. He's locked up, my uncle's locked up, my relationship with my aunt and cousins is pretty much in the crapper— where's the good part?"

"How are you and David?" asked Adara.

"Okay."

"Has this brought you closer in any way?"

Tsara rolled her eyes. "No. This isn't *Reader's Digest*."

"*Reader's*—"

"Oh, you know, they always have these revolting stories about people who discover the true meaning of happiness after they, like, lose their limbs to flesh-eating bacteria—oh, hey, I'm sorry—" She handed Adara a napkin.

The rabbi wiped her eyes. "You had me at flesh-eating bacteria."

"Sorry."

Adara put the napkin down. "I want to be serious now," she said. "You're very funny and witty because you always are, but I'm afraid we might enjoy ourselves so much that we won't get to what's bothering you. For the next few minutes I'm your rabbi." She settled back in her seat. "Go on."

"Okay." Tsara marshaled her crises. "Well, basically, my life is not so much more meaningful now that I've gone through all this crap. It was good *before*. David is now married to an irritable insomniac given to bouts of weeping. I'm in therapy, I'm getting better, but anyone who thinks something like this would be helpful for a relationship is full of shit. We *had* a good marriage."

Adara straightened up with a spark of panic. "Do you mean you're—"

"No. It still *is* good. But I won't lie to you. This has been a strain. I don't get why it happened—I don't think there's a reason. But now I need to figure out how to live in my new normal."

Forgiveness, thought Adara. *Atonement. These are questions a shrink can't answer. I hope I can.*

"Do you think he got a fair trial?"

"Yes. We were there for most of it."

"Then I think you need to make that part of your own process. The fact that he's receiving a fair punishment through the criminal justice system takes a big part of the responsibility off you."

"Why?"

"Because the wrong has been recognized, and there's been a sincere attempt to make things right."

"In a court of law."

"Yes. Which brings us to Jewish law."

"How does it—"

"Work with me." A rabbi was always ready to make a connection. "I've had the impression several times today that you are adding burdens to yourself because you think Jewish law demands it. That's not what our Law is for."

"It's not designed to crush us when we're down?"

Adara didn't smile. "It's our attempt to make life livable within the context of a moral relationship with God and humanity."

"What about Jewish atheists?"

"Plenty of Jewish atheists take the Law very seriously because they find it addresses life's biggest questions. Which brings us to you." Rabbis love a good segue.

"How?"

"He did what he did in order to rescue a child, right?"

"His son."

"And what are the chances he would have retrieved the boy in any other way?"

"He'd tried everything else. Or thought he had."

"So your part in this drama resulted in the saving of a child," said Adara.

Tsara put her hand down next to the mug. Her mouth softened and her eyes relaxed. "I never thought of that."

"Maybe the child *is* the repentance. Could he be what helps you forgive his father?"

"How?"

"Could you help the boy in some way? Do the repentance for the father?"

"I've been thinking about that," said Tsara slowly. "Because I hate like hell the fact that after—even after all this the kid still doesn't have his daddy."

Adara reached across the table and touched Tsara's hand. "If you want a happy ending," she said gently, "I think you may have to write it yourself."

When Tsara got home David held open the door for her. The house was quiet. She unwound the scarf from her neck and looked around. "What have you done with my children?"

"They're at my mom's. I figured you'd want to drive up to Madison tomorrow for the sentencing." When she didn't answer he went on, "I also figured if I'm wrong we can go out for dinner and a movie."

"Your mom's a goddess," said Tsara. She sat on the painted wooden bench and pulled off her boots.

"So what do you want to do?"

Tsara considered. "Dinner out, no movie, Madison tomorrow. That way we can get to bed early and hit the road before traffic gets too godawful."

So they went to Friday's and came home and, by a Herculean effort of will, resisted the temptation to stay up and watch *The Daily Show*. They were in bed with the lights out by ten-thirty.

Tsara stared into the darkness. She tried to be still so David could sleep, but first her nose itched and she had to scratch it. Then she had to rearrange the covers to slide her arm back under. Then her hair was tickling her face and needed to be smoothed away. Her back was tired of her lying on that side, so she very quietly rolled over, careful not to move the bed and disturb—

"You are just not going to sleep tonight, are you?" said the dark lump that was David.

"Why start now?" retorted Tsara. Abandoning all pretense she got out of bed, pulling on the flannel bathrobe David had given her for her birthday five years earlier. She walked over to the window and pulled up the shade. The sky was clear, and the backyard was a silverscape of ice and moonglow.

Behind her, sheets rustled as David got up and pulled on his own bathrobe. Then he was at her side, not quite touching her.

"This will all be over soon," he said.

"Why? Because of the sentencing?" Tsara rubbed her lip with her thumbnail. "That doesn't make it over."

"Well …." David was clearly at a loss. "What would, then?"

"I don't know," she said miserably. "I keep waiting for the happy ending."

"That's the thing about real life," said David. "It's not tidy."

Tsara hugged herself. The bedroom was cold. "Adara says if I want a happy ending I'll have to write it myself."

David stepped behind her. His arms went around her, and his chin was on her shoulder. "You're home and you're safe," he said. "Isn't that happy ending enough?"

Tsara shook her head. The feeling came over her again, as it had so often in recent days: an overwhelming sense of the wrongness of everything.

"Want to know something?" David's voice was soft, as though the kids were asleep in their rooms instead of at Grandma's house twenty minutes away. "For tidy endings …." His voice misted away.

"What?"

"I wanted to kill him," he said. "That first day in court, when you testified—when I saw him stand up, and I thought about what he—I just—" He stopped, but he held her tight and through her bathrobe Tsara could feel his heart thumping. "I wanted to kill him."

Tsara's eyes were still fixed on the mounded snow on the pines outside the window. "I know," she said. She put her hands over his. "But he thought … what would you do if someone took Josh or Abbie?"

"I wouldn't have kidnapped his wife."

"Of course not. She's been dead for five years."

"You know what I mean."

"Yeah." Tsara stared at the play of dark and gleam outside. "I wish he were just evil," she said. "I wish he didn't have a kid. Or that the kid were a total shit."

"Seems like a good kid," admitted David. "I hate that."

Tsara leaned her head toward his. "Because?"

"You know why."

She sighed.

"I'm conflicted about him," said David.

Tsara snorted. "You think *you're* conflicted," she muttered.

David unclasped his arms and stepped to one side so he was standing next to her again. "What do you want to do?"

"I don't know," she said wretchedly. "I just don't see what good it does to have him go to prison for the rest of his life—I just want something not crappy to come out of all this."

For a moment longer they stood in the glimmer from the window. Then David went to the door and opened it. "C'mon. I'll help you pick the stationery."

"How did you know?" said Tsara in amazement.

"Oh, good God. I know you." David tightened the belt of his robe. "You probably have the whole thing written out in your head in five-paragraph form."

"Certainly not." Tsara took his hand as they walked to the study. "I'm having a terrible time with paragraph three."

Early next morning David and Tsara sped north on I-93. Tsara glanced at the linen envelope poking out of her purse.

"Did you email him a copy?" asked David.

"I did. But you never know—the server could be down, or it goes in the spam file."

"We have plenty of time."

They were going against traffic, and the highway unspooled like a ribbon in front of them. As they drove, Tsara felt her heart lighten in a way it hadn't since a certain weekend in early October.

The parking lot to the courtyard was full when they arrived. David let her out. "Save me a seat." He pulled away, his wheels flinging up lumps of brown slush.

Fifteen minutes later, David sat down next to Tsara in Judge Nordlander's courtroom. His cheeks were red and he had unbuttoned his coat. "Did you see him?"

"I gave it to his clerk and made him promise to give it to him."

David straightened his tie. "Okay, then."

Judge Nordlander entered and took his seat. As the spectators retook theirs, Tsara saw that the judge held a sheet of linen stationery, tri-folded. Her stomach fluttered. Crews from the local television stations hoisted their cameras onto their shoulders as he began to speak.

"Good morning," he said. "As you know, we are here for the sentencing of Mr. Michael Westbrook in an unusually high-profile case.

The court will pronounce that sentence momentarily." He looked at the defendant's table. "Mr. Westbrook. Please stand."

Mike stood up.

"Do you have anything to say before the court pronounces sentence on you?" said the judge.

"Yes, Your Honor." Mike's voice was steady. "I would like to apologize for the pain my actions have caused Mrs. Adelman and her family." His eyes went to Tsara. "I'm sorry," he said.

Tsara's palms began to sweat. She felt dizzy.

"Do you have anything further to say?" asked the judge.

"No, Your Honor."

"Very well." Judge Nordlander unfolded the piece of paper in his hand and looked out at the courtroom. "A few minutes ago I received a letter from one of the people involved in this case. I've decided to share it with you before sentencing."

Oh, God, thought Tsara. She ran over the letter in her mind, wondering if she had made any errors. Well, too late for that now ....

"Dear Judge Nordlander," read the judge.

> *First, let me assure you that no one is making me write this; and furthermore, that in the opinion of the mental health professionals whom I now see regularly, I am not suffering from Stockholm Syndrome or any other mental disturbance that would impair my ability to think lucidly about this or any other matter. I state these facts because I expect you will be very surprised at my reason for this letter.*

> *I am writing to ask the court for mercy for Mr. Michael Westbrook.*

> *Let there be no mistake: Mr. Westbrook displayed appalling judgment toward me. That he broke into my room and, with an accomplice, abducted me has been thoroughly established. He himself does not deny it. Furthermore, I am viscerally aware that with but slight tilts in the angle of fate, events could have turned out quite differently for me, and far worse.*

> *And yet I would point to several mitigating factors.*

> *First, I did not experience any physical hurt at Michael Westbrook's hands beyond superficial scrapes and bruises. I have literally suffered worse from slipping in the bathroom.*

Furthermore, Mr. Westbrook repeatedly put himself in harm's way for my sake, placing my safety before his own. I feel no need to repeat the voluminous testimony we have heard regarding Jordan and Arnold Stone, so I will summarize by saying that I believe they intended to kill both Mr. Westbrook and me, and that his actions prevented them.

In short, despite the extreme nature of the events of that October weekend, Mr. Westbrook never displayed any malice toward me. His actions were desperately misguided, but I believe that he genuinely felt he had no other way to protect his only child.

This brings me to my final point. A young boy is at the heart of this case: a six-year-old who has never known any other parent; and who, throughout his own ordeal that weekend (an ordeal I am sure was far more terrifying than my own, if only because the boy is so young), clung to hope only because he knew with a child's certainty that his father would rescue him.

I must ask the court, how is it in the best interests of this child to separate these two?

For all these reasons, I ask the court not for clemency but leniency in sentencing Mr. Michael Westbrook.

Thank you.

Sincerely,

Tsarina Abrams Adelman

As Judge Nordlander read, Tsara glanced surreptitiously at Mike. For once his composure had abandoned him, and he started as though someone had hit him. As the reading went on he turned slowly toward her, eyes wide. She looked away.

The judge put down the paper. "Mrs. Adelman," he said, "did you write this letter?"

Tsara stood up. "Yes, Your Honor."

"It's very common for the court to receive letters on behalf of a defendant," said the judge. "But not from the victim of his crime. That is unusual, to say the least." He glanced at the letter and back at her. "You may be seated. I thank you for communicating with the court." As

383

Tsara took her seat again, the judge continued, "It seems everyone has had his or her say. Therefore, the court will now sentence the defendant."

Tsara swallowed. She put her cold hand in David's. Would her letter have any impact? Or would it just be a curiosity the judge would chuckle over later?

"Mr. Westbrook," said Nordlander, "you have been found guilty of trespassing, breaking and entering, and aggravated kidnapping. This court has established that you committed these acts under unexpected, not to say remarkable, circumstances. I have no doubt that you believed yourself to be acting in an honorable manner. You were not."

Mike bowed his head. Tsara's grip tightened on David's hand.

"That being said," continued Nordlander, "the fact remains that a number of these circumstances, though not perhaps mitigating, do give the court a certain measure of sympathy for the acts of a desperate father. Furthermore, Mr. Westbrook, the court has received numerous letters in your support. Your former commanding officer, fellow Marines who served with you, and many of your associates in Libertyville. You seem to have a lot of friends, sir.

"It is common for the court to receive such letters. As I stated before, however, it is downright extraordinary to receive one from the defendant's victim. Mrs. Adelman has told us she finds you deserving of mercy. I shall weigh her words most carefully as I pronounce your sentence.

"In the matter of the trespassing, the court sentences you to time served.

"In the matter of breaking and entering, the court sentences you to three years."

Tsara felt sick.

"To be served concurrently with the sentence for kidnapping," said the judge.

What?

"Finally, in the matter of aggravated kidnapping, the court sentences you to a sentence of not more than six years and not less than three, to be followed by probation for another seven years."

"Oh, my God," said Mike. He seemed almost to sway where he stood. "Thank you."

He looked at Tsara. "I—thank you."

A shaky smile lifted her lips. A glow seemed to emanate from her core, and her fingertips grew warm.

That afternoon David and Tsara ate their final lunch at the Big Band Café. Annette and Kevin had insisted that the entire meal was on the house, and the Adelmans were just finishing dessert. David leaned back and surveyed his wife. Tsara had never had French Chocolate Pie before, and she seemed to be enjoying it. Her shoulders were relaxed for the first time in months, and the twitches that had become part of her daily repertoire had dissolved. Her mouth was soft when she smiled. "I don't think I realized how much tension you were carrying around till now," he said.

"I feel good," said Tsara. "I feel …." She drifted off and had another bite of pie.

"Good, like you knew that you would?"

She took her time chewing. "Like I matter again."

Annette came to the table, coffeepot in one hand. "How you folks doing?" she said. "Guess we won't be seeing much more of you."

"Probably not," agreed David. "But thanks so much for everything you've done." He handed her a sheaf of envelopes. "Do you mind? Should be the last ones."

"No problem at all." She turned and shouted to the kitchen. "Hey, Kevin! Keep saving the papers!"

"Save the papers. Got it," called Kevin.

"Are you making a scrap book?" said Annette.

"I'd never get around to it," said Tsara. "I've just been keeping them in a box."

"Want me to make one for you?" asked Annette. "My cousin is good at it. We could do something real special for you."

"Oh, you don't have to do that."

Annette laughed uproariously. "Yeah, I know I don't have to. Do you *want* me to?"

Tsara grinned in helpless amusement. "If you insist, I'd be a fool to say no."

"Yeah, you would," called Kevin.

"Great," said Annette. "I love projects like this. I'll try to get it to you by Christmas, okay, doll?"

"Great."

As they were preparing to leave, Tsara stopped by the counter to drop a ten into the Jimmy Fund jar by the cash register. They had taken to doing this at every visit. It was their way of showing their appreciation for the long string of free desserts and meals they had enjoyed courtesy of Kevin and Annette.

"You must be feeling pretty relieved about now," said Annette, leaning over the counter. "What with that guy heading off to jail and all." She shook her head. "What a bastard."

"I feel pretty good." She smiled at Annette. "But y'know—he wasn't totally a bastard."

"No kiddin'?" Annette wiped down the counter with a rag. "Well, I guess you'd know better than anyone."

"Yeah," said Tsara. "I guess I would."

EPILOGUE

Tsara stood in an olive-drab hallway holding a little boy's hand. She had already relinquished her purse and cell phone and the clip in her hair and all of her jewelry except for her wedding band and the necklace with the Star of David medallion; but with a little pleading they had let her keep her copy of *People.* The boy held a folder full of his school projects. "I can't *wait,*" he exclaimed for the third time in five minutes. Tsara squeezed his hand gently.

It must be great to be six, she thought. He didn't care where they were. All that mattered was whom they were going to see.

The corrections officer opened the door and they stepped into a large, cinderblock room with high windows and a linoleum floor. Benches lined the walls, and tables were placed throughout the middle. It was visiting day and several families were there, some speaking in urgent undertones, most chatting easily.

"Daddy!" bellowed Aiden. He slipped his hand from Tsara's and barreled into the room.

At a table close to the door Mike stood up. His big shoulders filled the prison uniform. The boy ran into his arms and Mike swept him into the air, burying his head in his son's shoulder.

"Aiden!"

Tsara stepped forward. "They wouldn't let him come in without me," she said. "I'll just let you two visit." Before Mike could say anything she turned away and settled herself on a bench at the next table and opened her magazine.

"I have projects to show you," confided Aiden.

"Yeah? You show me, buddy."

The Westbrook boys went through every scrap of paper in the folder while Aiden explained the history and significance of each one. His teacher was nice. There were eleven kids in his class. He was the third tallest. And Grandma got grumpy if he didn't brush his teeth. Mike opined that Grandma was right about that, although under withering cross-examination he confessed that when he was six he hadn't always brushed his teeth either.

When they were done with the folder they went over to the meager supply of plastic toys in one corner. Aiden found a couple of Matchbox cars, and Mike promptly sat on the floor and rolled up his sleeve, bunching the muscles in his arm. Aiden rolled the cars over his father's biceps, one chasing the other around the bulges.

"Westbrook! Contact!" barked the guard.

"Right." Mike stood and set his feet apart and Aiden ran the cars around his father's ankles. Given the setting Tsara found his choice of siren noises rather odd, but Mike didn't seem to mind. She wondered if the prison would let her donate some of Josh's toy cars. He had so many.

Finally Tsara walked over to them. She had read the magazine twice and memorized the beauty secrets of the stars. Astonishing how many of them got by with moisturizer and a good night's sleep. "I hate to break this up, but it's time to go."

Aiden's face wrinkled. "But we just *got* here."

"None of that," admonished Mike. "When it's time to go it's time to go. Be a good boy now." He spoke lightly, but a tightening of his brows belied his tone. Back at the table he gathered the papers and slid them into the folder. "Don't forget your projects."

"Daddy!" Aiden was aghast. "They're for *you.*"

Mike's eyes creased in a smile. "Awesome, dude. I'll show all my friends." He put the folder under his arm and the three of them walked to the door. The guard opened it and Mike spoke to him suddenly.

"I need to speak to the lady in private." He gave a quick look at Aiden and back to the guard.

"Do I look like a babysitter, Westbrook?"

"Two minutes. Please. "

The guard looked at Tsara. "Is that okay with you, ma'am?"

"I guess so." Her fingers curled around the magazine.

"In that case," said the guard, "maybe the kid needs to use the bathroom." He looked down at Aiden and almost smiled.

"No, I don't," said Aiden.

"Yes, you do," said Mike. "C'mon, buddy. Bathroom's over here."

"It's a good idea right before a long car ride," said Tsara as she walked over with them.

Aiden stepped into the bathroom. The door closed behind him and Tsara looked up at her former captor.

"I knew you were coming," he said.

Of course he knew, she thought. He had had to put her name on a list. After a heartbeat he went on. "But what I don't understand—" His eyes narrowed in confusion. He cleared his throat. "After everything I put you through—why?"

"Oh," said Tsara. "I just decided … if anything good were going to come of this, I had to make it happen."

Mike looked at her. He wanted to ask if the nightmares were getting better, but he knew he didn't have the right. Instead he said, "Thank you."

"You're welcome."

"I am sorry," he said.

"I know."

Through the door came the sound of a toilet flushing. They had a few seconds. "Do you forgive me?"

Tsara thought of the box where she'd put the experience, as per the rabbi's instructions.

"No. Not yet."

The door opened. "I washed my hands," said Aiden. He held them up. "See? They're damp."

Mike turned his head away from Aiden. "Can you check?" he breathed. "I'm not allowed to touch him except at the beginning and the end."

Tsara ran a finger over Aiden's moist skin. "Looks good to me."

They walked back to the door. Mike gave Aiden a last hug and set him down. His fingers slid softly over the boy's hair before he pulled his hands away.

"Thanks."

"I didn't do anything," said the officer. But Mike had been looking at Tsara when he spoke.

She stepped through the door. "I'll try again for next month," she said, "but I can't promise anything."

"'Bye, Daddy," called Aiden.

"'Bye, buddy. Be good."

Tsara and Aiden walked into the prison parking lot. It would be spring soon, but sunset was still early. Darkness thickened around them, and slush squished under their feet as they made their way to her minivan.

It had been a long trip.

But worth it.

ACKNOWLEDGEMENTS

It takes a village.

First and foremost, I have to thank Mike Marano, whose merciless evisceration of what I had thought was my final draft gave me the tools I needed to take *Wrong Place, Wrong Time* to a level I could never have reached on my own. I'm grateful that Mike spared no pains to tell me what was wrong and, occasionally, what was right about my manuscript. (Sample marginalia: "AAAARRRRGHHH! You *know* better than this!")

Next are Bradley Bryant and Steve Grassie of the Violent Crimes Unit at the FBI, who provided a stunning trove of information about the FBI and kidnapping cases. The fact that they were able to refrain from bawling with laughter as we dove through the Mariana Trench of my ignorance is a testament to American law enforcement everywhere. Any humanity, not to say accuracy, in Spaar and Galen is due to them. Any deficits are my fault.

Thanks also to Linda Wilkins of the Office of Public Affairs at the FBI, who set up not one but two interviews with the agents for me, thereby making me a pariah among my writing friends, who were so jealous they could barely be civil.

Karl Colón practically deserves co-writer credit. It is good to be friends with a former prosecutor turned librarian, especially when one is writing dramatic courtroom scenes. This is especially true if one's legal training is limited to having watched *LA Law* back when it was in syndication. I might add that, unlike Brad and Steve, Karl did not actually refrain from giggling at me. I guess he is entitled.

Don Avey, retired cop of Marlborough, MA, told me everything I needed to know about gunshot wounds, and had the good sense to clam up whenever my four-year-old toddled into the room.

Marine Lance Corporal Tom Whitmer provided tremendous details about his time battling terrorists in Iraq, giving me information I simply could not have gotten elsewhere. I can only add my thanks to the chorus of a grateful nation.

Rabbi Sally Finestone answered all my Jewy questions with her customary humor and élan. She had very definite ideas about which *yeshiva* Yoda would have attended.

Sara Sullivan educated me in the details of sign language. It was a delight to name my court interpreter after her.

Way, way too many thanks for Natasha Hatalsky, my expert on everything equine, my sometimes babysitter and occasional date for tea at the Ritz.

Nancy Antonietti and Elizabeth Morana read my stuff and gave me constructive feedback and rousing cheers in almost equal measure. Way to be an online support group, ladies!

Grub Street is known as "Boston's Premier Writing Organization," and it ain't braggin' if you can do it. There is nothing like being surrounded by a community of writers. Mike Marano's Smart Page-Turner class at Grub was another source of support and insight. I put the plot of this book through a Cuisinart several times based on their and Mike's recommendations. Painful, but in a good way.

The Office of Letters and Light runs National Novel-Writing Month every November. Got a great idea for a novel? Take a month and get that sucker down on paper. I can't say enough about these people and their outstanding program, except to say that thanks to them I finished the first draft of *Wrong Place, Wrong Time* in seven weeks. The fact that at that point most of it read like Nancy Drew on a very bad day is hardly their fault.

I absolutely must thank Burt and Virginia, who gave me the idea that started it all.

And finally, I have been blessed beyond all measure with my husband, Doug Jacobs. While I was going hell for leather on the first draft, he took over my usual childcare and household tasks. He read three different iterations of the manuscript out loud to me, beautifully, with expression and different voices. He seemed almost as fascinated with the characters and their story as I was, and we discussed them endlessly. Because of him, writing this book was never a solitary task. The only thing he never gave me was any doubt that I would succeed. Thanks, Doug, today and every day. You're my guy.

About the Author

Tilia Klebenov Jacobs holds a BA from Oberlin College, where she double-majored in Religion and English with a concentration in Creative Writing. Following an interregnum as an outdoor educator with the Fairfax County Park Authority in Virginia, she earned a Master of Theological Studies from Harvard Divinity School and a Secondary School Teaching Certification from the Harvard Graduate School of Education. Despite lacking the ability to breathe fire except in the strictly metaphorical sense, Tilia has taught middle school, high school, and college, and has won numerous awards for her fiction and nonfiction writing. She is a judge in the Soul-Making Keats Literary Competition, and she teaches writing in Massachusetts state prisons. Tilia lives near Boston with her husband, two children, and two standard poodles.

Questions for Discussion

1. Tsara is a mother. To what extent does that guide her actions?

2. What qualities make Tsara an excellent mother? What personality traits does she share with her own mother?

3. How is loss of a loved one a theme in this book?

4. The novel is told from multiple points of view, so we see the situations from almost everyone's perspective. Did this change your understanding of why the characters acted as they did? Were you surprised at any point to find yourself sympathizing with a character you had previously disliked?

5. Tsara's discussions with her rabbi help her to find a path to internal peace. Have you had a spiritual leader or other friend who helped you toward a resolution of an internal conflict?

6. Adara gives Tsara advice about forgiveness. Did the advice surprise you? Is Adara's concept of forgiveness the same as yours?

7. At the start of the book, Tsara reads letters from her mother. At the end of the book, Tsara writes a letter which has a dramatic impact on Mike's life. What does the act of writing this letter mean to her?

8. What do letters offer that no other form of communication (phone calls, email) can?

9. Unlike many abduction novels, Tsara and Mike do not end up in bed together. Is this a relief or a disappointment?

10. How would you describe Tsara and David's relationship? What keeps them together during the difficult times following Tsara's abduction?

11. How is Mike different from the other men in Tsara's life?

12. Does this book have a happy ending?

13. Do you think Tsara continues to bring Aiden to visit Mike? How would David feel about this?

14. Is Mike's sentence fair?

15. Tsara finds her own path to her internal healing. Would you have done something different? Do you think you would experience the same internal struggle if you had been through her ordeal?

16. The self-defense classes Tsara takes before the story starts give her the confidence and know-how to fight against her various attackers. Though Mike's training and experience give him an advantage, Jim and Jordan don't fare so well. Have you taken classes geared for women as Tsara has? Would you now consider it? Perhaps you and your book club would like to take such a class together as a group.

25470539R30244

Made in the USA
Charleston, SC
30 December 2013